George P. Pelecanos is the author of *The Big Blowdown*, *King Suckerman* (shortlisted for the 1998 Crime Writers' Association Golden Dagger Award), *The Sweet Forever*, and *Shame the Devil*, which make up his DC Quartet (the first three are published by Serpent's Tail), and of a trilogy featuring PI Nick Stefanos, *A Firing Offense*, *Nick's Trip*, and *Down by the River Where the Dead Men Go*, published by Serpent's Tail. Pelecanos has been hailed as "the coolest writer in America" (*GQ*) and "a literary Tarantino with added heart" (*Mail on Sunday*) who "makes Jim Thompson look like Barbara Cartland" (*Mirabella*).

Pelecanos lives in Washington, where he "has carved out a territory— the seedier suburbs of Washington, D.C.—and a language of danger and sadness all his own" (*Chicago Tribune*).

THE BIG BLOWDOWN

George P. Pelecanos

To Pete Frank and Alice Frank

Acknowledgments

I would like to thank the following individuals who were of help in the writing of this book, the staff of the Washingtoniana Room of the Martin Luther King Memorial Library in Washington, D C, Jim and Ted Pedas; James Boukas, Gordon Van Gelder, Sloan Harris, and Emily A special thanks to my parents, Pete and Ruby Pelecanos.

A complete catalogue record for this book can be obtained from the British Library on request

FT
Pbk

First published in the USA in 1996

First published in the UK in 2000 by Serpent's Tail, an imprint of Profile Books Ltd, 3A Exmouth House, Pine Street, London EC1R 0JH

First published in this 5 star edition in 2001

Website: www.serpentstail.com

Printed in the UK by CPI Bookmarque, Croydon, CR0 4TD

10 9 8 7 6 5 4

Mixed Sources
Product group from well-managed forests and other controlled sources
www.fsc.org Cert no. TT-COC-002227
© 1996 Forest Stewardship Council
FSC

Introduction

Each moment of our life, each action we take, celebrates both our own uniqueness and the extent to which we manage to abridge that uniqueness in forming connections to others. Similarly, the greatness of any writer may lie in his capacity to confront contradictions within himself: to express among other things, out of the well of his absolute individuality and that of his characters, the many ways in which we are all alike.

Having written that, I peer out into yet another spectacular Arizona sunset (so far away from this world according to Pelecanos), sip coffee, put down my pen.

George Pelecanos now has published seven novels of rare ambition and complexity. And though you are not likely to find him listed among today's hot tickets—on the approved canon of properly serious young writers, say, or in line for foundation grants—he is among the finest ten or twelve novelists working in the U.S. today. So what do I say here? I've been given a bean-shooter, six hundred words, to stand against a lion.

Do I write about the Pelecanos who started off playing such games with conventions of the detective genre, wearing them inside out, sleeves ripped off, nothing underneath? Or the one who wrote a lean, classically noir book just to see if he could do it? About the dedicated chronicler of inner-city Washington, D.C.? The Balzacian figure so intent upon rendering this nation's whole ramshackle, impossible urban life over the past half-century?

Or about how all these are curiously one?

I recall, some years back, the much-trumpeted arrival of a new novel from one of our "A" list writers, and a single calm voice floating to the surface. By book's end, this reviewer said, the protagonist's self-absorption and self-pity, his fear that any break in the day's routine could lead to unspeakable dread from which he'd never recover, may well come to seem like the American experience, rather than the circumscribed experience of the white suburban male; maybe nobody more than a provided-for white guy could be so certain that his crises were those of the world.

It's not a charge ever likely to be leveled on George Pelecanos as he goes quietly about his work.

He writes of immigrants, of blacks, of the young, of all the damaged and disadvantaged and discarded shut away in rented rooms or shuttled aside into bars and diners reeking of stagnant time till, their moment come round at last, they erupt, burn furiously, and expire.

He works hard and shows a rare dedication to that work, continuing with each book to go after what eluded him, what he may have missed the last time out, writing, through the lives of some of its meanest citizens, the whole history of this strange new land, this America where we have murdered ourselves into democracy. True to self and material, he's burrowed in and found direction in the work itself, letting it grow organically, following where it takes him. He's become, in Isaiah Berlin's phrase, both the fox that knows many things and the hedgehog that knows one thing deeply.

At its heart all art asks the same question: How should we live, and how counter the self-destructive nature of ourselves and our history? And at the heart of each Pelecanos novel, that is the theme.

An old friend, Mike Moorcock, recently wrote me that sometimes these days he feels like Big Mama Thornton at an Elvis retrospective. So it is with George Pelecanos. He's the real thing, a powerful and intensely original writer who calls his own tunes and makes us all, bears and people and, yes (as Flaubert said), sometimes the stars alike, dance to them.

You are about to read *The Big Blowdown*, a novel of rare and spectacular achievement.

Treasure this book and its author.

I do.

—James Sallis

Phoenix, Arizona

PROLOGUE

Washington, D.C.
1946

Peter Karras dreamed. He dreamed of his Murphy bed, and a plate of his mother's beans *me selina*. He could smell the richness of the food, see the brown around the black-eyed peas and stewed tomatoes and the pale-green celery as if he were sitting at the old table at 5th and H. He dreamed of sirens and Jimmy Boyle, Boyle in his blue uniform, looking down on him with concern. He watched the white moon, saw lights color it and swirl across the sky. He dreamed he had raised his head and looked at his leg. He dreamed the foot at the end of it was flattened, without shape, smashed into a swollen mound on the stones, twisted in a funny kind of way. In between the dreams came blackness; in the blackness came naked screams.

"Jimmy," said Karras.

"I'm here, pal."

It was Boyle again, in uniform, crouched over him, back in the dream. The siren was loud in this dream. Boyle held his hand. They were in a small space, and someone was in the space with them, someone wearing white. They were moving, rocking back and forth.

"We're on our way to the hospital," said Boyle.

"The hospital."

"Yeah."

Karras's mouth was awfully dry. "How does it look for me?"

"Huh?"

"Turn your good ear my way, Jimmy." Boyle did it. "I said, how is it?"

"You're gonna make it."

"I asked you how it was, Jimmy."

Boyle lowered his eyes.

Karras had a sudden shock of pain that arched his back. Boyle squeezed his hand until the shock receded. The one wearing white blotted a rag on Karras's head.

"We're almost there, pal," said Boyle.

Karras licked his lips. "How'd you get in on this?"

"My beat." Boyle smiled sadly. "You got lucky, I guess."

"Luck. I'm lousy with it, Jimmy."

The ambulance made a severe turn. Boyle steadied the gurney, yelled something at the driver. He looked back down at Karras.

"Who did this to you, Pete?"

Karras thought of Joe Recevo, the image of the Mercury pulling away, clear and pounding in his head. "I got yoked, that's all. Some guys jumped me. I didn't see their faces. Maybe you ought to ask the old-timer that runs the market."

"We will."

Karras looked at his friend, smiled at the rolls of fat spilling over the collar of Boyle's shirt.

"You put on a few pounds, Jimmy."

Boyle blushed. "Aw, hell, Pete, you know I like to eat."

"I know, chum. I know."

The driver cut the siren as the ambulance slowed.

"Pete," Boyle said. "When I found you, you were talkin' Greek. *Mana mou, mana mou,* you kept sayin'. What the hell was that?"

Mana mou. Karras looked away. He had been calling out for his mother in that alley. So that's what a tough guy like him did when things got real good and rough.

"Crazy talk," said Karras, "that's all it was."

The ambulance stopped, and Boyle patted Karras's hand. "All right, pal. Now they're gonna fix you up."

The back doors opened. A couple of guys leaned in, grabbed the gurney. They lifted him out into the night air, the smells and sounds of the city strong and then gone as he was pushed through a set of swinging doors.

Karras stared at the white rush of ceiling overhead.

"Joe," he said.

Karras went to sleep.

ONE

Washington, D.C.
1933

1

Peter Karras learned to swim one afternoon at the tail end of a heat wave in early June. The heat had come upon D.C. like a bad dream and had killed several old-timers and a few who were not so old. Two had succumbed from it the day before.

The first was a tourist from San Francisco, a Swede in his middle years who collapsed at the corner of 2nd Street and Virginia Avenue, dead of an exploded heart before he hit the sidewalk. The second was a crewman on the *SS Veedol*, which was tied up that summer at the Alexandria docks. The young man had stood on the gunwales and leaped into the Potomac in an effort to cool down, despite the fact that he knew he could not swim. The crewman, whose name was Elridge Kruse, plunged into the water and went straight and swiftly to the bottom. A witness told the papers that Kruse went down so quickly it looked as if his pockets had been filled with stones.

Karras wiped sweat from his brow and tried not to show his discomfort while quickening his step. He was trying to keep pace with Steve Mamakos, a comer around town who was becoming well-known in the boxing ranks. Mamakos was not much taller than Karras but thicker to the tune of thirty pounds, with a squat build and a nose that one could see had already been hit. Karras was eleven years old to Mamakos's sixteen, the difference between a boy and one who is nearly a man. The difference showed as they walked side by side.

Mamakos could fight; he favored his right, possessed a good sense of the ring, and had moderate quickness in both hands. Far from a technician, he was rather a straight-up boxer, with few tricks in his arsenal. On paper,

7

his deficiencies seemed overwhelming: He dropped his left too often, rarely used it, and pawed with it when he did use it. His true strength— and it was a strength, indeed—was that he could take three to land one. Some guys who knew something about it said that Mamakos could go all the way.

In the Boy's Club at 5th and G, Mamakos and his trainer, "Buster" Brown, had spent the better part of the morning teaching Karras how to box. Mamakos had barely pulled his punches, and once, when Karras had been hit dead in the nose, Karras's eyes teared up, and the room tilted in front of his face. The only thing he cared about then was that Mamakos not mistake his tears for the crying kind. Peter Karras didn't mind that Steve Mamakos didn't pull up; hell, he was proud of it. And proud to be walking next to him now.

Mamakos had the change for the streetcar, but Karras preferred to walk, and the two of them went downtown and across the Mall and into the neighborhoods and alleys of Southwest, where Negroes watched them pass but did not meet their eyes. Soon they had reached the fruit and vegetable stands and fish vendors that lined the Washington Channel along Maine Avenue. They were just walking, with the vague idea of getting to the water, where they thought that there might be a breeze. Their shirts were soaked through as they crossed the road.

Along the waterline, restaurateurs and cooks, shopping for their evening menus, picked through the produce of the vendors' carts. Karras recognized Lou DiGeordano, standing behind his fruit cart, his shirtsleeves rolled to the elbow. DiGeordano, short and wire thin, with a black moustache and a high black pompadour, used his thumbnail to pick food from his teeth. Karras's father knew DiGeordano, claimed that he ran numbers on the side.

DiGeordano lived in the same area of Chinatown as Karras, at 5th and H. His apartment building, all three floors of it, housed strictly Italians, the way it worked, as people usually drifted to their own kind. Joe Recevo, Peter Karras's best friend, lived in that building with his folks. So did the Damiano and Carchedi families; Karras went to Catholic school with a couple of the kids.

"Hey, Karras Jr.," said DiGeordano, as Karras walked in front of the cart.

"Mr. DiGeordano," said Karras with a nod, as he and Mamakos passed.

They walked behind DiGeordano's cart and had a seat on the edge of the bulkhead, their legs dangling over the side. A rowboat was tied off on a piling to their right. The water was not so clean here as it was downriver at Mount Vernon and at Marshall Hall.

8

"Hot," said Mamakos.

"Damn hot," said Karras, happy for the chance to curse in front of Mamakos but wincing at the sound of his own high voice.

Mamakos looked down at the rowboat, then pointed his chin towards Hains Point. "What we ought to do, maybe we ought to take that over to the Speedway, go for a swim while we're at it."

"I can't swim," said Karras.

"Sure you can."

Peter Karras spat between his feet, watched the spit hit the water with a soft click. "I can't."

Mamakos nodded, glanced thoughtfully across the channel. "So who's gonna win the fight tonight?"

"My pop says Schmeling. Says Max Baer ain't nothin' but a *bufo*."

"Your pop says."

"That's right."

"He thinks Baer's a clown? Maybe. But he's a clown with a right."

Karras squinted in the sun. "You gonna listen to it?"

"Yeah. You?"

"Uh-huh."

Mamakos looked over at Karras, smiled as he studied the mop of blond hair, the blue eyes. "You don't look much like a Greek, you know it, Pete? Except for the *ilia*, maybe."

Karras touched his finger to the prominent black mole to the right of his lip. "My pop's village, in Sparta, they all look like this. Pop says we never got overrun by the Turks. It's the Turk blood makes other Greeks dark—"

"Your pop says." A drop of sweat fell from the blunt tip of Steve Mamakos's nose. "Sure is hot, though. We ought to take that little boat out."

Lou DiGeordano had been listening to the conversation. He turned around, made a kind of pushing motion with his hands. "You wanna take the boat, take it. I know the guy who owns it. He owes me a few dollars, anyway. But bring it back soon. You hear, Karras Jr.?"

Mamakos had lowered himself down into the rowboat before Peter Karras could protest. Karras followed, freeing the loop of line from the piling. He pushed off on the bulkhead, noticing the meager flex of his biceps. They floated out into the channel then. Mamakos peeled off his shirt and took hold of the oars. His arms rippled on the stroke. Karras pulled his shirt over his head and dropped it in the boat, and kicked his shoes off as well. He looked at the thinness of his own arms, told himself that he would grow.

"I'm telling you," said Mamakos, "it's going to be Baer. Then Baer will take the title from Carnera after Carnera beats hell out of Sharkey in July."

"I hear you," said Karras, who suddenly felt closed in on the boat. It reminded him of the Murphy bed he slept on in his parents' apartment.

"You looked good in the gym this morning, Karras. Maybe you got a little Max Baer in you, too. But you got to remember to keep your hands up, and breathe. Breathing's real important."

"Okay, Steve." The boat rose and dipped over the wake of a passing skiff, and Karras felt a flutter in his stomach. Now that they were out in the channel, it didn't seem so cool after all. Karras still felt hot and a little bit sick.

"This is good enough," said Mamakos, pulling the oars from the water.

"What're we gonna do now?" said Karras.

"Now," said Mamakos, "I'm going to teach you how to swim."

"I can't. I *know* I can't."

"Sure you can. Once you're in there, you make like a dog. Move your hands and feet like hell. Kind of paddle, like, and keep paddlin'. It's simple."

"I can't, Steve."

"Stand up, boy."

"Steve—"

"Stand up and jump off the front of this boat."

Karras went to the bow, stood there. He knew that he would do it, on account of being a chicken in front of Steve Mamakos was the last thing he would ever want to be. And it did feel awful close in the tiny rowboat, real close and uncomfortable. He wanted to take a deep breath first, but he couldn't seem to keep one in. He would do it, but not just yet. He needed to wait.

The easy laughter of Mamakos filled the air as Karras felt the weight of a large hand on his back. He was falling then, and almost as he touched the water he slipped beneath it, and he waved his hands and kicked his feet frantically, and just as quickly as he had gone under his head came out. He heard his own voice, a kind of humming sound. His hands swirled and his feet kicked. He saw the green of Hains Point, the gulls gliding at its edge, the white puff of clouds against the perfect azure sky. He took the warmth of the sun on his face, and felt the stretch of his own smile.

"Swim, you Greek bastard!" said Mamakos.

Swim. Yeah, it was simple.

2

██████ Peter Karras pushed the covers off his bed. He sat up and touched the bruise at the edge of his temple, the bruise given to him by his father the night before. Dimitri Karras, who worked a fruit and vegetable stand at the head of an alley on the 1700 block of Pennsylvania, had heard from one of his friends on Maine Avenue who had seen his son swimming in the channel. Dimitri had come home that night with the idea of teaching the boy a lesson. He had taken off his belt, and he had beaten his son with it, and the buckle had caught the boy on the side of the head. Dimitri Karras stopped when he saw what he had done. During the whole thing, the boy had never cried.

Karras glanced over at his father, sitting at the table wearing only his union suit, his hand touching a cup of Turkish coffee. His father did not look up. At the foot of Peter Karras's bed, a lobby card from a movie house lay on the wood floor. The photograph, bent and wrinkled, showed two actors, James Dunn and Zasu Pitts, from a picture called *Hello Sister.* So his old man had gone up to the Savoy to see a late show, and taken the photograph off the wall. And then probably gotten drunk. A present for his son, and a cockeyed one at that, as if Karras would want a photograph of Zasu Pitts. What would he do with it, anyway? Well, it was a gesture, at least. It was something.

At the kitchen stove, Georgia Karras crumpled feta cheese into the frying pan which held the scrambled eggs she cooked for her husband. She wore a dark housedress, one of three identical housedresses she owned, with her long brown hair tied up tightly in a bun. On her feet she wore a pair of cord-fabric sandals with leather soles and Cuban heels, which she

11

had saved for and bought at Goldenberg's for a dollar and nineteen cents. A cat sat beside her, its nose touching her calf, listening to the hiss of the eggs congealing in the pan.

"More *cafe*, Yiorgia," said Dimitri.

"It's coming," Georgia said tiredly. "I'm going to bring the eggs and the coffee together. I'm going to give it to you all at once."

"Uh," said Dimitri.

"Ella na fas, Panayotaki," said Georgia to her son, with a come-on gesture of her hand.

"Don't have time to eat, Ma," said Peter as he tied his shoes and pulled on the shirt he had worn the day before. "I'm gonna meet my friends."

"What friends you gonna meet?" said Dimitri.

"Perry Angelos, and Billy Nicodemus. Jimmy Boyle, and Joe Recevo."

"Recevo," said Dimitri. "The *Italos.*"

Georgia served the eggs to Dimitri and refilled his coffee. She wiped her hands dry on her housedress.

"Come into the bedroom, Panayoti," she said, "before you go."

Peter Karras remade his bed and pushed it up into the wall. He passed his father, who smelled of coffee and cigarettes and booze, and faintly of the Wildroot tonic he wore in his thick, graying hair, and went into the apartment's sole bedroom. The shades were drawn, as they were drawn in all the rooms, the red light coming from a *candili* suspended from the ceiling in front of several icons hung on the wall. Among the icons was a framed magazine photograph of FDR.

His mother stood by his father's dresser, pushing coins off the top of it into her hand. Peter stood beside her, admiring his father's Bowie knife, which he kept on the dresser. Next to the knife sat an American-Bosch radio, and next to that two empty bottles of Gunther's beer. Georgia reached over and took her son's face and turned it in the light. She looked at his bruised temple and sighed.

"It's okay, Ma. It don't matter."

"O patera sou eine kalos anthropos. Acous? Don't be mad at him, boy. He only wants you to be safe. He worries, Panayoti, thas all. Hokay?"

"Then birazi," he repeated in assurance.

She blinked her eyes and pressed the coins into her son's palm. "Pick up a chicken from the butcher on your way back home. I'm gonna boil it, make an *avgolemono* soup for tonight."

"I'll get it at the Piggly Wiggly, Ma. They got 'em fresh killed."

"They all say fresh killed. Get it from the butcher down the block, it's cheaper." She pushed him softly on the back of the head. "Go on, boy. *Pas sto kalo.*"

Peter walked from the room. She watched him go.

Out in the living room, he passed his father once more. Dimitri pushed his empty plate to the side and struck a match to a tailor-made cigarette. He looked at his skinny son, getting taller now, almost ready for his balls to grow heavy, to get the feelings of a man.

"You see the *photographia?*" said Dimitri.

"I saw it," said Peter. "Thanks, Pop." Peter kept walking, opened the front door.

"Don't forget about the chicken," said Dimitri, as the door closed.

Outside the door, the iceman, a narrow-chested American in white duck trousers, arrived. Karras faked a punch as he passed. The iceman flinched, mumbled something about Greeks. Karras laughed, headed down the stairs, thinking that he caught the scared little guy the same way every day. It was easy to take control, if you acted like a guy who didn't care.

Billy Nicodemus lived in the same building as Peter Karras, at 606 H. Karras picked him up at his door on the second floor and said hello to Billy's parents, a quiet couple who ran a soda-bar concession downtown. Steve Nicodemus, Billy's older brother, smacked Billy on the back of the head as he was going out the door. Billy Nicodemus was a husky, kind kid, with the essential good nature of his father. He never saw the point of a fight.

"Say," said Billy, "what'd you have to go and do that for?"

"A love tap," said Steve, and tilted his chin up at Karras, who he knew would understand.

Billy, crazy about baseball, had his mitt under his arm. He and Karras went down the stairs and out onto the street.

They went around the corner to 703 6th, and took the stairs up to Perry Angelos' place. On the way up, Karras saw Helen Leonides, one year his junior, playing jacks outside her parents' apartment while the landlord, Leo Bernstein, stood at the door collecting rent. She smiled at Karras, who looked away.

Perry, a small, rather homely child with long ears and large, sad brown eyes, was nearly ready when the boys came to pick him up. Karras and Nicodemus talked to Perry's mother for a while, who offered them some *gleeka.* They ate the sweets standing at the door of the bright apartment. Perry's father, who owned a kind of coffeehouse for Greeks near the Navy Yard, worked seven days a week and came home only to sleep and change

13

clothes. The other boys rarely saw him, but imagined they knew the father well, as Perry described him to them all the time.

Perry gave his mother a kiss. On the way downstairs, Perry saw Helen Leonides, and said hello.

"Hello, Perry," said Helen. And then, musically, "Hello, Pete."

Helen made Karras nervous, in a funny kind of way. He didn't respond to her greeting, and he and Perry and Billy took the stairs quickly to the street.

Joe Recevo sat on the stoop and grinned as the boys approached his building at 5th and H. At twelve, Recevo was the senior member of the group, but had been held back in a year in school for poor performance. The year meant something: Recevo was taller than the others, had a downy row of moustaches, and in the past few months witnessed his voice deepen by a shade. With his dark, dense wave of hair and deep brown eyes, he had it over them in the looks department as well.

Recevo jumped down off the stoop onto the sidewalk, tilted his newsboy's cap back on his head. The boys stood around him.

"Fellas," he said, and he reached out and flicked a finger at the lobe of Perry's right ear. It stung a little, and Perry rubbed it. "I didn't hurt you, did I, Pericles?"

"Leave him alone, Joey," said Karras.

"Sure, Pete, I'll leave the little bookworm alone."

Recevo pushed on Karras's shoulder a little. Karras brushed Recevo's hand away. They smiled at each other, neither of them stepping back.

"So where we headed?" asked Recevo.

"Let's get over to the playground," said Karras. "Boyle ought to be there. Maybe get up some stickball."

"All right!" said Nicodemus, punching a fist into his mitt.

Walking through Chinatown, they came upon a kid named Su. Recevo warned Karras once that Su's pop was in with the Hip Sings, but Karras didn't know what that meant, and didn't care. Karras played often with Su in the alley, and thought him to be a good little athlete. The boys asked him to come along.

"What about Baer and Schmeling?" said Nicodemus as they headed east. "Wasn't that somethin'?"

"It was a wild right," said Recevo, "that's what it was. Schmeling turned right into it."

"Knocked him colder than a pawnbroker's heart," said Perry Angelos, who had read that expression exactly in the morning *Herald*. He had memorized it after he had finished poring over "Buck Rogers", "Barney Google", and "Gasoline Alley"—his favorites—in the funny pages.

"Steve Mamakos called it," said Karras. "He said yesterday that Baer was gonna win."

"Mamakos," said Recevo. "What're you, in love with the guy?"

"I said he called it, that's all."

"Max Baer!" said Su, who threw a left hook and a straight right at the air as he walked.

"What's a Chink know about boxing, anyway?" said Recevo.

"I know, Lecevo," said Su.

" 'Lecevo'," said Joe, with a chuckle. "Yeah, you know, all right."

"I bet George Zaharias could beat Max Baer," said Angelos.

"Zaharias is a wrestler, Pericles," said Recevo. "What a dumbhead."

"I know it," said Perry. "And he's a Greek, did ya know *that?* Real name is Vetoyanis. He's wrestlin' Jim Londos next week at Griffith Stadium."

"Like we need another Greek visitin' D.C.," said Recevo. "The town's already lousy with 'em."

Perry Angelos and Billy Nicodemus said nothing. Recevo looked over at Karras, who seemed to be grinning a little, maybe at the exchange, or maybe just because the guy was enjoying the day. With Karras, Recevo couldn't tell.

Jimmy Boyle stood waiting on the playground at 3rd and F when they arrived. Boyle wore threadbare clothes and shoes with holes in the toes and holes in the socks that poked through. His nose ran frequently because he was often sick, and his cheekbones stood out from the set of his face.

The boys were poor, all of them, Boyle poorer than the rest. They knew there was something called a Depression going on, but the word was just a word to them. They had heard their parents talk about it and argue about it late at night, or the few that read the papers had read about it or had it read to them. The Greeks were better off than most, because they had their relatives and their *patriotis*, and they were willing to work service and food-related jobs for low wages, and sometimes the food from those jobs came home with them and made its way to the kitchen table. But they were all poor. They were poor and they didn't really know it, and if they had known it, they wouldn't have cared.

They wouldn't have cared because they were boys. They had beds to sleep in, and friends, and when they felt hungry there was usually something to eat. They knew nothing of sickness or death but to joke of it. The night seemed very far away.

Recevo kidded Boyle that his shoes were dead man's shoes, and everyone laughed. They all knew that Boyle's dad worked as an assistant in the City Morgue. The thing of it was, Boyle's father had stolen the shoes off the corpse of a boy close to Jimmy's age, just the night before. Jimmy Boyle smiled uneasily at the comment, then tried to retaliate with an insult directed at Recevo. Recevo lowered his voice to a whisper, asked Jimmy to "come again." This was a joke they could all appreciate, as Boyle was nearly deaf in one ear. He had caught the fever real bad as a kid.

"Well?" said Angelos, when they were done laughing. "What're we gonna do now?"

Billy Nicodemus punched his fist into his mitt. "Let's play a little ball."

"Babe Wooth," said Su, who took a swing at the air.

3

The boys played stickball against the brick wall of a schoolhouse for the balance of the morning, then had a quick lunch at Nick Kendros's place, the Woodward Grill on 15th. They were due to meet some Negro boys from Southwest down at a field on D Street near 5th. They had rumbled with them in June, and promised to meet on the same day in July to rumble again.

On the walk downtown they lost Su, who had to get to his father's laundromat for work, and then Nicodemus, who mumbled something about helping his brother Steve with a soapbox he was building in the alley. They let Nicodemus go, and soon they were on G Street, in front of Murphy's 5 & 10.

"I'm gonna go through to F," said Karras. "I'll meet you guys there."

"Get me some Nigger Babies," yelled Boyle, always hungry, as Karras pushed open the glass doors. Boyle knew Karras had no money for candy but felt it was worth the try.

In the Murphy's, Karras at once caught the warm, brown smell of roasted nuts, and found the concession run by a smiling Tom Andros, known to the kids around town as the Peanut Man. Andros scooped some peanuts into a small paper bag and placed the bag in Karras's hand. He knew the Karras boy from church.

"Thanks," said Karras.

"*Ande, boy,*" said Andros, with a sweeping motion of his hand.

On the street, the boys shared the nuts and walked east and then south. Around the Negro neighborhoods of New Jersey Avenue, Jimmy Boyle noticed a girl with thin brown arms and a bright and beautiful smile.

17

Recevo caught the look in Boyle's eyes, and made sure to rib him about it once they had gotten out of the neighborhood. Boyle just shrugged it off. A '32 Chevy went by on the street, a two-door model with olive-green finish, and Joe Recevo had to stop and stare. Recevo loved cars, couldn't wait to grow up and have one of his own. His father had recently bought a '29 Dodge sedan on time from the Trew Motor Company on 14th, but this Chevy, this was the cat's meow. Perry Angelos's father owned a Chevrolet Rumble Seat Coupe, tan with full-coat nickel trim, though Perry did not brag about it to his friends. The fathers of Karras, Nicodemus, and Boyle did not own cars. Cars didn't interest Karras, as he felt that the way to see the city was to get out into it and walk on its streets.

Soon they found themselves on D Street, at the edge of a rockstrewn field. The boys from Southwest stood in the middle of the field, four of them, an even match, if numbers made things even. Perry Angelos felt his stomach flip at the sight of them, while Recevo and Karras experienced a kind of satisfaction at the recognition of their own fear. Boyle's palms sweated, and his tongue stuck to the roof of his mouth.

"That's them," said Recevo.

"I heard they were Bloodfield boys," said Angelos.

"We said we'd meet 'em," said Boyle. "So let's go."

They walked towards them across the field. Joe Recevo took his newsboy's cap from his head and tossed it to the side.

"I'm gonna take the skinny one," said Karras to Recevo.

"He ain't the strongest," said Recevo, "but he's the quickest. Remember?"

"I remember."

"I got the tall one, with the high-buttoned shoes."

"He likes to wave his right above his head to get your attention. But he's gonna strike with his left, Joey. Hear?"

"I hear ya," said Recevo.

They were moving fast now, almost running to the group of boys who stood still and glaring in the middle of the field.

"Perry—" said Karras.

"Don't worry about me, Pete."

The tall Negro boy with the high-buttoned shoes yelled, "Southwest!"

Recevo laughed and screamed, "Northwest!" His laughter inspired them, and they followed Recevo's charge.

They were all mixed together then, grabbing and pushing and punching at each other close in. The first to fall was Perry Angelos. Karras let his guard down to rabbit-punch the wiry boy who had knocked Angelos to the ground with the first blow. He was tackled at chest level by the skinny

18

boy, who rammed the top of his nappy head into Karras's stomach and pushed him to the ground. Karras felt a rock dig in above his buttocks on contact. Recevo ran over and kicked the skinny boy off, and then Recevo was grabbed by the tall one, and then he was standing toe-to-toe with him, trading blows, both of them yelling loudly with each one. Boyle and his opponent were on the ground, rolling and flailing at each other in a rising cloud of dirt and dust. Karras got to his feet.

"Come on, boy," said the skinny one, both his hands up, wiggling the fingers of one hand at Karras.

Karras came in, took a punch in the gut from the skinny boy, brought his elbows in and took two more on his arms. He felt a little dizzy, breathed, felt better for it, uppercut at the second the next punch came in. That one caught the skinny boy on the chin, pushing him back. Karras went in, saw the shape of Angelos on the ground, the wiry boy on top of him, pummeling him with weak blows. The distraction made the skinny boy go for Karras's legs and knock him off his feet. They both went down, rolled twice, with Karras coming out on top. He sat on the skinny boy's chest, grabbed the front of his ripped shirt with his left hand, made a tight fist of his right, and prepared to bring it down in the boy's face. He looked in the skinny boy's eyes, and the skinny boy looked back with blank and unafraid acceptance of what had to happen next. But Karras noticed then that there was little sound around him, and that the other boys—his and theirs—had fallen away and were lying on the ground, some of them holding themselves where they hurt, all of them at rest. Karras released his grip on the skinny boy's shirt, lowered his fist.

Karras stood up, brushed himself off. The others did the same. Eight boys stood there with winded lungs and cut lips, and the beginnings of bruises which they would hide from their parents later that night. No one had won.

The white boys from Northwest began to move out. Then the skinny one said, "Hey, you with that black mark on your face." Karras turned around.

"Yeah," said Karras. "What d'ya want?"

"What's your name, anyway?" said the skinny boy.

Karras softened his glare. "Pete Karras. You?"

"My daddy's name is Oliver. Around my way, they call me Junior Oliver."

Karras nodded, and the one called Junior Oliver blinked his eyes. They turned, and joined their own. The Negroes walked back towards Southwest. The boys from Northwest went in the direction of their homes.

19

"You all right, Perry?" said Karras.

"Fine," said Angelos, smiling a little in relief, blood smudged pink on his teeth.

"Jimmy?"

"Yep," said Boyle, brushing dirt from a scrape on his cheek.

"Those nigger boys could fight," said Recevo.

"Yeah." Karras put his hand on Recevo's shoulder. "Thanks for watchin' my back, Joey."

"Count on it, Greek," said Recevo. And Karras had no doubt.

"Where we goin' now?" said Boyle.

Recevo picked up his newsboy's cap where he had left it, slapped the dust off on his trousers. "Let's find Nicodemus," he said. "Maybe we can get in on that soapbox deal."

Karras shook his head. "I can't."

"Why not?" said Recevo.

"Gotta pick a chicken up for my ma," said Karras. "She's makin' a soup."

4

■■■■■ To Peter Karras, the long days of summer seemed to drag. Yet soon enough they had passed, and he and his friends found themselves in school, daydreaming about the season gone and looking to the one ahead.

At St. Mary's, Karras spoke to the nuns only when called upon, and responded to their lessons with barely masked inattention. Often he looked through the smudged glass window next to his desk at the oak that grew alongside the church, watching the gradual turn of its leaves. His grades were only adequate, better than Recevo's, and on par with Nicodemus's and Boyle's. Perry Angelos, who already talked about college as the clean path to making a buck, placed far ahead of the rest.

"Hey, Pete," said Recevo one morning, as Jimmy Boyle entered the classroom, a gaping rip in the knee of his trousers. "Looks like Boyle just checked out of a Hoover Hotel."

"His old man got his walking papers at the morgue," said Karras. "He'll get his job back, once things get better. My pop says Roosevelt's gonna turn things around. Says he's gonna put the men back to work, the ones that wanna work and even the ones that don't."

"Your pop says. All you Greeks are in bed with Roosevelt."

"Yeah," said Karras. "I guess."

During the lesson, Recevo set fire to a book of matches, then quickly blew out the flame. Their teacher, Sister Cumilliana, asked who had done the deed, and a girl named Linda McCabe pointed to Joe. Sister Cumilliana walked over to Recevo, stood over him, and rolled up the right sleeve of her habit.

"Hold out your hand," she instructed.

Recevo, his eyes fixed on the right hand of the nun, did not comply. The nun's left hand slashed out of nowhere, slapping him sharply across the cheek. Recevo rubbed the red mark as the children laughed. Sister Cumilliana walked back to the head of the class, a smile in her eyes.

You shoulda watched the left, Joey, thought Karras. *You shoulda watched out for the left.*

The days went on like that, with Recevo and Karras in and out of trouble and getting little from their schooling. Perry Angelos applied himself and concentrated on his studies, though he could not fail to notice that the girls of the class admired the antics of Recevo and Karras more than his own academic accomplishments. But it was not in Angelos to misbehave. Boyle and Nicodemus talked big out on the playground, but remained quiet and virtually invisible within the walls of the church. Outside the smudged window, Karras stared at the branches of the oak, now stripped bare.

■

An early snow came the second week of December. On the Sunday morning after the storm, Karras went to church service at St. Sophia's, on 8th and L. It was usually Karras and his mother in church, while his father slept off his Saturday-night drunks undisturbed. Karras sat there, listening to the nasal chanting of Father Papanicolas, watching the other families in the pews through the heavy haze of incense, thinking, as he tended to do in church, of how he did not belong. He had always felt apart from the rest of them, with their large numbers of relatives and their brothers and sisters. Years ago his mother had given birth to a little brother, Theodoros, who had died in his crib just after his sixth month, and Karras had remained and would remain an only child. As for relatives, his father had broken off relations with his own sister and cousins in D.C. long ago. Peter Karras could not see himself as an adult, with his own wife and children. It was not something he could picture in his mind.

After church, Karras met his friends at a garage in the alley, where they had hidden an air rifle they had saved for and bought together in the fall. They knew the man who sold it to them had stolen it himself, and they used that knowledge to bargain out a good price.

"You pump this baby up, say fifteen times," said the man, "and what you boys got here is as powerful as a twenty-two." The boys knew that the man was selling them a load of baloney, but they wanted that rifle awful bad.

The day was not warm, but the sun had come out and the snow had melted from the streets, though it hung in the pockets of the branches and

22

capped the roofs of cars. Walking across town, the boys took turns carry-ing the rifle in their pantslegs, which afforded each one of them the oppor-tunity to affect the tortured movements of a cripple. This provoked a new joke within the group each time the rifle changed hands, jokes at which Peter Karras could not laugh; he had seen a cripple once, a real one, beg-ging for money downtown, and the sight of it had caused him a series of tortuous nightmares. He would rather be anything, maybe even dead, than that.

It took a few hours for them to make it to the other side of Northwest. In Georgetown they lost direction, and asked help from a man who was dumping something chunked and brown from a pot behind a restaurant. He pointed them to the bridge. Boyle, who smelled the roasted meat com-ing from the back door, could not resist asking the man for a bite of food.

"I'm workin' for my dinner my *own* self," said the man. The boys went on their way.

They walked over the bridge from Georgetown to Virginia. It was all field and forest there, with woods at the edge of the field. The sun hung weak and pale yellow against the sheeted gray sky.

Karras looked back at the city as they walked off the bridge through the snow and to the middle of a field. Though this was not the country, it was close enough, and he did not like to be away from the car sounds and restaurant smells, to be without the solid feel of asphalt beneath his feet. He had gone with his parents into Maryland one summer day, driven in a friend's borrowed car toward a place called Soloman's Island, and they had tried to find a beach where they could sun themselves and where his father could swim. His father had been turned away at the gate, where a sign said NORTHERN EUROPEAN WHITES ONLY. Karras did not like the feeling he had when he left D.C.

"Give me the rifle, Perry," said Boyle, whose feet stung from the cold and who wanted to get on with it. Boyle had worn two pairs of socks but the snow had entered a split in the leather of his shoe.

Angelos grabbed the butt, which protruded from his waistband, and slid the rifle out. The sight had caught him on the thigh and made the spot raw. Boyle took the rifle, loaded it with a pellet, and pumped it several times.

"My dad shot a rabbit out here with his pistol," said Joe Recevo. "We ate the stew. My dad says there's enough rabbit runnin' around here to feed a family all year."

"We ought to be able to see 'em good," said Nicodemus. "Against this snow, I mean."

Karras rubbed the back of his hand across his lips, wiped off snot that had dripped down from his nose. "They gotta come out for us to see them, though."

"Good target practice for you, Jimmy," said Recevo to Boyle, "for when you go to be a cop."

"My uncle's one," said Boyle. "I'll be one, don't worry."

"Maybe you'll just end up washin' off the slabs down at the morgue," said Recevo, "like your old man. When he still had his job, that is."

"I'll be a cop," said Boyle. The comment about his father hurt him deeply, but he bit on his lip and let it pass.

A rabbit dashed across the field. Boyle took aim, and missed.

They did not see another rabbit for some time. Joe Recevo pulled a rolled cigarette built of Bull Durham tobacco, which he had stolen from his father, out of his jacket. He lighted the cigarette with a straight match, and the tobacco went around the group. Soon they began to fire the rifle at birds and at trees, and when they became bored with that they fired the rifle at each other, the pellets bouncing off their heavy jackets and stinging at their legs. Then, while Billy Nicodemus held the rifle, a rabbit appeared from a hole at the beginning of the tree line, and Nicodemus aimed and fired. The rabbit fell over on its side.

They ran to where the rabbit had fallen, and stood grouped around it. The rabbit, brown with irregular white spots, lay there breathing heavily, one fading brown eye staring at the snow in front of it, the pellet embedded and showing behind the eye. They could see the heart beating in the rabbit's chest.

"I didn't mean to hurt it," said Nicodemus.

"Gimme the rifle," said Recevo. He took the rifle from Nicodemus, loaded a pellet into it, and pumped it ten times.

"I didn't mean to," said Nicodemus.

Recevo put the barrel to the rabbit's head and pulled the trigger. The pellet made a steaming hole near the rabbit's mouth. The rabbit kicked a little, its eye filming over.

"It's still breathin'." Perry Angelos spread his fingers wide. "What are we gonna do, Pete?"

"It ain't dead," Boyle said. "We ought to just kill it."

"The joker who sold this rifle to us said it was just like a twenty-two," said Recevo. "But this here is no twenty-two. A twenty-two woulda killed it."

"Pete," said Angelos, "you gotta do something."

Karras took the rifle from Recevo's hands. He raised it up, and smashed the butt down into the rabbit's skull two times. He wiped the butt of the rifle off on the ground, leaving a chunky streak of red and brown in the snow. Then he slid the rifle inside the leg of his trousers.

Recevo smiled at Karras. Billy Nicodemus wiped a tear from his cheek as Karras looked away. A wind came through the woods, rustling the few leaves that remained.

"I'm gonna be late for dinner," said Angelos.

"Come on, then," said Karras. "We better be gettin' home."

They walked along the edge of the field toward the bridge. The sun behind the trees made crawling shadows at their feet.

TWO

Leyte, The Philippines
1944

5

Peter Karras had the first man he ever killed in his sights for ten minutes before he managed to pull the trigger. The man was a sniper who had taken out a Marine in Karras's unit, a private named Slocum from Apple Valley, Minnesota. Slocum had tried to bolt from his foxhole to the L-shaped trench that ran to the division's 55mm gun, when the sniper's slug caught him in the chest. A medic had gotten to Slocum and had begun to administer the morphine that would quiet him down. But Slocum's lungs had rapidly begun to fill, and Slocum knew that he was done.

Karras noticed the sniper resting in the crook of a coconut palm at the edge of the jungle when the sun flashed off the sniper's cartridge belt as he moved to reload, a quick wink of white light against the wall of green. Karras hefted his M-1, leaning out of his foxhole. He got the soldier in his sights.

A soldier, just like him. The uniform different, maybe—khaki, they called it, though it looked more to Karras like dirty yellow, the color of the mustard he had squeezed on the hot dogs at Griffith Stadium all his life—but a soldier, just like him, the difference a color of uniform.

The day, like every day, hung wet and hot. A drop of sweat snaked down from beneath Karras's helmet and stung his eye.

Karras could remember watching war movies, working as an usher at the Hippodrome at 9th and K, after classes let out at Central High. Movies set in the first war, dogfight movies mostly, smiling, long-scarved flyboys with Errol Flynn moustaches whose women waited with patience and bright-eyed admiration on the ground. He always wondered, watching the pictures, what about the ones they shot down, the ones who wore the different uniform? Didn't they laugh, too? Didn't they have women who waited, who admired them and loved them too? Didn't they have mothers who held them as babies once, too?

Karras knew that Slocum had a mother. Slocum had talked about his mother and her cooking constantly, until the other men in the unit had to walk away. Slocum, who was yelling abusively at the medic now, obscenities at first and then begging the medic to stay.

Karras took one hand off his rifle, and nervously fingered the checkered handle of his father's Bowie knife, which he kept sheathed to this hip. The blade of the knife, double-edged stainless steel, could cut paper in midair; it was a knife to show off in times of boredom, one that the other men in the unit would talk about and admire. Dimitri Karras had burned his son's initials into the handle before he shipped it overseas.

Peter Karras wiped at his face, then curled his finger back inside the trigger guard of his gun.

You could talk about Corregidor and Bataan, and all the things they had done, things too terrible to repeat. Well, we had done some bad things, too. Everything came out in the wash, and in the end it was just two groups of men fighting and killing over a piece of land that everyone but the dead would walk away from when the shooting was done.

This rifle sight's a little low, thought Karras. He raised it up an inch.

Slocum, who had a mother, made choking sounds as he began to drown from the fluid filling his lungs. Did the man in the coconut palm have a mother? Slocum, who had spiky blond hair and rounded his vowels in a funny kind of way when he spoke, had a mother for sure. Slocum had described her in detail to Peter Karras, just the night before.

Karras squeezed the trigger on his M-1. The man in the coconut palm, who was no longer a man, fell to the ground and bounced one time.

6

Peter Karras always said that he chose the Marine Corps before the Army could choose him, and though he came to say it in a joking manner, he spoke the truth. His best friend Joe Recevo had gone to the Army early in the draft—Karras had listened to Recevo grouse about it all the way—and Billy Nicodemus had been shipped off to Europe in 1943. His other friends fared better: Jimmy Boyle managed to pull a Four-F on account of his bum ear, and Perry Angelos, who had completed his degree at Catholic University, drew desk duty with the Army Corps of Engineers. Karras was the last one left uncontacted, and knew that his time was near.

He wanted only to have a choice; Karras feared naval duty over anything, especially feared the prospect of facing death within the confines and close quarters of a ship. And the idea of being a dogfaced grunt, regular infantry in the U.S. Army, did not appeal to him in the least. After all, he had been told throughout his life that he was a Spartan, believed the warrior implications that went with the tag, and simply felt that the Army was not in any way the equal of the Corps. There was also the element of living up to a certain image in his father's eye. Karras's mother had tried to keep him from the service with a phony Greek birth certificate that she had used for other purposes on several occasions, but Karras would not be one of the men who walked the streets of Washington without a uniform, men who were frankly considered less than men by most of the women around town. So he did not wait. He enlisted in the Marine Corps, and tuned out his mother's anguished cries, and endured the unreadable, watery-eyed stare of his father. He was twenty-two years of age, and off to war.

After twelve weeks of basic training at Parris Island, Karras returned to D.C. on a ten-day furlough, fifteen pounds heavier, all of it muscle, with a new, handsome hardness to his tanned face. On the first night home, he had dinner with his parents—his mother had prepared a lamb—and then met some friends at a pool hall and beer garden at 5th and G. The next day he rang up a girl named Eleni Triandokidis, the younger sister of a friend from Central High whom he had had an eye on for some time. On those rare occasions when Karras had found the privacy to masturbate while at boot camp, it had been Eleni to whose image he had returned most.

She was a shapely brunette with thick ankles and rather large calves for a girl her age—Eleni was seventeen when Karras first courted her—and a nose that crinkled when she smiled. Eleni's people were from the Peleponese, not Sparta, so Karras's parents would not have approved. Peter Karras would not have taken their advice in any case, as after their first date, dining under the stars on the patio at the Roma on Connecticut Avenue, he convinced himself that he had fallen for her, that he maybe even loved her in some detached, dispassionate way. What he loved, of course, was the image of being with her, to taste the salt of sweat on her breasts and lie between her muscled thighs. Karras had his way with her the night before he shipped back out, in the basement of her parents' house off Kansas Avenue in Northwest, his hand over her mouth at the end to keep her from waking the old man. There was the mumbled promise of an unofficial engagement before he went out her door for the long walk home.

Back on Parris Island, he was recommended for and accepted the position of DI, a favorable situation on the surface in that it kept him in the States. But he soon found that he was working seven days a week and pulling extra shifts for a sergeant who was often out drinking beer. After thirty days of that, and with the vague desire to test himself in some unforeseen way, he requested and was granted overseas duty. He shipped out to Norfolk, then to Hawaii, where on the island of Kauai he found himself training in an artillery outfit that specialized in 55-millimeter guns.

After zigzagging across the Pacific for almost two months, he landed in Guam and was told that his outfit would continue to train. Somehow Karras managed to get on the wrong side of a Sergeant Skinner, a real SOB from the old school, so Karras pulled a three-month duty repairing belly stoves. But the tedium was relieved by rugby games on a stone-filled field, and the assemblage of a crack baseball team, on which he played catcher. Eventually, he and his unbeaten teammates were flown to Saipan, where they played opposite Cecil Travis, the Senators' shortstop who was on an island-hopping tour designed to boost troop morale. Beating Travis and his boys was the highlight of Karras's tour of duty; it made him wish he could see his friend Billy Nicodemus, who loved baseball as much as life. He had not heard from Billy in more than a year.

On returning to Guam, the outfit threw what had become their weekly party, in which the six members of each tent pooled and drank their beer rations in one night. As the night progressed, the humor grew crueler and there was at least one fight. A private from Kentucky named Valin, who went on incessantly about his Louisville fiancée, was encouraged to drink more than the rest, the idea being that a passed-out man could not talk. The atmosphere was meaner than usual that night, as there was a feeling among the men, a feeling fueled by strong and repeated rumor, that they were to be shipped out for combat very soon. Valin did not pass out, kept on bragging about his girl, and late in the party a couple of guys in the outfit held him down while another poured Listerine down his throat. He vomited immediately and fell flat on his stomach into a deep sleep. Then someone pulled Valin's pants down around his ankles, and another fellow crouched behind him, and a third brought out a camera, and from just the right angle took phony bugger pictures to the laughter of the remaining men. The photographs were sent to Valin's fiancée the next morning. Karras did not participate, but did not move to stop them. This episode was not mentioned again, not even that afternoon when they had sobered up. And it was not mentioned three weeks to that day, when a Japanese shell cut Grayson Valin clean in half.

The night after the beer party, Karras, who felt the need to get away from the men in his outfit, hopped a ride on the back of a supply truck to a division two miles down the road, where a movie was set to be shown in the main tent. The schedule called for a Rita Hayworth picture, but it turned out to be an Abbott and Costello, which drew boos initially and then uninterrupted laughter once the projector rolled.

After the show, Karras stood outside the tent and lighted a cigarette. He heard a voice that sounded familiar in tone and accent.

"Hey, Marine," said the voice.

Karras turned. The voice belonged to a fellow named Tommy Rados, a Washingtonian with an easy style, a great dancer and storyteller who was well liked in the Greek community by both men and women.

"Tommy," said Karras. "How you doin', chum?"

"Real good," said Rados, who shifted his shoulders and smiled.

"Seen any action yet?"

"Uh-uh. You?"

"We're fixin' to, I think," said Karras.

Rados hummed a few bars of a popular tune, kicked some dirt at his feet. "Say, I've got an army buddy in the infantry, made it off Guadalcanal. He wrote a letter to me, mentioned a local boy in his outfit, guy named Recevo. Didn't you used to pal around with a fellow named Recevo?"

"Joe Recevo, yeah. Why, he's all right, isn't he?"

"Far as I know. 'Course, the letter's kinda old now."

"Uh-huh," said Karras, who pitched his cigarette out into the night.

"Yeah," said Rados, with a reassuring smile. "Well, I gotta get back. Stay safe, Pete."

"You too, Tommy. See you in D.C., hear?"

Karras liked Rados, thought he was a good Joe. Five years later, when he saw Tommy Rados cutting it on the dance floor at the Casino Royal back in town, he felt glad to know that Rados had made it through.

Karras walked back down the road through the thick starless night. The next morning, he shipped out for Leyte, one of the Visayan Islands in the Philippines, somewhere between Samar and Mindanao. It was late October 1944.

Though the landing met little resistance, the fear level was as high as it would get for the men and boys, who for the most part were facing combat for the first time. Going in, there was talk and some derisive laughter over MacArthur's wade in the surf at Red Beach near Tacloban, the true story having gotten around of the famous image being staged. But any laughter during the landing was short and forced, as each man sweated tightly through his own thoughts. Next to Karras on the boat a fellow named Begonia tried to expel gas but instead shit his pants; Karras breathed sparingly, wanting only to get away from the cramped quarters of the LCI.

Once past the beach, they hiked into the jungle, dense with large-leafed vegetation and palms. Despite the shelter of the jungle's green roof, or because of it, the air felt stiflingly damp and hot. The men soon found that there was no place on Leyte to escape the heat, or the rains that came every day. Karras, who had only been out of the city a couple of times in his life, preferred to be away from the jungle, under the open blue of the sky.

They settled in a clearing near a river, a position that they were assured was three miles in front of enemy lines. Machete-wielding Filipinos had done a fair job of scouting the area and freeing it of brush and debris. The men dug their foxholes individually and then collectively cut an L-trench to their 55-millimeter gun. Karras had been named gun captain on Guam.

Sniper fire commenced almost immediately, and the unit was mortared with frequency each day. Soon it became clear that the Japanese were closer than at first anticipated; in fact, their lines were only a couple of thousand yards away.

Three days after they arrived on Leyte, Karras made his first kill, a sniper who had chest-shot a private named Slocum from Apple Valley, Minnesota. Eventually each U.S. soldier killed his first Japanese. Thereafter they ceased to ponder the morality of the act.

As gun captain, Karras felt responsible when a worn breech was discovered in the 55-millimeter gun. A breech from a 155-millimeter Army howitzer, located across the river, was found to be available, but the bridge over the river had been blown by the American army itself to prevent the Japanese from following their path. Karras volunteered, along with two other men, to swim the hundred-odd yards across the river and return with the needed breech. The three of them left that night. One of the men got lucky, contracted elephantiasis after swallowing a mouthful of water, and from that earned a ticket back to the States. Karras did not get sick, and was awarded the first of several medals that he would receive in the course of the war. He would remain most proud of the medal for the swim across the river, which required bravery along with physical endurance and skill. The other medals he received were for killing men.

Despite the K rations and a nagging, fragile stomach which persisted during his Philippine tour, Karras grew stronger and gained more bulk. Daily he lifted the ninety-nine-pound shells, gunpowder canister, and detonator into the tube of the gun. As his strength increased, so did his confidence. Karras had by now seen every kind of combat. He had seen the deaths of many of the men he trained with, some of them friends, some not; as yet, Peter Karras had not received so much as a scratch. But he was still afraid. All of them were still afraid.

Since snipers were everywhere, it was unwise to move around, and foolish to smoke. When Karras wasn't on the gun, he was down in his foxhole, sitting in the water that would rise from the earth after the daily rain. On patrol in the jungle, his unit would meet the enemy face to face, where they would either kill in the most unthinking way, or die. Karras fought hand to hand, taking the life of more than one man like that, looking into their eyes, sometimes filled with fear and sometimes showing nothing at all. He stabbed them and shot them at close range, and beat them to death in their narrow, jaundiced heads with the butt of his M-1. They were the toughest men he had known or would ever know. And while he began to respect them, he hated them, had to hate them so he would not hesitate to do what he had to or think about what he had done.

In those times in the jungle, he fought without a bayonet. He had seen a friend die, his bayonet stuck in a man he had just killed, frantically trying to pull it out as a Japanese soldier shot him in the back of the head. So Karras used his father's Bowie knife instead. He used it until he left it in a man who had come into his foxhole with him one black night. Karras had seen him crawling towards him, and he had called for the man to identify himself. The man did not answer, and Karras, without deliberation, buried the knife in the man's throat. Karras crawled to another foxhole, and in the morning did not go back for the knife. He never knew or cared to know if the man had been American or Japanese.

By late November, it became obvious that the Philippine campaign, predicted as an easy mop-up by MacArthur, was becoming far more costly, bloody, and protracted than anyone had imagined. It was said that the Japanese lieutenant general had abandoned the island to twenty thousand of his own troops, and now the soldiers—sick, starving, resigned to their fates, and living on sea salt and plants—were ready to die in the only way they understood.

December came, and the shelling and sniper fire increased along with the nerve-fraying shouts and taunts from within the jungle. Peter Karras sat in the rain of his foxhole, his M-1 across his lap, his eyes heavy-lidded and hard. He knew, they all knew, that the Japanese had encircled their division. He sat there, trying to recall the smell of his mother's soup, thinking of Eleni Triandokidis and her warm, wet pussy, the thought of Eleni naked hardening his cock. The only thing to do now was think about things like that, things that made him feel good and made him forget. Think about things, and wait.

7

Peter Karras heard the flutter of the first mortar shell leaving its tube in the middle of the afternoon rain. He had come to duck at the sound of it, the sound like the flap of pigeon wings, dirty gray birds lifting off F Street on Saturday afternoons. The shell and then another exploded nearby. Karras balled up until his cheek touched the water that had risen in his foxhole. He felt mud and dirt shower down heavily on his helmet, heard rifle fire and a boy named Maxson scream. Nearby, the radio man, Rubino from Illinois, called in their position and advised that they were under attack.

Karras laid his M-1 outside the foxhole, caught the warm spark of a round on his hand as a bullet glanced off the stock of his weapon. He mumbled something to himself, raised his head slowly so that his eyes cleared the edge of the hole. The Japanese were coming out of the jungle, through the sword grass, and into the clearing in numbers.

From a foxhole up ahead a machine gun chattered, spent shells arcing lazily amidst a widening cloud of smoke. That would be Harper. Harper, from Cuyahoga River country in Ohio, laying rounds into the clearing towards the torsos of the charging Japanese.

Karras got a khaki-mustard uniform in his gunsights and squeezed off a round. The man threw his weapon to the side, arched his back, and waved his hands dreamily as he drifted down into the mud.

"My arm!" yelled Maxson. "God . . . *damn* you, you bastards. My arm . . ."

The sickening flutter of a mortar launch cut the air. Karras had the strange and sure feeling that this one had his name on it—*his* mortar shell,

37

he knew. He rolled out of his foxhole, the mortar exploding somewhere behind him, sending a violent eruption of water and mud into the sky. A wall of air pushed heavily at his back.

Karras had left his M-1 in the hole. He stood, moved a few steps forward, drunk with confusion. Then he looked down. His sergeant, a man named Shelby, lay dead in the mud. Karras bent forward and wrenched Shelby's .45 from his hand.

Karras heard a scream and turned. A Japanese officer, waving his sword, his rotten teeth bared, eager to leave his world and in love with death, ran straight toward him with a caterwauling howl. Karras fired the .45, emptied it, dropped the man several feet short of his mark. Some pieces flew away from the officer's head as he was blown back off his feet.

I'm not going to die today. Today is not my day to die.

Maxson had crawled from his foxhole, in shock now or dead, not moving at all. A jagged piece of bone jutted out from a frayed sleeve, black with blood, where his right arm had been. Karras moved past Maxson, looked up toward the buzz of an engine and the whir of props. Two B-25s rose over the hills and descended into the valley, flying above the coconut palms. Black bombs dropped from beneath the planes, the bombs tottering as they fell. The edge of the jungle erupted in sudden flame. Then the planes strafed the clearing as they passed overhead. Men dove for cover, were shot, or fell to their stomachs shaking, all of them illuminated from the bomb flames that rose like torches in the gray afternoon light. Karras dropped the spent .45 from his hand and ran.

He leaped into a foxhole where Harper sat hunched over his machine gun. Karras put his boot to Harper's side, pushed him away. A clean, black star sat square in the middle of Harper's forehead. Below his useless helmet, the back of Harper's head was pulp.

Not today. I'm not going to die today. Goddamnit, man, look at me. Look at me! I haven't even got a scratch.

Karras laughed.

The bombing had been like setting fire to a beehive. Karras could hear the rest of them coming out of the trees now, running across the field. The Japanese were shooting into foxholes as they ran, then jumping in, thrusting with their bayonets.

Karras put his hand out of the hole, pulled the machine gun in with him. He took the feed belt from the cartridge box, unraveled it, and draped the belt back over his shoulder. Within the confines of the foxhole, it was very hot. He wanted to be out. In the hole, he found it hard to breathe.

Not today. Not in this tiny hole, with someone running by, shooting down at me. Shooting down at me like some kind of animal. Not in this hole. Not today.

Karras pushed off with his legs, lifted the machine gun into his arms, cradled it. He sprung from the foxhole and landed on his feet, landed as softly as if he had jumped into water. He breathed deeply as the rain cooled his face.

They were there, running toward him now, four of them, less than thirty yards away. The crazy screaming bastards were charging, fire flashing from the muzzles of their guns. Karras heard himself hum as his finger locked on the trigger. Puffs of white moved across a perfect azure sky as gulls glided down through the smoke and ejecting shells of the weapon dancing wildly in his arms.

The men before him jerked and fell. Their uniforms ripped open where red flowers bloomed on their khaki-mustard chests.

THREE

Washington, D.C.
1946

8

Peter Karras woke to the gnawing sound of "Baby Snooks" on WTOP coming from the radio on his nightstand. He reached over and turned the damned thing off, adjusting his eyes to the fading light of the room. Had he been sleeping all afternoon? And if he had, well, why the hell not? He draped a forearm over his eyes, and began to drift back off. Then he remembered: the fights. Me and Joe've got tickets to the fights. Archie Moore, no less. He swung himself up, sat on the edge of the bed, and rubbed his eyes.

In the bathroom, Karras took a long leak, then lathered some Barbasol on his shadow and shaved. He could hear Eleni's off-key voice coming from the kitchen, singing along to a Perry Como record—"Dig You Later (A Hubba, Hubba, Hubba)"—that she had bought over the weekend at Super Drugs on 13th and H. At least it wasn't the new Vaughn Monroe, a record she had brought home the same day. Karras had had it up to there with Monroe.

He showered, and when he came out Eleni was singing the Como all over again. Karras could smell her cooking now, a chicken roasted in a pan of *manestra*. He was going to have to disappoint her about dinner. He had a busy night ahead of him, and she'd have to understand.

Karras looked in the mirror as he ran a little Vitalis through his dirty-blond hair, combing it back. Twenty-four years old, and already a little gray in the temples. Like his old man, who was nothing but gray now with a *yero*'s white moustache. Anyway, it didn't stop Karras from getting the looks as he walked down the street. If he had grown up in a different place, and if not for the prominent black mole near his mouth, he maybe even could have been a movie star. He was that kind of handsome, he knew. And not the loverboy, loved-boy, Tyrone Power kind of handsome. More like John Hodiak. Yeah, like a blue-eyed Hodiak. He always liked that guy.

Karras put on a powder-blue shirt, and with it a blue serge suit with pleated trousers. He found a maroon tie decorated with gold diamonds outlined in blue, the blue the same shade as the suit. He laced on a pair of cordovan wingtip brogues, fresh out of the box from the Hahn's at 14th and Park Road, and checked himself out in the door mirror: sharp, and ready to go.

Karras went out to the kitchen and came up behind Eleni, who stood over the stove, stirring the orzo in the pan. She wore a print housedress, her brown hair down and fluffed about her shoulders. Her plump, swollen ankles pushed out on the strap of her sandals. Karras put his arms around her waist, felt her relax.

"How's it going, sweetheart?" he said. He bent forward and kissed the raised pink birthmark on the side of Eleni's neck, brushing his lips on the two or three hairs which grew from it, tangled in a clump.

"It's goin' good now," she said, shifting her thick body beneath his fingers.

"You better be careful, listening to that Como all day. You might fall in love with him."

"I've got enough to keep me busy right here with you."

"Don't forget it." Karras rubbed a hand across her belly. "You feelin' okay?"

"I threw up a little this morning. But I'm all right."

"Good. It's going to be fine."

"I know it." She moved the wooden spoon around in the *manestra*. "We're gonna have a good dinner tonight, Pete."

"It's going to have to wait till I get back," he said, and as he did she stiffened beneath his grip. She did not turn around.

"Why, Pete? Why can't you eat something before the fights?"

"Me and Joe got to go see somebody first. Business, is all it is."

"Business," she said, with a toss of her hair.

He brought his hand up to her right breast, rubbed it slowly until her nipple hardened beneath the cloth. He pushed himself into the small of her back.

"Pete," she said, "I want to you to stay." He caught a side glimpse of her frown, but the edge had left her voice.

"Save it for me, sweetheart. Keep it all warm for me till I get home." He

44

kissed her on the side of her mouth, tasted the grease from the chicken. He rubbed the grease off with the back of his hand.

Karras walked to the door, lifted a deck of Luckies and a book of matches from an end table that stood there, slipped them into the inside pocket of his jacket. He took his black topcoat off the rack and shook himself into it.

"Wait a second, Pete," said Eleni from the open kitchen. She was spooning some *manestra* into a black pot.

"Aw, no, I'm not goin' anywhere with that. I'm not walkin' down the street in my best suit, carrying a *katsarola.*"

"It's for your mother. I told her you'd run it by."

"All right, damnit. Give it to me."

"What're you gettin' so sore about?"

"Nothin'. Just give me the pot."

Eleni crossed the room, put the pot in his arms. She gave him another kiss.

"Try and get home early," she said.

"I will."

She opened the door for him. He stepped out into the hall.

They lived on 6th, up from H, in the same apartment house where Perry Angelos had grown up. Perry's folks still had the same place, and Perry and his wife had a two-bedroom one floor down. Peter Karras didn't mind living in the same neighborhood where he had been raised. It made Eleni a little uncomfortable sometimes, when the hookers and the runners and the bookies flooded into Chinatown after hours every night. But Karras liked the action, and he liked the noise. It was what he was used to, all he knew. Year round, he slept with the window cracked open; the street sounds down on H were his lullaby.

Perry's door was open as Karras headed down the stairs. Perry stood leaning in the frame, reading the *Times-Herald*. The sound of a baby crying reached into the hall from behind him. Karras took the landing to where Perry stood, and put the pot down on the tiles.

"Perry."

"Hey, Pete! What d'ya know?" Perry smiled, his large ears jacking up with the action. He had begun to lose his hair on top, and his work schedule and the new baby had left heavy baggage beneath his eyes.

Karras nodded at the newspaper in Perry's hand. "Anything good?"

"Just readin' the funny pages before I get back to work. 'Gasoline Alley.' Can you believe it, Pete? Skeezix has a kid! We must be gettin' old, buddy."

Karras shuffled his feet. "Still working for your old man?"

"Pullin' double shifts down at the coffeehouse. Just until I can get enough for my own place. I've got my way of running things and he's got his. It's gonna be better when I get out on my own."

"Put all that stuff they taught you in college to good use."

"Yeah, I guess."

Helen walked up behind Perry, jiggling their baby girl in her arms. The baby continued to cry, reaching blindly for her mother's breast. Karras noticed that Helen had gotten her figure back in just two months. She was all made up, too, her bottle-blonde hair falling down across her face on one side. Helen, still doing that Veronica Lake number a couple of years too late. Well, she probably didn't know the Lake look was long gone. Helen didn't get out much anymore.

"Hello, Pete." Her red lips parted in a smile.

"Helen. How's Evthokia?"

"Keeping me busy." She looked him over. "Where you off to, all spiffed up?"

"Me and Joe got tickets to the fights."

"The Moore fight?" said Perry.

"Yeah."

"Damn," said Perry.

"Want to go?" said Karras. "We could probably get you a ticket outside Turner's."

"No. I gotta work." Perry tapped the newspaper excitedly. "Dick McCann says that you're not gonna be able to tell Moore and Parks apart, on account of they're both gonna be wearing purple trunks, and they're both the same shade of brown."

"McCann's an idiot," said Karras. "Don't take everything in that newspaper for gospel, Perry."

Helen chuckled and rolled her eyes. Karras felt a stab of guilt at making Perry look like a sap in front of his wife.

"I gotta feed this baby," said Helen. "Enjoy yourself, Pete. Stay out of trouble." She undid the first few buttons on her blouse, gazing back once at Karras as she drifted. His eyes took in the round tops of her breasts, the sight of them bringing back the memory of the rest of her. He knew better, but he couldn't look away.

"Yeah, Pete," said Perry, not catching a thing. "Have a good time."

"Don't work too hard, chum," said Karras. He picked the pot up off the floor and headed down the stairs.

Out on the street, Karras tried to look as smooth as possible for a guy carrying a big black pot of food. On H, a couple of seagulls hovered above his head, followed him all the way. Seagulls, in the middle of the city. It always surprised him to see it, until he thought of the rivers, and the nearby bay. But the sight of gulls in the city always made him stop, just the same.

At 606, Karras took the steps up to his parents' apartment. The door was open, and he pushed his way in. The place was dark, as it always was, and smelled of incense and garlic. His Murphy bed was up, a table pushed against it, but his old dresser was in place, probably still packed with his old clothes. Dimitri Karras sat in his white T-shirt at his normal spot at the eating table, a bottle of *mastica* in front of him, a cigarette burning in the tray. His mother stood in the kitchen stirring something over the stove.

"*Pos eise, pethi mou?*" said his mother.

"I'm okay, Ma," said Karras, as he walked into the kitchen and put the pot in the sink. "I brought some *kota* and *manestra* from Eleni."

"Hokay, boy," she said.

He kissed her on the cheek. "You look good, Ma."

"Ah," she said, with a flip of her hand.

"Where you goin'," Dimitri said, "all pretty like that. You gotta date?"

Karras looked over at his father, who was staring straight ahead, chuckling at his joke. His eyes were glassy, and his tonicky hair had fallen down about his face. Drunk, and the sun had not yet fallen.

"I'm goin' to the Archie Moore fight, Pop."

"Archie Moore. Thas' one strong nigger." Dimitri coughed, wiped at his moustache with his hand. "*Yiorgia*, when we gonna have a little *fayito?*"

"It's coming, Dimitri. I'm heating it up."

Karras looked at his mother, her graying hair braided and pinned up behind her head. She was on the heavy side, built for work, with thick, calloused hands, and a weak brown moustache across her simian upper lip. But when she brushed her hair out at night, let it fall behind her back, her green eyes shining and relaxed at the end of the day, Karras thought she was as beautiful as any woman he had ever seen.

He'd do anything to protect her. Once, before the war, when some American boys on the corner were making fun of her, calling her a "wop" and a "white nigger" as she walked down H carrying groceries, something had gone black inside him. He had called Joe Recevo, and the two of them had waited across the street from the poolroom where the American boys had gone inside, and when the Americans came out they followed them to an alley, and he and Joe had beaten the hell out of all three, busted them good and bloody with a baseball bat and a pipe. He could take care

47

of things like that on the outside. The only thing he couldn't do was protect her from the old man, in here.

"Yiorgia, the food!" said Dimitri.

"It's comin', Pop!" said Karras.

"I wasn't talkin' to you," mumbled Dimitri. "Big Marine, now he's gonna tell me what's what."

"Siopi," whispered Georgia to her son.

All right, Ma, I'll shut my mouth. Just let me get the hell on out of here.

"I gotta go," Karras said to both of them. "I'm gonna be late."

"Fight's not till later," said Dimitri. "What, you gotta go meet the *Italos?"*

"Yeah, me and Joe have to do a little business."

"What kinda business?" said Dimitri. "Shakedown business? Like some kinda goddamn gangster? Huh?"

"I gotta go," said Karras.

"When you gon' get a real job?" said Dimitri.

"See ya, Ma," said Karras, and he kissed her again on the cheek.

"Adio, Panayoti. Have fun."

Dimitri stood up from his chair, walked unsteadily but quickly across the room. "What, you don't have t'answer your old man? Big Marine, don't have to answer his old man no more." Dimitri reached Peter Karras, shoved him in the chest with the flat of his palm. "Huh?" He shoved once more. "Huh?"

Karras did not step back. "I gotta go, Pop."

"You too good to talk to me now? In your gangster suit?"

"Dimitri—" said Georgia.

"Shutup!" Some spit flew from Dimitri Karras's mouth.

"Relax, Pop."

"I'm gonna relax when I wanna relax! You're not gon' tell me nothin'!"

Dimitri raised his open hand, brought it down towards Peter's face. Peter grabbed his father's wrist, twisted, pushed away. Dimitri lost his balance and fell heavily to the hardwood floor. He stayed there on his side, looking up at this son, his watery brown eyes a mixture of hurt and anger and shame. Karras looked away.

"Fiya apo tho!" his mother screamed, gasping for air through her sobs.

Karras did as his mother asked, and walked from the apartment. On the stairs, he heard the door close softly behind him. He went out of the building, and stepped out onto the sidewalk. He looked back up at his parents' apartment, and saw the curtain move from his mother's bedroom window.

Karras found a phone in a Chinatown restaurant, dialed Joe Recevo. He lighted a cigarette and drew on it while he waited for someone to pick up.

"Hello."

"Joe, it's Pete."

"Hey, Greek, been waitin' by the phone."

"Here I am."

"What's wrong?"

"Nothin'," said Karras. "I'm just anxious to get out, that's all."

"Where you at, I'll pick you up."

"I'm gonna grab a little dinner first. Why don't you swing by Nick Stefanos's grill, say in about an hour."

"Fourteenth and S, right?"

"Yeah."

"Hell, what are you, in Chinatown? That's a long way on foot. I'll pick you up now, we'll drive over."

"That's all right, Joe," said Karras. "It's nice out, not too cold. I think I'm gonna walk."

Karras cradled the receiver, stepped out of the restaurant, buttoned his topcoat as he headed west, pigeons fluttering at his feet. The sun had gone down behind the buildings, leaving long shadows in the golden cast of dusk. He closed his eyes, breathed in the city smells, tried to let things slow down. It was better now, alone out here, walking on the streets.

9

Peter Karras had broken a sweat beneath his topcoat by the time he reached 14th. He turned north, going by Pete Frank's restaurant, a place called the Sun Dial, at R. Frank—Frangis was his name before he Americanized it—was a large Greek from Comosta, a mountain village outside Sparta proper. Karras could see Frank's wife Alice, a stylish woman in her early forties, behind the counter as he passed. He nodded, and caught a smile in return.

Nick Stefanos's grill stood one block up, on the corner of S. An oblong sign hung above the door, blue with red lettering encircled by white bulbs, lit now in the growing darkness like a theatre marquee. NICK'S was all it said. Karras pushed on the door and stepped inside.

Nick's was a plain eat house with eight backless stools up against the lunch counter and three wood-benched booths along the wall. Behind the counter ran a grill and sandwich board arrangement with a soda fountain, coffee urn, and ice cream cooler to the side. A full kitchen sat to the back, and beyond that lay a warehouse area with a private head and a bolted door that led to the alley.

Karras removed his topcoat, hung it on one of the trees that adjoined the booths, and had a seat on a swivel stool cushioned in red, the cushion veined in black. He took his smokes with him.

"Yasou Panayoti!" said Nick Stefanos, walking down to Karras behind the counter, rubbing his hands on a stained apron.

"Yasou Niko."

Karras took Stefanos's hand, leathery and large as a boy's first mitt, and shook it. Stefanos was big for a Greek, barrel-chested and broad, with a wide open face to go with his size.

"What're ya gonna have?" said Stefanos.

"What's the dinner special?"

"We got a nice little lamb. Costa cooked it this afternoon."

"I don't think so. Make it a plate of franks and beans."

"Anything to drink? How 'bout a bottle of beer?"

"Just a Co-cola," said Karras.

Stefanos turned his head toward the slotted hinged doors that led to the kitchen. "Costa," he yelled, "a plate of franks and beans out here! *Grigora!*"

Costa, short and stocky with a great head of black hair and a thick black moustache, pushed through the doors excitedly. The only other customer, an old-timer wearing a chesterfield coat, glanced up from his soup at the sound of the doors crying on their hinges.

Costa looked at Karras. "What, you tellin' me these hot dogs for you, Pete?"

Karras nodded. "That's what I want, Costa."

"You think you at the ballpark or somethin'? Huh? I got a nice little lamb in the back!" He tossed the carving knife that was in his hand up into the air. It rotated once, came to rest cleanly in his grip.

"Give him what he wants," said Stefanos.

"*Entaxi.*" Costa snorted, cursed floridly, turned back toward the kitchen.

"You got no problem," said Stefanos, "do you, Costa?"

"Me?" said Costa. "I don't give a damn nothing."

Stefanos reached into the cooler, fixed a nice plate of calamata olives and feta cheese. He put the plate and a bottle of Coke on the counter in front of Karras.

"Here you go, *vre*," said Stefanos. "Have a little *meza* while you're waitin'."

"Thanks, Nick."

Karras popped an olive into his mouth, stripped it, spit the pit into the plate. He looked past Stefanos's wide head to the large blue sign that hung on the wall—MANN'S POTATO CHIPS, YEAH MANN!—and listened to the show coming from the radio that sat on a wooden shelf next to the sign. An actor was being interviewed by a ventriloquist's dummy. Karras had to smile.

"Who's that on Charlie McCarthy?" said Karras.

"What's that guy," said Stefanos, "the guy plays a drunk."

"Ray Milland," said Karras. "You seen *The Lost Weekend* yet?"

"I go to the pictures, I wanna be happy. See a good Western, maybe. What I wanna see a movie 'bout a boozer for? I got enough problems of my own, right here."

"What kind of problems you got?"

Stefanos made a sweep of his hand. "Just look at my dinner business. There isn't any. The car agencies across the street, they had to close on account of the war."

"Well, they didn't have any cars to sell."

"I know, but . . . what I got left is the phone company business, and it's not enough. I'm telling you, I'm thinkin' about turning this into a place for the *mavri*."

"You're gonna make this into a colored joint?"

"I'm thinkin' about it. Hell, Pete Frank's gettin' ready to do it, right down the street. I can't let him get all the *mavriko* business from U Street, can I?"

"Frank's a good man."

"All right, he's good. But what the hell, I'm not gonna let him get all the goddamn business."

Costa came from the kitchen and dropped a steaming plate of food in front of Karras. He reached under the counter and married a fork and knife setup to a napkin. He slid a bottle of ketchup down next to that.

"Here you go, boss," said Costa. He walked away.

"So what about you?" said Stefanos, leaning his bulk against the counter. "What're you gonna do, now you're back from the war?"

"I don't know," said Karras. "Little bit of this and that, I guess."

"Uh," said Stefanos.

"Gotta find something I like. Don't wanna end up behind a fruit cart like my old man."

"Well, when things pick up around here, and you get tired of relaxin', you come see me. I'm gonna be needin' a little help, a strong set of arms now that me and Costa are gettin' up over forty. And you got a kid on the way now. You gotta think about that, too."

Karras swallowed some food, looked straight ahead. "Sure, Nick. Maybe you and me, we'll have a talk."

The bell over the door chimed, and Lou DiGeordano stepped into the store. He had come directly from his fruit cart, wearing a threadbare jacket over a plain white shirt. His hair was slicked back, his thin black moustache greased as well. A few stray grays sprouted from the black.

"Karras Jr.," said DiGeordano, clapping Karras on the shoulder. He chin-nodded Stefanos. "Nick."

"Lou," said Stefanos.

"How's your old man?" said DiGeordano.

"He's okay," said Karras.

"He's some kinda proud of you, boy. Always talkin' about his son, the war hero."

Karras stabbed his fork into a frank.

"Wanna beer, Lou?" said Stefanos.

"Ballantine Ale," said DiGeordano.

"What's the line on the fight tonight?" said Karras.

"I'm strictly numbers," said DiGeordano. "I don't make book. But if you take Parks, you got a screw loose somewheres. You see the chest on Archie Moore?"

"Some guys around town say that Moore could go down," said Karras.

DiGeordano curled his lip. "Those guys don't know shit from apple butter."

Karras nodded. Stefanos took two bottles from the cooler, and motioned his head in the direction of the kitchen.

"If you're gonna be back there a while," said Karras, "leave me somethin' to read, will you, Nick?"

Stefanos put an *Evening Star* on the counter. He went back to the kitchen, and DiGeordano followed.

Karras finished his dinner, put fire to a smoke as he read the front page. MacArthur was set to execute some Japanese officer from the Philippine campaign, and the hearings on Pearl Harbor were ready to begin. Below the fold, he read about a woman of no fixed address found dead in a house on New York Avenue, cut wide open from sternum to groin. So another working girl went and got herself killed. There had been plenty of crime in town since the war, a few murders now and again, retribution deaths, final settlements on long-cold gambling debts and the like. But these whore murders were a new brand of slaughter: vicious, senseless. These whore murders were just something else.

Costa came out of the kitchen and took Karras's plate. He wiped the area clean with a wet rag.

"Hey, Pete," said Costa, "I was wonderin'. You bring back any kind of knife from overseas? Switchblade, anything like that?"

"I left the only knife I had on the island of Leyte," said Karras. "One of those Filipinos over there, he gave me his machete. That's about it."

"I bet you seen some good knives over there, though. Right?" Costa's eyes were bright.

Karras just shrugged. Costa stared at him for a second or two, then took his plate and the empty soup bowl from the old-timer and went away.

Lou DiGeordano came from the kitchen, using the sleeve of his jacket to wipe foam from his moustache as he walked.

"See you later, Karras Jr."

"Okay, Mr. DiGeordano. See you around."

The chime sounded as DiGeordano went out the door.

Karras took a last drag off his smoke, stubbed it out in the ashtray. The old-timer had hit the road, left two bits on the counter before he buttoned his chesterfield and shuffled out. Nick Stefanos walked from the kitchen, hiking up his trousers as he moved.

"What do I owe you, Nick?"

"Let's see . . . franks and beans, a bottle of Coke. Seventy-five cents."

"All that, huh?" Karras pushed a buck across the counter. "You play a good one with Lou?"

Stefanos spread his hands. "They're all good, till they don't come up. I had a dream about this one, though. My mother was in the dream."

"I never dream about the dead. Anyway, you're not supposed to."

"That's right. But she wasn't in the dream, exactly. I mean, I didn't see her. I heard her voice, though. I was listenin' to her from behind a door. There was a number on the door, like some kind apartment number—"

"So you played the number."

"Yeah. I put a fistful on it."

"You'll win a bundle if it hits. What're you gonna do with it if you win?"

"I dunno. Send some to my boy in Greece, I guess. Or maybe use it like bait to get him over here. Anyway, I don't hit the number, I'm gonna win it back from Lou on Saturday night."

"You still have that card game at your place every weekend?"

"Yeah, sure. Lou and Costa are regulars. Pete Frank and his wife Kiki, they're gonna come too. Pete's brother-in-law, George Boukas—"

"That the guy who used to be a fighter?"

"Went by the name of 'Kid Boukas' in the ring. Worked down at the Willard as a busboy, long time. Has a flower shop now."

"Yeah," said Karras. "I heard of that guy. A lightweight, wasn't he?"

"Good little boxer," said Stefanos. "Good athlete, all the way around."

A horn sounded outside the plate-glass window of the grill as a Mercury coupe pulled over to the curb. Karras stood, grabbed his topcoat, smoothed out the lapels as he put it on.

"That's my ride, Nick."

"You chew on what I told you, *re*. Fun and games is all right, but now you gotta think about a little honest work."

"I'll think about it."

"Call me," said Stefanos. "Adams four, sixty-four-eighty."

Karras smiled. "Okay, Nick. We'll talk."

The chimes sounded as Karras went out to the street. Nick Stefanos watched him open the passenger door of the coupe and climb inside.

"Yeah," said Stefanos to an empty store, rubbing a thick, calloused hand across his face. "We'll talk. But first, young guy like you? You gonna go out and have a little fun."

10

Joe Recevo pushed the shifter into second, gave the Mercury some gas. He looked over at Karras, fiddling with the dial on the radio. An old, English-accented voice came through the dash speaker. The sound of it made Recevo wince.

"Find some music on that thing, will ya?"

"That's Fred Allen's show," said Karras. "What's wrong with that? He's got this British comedian . . . *comédienne* on tonight. Beatrice Lillie is her name."

"I don't care what her name is. I need to hear some old broad yappin' like a submarine needs a screen door."

Karras spun the dial, landed on the lilting vocal of Dinah Shore—"Personality" was the tune. He kept his hand on the knob, glanced across the bench at Recevo: a chocolate-brown suit with a matching tie, and a camel hair topcoat over the whole rig. On his head, a brown fedora with a chocolate-brown band, a small red feather tucked in it. Recevo, always with the hats.

"This okay?" said Karras.

"Yeah, Dinah Shore is top shelf." Recevo sideglanced at Karras. "They say she's high yellow. You know that?"

"Oh, for God's sakes, Joe."

"Got a strain of jig blood in her. It ain't no secret."

"That's a bunch of horseshit."

"What, did I offend you, Mrs. Roosevelt?"

"It's stupid, Joe, that's all."

Recevo grinned a little, fished a deck of Raleighs from his coat, blew into the open top of the pack. A cigarette popped out from the rush. Karras lighted a match, heated up a Lucky for himself, extended the match to Recevo, lighted his. Recevo extinguished the flame on the exhale. Karras cracked the window, tossed the match out into the night.

"Have a good dinner with your pals?" said Recevo.

"Yeah."

"You and all them JCOs, talkin' away. That must of been a sight."

"JCOs?" said Karras. "They didn't 'just come over.' Hell, Joe, they been here over twenty years. Came the same time as your old man, and mine."

"They don't sound like it. The little one, Costa—"

"He's all right. Just has an excitable personality, is all. And Nick Stefanos is all aces."

"Stefanos is Jake. I know one thing, I'd hate to be on the receiving end of one of his punches. You ever get a look at that guy's hands? Like pie plates."

"He offered me a job in his place."

Joe smiled. "I'd like to see that. You in an apron."

"Yeah," said Karras. "That would be somethin', wouldn't it?"

Recevo slowed going by the Lotus Club, where a small line had formed outside. Karras craned his neck.

"What're they, givin' away drinks?" said Karras.

"No cover tonight," said Recevo. "The usual revue. Burlesque, with an orchestra. The Baron Twins—"

"I seen 'em," said Karras. "One's all right, but two is overkill."

Recevo hooked a left onto New York Avenue, downshifted going into the turn. Karras lurched forward, ashes dropping onto his coat.

"Shit, Joe, can't you control this oil can?"

"It's that Flathead V-8 under the hood. A little too many horses for the car."

"Maybe you ought to get yourself a nice, quiet sedan."

"I got my eye on the new models when they come out. A Hudson, maybe. Anyway, I don't need advice from a guy who doesn't even own a set of wheels."

"I like to walk, is what it is."

"Yeah, you took a good one tonight. You know, you coulda caught a streetcar, Pete."

"You seen the streetcars lately? Too crowded for me. They all look like the Toonerville Trolley, everybody hangin' off the sides. This whole damn town's too crowded. They said things would clear out after V-J Day, but you wouldn't know it, lookin' around D.C."

"You can't complain about the women, though, can you. My God, there's enough of 'em."

"I noticed," said Karras.

"Sure you did," said Recevo. "Gash-hound like you."

Karras dragged on his cigarette, blew smoke through his lips and watched it shatter on the windshield. He looked down on the hand that held the cigarette. A wedge of yellow light passed across his fingers, disappeared and returned as they drove beneath the streetlights. The veins along the back of his hand reflected blue in the light.

"Where we headed now?" said Karras.

"To see Mr. Burke," said Recevo. "He's got something for us to take care of later on. It won't take a minute. He's just gonna give us our marching orders, and then we're gonna be on our way."

"I took all the orders I ever wanted to take in the service."

"It kept you alive, didn't it?"

"Luck kept me alive," said Karras. "Plain dumb luck."

"Well, I'll do any talking if it's called for. You just smile and nod your head. Think you can do that?"

"Sure, Joey," said Karras. "I'll just nod my head." He took one last drag off his cigarette, and pitched the butt end out the window.

Sinatra's latest, "Day by Day," came smoothly through the radio. Recevo reached over and gave the volume a quarter turn. He tossed his cigarette, settled into his seat, smiled, and began to sing along. Karras let him do it. The truth of it was, Joe had a pretty nice voice.

"You know, they say it's gonna be all singers now," said Recevo at the break in the vocal. "The big bands are through."

"That's what I hear."

"I loved the bands, you know? But if all the singers sounded like Sinatra, I wouldn't mind if I never heard another instrumental number in my life." Recevo tapped Karras's arm. "Hey, you remember the first time we saw him?"

"U-Line Arena," said Karras.

"Nineteen-forty. He was with the Pied Pipers. Sang 'Just Look at Me Now.' My God, the girls went nuts. One minute we were dancin' with a couple of broads, and the next we were standing alone in the middle of the floor. Hell, we barely even knew who the guy was."

"Looked like just another greaser to me," said Karras. But Recevo was off somewhere, and the comment didn't sink.

"But the best night," said Recevo. "The best night! That was when we took those canoes down from Fletcher's Boathouse, floated down the

58

channel to the Watergate barge. Sinatra was playing for free that night, under the stars with a full orchestra. Sang 'Ol' Man River,' right? It's like the whole crowd was hypnotized or somethin'. Man, those women were all googoo-eyed, hangin' off the Memorial Bridge."

"Just before you shipped out."

"Yeah. I was with that Lawson girl—what the hell was her first name?"

"How would I know? She was your girl, not mine."

"And you were with Helen Leonides. *Goddamn*, did she look put together that night. A brick shithouse don't begin to describe it—"

"Knock it off, Joey."

"Sorry. I forgot, you're married now. And your buddy Pericles is married to Helen—"

"Forget about it."

"What, now you're gonna tell me you never had any of that? Shit, Greek, you told me the next day that you jazzed her all up and down—"

"I said, knock it off!"

"All right."

They drove without speaking for the next couple of miles. A Phil Harris record replaced the Sinatra. Karras rolled the window down an inch and let himself cool off. It wasn't Joe he was mad at, anyway.

"As a matter of fact," said Karras, "I saw Perry earlier tonight."

"How's he doin'?"

"He's good. He's working hard, lookin' to open a place of his own. He'll probably have a few of them when he's done."

"See the new baby?"

"Uh-huh. The baby's fine."

"And how about Helen. You see her too?"

"I saw her."

"Yeah?" Recevo cleared his throat. "How'd she look?"

Karras looked over at Recevo. Both of them broke out in laughter. Karras punched Recevo's arm. Recevo put one hand up to stop a second blow, and the Mercury swerved over the center line. They hit the Negro blocks around New Jersey Avenue, still laughing as they reached a cross street with a few row houses occupied by whites. Recevo pulled over to the curb and cut the engine.

"Remember what I said, Pete."

"Smile and nod."

"Right."

They got out of the coupe and crossed the street. Karras and Recevo were roughly the same height, moved similarly with fluid, sharklike intent.

When they walked together, side by side like that, it was as if they were two halves of one man. Recevo had angular, set-in, pockmarked cheeks, and he was dark of complexion with black, wavy hair. Nobody ever called him handsome like they did Karras. Street handsome was more like it. But Recevo did all right.

They took the steps up to the row house door. Like several corner row houses scattered around D.C., this one was topped with a castlelike battlement. A crenellated wall crowned its turret. Recevo pointed it out to Karras.

"What, is Burke splittin' the rent with King Arthur, or somethin'?"

"Yeah," said Recevo. "And there's Basil Rathbone. He's up there, threadin' an arrow's got your name on it."

Karras laughed. While he was laughing, he looked down at Recevo's feet.

"New brogues?"

"Flagg Brothers, four dollars and ninety-five. You like?"

"Yeah," said Karras. "They'll do."

Recevo knocked on the front door. He took off his hat, smoothed back his hair, flicked at the dent of the fedora, replaced it on his head. He ran a thumb and forefinger along the brim. A shutter opened on the door, a large pair of blood-rimmed eyes appearing in the space.

Recevo moved his face into the light. "Karras and Recevo, here to see Mr. Burke."

"Hold on."

The shutter closed, and then the door swung open to a huge ugly man standing in the frame. Karras looked him over, thinking, the only way to drop him is to hit him low. Cut him down like a big tree.

"Come on," said the man, who everyone called Face.

They went into a small foyer which introduced a banistered staircase on the left. To the right, an open set of French doors gave to a large living room where three men in suits and a woman in a bolero jacket and slacks sat around in cushioned furniture sipping highballs and huffing cigarettes. The woman looked brittle and cheap; Karras smiled at her anyway, from habit. Her shoeless, stockinged feet rested on top of a kidney-shaped marble table. Next to her feet, a blue-black revolver lay on its side.

"Hey, Face," said Karras, "how's the family?"

"They're good, Karras. Thanks for askin'."

Recevo said, "Your kids look like you or your wife?"

Face thought it over. "My wife, I guess."

Recevo grinned. "They oughta thank God."

"Go on up," said Face, jerking a thumb thick as a divot toward the ceiling.

Recevo and Karras took the stairs. Karras ran his hand along the stained oak of the banister.

"Face just called you a pussy behind your back," said Karras. "I heard him clear as day. You gonna take him on when we're done with Burke?"

"Yeah," said Recevo. "And right after that, I'm gonna wrastle Mighty Joe Young."

They reached the landing at the top of the stairs, turned right and went through an open door into a large area that had been a couple of bedrooms before Burke's men had knocked out the walls. Burke, sitting behind a clean oak desk, did not look up as they entered. Karras noted the locked gun case against the wall, a Thompson gun racked behind the glass.

A woman, an unremarkable brunette, sat at the end of a divan pushed against the wall. The wood of the divan was scraped and chipped—Face had knocked it around, most likely, carrying it up the stairs on his back. The rest of the divan was taken up by Gearhart, Burke's brain and counsel, all three hundred hawk-nosed pounds of him. He strained a smile at Recevo, showing more gum than teeth, his fingers playing with a watch chain that ran from vest to trouser pocket, pushed out in the middle at the bulge of his lap. Karras could see the usual two-toned, brown and white gibsons on Gearhart's pudgy feet. A dandy all the way, and a fat one at that—the worst kind.

A plain, heavy dining table stood in the middle of the room, four high-backed chairs grouped around it. Reed, Burke's top muscle, sat at the head of the table, rolling an unlit Fatima around in his fingers, sizing up Karras as he crossed the room. Recevo and Karras each took a chair away from the table, pulled them over to in front of Burke's desk. They had their seats. Recevo removed his hat, smoothed back his hair, placed the hat in his lap.

Burke laced his fingers together, rested his hands on the desk. "How's it going, Joe?"

"Things are all right, I guess."

"Karras," said Burke. "Glad you could come."

Karras nodded and smiled. He forgot which one he had agreed to do first.

"You boys going to the fights tonight?"

"Uh-huh," said Recevo, glancing at his watch.

"Got money on Moore?"

"Not worth the time it takes to place the bet," said Recevo. "I just don't think Parks is gonna give him much of an argument. I got a little cash on the undercard, though. Morales against Russell."

"You took Morales, I hope."

"Yeah."

Burke said, "Smart boy."

Karras, fidgety as a kid in church, looked around the room. His eyes landed on the brunette. He followed her legs down to her shoes, platform slingbacks with silver nailheads along the sides of the soles. He had seen them in the window at I. Miller's on F, when he was looking around for a little something for Eleni. He wondered idly who the woman was with, if anyone, or if she was just around for decoration. Twelve dollars and ninety-five cents for those shoes. He wondered if she was worth the price.

"We gonna talk business, or what?" said Reed, in that too-loud way of his, like talking loud would make someone care about what he had to say. Karras had known guys like him in the service. Not that Reed had ever been in uniform; the word was that he had flunked the psychiatric. He was just a mean one, with the small eyes of a pig and the shoulders of a full-back. As a kid, he had done reform time for pouring gasoline on a neighbor's cat. Later, as an adult, he had pulled a year's stretch for slapping a girl on a bus.

"Yes," said Burke, "we need to talk. Don't want you two to be late for the main event."

"If it's business," Reed said, "then maybe the twist ought to leave the room."

The twist. Karras grinned. Reed hadn't gone to the pictures since 1939. *The Roaring Twenties* had been the last one he'd seen.

Burke nodded at the woman, who rose quickly but with some dignity. She threw a hurt look at Burke and flicked her eyes over Karras as she walked across the room. The slingbacks made a clapping sound on the hardwood floor, then were muted as she hit the carpet of the stairs.

"So," said Recevo, "what've we got?"

"A fellow named George Georgakos owes me a few bucks. Old bird paid me the principle, but we're having a little disagreement over the interest. He claims he's going to get around to it, but so far, nothing. I thought you and Karras would go see him tonight, collect some of my money. It might convince me that he's sincere."

George Georgakos—a gypsy type from the ghettos of Athens via Smyrna. Karras knew him vaguely as a guy who hung out late at night at the Greek clubs in Southeast, playing cards and drinking *mastica* with his old man. Hanging out at the clubs, after his bus shift at the Hotel Washington, where he took home fifteen, maybe twenty bucks a week. Karras looked at Burke's hands, tented on the desk. On the outside, Burke seemed fit, his posture always ramrod straight, his stomach flat beneath the vest of his suit. But the hands were soft, the grip lazy and without character. Karras remembered wanting to wash off, the last time he shook Burke's hand.

"How much do you want us to collect?" said Recevo.

"Forty ought to do it for now. We had a little communication problem in the past. Maybe he was kidding me, but I couldn't understand much of what the old guy said. Typical, with these immigrants—they don't even bother to learn the language."

That's because they've been too busy workin', tryin' to feed their families. Workin' like dogs, as if a dog could ever work that hard. Not that any of you snow-white bastards would understand the meaning of the word—

" . . . That's why I thought it might be a good idea for Karras here to go along. That sound good to you, Karras?"

Karras smiled and nodded. He thought he'd mix things up this time.

"Yeah," said Reed. "Karras and this Georgakos bird, they speak the same language. The two of them can just sit around together all night and grunt."

Gearhart snorted, issued a gassy grin. Karras heard Reed strike a match to the Fatima behind his back. The smoke from it crawled across the room.

"Forty dollars," said Recevo, trying to cut the chill. "That should be a walk in the park, right, Pete?"

"Not a problem," said Karras.

"Hey, Karras," said Reed. "Be a good little colored girl and fetch me that ashtray offa Mr. Burke's desk."

"I'll get it," said Recevo, but Karras held him back with his arm.

"I asked Karras to get it for me," said Reed.

Karras pointed his chin in the direction of Gearhart. "Ask Laird Cregar over there to get it for you, Reed. He's a little closer."

Gearhart's grin turned down. He didn't make a move for the ashtray, and neither did Reed.

Recevo drummed his fingers on the arm of his chair. He shifted in his seat. "Mr. Burke, what should we do if this Georgakos gives us an argument?"

"He won't give you an argument," said Burke, keeping his eyes locked on Karras. "He wouldn't give an argument to a couple of boys who've seen the action you've seen. Would he?"

Burke himself had seen no "action," as he was on the brown side of thirty. But he had a brother who had fought in the European theatre, and

63

being a veteran meant something to Burke. There were points to be had there, Karras figured, and some degree of slack.

"We'll take care of it," said Recevo, and he and Karras rose from their seats.

"Hey," said Reed. "I got an idea. Maybe you ought to wear your uniforms over to the Greek's place. Wear your medals, too. Maybe that would help."

"Maybe you'd like to go with them," said Burke, with a touch of acid in his voice.

"Reed might have a little problem there," said Karras. "He'd need a uniform, too. And the last time I checked, they weren't handin' out uniforms to Section Eights."

Reed stood from his chair, blood coloring his face.

"Hold it," said Burke. "You two can play if you want, but not in here."

"Guy kills a few Japs," muttered Reed, "he thinks his asshole squirts perfume."

Burke raised his voice. "Shut your mouth, Reed, and sit down. You can thank me later."

Reed sat, dragged deeply on his cigarette. Recevo placed his hat back on his head, cocked it just right. Karras shifted his shoulders to comfort beneath his topcoat.

"You've got an address for us, Mr. Burke?" said Recevo.

"Yes, I'm going to give it to you now." Burke looked at Karras. "Will you excuse us a minute, Pete? I've got a private matter to discuss with Joe here."

"I'll meet you down in the foyer, Joe."

Karras turned and went through the open door, a kind of spring in his step. Reed smiled at him, followed his movements with narrowed eyes. Karras's heavy footsteps faded as Burke jotted down the address on a slip of paper.

"Here," said Burke, passing the paper to Recevo across the desk. "There's not going to be any trouble tonight, is there?"

"No," said Recevo. "No trouble."

"Because I'm remembering the screwup with Mr. Weinberg. That tailor who owed me protection money, over on Seventh."

"That was just a special case," said Recevo. "The thing of that was, Pete knew the guy, from the neighborhood. He outfitted a lot of Greeks on credit in the old days. I think he even sold a suit to Pete's old man—a dollar a week, for fifteen weeks, no interest, something like that. Altered the suit for him on a handshake. So Pete had a personal connection there—"

"I'm not interested in your boyhood connections. This Weinberg character, we lost him right after you gave him breathing room."

"The Jew bastard skipped," said Reed.

"We lost him because you allowed Karras to turn soft," said Burke. "And you can't allow anyone to be soft when you're trying to build this type of business."

"I understand, Mr. Burke."

"Listen. I'm giving you another chance because the two of you did your part overseas, and you know with me that means something. And because I see promise in you, Joe. The people who start off with me are going to go all the way. Understand?"

"Sure."

"Good. Enjoy the fights. Phone me later and let me know how things went. I'll be waiting for your call."

Recevo tipped his hat to Burke, walked toward the door, gave nothing, not even an eye-sweep, to Reed. The way to hurt Reed was to not give up a thing. You held the steak outside the cage with that one, but you never slipped it through the bars.

Recevo left the room and no one said a thing. In a minute or two they heard the door close from the front of the house.

Reed dropped his cigarette to the floor and crushed it beneath his shoe. "Greeks and Italians," he said. "I'm tellin' you, we don't need any part of 'em. The next thing you know, we'll be walkin' around here in tuxedos, servin' dinner to niggers."

Gearhart fingered his watch chain, moved his turtle eyes curiously beneath their lids. "The Greek's going to stumble," he said. "It's in his nature. You know that, don't you?"

Burke nodded. "Of course. But this isn't his test. It's Recevo's."

Gearhart raised an eyebrow. "What about the Greek, then?"

Burke exhaled heavily. "The Greek's done."

Out on the sidewalk, Recevo stopped under a streetlight to strike a match to a cigarette. He blew smoke in the direction of Karras, who stood beside him, looking up at the starless sky.

"Pete, Pete, Pete," said Recevo. "What the hell am I gonna do with you?"

"What?"

"I thought I told you to keep your mouth shut."

"Oh, for God's sakes, Joe. It was a laugh, wasn't it? I mean, don't take those guys so seriously. Anyhow, I wasn't so out of line, was I?"

"Calling Reed a Section Eight? And then that Laird Cregar crack with Gearhart."

"Relax." Karras pulled on Recevo's arm. "Come on, we're gonna miss the undercards."

They walked to the coupe and climbed inside. Karras found a station on the radio while Recevo turned the ignition and revved the engine.

"Gearhart," said Karras. "You gotta admit, that fat sonofabitch does look a little like Laird Cregar, doesn't he?"

"Cregar's better lookin'," said Recevo.

They were laughing as the coupe pulled away from the curb.

11

Karras rolled his window down a quarter turn, aimed the exhale from his cigarette in the direction of the crack. The radio played "The Frim Fram Sauce" by the King Cole Trio. Karras had seen Nat Cole at the Casino Royal late one night. He had really liked Cole's style.

"I don't want to bring this up again—" said Recevo.

"Then don't."

"But your attitude back there—it just wasn't right."

"Uh-huh."

"The thing is, you gotta take this work we're gettin' with Burke a little more serious."

"Oh, yeah? Why's that?"

"Because we're gettin' in on the ground floor here, Pete, that's why. Burke's got plans to expand his organization."

Karras dragged on his cigarette. "He gets too big, he's gonna get crushed. The rackets are already sewed up. Snags Lewis runs the wire service, and Pete Gianaris controls the numbers game. Meyers is dice. All of it flows to Jimmy La Fontaine. And a wire runs from La Fontaine to Frank Costello in New York. You think the New York mob's gonna let a bunch of rogues take a piece of the action?"

"You miss my point. Burke's not interested in numbers, or dice, and he ain't interested in the ponies. His grift is protection, high-interest loans. There's a whole lot of people out there, they want to start a business, whatever—"

"Immigrants, you mean."

"Immigrants, yeah, and some others, too. The banks won't give 'em a second look. It's a kind of service Burke is providing."

"Burke and his men, they're not going to last. I'm tellin' you, you're puttin' your chips on the wrong color. He's gonna get crushed."

"There's a hole out there, and Burke is filling it. Pete, this town is wide open. Somebody's going to come along and pick up the money that's just lyin' in the street. We could be a part of it, you and me."

"I don't want to fall in with those guys," said Karras. "I'm tellin' you, I just don't."

"Sure you do. And if you keep it up with this attitude, Burke's gonna think twice about moving us up."

"I don't give a good goddamn what he thinks."

"Okay. But what the hell are you going to do if you don't do this?"

"I don't know. I'll find something. Maybe I'll take the civil service exam."

"A government man," said Recevo. "That's a laugh. You'd have to get up before noon, you ever think of that?"

"I could do that."

"Sure you could. Listen, you and me, we're Washingtonians. Real Washingtonians, born and raised. We got nothin' to do with those government types. Tourists is what they are. Anyway, you never gave two shits about it before. You never even voted. I mean, you ever visited the Capitol? Ever taken the White House tour?"

"I went to the Lincoln Memorial one night."

"That was to neck with some broad."

"I went, is all I'm sayin'."

"And all I'm saying is, you got to stop bein' so cocky, Pete. You got a kid on the way, don't forget."

"I know it," said Karras. "But I'm gonna work it out myself. I don't want to be falling in with someone like Burke."

"Do me a favor, then. Play things straight tonight. Help me out with this Georgakos character, all right? You're gonna see, things'll fall into place after that."

"Don't worry, Joe." Karras dropped his cigarette out the window. "I won't screw up."

■

They were turning them away on W Street, outside Turner's Arena. Recevo found a spot to park the Mercury, and he and Karras went inside.

Recevo's tickets were close to prime, eighteen rows up from the ring. Most of the crowd sported shirts and ties, guys going solo mainly, with only a smattering of dates. A haze of cigar and cigarette smoke hovered like a fog down below. They bought a couple of beers on the way to their seats.

Karras lighted a smoke. He lighted one for Recevo off the same match. They had come in on the middle of the prelims, a five-round match between two local boys, Artie Brown and Flattop Cummings.

In the fifth, the boxing got furious close in, and Cummings's trunks began to fall below his waist. The referee tried to step in and pull the trunks back up, took a good one on the chin from Brown for his troubles.

"Would you look at that!" said Recevo, elbowing Karras in the ribs. "Brown clocked the ref right in the kisser!"

"I'll be goddamned," said Karras.

Brown won on points, and in the dead time before the next bout Karras looked around the plant. Chief Barrett was seated down at ringside with a couple of his lieutenants. Nearby was Emmit Warring, one of the better-known professional gamblers around town. In the row behind them, Karras could see Steve Mamakos, seated with his manager.

"Hey, Joe, there's Mamakos!"

"Where?"

"Second row back from the ring."

Recevo looked over at Karras. He was smiling, leaning forward, his eyes wide as a kid's. Recevo hadn't seen that look on Karras since way before the war.

"Maybe your boy Mamakos is thinking of steppin' into the ring someday with Archie Moore. He's studyin' him, like."

"Stop kiddin'. Mamakos is a middleweight all the way. Pound for pound, though, if all things were equal, I bet he could give Moore a fight."

"Like he gave Tony Zale?"

"Knock it off. Zale decisioned him in thirteen in that first fight. Then it took Zale another thirteen in the second fight to drop Steve. In that one, Mamakos had both of Zale's eyes shut at the end. I don't think any fighter gave Zale a tougher time than Mamakos. Billy Conn didn't. Not even Graziano."

"All right, I get it. You don't have to keep yappin' about it."

"It's not over yet for Mamakos."

"I said, 'all right.'" Recevo stood from his seat. "I'm gonna go get a couple Nationals. You want?"

"Yeah, I want."

The featherweight semiwindup, Chico Morales against Danny Russel, got under way as Recevo returned to the seats. Morales went inside quick, punctuating each combination with the snap of a short right. He kept at it, and Russel began to tire by the third.

"The Cuban's fast," said Karras. "You got money on him?"

"A little."

"The Cuban's gonna take him out."

Morales chilled Russel in the fourth. Recevo and Karras drank their beers and smoked a couple of cigarettes. Jimmy La Fontaine and his lawyer, Charlie Ford, arrived at their ringside seats with a flourish just as the announcer was pulling down the mike to bark out the stats for the main event.

"La Fontaine looks old," said Recevo.

"He's what, close to eighty?"

"Around there, yeah. I hear Jimmy Boyle is workin' the door for La Fontaine at night, over at Eastern Avenue."

"It's no secret."

"A D.C. beat cop, workin' the biggest gambling joint in the county. A little dangerous, playing both sides of the street like that, don't you think?"

"Boyle knows what he's doing. He's not dirty, if that's what you mean. La Fontaine likes to have a few cops on the payroll, makes him feel secure. Anyway, this isn't Chicago. The payoff money funnels up here, not down to the cops in uniform. Boyle's just ambitious. And you hear things, workin' in a place like that."

"If Boyle really wants to get off the street, get his detective's badge, maybe he oughta look into solving those hooker murders. The suits they got on the case, they haven't turned up a thing. That one last night was the second this year."

"Boyle's wanted to be a cop since he was a kid. If there's any way for him to advance, he'll find it."

The ring announcer introduced the fighters. Archie Moore looked slim in the hips, solid up top, his face smooth and unmarked. A loud applause went up for hometown boy George Parks.

"My God, Parks is some kind of big."

"Moore's giving away fifteen pounds," said Karras. "But just you watch."

At the bell, Archie Moore came out with a series of left jabs. Then a left hook connecting to Parks's jaw, and a straight right after that to the same spot. Moore followed with the exact combination and sent Parks into the ropes.

Recevo pointed at the referee. "Gallagher's gonna stop it."

But Moore beat the ref to it and put Parks down to the canvas with a hard right. Parks took a nine count, stood up. He was bleeding freely from his nose and couldn't find his feet.

"Parks is on Queer Street," said Karras.

"Yeah," said Recevo. "Parks is done."

Moore gave Parks another flurry and Marty Gallagher stopped the fight. There were boos heard in the auditorium as Karras and Recevo filed out.

"Two minutes and change into the first round," said Recevo. "Can you believe it?"

"What did you think was gonna happen? Anyway, we saw a couple of good fights. You win anything on Morales?"

"A couple of bucks."

They walked out of Turner's, hit the night air. Karras reached into his topcoat, withdrew an empty pack of Luckies, crumpled the pack.

"Gimme one of those Raleighs, will you?"

"Here."

Karras struck a match, drew in smoke. He made a sour face, tossed the match into the street. "How the hell do you stand these things?"

"What, they're good enough for Babe Ruth and Ed Sullivan, aren't they?"

"Ed Sullivan," said Karras, and shook his head. "Where we off to, Joe?"

"To see Georgakos, I guess. Get that out of the way."

"Georgakos hangs out at the Hellenic Club most nights. He won't be in till late."

"All right then, we'll wait."

"What are we gonna do in the meantime?"

"Find ourselves a drink, I guess."

"Make it Kavakos's," said Karras.

Recevo grinned, put the Mercury in gear.

12

■■■■■■ They drove into Northeast, parked on H, approached the club on the 8th Street side. The sound of the place was spilling out onto the sidewalk, people laughing and shouting over the amplified voice of Frankie Donato, the house emcee. Karras removed his wedding band, dropped it in his trouser pocket. The doorman, a guy named Jerry Tsondilis, let Karras and Recevo in on sight.

It was jumping for a weeknight, the bar near full, all the tables of the nightclub occupied. Karras stepped up to the stick. Recevo elbowed his way to a spot on Karras's right.

Karras signalled Bill Kavakos, who stood drawing a draft beneath the tap. His brother Johnny leaned on the other end, wiping down a puddle where some booze had spilled.

Bill Kavakos stepped up, nodded at the two of them. His eyes lingered on Karras without emotion. "Pete. What's it going to be?"

"A bottle of Senate for me," said Karras. "And a shot of rye."

"What flavor on the whiskey?"

"Pete Hagen's. The hundred proof if you've got it."

"How bout you, friend?"

"The same way," said Recevo.

Bill Kavakos went and put together the order while Recevo lighted a smoke. He blew into the pack, sent another one out, pushed the pack in the direction of Karras. Kavakos returned with the drinks, set them down. Karras floated a couple of ones onto the bar.

Recevo lifted his glass. "Success, buddy."

"I'm for it, chum."

They knocked back their shots at once, chased the rye with a swig from their bottles. Karras took in a lungful of smoke, let it out slowly. He looked around the bar.

Kavakos's bar didn't seem much different from years ago, when it had been a low-ceilinged, straight saloon, with a film of sawdust on the floor and the smell of stale beer locked in every split of wood. Peter Karras had often walked here from across town as a child, sent by his mother to find his father, to bring him home for dinner. More often than not he did find his father here, watery-eyed and belligerent, his arms folded on the bar. Fifteen years later, here was Karras, doing the same damn thing. He wasn't his old man, though. Not by a long shot.

"There's Steve Nicodemus," said Recevo. Nicodemus was down near the end of the bar, visibly drunk, trying to get Johnny Kavakos's attention.

"I see him." But Karras was already looking past Nicodemus to a blonde who sat beyond him, reading a paperback novel, a cocktail glass in front of her.

"Want to go talk to him?"

"Maybe later," said Karras, finishing his beer. "Let's have another round."

"We got work to do tonight. And you ain't much of a drinker."

"I need more practice at it, that's all."

"Whatever you say." Recevo caught Bill Kavakos's eye. "One more time over here!" he said, swirling his finger above their empty glasses.

They had their shots and dented the beers. Recevo saw a girl he knew, Lois Roman, walk into the nightclub with an older guy wearing a herringbone topcoat. Lois wore a muskrat topper, which Recevo figured went for a couple of hundred bucks. He wondered if the guy with the gray temples had sprung for the coat.

"I'm gonna head into the nightclub," said Recevo. "You coming?"

"Nah. That Donato guy gives me a headache. Your grandmother was laughing at those jokes when she was in diapers."

"Not unless she heard 'em in Sicilian, she wasn't."

"You go ahead. I'll be along."

Karras took his beer down the bar to where the blonde sat. He stood next to her, leaned over, rested one forearm on the pocked oak. Even through the tobacco curtain and the stink of booze he could pick up the clean smell of shampoo coming off her long blonde hair. She wore no perfume, and he couldn't stand it when a woman did. He wondered, how in the hell could a dish like this be all alone?

She wore a blue slack suit with wing sleeves on the drop-shouldered jacket, a white silk blouse underneath. Karras checked out her feet: cobra-skin sling pumps, open-toed. A matching handbag sat on the bar next to a pack of Camel cigarettes.

"Snake charmers," said Karras.

"Excuse me?" she said, without looking up from her book.

"Your shoes. I saw them down at Hahn's. They had a little card set up next to the display. 'Snake Charmers' is what it said on the card."

She glanced up into his eyes for a second or so, and then at his hand on the bar. She had a small, tidy nose and a wide mouth that curved kind of nicely and didn't seem to move too much when she spoke. Her own eyes were a kind of sea green, crystalline at times when they picked up the light from the fixtures above the bar. He could see that much in those couple of seconds, and knew right away that he liked what he had seen. She returned to her book, spoke to him again without so much as a movement of her head.

"So what were you doing shopping for women's shoes?"

"It's a hobby of mine."

"Or maybe you were thinking of picking up a little something for your wife. Men surprise their wives with gifts when they've got to take a load off their consciences, don't they."

"I guess you got me," said Karras, throwing up his palms in surrender. "Yeah, I've got a wife. Truth is, I'm as married as a drunk to his bottle."

"Well, at least you're honest. You're awful forward, but you're honest, I'll give you that. It's an unusual combination in this town."

She had a gravelly quality to her voice, worn and frayed. It was the cigarettes that had done it, that and the bars, if bars were where she spent her nights. Tiny lines flowered off her eyes, and a nice long one arced around the side of her mouth. Her life was beginning to show itself on her face. Karras figured she had two, three years on him. He didn't mind.

"How'd you know I had a wife?"

"You've got a sun line on your finger. You didn't figure that, did you."

"Can't say I did. Anyhow, we got that out of the way nice and quick. Why don't you let me buy you a drink?"

"What am I going to have to do for it?"

"Oh, I don't know. Take your head out of that book, for one. It must be something, the way you're buried in it."

"It's *The Fountainhead*. Have you read it?"

"I'm not big on books. Any good?"

"It's long, anyway. It's about . . . well, it's about Freud and Nietzsche, when you get right down to it."

"Nietzsche? Nietzsche, geechie, what do I know?"

74

"He's a philosopher. You know, Man and Superman."

"Superman? Him I know. I've seen the cartoons."

She laughed, put the book down on the bar, tossed her hair off her shoulder as she looked his way. She studied him this time.

"All right," she said. "I'll have that drink."

"What's it gonna be?"

"Scotch rocks, with a splash."

Karras ordered her drink and a fresh bottle of beer for himself. One of the Kavakos brothers—Karras didn't notice which one—served the order. Karras reached across the woman for her pack of cigarettes.

"You mind?"

"Go ahead. But you might not like it. They use Turkish tobaccos in those."

"I get it. Like a joke, on account of my people can't stand the Turks." She was wise to go with the rest of the package. He liked that, too. "Who told you I was a Greek?"

"You don't look it exactly. You're kind of on the blond side. But you don't exactly look like you grew up milking cows for Farmer Brown, either. Anyway, it wasn't much of a longshot to peg you for a Greek. In this place, you call out the name 'Nick' or 'Pete' or 'George' and ten heads are going to turn around."

"So what are *you* doing here, then?"

"I like to drink, and I don't like to do it alone. This place is as good as any."

Karras tapped his bottle to her glass. "Cheers, sweetheart," he said.

Clint Hobbs's orchestra started up in the nightclub, kicked off with a Woody Herman number. They didn't sound much like the Thundering Herd, but the tune was recognizable, the rhythm section tight enough to empty the tables. Through the doorway, Karras could see Recevo leading Lois Roman to the dance floor, the old gent sitting placidly at his chair.

"You care to dance?"

"Maybe a little later."

"How about the pictures? We could sneak out and see a picture right now. There's a late show playing at the Keith's. *Scarlet Street*, I think it is. Eddie Robinson and Joan Bennett. Dan Duryea plays a heavy—"

"What else *would* he play? Anyway, I've seen it."

Karras dragged on his cigarette. "All right, then, how about we get some air? Take a walk."

He was closer to her now and didn't know how he had gotten there. Her breasts hung down and curved up again and the points of them pushed out

75

against the fabric of the shirt. Karras had gotten hard standing there, just looking at her. She caught the blackness in his eyes.

"You're moving too fast, soldier."

Karras stood straight, backed off a step. "Hell, I didn't mean anything. I didn't mean to rush you. I'm just having a little fun, that's all."

She closed her eyes slowly, opened them, spoke softly and with patience. "You guys. You guys come back from the war, you think because you made it out alive, everything and everybody's got to lay down right in front of you. Everything's a gift now, wrapped up special with a bow on it, just for you. You think because you've made it, you're never going to die. But I'm telling you, it's only a reprieve that you got. Just a reprieve. Guys like you, you just don't get it."

He saw her hand shake as she tilted the glass back against her lips. "Settle down, will you? You lose someone in the war? Is that it?"

"No one in particular. I'm no different or better than anybody else."

Karras stubbed out his cigarette. "Listen, I'm sorry. We got off on the wrong foot tonight, I guess. Maybe we can try some other time."

"Soldier, I don't even know your name."

"Pete Karras."

She extended her hand. "Vera Gardner."

Karras shook her hand, rubbed his thumb down the softness of her forefinger. He let it go, dropped a few dollars on the bar.

"How about I call you some night?"

"I don't give out my number in bars."

"Then how about this. If you want, you call me. You can leave a message for me at Adams four, sixty-four eighty. You want to write it down?"

"I'll remember it if I want to remember it."

"I get it. So long, then, Vera."

As he began to turn, she reached out and touched the mole on his face. "What is this, Pete?"

"Just a birthmark," he said. "Why, you think it ruins me?"

"No," she said. "It suits you."

He walked toward the nightclub, stumbling briefly on the uneven planks of the wood floor. He looked back once, past the back of Steve Nicodemus. Vera had stood now and was sliding her cigarettes into her handbag. Karras wished he had been smarter with her. He wished he hadn't had so much to drink.

■

Karras found Recevo and Lois Roman at a table in the club. The old guy's seat stood empty, and his herringbone topcoat was gone as well. Recevo winked at Karras, ordered everyone another round. They had a few laughs over the drinks and cigarettes. Karras liked Lois all right, who was sharp-witted but otherwise not awfully bright. In that respect, she and Recevo made a good pair. Lois went off to rearrange herself in the ladies' room. Recevo and Karras watched her walk away.

"Beautiful," said Recevo. "It's beautiful, isn't it? I'm tellin' you, Pete, that ass of hers has a life of its own."

"Nice girl," said Karras.

"Yeah, she's nice. But I'm talkin' about her ass. I could live down there, pal, change my address. Slip a napkin under my chin and just dig right on in—"

"Nice girl. Where's her date?"

"The gentleman had a 'previous engagement,' he said. Bowed out real graceful. He'll get his chance another night. But not tonight. Law of the jungle, buddy." Recevo tapped the ash off his cigarette. "How'd you make out with Lizabeth Scott?"

"You think she looked like Lizabeth Scott?"

"Damn right."

"I liked her. But I tried to reel it in too quick. I let her get away from me."

"There'll be others."

"I know it." Karras pointed to a small brunette on the dance floor, cutting it with a thin fellow in a brown suit. "I got my eye on that one right there."

"Forget it," said Recevo. "She's been with that joker all night, both of them smilin' like they're all hopped up on somethin'. Just forget it."

It was Vera who Karras couldn't forget.

Lois Roman returned, and they had another round, and that beer only pushed Karras the wrong way. He stood from his seat, bumped into the adjacent table as he went toward the dance floor. The band was murdering Charlie Barnet's latest, and all the couples were jitterbugging to it across the floor. Karras found the guy in the brown suit, tapped him on his shoulder. The guy turned around, smiled, shook his head, and he and his toothy girlfriend kept dancing on their way. Karras followed them, tapped Brown Suit's shoulder, rougher this time. When the guy didn't respond, Karras gripped him on the shoulder and pulled him away from his girl. Karras stepped in, grabbed the brunette's hands, began to move her around the floor like she was filled with straw. She was trying to get her hands free when Karras was pulled off from behind.

He turned around, faced the guy in the brown suit. A couple of Brown Suit's buddies were coming fast across the floor. Brown Suit reared back his fist like he had seen it done in the Westerns, just what any amateur would have done. Karras swatted away the punch with his left, dropped the guy to the floor with a straight right. The guy's friends were just about on him now. So was Recevo; Karras could feel him by his side.

"You wanna try me, sister?" yelled Recevo over the music to the biggest of the friends. "Come on and try me!"

Karras had his fists balled, his right tight against his chest. He laughed.

Tsondilis came into the crowd, put himself between the two groups of men. He stepped up to Karras, shoved his face close in.

"*Siga, vre,*" said Tsondilis.

"Okay, *Kiriako.* I'll take it slow."

"You and your buddy, go cool off in the bar."

Karras and Recevo stepped off. Karras smiled at the men and gave one to the brunette as he walked away. Tsondilis helped Brown Suit up, gave him a cloth napkin to wipe the blood from his mouth. The orchestra went into a Guy Lombardo number, and things began to slow down.

Lois Roman met Karras and Recevo at the bar. They ordered more drinks, and drank them slowly and quietly as the place thinned out. After about fifteen minutes, Recevo shook himself into his topcoat.

"I'm going to drop Lois off," he said. "I'll swing back in about fifteen, pick you up."

"All right."

"Here." Recevo slipped a couple of cigarettes into Karras's suit pocket.

"Thanks for watching my back, buddy."

"No problem."

"So long, Lois."

"See ya, Pete." She planted one on his cheek, and she and Recevo went out the side door.

Karras smoked one of the Raleighs and drank down half of his beer. It was only him at the bar now, and Steve Nicodemus, kind of slumped over at the other end.

"Oh, what the hell," said Karras.

He picked up his beer, walked down to the end of the bar, had a seat next to Nicodemus. Nicodemus looked over, tried to focus, did it enough to recognize Karras. He straightened up a little, pushed at the knot of his tie.

"Pete."

"Steve. Buy you a drink?"

"Sure, why not. I'm havin' bourbon, straight up."

"Hey, Johnny!" said Karras. "A shot of Old Blue Springs neat, for Steve, here."

"The house rotgut is okay by me."

"Relax, Steve, it's on me."

Johnny Kavakos served the whiskey. Karras put fire to a cigarette.

"How's your mom and dad?"

"You know. They're okay, I guess."

Yeah, Karras knew. He had seen Steve Nicodemus's mother several times on the street since the war, gray hair pinned up, silent, wearing black. Always wearing black.

"My mother," said Nicodemus, "she misses him all the time, you know. She can't get her baby boy out of her mind. Goddamnit, Pete, I miss him, too."

"I know it, Steve. I think about him every day."

Nicodemus tried on a weak smile. "I used to smack him all the time, remember? It was to make him tough. Because he wasn't tough, see? He never wanted to hurt anybody or anything. He only wanted to go to Griffith, watch the Nats, or listen to the ballgames on the radio when they were away. When he went into the service he was kind of excited about it, 'cause he figured it was just another chance to play a little ball. He could have drawn desk duty, too, if he hadn't been such a good shot. A marksman, is what they called him. So they gave him a carbine instead of an M-1. A carbine—what is that, anyway, some fuckin' toy?"

"It's a light gun, all right," said Karras, who could think of nothing else to say.

"And then they landed him and all the others on that beach at Anzio. Soon as he hit the beach, they got him. I bet he never even fired his weapon. He caught a bullet, right in the mouth."

"Steve—"

"But Billy, like I say, he wasn't tough. When you guys were kids, you used to rumble with them nigger boys from Bloodfield, remember? He'd make some excuse, tell you he had to come home, help me work on some soapbox I was buildin' in the alley. Shit, Pete, there wasn't any soapbox. Billy just didn't want to fight. That's all it was. He just plain didn't want to fight. So what'd they do? What'd those motherless bastards do? They gave him a carbine and dropped him on a beach. A goddamn, fuckin' carbine."

"I know it, Steve. It's tough, buddy. It's tough."

Nicodemus's shoulders began to shake. A thread of mucus dripped from his nose and settled in his brown moustache. Karras put a cocktail napkin in Nicodemus's hand.

"Yeah," said Nicodemus, wiping the napkin across his face, "I used to smack him around. It was to make him tough, that's all it was. But if he was here right now, I'm tellin' you, I'd never lay a hand on him again. If Billy walked through that door right now—"

"All right, Steve. Forget it."

"You're right. I gotta just forget it." Nicodemus tilted his head back, let the bourbon drain from the shot glass and down his throat. He closed his eyes, set the glass down on the bar. He smiled a funny little smile then, without an ounce of happiness in it at all. "Must be nice, to be able to afford good whiskey."

"I'm doing okay."

"Yeah, you and that Italian boy, you guys are doin' all right. The Greek community around town, they're all talkin' about how good you and your Italian friend are doing. Real interested, like. They're talkin' all about it, Pete." Steve Nicodemus stared at Karras, kept the stare fixed.

Okay, here it comes: Why was it my brother on that beach, and not you? Why did Billy have to go out like that, and not you—a guy rousting immigrants for loan-shark money and running muscle for the protection racket. Why'd my brother Billy have to die, a guy with a heart as wide as a mile. Why him, and not a guy like you?

Karras stabbed out his cigarette. "I got to get goin', Steve. You take care."

"Sure, Pete. Say hello to Eleni for me. Thanks for the drink."

Karras left money on the bar, went down to the other end and found his topcoat on a stool where he had left it. He looked back at Nicodemus staring straight ahead, his hand around the empty shotglass. From across the room, he could see that Steve Nicodemus had begun to cry. Karras looked away, said goodnight to Johnny Kavakos behind the bar, nodded to Jerry Tsondilis at the door. He stepped out to the street, walked to the Mercury idling at the curb. He got inside.

"I've been out here ten minutes," said Recevo.

Karras settled into his seat. "I was talkin' to Steve Nicodemus."

"How's he doin'?"

"You know."

"Yeah." Recevo lowered the volume on the radio. The two of them sat there for a minute or so, not speaking, not hearing the tune. Recevo said, "You wanna know somethin'? I was scared over there, Pete."

"What?"

"I never told you this. But on Guadalcanal—when things really got out of control—man, I was just plain scared."

"We were all scared."

"But I was scared frozen, buddy. One day, when they ordered us to go over this hill . . . well, there was this Jap machine-gun emplacement on the other side. All the guys that had gone before us had bought it. We could see them droppin' from where we were. When I got so close to my own death that I could smell it, I just froze up. I made a promise to myself that if I ever got out of it, got back home, that I'd do anything to live to a ripe old age. In the war, I found out that I was just like anybody else, Pete—so afraid, like everybody else. So goddamned afraid to die."

"But you made it. You got over that hill and you made it home."

"Yeah, I made it. But I found a few things out about myself that I didn't like." Recevo swallowed hard. "How about you? What was it like that day when you killed all those Japs?"

Karras shrugged. "I just . . . hell, I don't know. It's funny, Joe, but I knew that it wasn't my day. I think you know when it is. And I knew that it was just not my day."

Recevo put the shifter in gear. He checked the rearview, then looked over at Karras.

"How'd Billy get it, anyway?"

"He took a bullet in the mouth."

"Those guys at Anzio really took a beating."

"Yeah," said Karras. "They caught hell on that beach."

13

George Georgakos lived in one of three furnished rooms in a private rowhouse at 3rd and Seaton Place in Northeast. Recevo pulled the Mercury to a stop beneath a streetlamp, a half block down from the house. He cut the engine, reached beneath the seat.

"What're you lookin' for, Joe?"

"I got a sap somewhere under here."

"You won't need it. Let me talk to the guy, work it out."

"You know him, huh."

"I've seen him around."

Joe kept at it beneath the seat. "Maybe he won't want to listen."

"Forget about the sap. Like you need it on some old man."

"You gonna handle it?"

"I said I would."

"Well, move it. I got to check in with Burke, and it's way late."

They got out of the car, moved together along the sidewalk toward the house. The place had been set up by the landlords with a separate entrance for the tenants. Karras and Recevo stepped into a kind of foyer which led to four closed doors and one open door leading to a common toilet and shower. The landlord's door was decorated with a fancy nameplate, etched brass, while the other doors had small metal cages on their faces holding slips of white cardboard on which the tenants' names were scrawled. A red sign hung on the wall next to the landlord's door, announcing a vacancy for a QUIET, OLDER, MALE GENTILE at thirty-two bucks a month.

"Thirty-two a month," said Recevo. "For this dump?"

"Over here." Karras stood in front of the door at the end of the foyer.

He looked at the name in the slot, the *E* in Georgakos lettered Grecian-style, curved like the head of a pitchfork.

"What's so funny?"

"Nothin'," said Karras. He knocked on the door two times. He could hear loud music coming from inside the room.

After a while the door swung open and Georgakos stood in the frame. He was a short Greek with closely cropped, unruly hair and a thick, wide moustache handlebarred at its ends. Karras looked at the low-slung build, the forearms thick and hard as slats of fruitwood. Georgakos wore a white shirt with two pens clipped in the breast pocket, and striped, pleated trousers cut from wool. He leaned against the frame, stayed there. He was drunk. They were all drunk.

"Yeah," said Georgakos.

"We're from Burke's outfit," said Karras. "We've come to get a payment on what you owe."

"Huh?"

"Chrimata. Yia to Kyrio Burke."

Georgakos looked at Karras, his moustache notching up a touch on one side. *"Ellinos eise?"*

Karras nodded. *"Panayoti Karras."*

"Apo pou?"

Now you want to know the rest, Georgakos. Where my people come from, and all that. And then you'll put me together with my old man.

"Sparti," said Karras.

"O patera sou eine Dimitri Karras?"

Karras nodded once again. *"Ne."*

Georgakos made a sloppy head move toward Recevo. *"Ke aftos?"*

"Aftos eine Italos. Fylos mou."

"Uh," said Georgakos.

"What are you two goin' on about?" said Recevo.

"He knows my old man. He wanted to know about you. I told him you were a greaser, but that you were all right. I told him you were my friend."

"Swell."

"Just gettin' us introduced."

"Fine. Can we go in now, or are we gonna get a shovel and plant our family trees right out here in the hall?"

"Ella," said Georgakos with a flip of his hand. They all walked into the room then, Recevo closing the door behind him.

The music seemed louder now in the confines of the room. It was a small room to begin with, a cot and a dresser and a sitting area and then a stove

83

and sink arrangement on the side. The place stunk of tobacco, with a haze of it hovering in the room. Georgakos's boxer shorts and a sleeveless T-shirt were laid out on the radiator to dry.

Karras recognized the music as *remebetica*, outlaw music from the Athens ghettos by way of Constantinople and Smyrna. His father listened to it once in a while, though not without deriding it as music for "hashish smokers, cocaine and opium users, bums like that." Karras had never seen powder himself, though he did get out of a carful of veterans one night when a joker in the front seat had lighted a reefer cigarette. He didn't want anything to do with guys like that. Being on hop to him was just as bad as being a cripple.

"Tell him to turn that shit down," said Recevo.

Georgakos just smiled, waved a finger to the fiddle dancing around the vocals. A 78 spun on the platter of the automatic record-changing phonograph that sat on a small endtable beside a cat-frayed chair. The woman was singing about a village girl whose mother had cut off her beautiful hair.

"Thelis kamio beera?" said Georgakos to Karras.

"All right, I'll have a beer. How about you, Joe?"

"No. Let's just get this done."

"You got to let me do it my way, Joe. Just relax."

"I get it from the *frigidairi*," said Georgakos. He went to the sink and began to wash out a couple of glasses.

"You see that record player?" said Recevo.

"I see it. So what?"

"They got that model down at Sun Radio, on Eleventh and E. One of those new Trav-ler models, go for forty-four bucks and change. If he can afford that—"

"He bought it on time, most likely."

"I don't give a damn how he bought it. He bought it, is what I'm saying. If he can buy a phonograph, he can give us our money. We're not walkin' out of here without it, get me?"

"I said I'd handle it, Joe."

Georgakos returned with a bottle of National and two water glasses in his hand. He placed the glasses on his eating table and carefully poured an equal amount of beer into each glass. He lighted a tailor-made and dropped the match into the neck of the bottle. Karras picked up one glass and Georgakos picked up the other. They touched the two together.

"Siyiam," said Georgakos. They both drank.

Georgakos went to the phonograph and started up the same record. He smiled as the *cymbalom* kicked in.

"For Chrissakes," said Recevo.

Recevo had a seat in the tattered chair, took an ashtray with him and sat it on the cushioned arm. He lighted a Raleigh, blew out the match. He watched Karras and Georgakos, standing around the table with the water glasses in their hands, splitting one lousy beer like a couple of hillbillies. His own father had done the same damn thing with his Sicilian buddies, in the old days when they used to drop by, before the old man died. It used to drive him nuts then, too.

Karras wasn't leaning too hard on Georgakos, at least it didn't look like it to Recevo. He wasn't even sure if they had gotten around to the money. Mostly the immigrant was moving his hands around, shrugging, winking when it was called for. Karras's hands were flying around, too. These Greeks, if you cut the hands off 'em, odds were they'd forget how to talk.

After a few more minutes of that, Recevo began to feel the tick of blood through his veins. He didn't feel so good any more from the booze; a dull, throbbing ache had pitched camp in his temples. He wanted to have the money in his hands and then get out of that stinking room. He mashed out his cigarette in the ashtray.

The song had ended again, but Karras and Georgakos were speaking Greek exclusively now; Recevo couldn't figure out if things were coming along. Georgakos went to the icebox for another beer, stopping to take a swig from a bottle of clear liquor he removed from a squat, wood cabinet.

"What's goin' on?" said Recevo.

"We're working it out," said Karras. "It might not be tonight, but he'll pay what he owes. I've got his word. He's got himself in a little financial trouble right now, is all it is."

"That's horseshit. We get the money tonight."

"You're not gonna get involved here, Joe."

"Watch me."

Georgakos returned, poured beer into the glasses. He drank deeply from the glass, looked at Recevo in a too-cheerful kind of way. Recevo stood out of the chair.

"All right—you've been given enough time, old man. We want the money tonight."

"Huh?" said Georgakos.

"You understand what I'm saying," said Recevo. "You understand everything just fine. I want that money—now."

"I'm gonna give it to you. But first I'm gonna have a dance. Hokay, *vre gamoto?*"

"What'd he call me?" said Recevo.

He called you a fuck, thought Karras. Karras said, "He called you his pal."

Recevo took his hat off, smoothed back his hair. Georgakos went to the phonograph, started the same record once again. He turned up the volume.

"Ah, no," said Recevo. "I'm tellin' you, Pete, I've had it with this shit."

Georgakos looked at Recevo, smiled. He began to sing: *"Ta mallia sou ta kommena!"*

As he sang, he raised his arms and started to dance. It was a solo dance, a *zembekiko*. Karras had seen his father do it at the Hellenic Club, or at home when he was happy or drunk.

"What the hell," said Recevo.

He watched Georgakos, snapping his fingers to the music, hopping on one leg, tilting his head in his direction as he smiled that goddamned smile of his.

"Opa!" yelled Georgakos.

The blood began to drain from Recevo's face.

"Ella, yiane tyn karthia mou," sang Georgakos as he danced. He moved very close to Recevo. His eyes were locked on Recevo's, and they were mocking and bright.

"The money!" screamed Recevo.

"Joe," said Karras. But it was too late.

Recevo grabbed Georgakos by the collar of his shirt and threw him violently across the room. The Greek crashed into the phonograph, knocking it from the table and tumbling with it to the hardwood floor. There was a feline screech as the needle ripped across the vinyl, and then the record was in pieces on the floor. The old man sat there looking at the broken 78 as Recevo advanced on him from across the room.

Karras stepped in front of Recevo. He grabbed the lapels of his topcoat, jerked them together, got right up in Recevo's face. They stood there inhaling the foul alcohol and tobacco smell of each other's breath. It had been like this so many times, going back to when they were kids; they couldn't hit each other; it would always end the same way.

The color came back to Recevo's face. Karras released his grip on the lapels. He smiled. Recevo looked away. He bent down to pick up his fedora from where it had fallen, straightening it on his head. He walked from the room. Karras followed, closing the door behind him. He didn't turn around, didn't stop to say a thing to the Greek.

"Hey, Joe!" said Karras. "Come on, Joe, slow down."

They were out on the sidewalk now, Recevo walking quickly and well ahead of Karras. Karras was shouting, getting no response. It was late, well past midnight, and quiet as a church. Their brogues made echoes as they slapped against the pavement. A light came on in a window down the block.

Recevo made it to the Mercury, got in, started it up. Karras slipped into the passenger side just as Recevo put the car in gear. Recevo pulled out, gave it too much gas against the clutch, left a little rubber on the street.

Karras laughed. "You keep driving this hunk of tin like that, it's gonna fly apart." Recevo didn't answer, didn't even smile. "Aw, hell, Joey, gimme a cigarette."

Recevo reached into the pocket of his topcoat, passed over the pack. Karras lighted one, tossed the match out the window. He smoked some of the cigarette down, settled in his seat.

"Listen, Joe. About that back there. I didn't mean to put my hands on you like that."

"Forget it."

"I thought you were gonna hurt the old guy, that's all."

"I said forget it."

"Georgakos, he plays dice games with my old man, down at the club."

"Your old man." Recevo's voice went low, stayed low and steady. "What the hell did your old man ever do for you anyway, Pete. I been hearin' about it all my life, and I'm tellin' you I'm sick of it. Your old man."

Karras dragged on his cigarette. "You don't get it."

"It's you that doesn't get it. I was doin' that old guy a favor back there. What I was gonna do to him is ten times softer than what Reed and his boys will do to him next. Not to mention what's gonna happen to us. When Burke finds out—"

"I don't give a good goddamn about Burke."

"Sure you don't. You don't give a good goddamn about a damn thing, do you? It's never gonna be your day. You're indestructible. That's it, isn't it?"

"Go on, Joe. Turn it off."

Recevo rubbed his cheek. "I gotta make a call."

Recevo got the Mercury off New York Avenue, put it on 14th. He parked around F, told Karras to wait in the car. He jogged across the street to the 400 Club, which he knew would be open late. There wouldn't be a cover at this hour, and they had a phone in a booth with a door on it that sealed nice and tight.

He entered the club, found the booth, had a seat on the triangular wood bench inside it. He shut the door. The sounds of Joe Masters's band died out. He rang Burke up, got him on the line.

"Burke here."

"Mr. Burke, it's Joe Recevo."

"Joe. You get it done?"

"Yes and no. We saw him, but we don't have the dough in our hands. We had a little problem—"

"That's too bad for you."

Burke sounded a little slow and slurry to Recevo. He knew Burke drank, heavily at times and mostly late at night. A hand went over the receiver on the other end. The hand came off to a trail of laughter from the others who were in Burke's office.

"So let me get this straight," said Burke. "You didn't get the money."

"No, but—"

"Karras queered it. Isn't that right?"

Recevo shifted in his seat. "He made a deal with Georgakos. He's gonna get the money from him in a couple of days. Three days, tops."

"If I wanted the money in a couple of days, I wouldn't have sent you over there tonight. Now I'm going to ask you again—did Karras get in the way of what I asked you to do?"

"Listen," said Recevo. "It just wasn't the right time, that's all."

Burke must have made a face or something, because there was an eruption of laughter on the other end. They were having fun with him, kidding him a little. That's what it was.

But then there was no laughter. And Burke said, "We need to have a talk with your Greek friend. Tonight."

A line of sweat slid down the back of Recevo's neck. "No disrespect intended, Mr. Burke, but I don't think that's necessary."

"Not necessary?"

"What I mean to say is, Pete's out. You don't need to talk to him, on account of he's gettin' out. This business ain't for him. He's not cut out for this line of work, that's all."

"He's out all right. We just want to give him a little retirement present before he goes."

"Mr. Burke—"

"It's like this, Joe. You have a kid, he does something wrong, you have to slap him every so often, so he gets the idea. You're doing him a favor, like. We're just going to slap your friend around a little bit, so he learns."

"Pete's not so easy to slap."

"Neither am I," said Burke, his voice losing some of its control. "Not normally, anyway. But your friend managed to slap me real good tonight. I have no choice but to give some back."

"Listen, M . . . Mr. Burke . . . " Recevo heard the stammer in his own voice, hated himself for it. "If it's me you're really tryin' to teach a lesson to, then how about this—I'll walk away from the business, too. Walk away clean. We part friends, with no hard feelings. How about that?"

"You misunderstand me, Joe. Anyway, who ever told you that you could just walk away? I can assure you that the alternative is much worse than you can ever imagine."

"What's that supposed to mean?"

"You saw a lot of death overseas, didn't you, Joe?"

"Yes."

"Then I don't need to spell it out for you, do I."

"Maybe you better, Mr. Burke. Maybe you better spell it out."

"Think of it like this. You play it like I ask, you're gonna save his life. You're gonna save his, *and* yours. The other way, you're both going to go down. Understand?"

Recevo didn't answer. He was thinking of the weakness that had seeped into his knees, and the heat inside the booth. He was thinking of that day on Guadalcanal, the feeling he had then, the same exact feeling he had now. He was thinking that he was a stinking coward. That he always would be. And that he knew he couldn't stand to die.

"Joe, are you there?"

"Yes."

"*Where* are you?"

"The Four-hundred Club. Fourteenth and F."

"There's a late-night market three blocks up, on the east side of Fourteenth. Right next to an alley. Do you know it?"

"Yes."

"Drop your friend off there in about fifteen minutes. When he's inside the market, drive away. It won't be all that bad. You'll see."

"But—"

"Don't fight us, Joe. Believe me, you'll lose."

Recevo closed his eyes, lowered his voice to a near whisper. "How am I going to get him to go inside?"

"Oh, I don't know," said Burke. "Send him in for some cigarettes. How's that?"

He's been out of cigarettes all night. He needs cigarettes.

"Mr. Burke. Mr. Burke, are you there?"

There was no one on the other end of the line. The line was dead.

14

"Gimme one of those, will you?"

"My last one. We'll split it, how about that?"

"All right."

Recevo lighted the cigarette, crumpled the empty pack in his hand. He rolled down the window of the coupe. Karras reached over, plucked the cigarette from Recevo's hand. He hit it, kept the smoke deep in his lungs. He took another drag before he exhaled the first, and let it all go at once.

"You're gonna get it all hot like that."

"Relax, Joe. Anyway, you don't look like you ought to have any right now. You look like you had a dizzy spell, or somethin'. Like you had too much to drink. You're all pale."

"I'm fine."

With their windows rolled down, they could hear the band from inside the club. From where they sat, it sounded like a pileup of brass, a collision of blare and no rhythm.

"That's Joe Masters's outfit, isn't it?"

"Yeah."

"They sound like one weak tit."

"It sounded something like music inside the club."

"You get a hold of Burke in there?"

"Yeah."

"And?"

"He ain't happy."

"I'll talk to him myself, Joe. Tell him how it was."

"Forget it."

91

"I'll talk to him, anyway."

"Gimme back my cigarette."

"Sure."

Karras handed it over. Recevo put it between his lips, let it dangle there. Except for the sound of the band, there was no racket coming from anywhere else. There wasn't a soul out on the street.

Karras breathed in the air. "It's nice this time of night. It's beautiful, you know it? I love this town when it's like this."

"I know you do."

"But D.C.'s different now, since the war."

"Different."

"Yeah. There's too many people. And the *people* are different. Like they always got something on their minds, with no time for nobody else. You notice that? I'm tellin' you, we lost something in that war. Not just guys like you and me, guys that shipped out overseas. Everybody lost something, I mean."

Recevo pitched the cigarette out the window. He turned the key on the ignition, pulled away from the curb. He swung the car around, kept it going north on 14th.

"Listen," said Karras. "I'm sorry about how things went tonight."

"Don't worry about it."

"We'll find our way, Joe. We'll find our way clear, and things'll be more simple. Like they were when we were kids."

Recevo pulled his hat down a little, so the brim of it shaded his eyes.

Karras smiled. "Remember when we used to spend every Saturday at the pictures? You remember that, Joe?"

"Sure. At the Earle."

"Four hours of entertainment. Fifteen cents if we got in before one o'clock. Selected short subjects, the Movietone news, and a feature. And the orchestra would rise out of the pit. Those dancers—"

"The Roxiettes."

"Yeah, them."

Joe laughed. "That one time, you had eaten some of that shit your mother always cooked on the weekends, that shit with all the garlic in it."

"*Scortholia.*"

"Whatever. That garlic was just comin' right through your skin. Little by little, everybody around us started to move out of their seats. They didn't know where that smell was comin' from. Goddamn, Pete, I'm tellin' you, you smelled somethin' awful."

"You didn't move, though."

"No," said Recevo, his voice cracking. "I didn't move."

Karras stared at him from across the bench. "You all right, Joe? You don't sound so good."

"I'm tired, that's all. Time for me to turn in. Let's pick up some smokes and head home. There's a market open, just ahead."

"Okay. I'll run in."

Recevo took his foot off the gas. He pulled to the curb, let the engine idle. Karras noticed a car parked in front of them, two lengths up.

"Joe, you see that car?"

"Yeah. It's a 'thirty-eight Packard. So what?"

"I seen that car tonight, somewhere else. I remember that straight-up grille, and the color."

"You don't know a damn thing about cars, Pete."

"I guess you're right."

"Get me a deck of Raleighs while you're in there."

"All right. Be right out."

Karras opened the door, stepped onto the sidewalk, closed the door behind him.

"Hey, Pete."

Karras leaned on the lip of the window. Recevo's eyes looked funny, hollow; his mouth was stretched back like he was in some kind of pain. Like he wanted to scream. He thought that Joe looked awfully strange in the light.

"What," said Karras.

"Nothing."

"Raleighs, right?"

Recevo hesitated. "Yeah."

Karras shook his head and laughed. "Man, you do need that sleep." He pushed away from the car, stood straight, and walked toward the market.

There was a tune coming from the open windows of the Packard: Tommy Dorsey's "Well, Git It." Karras liked that one, with its crazy clarinet solo and those two trumpets coming in together at the end. WTOP played the Dorsey Orchestra well into the night. Was it that late?

There was no one in the Packard that he could see, and he wondered then why someone would let the radio go on like that and have the battery run down with no one around to hear the music. But then he saw the suit jackets of a couple of guys moving around in the shadows of a nearby alley, guys who had ducked in, to take a leak most likely, or to shoot a little dice. Karras kept to his own business and entered the store.

The old bird behind the counter had to get up out of his chair, made a tortured face to let Karras know he didn't much like it. Karras looked around the candy section, his eyes lighting on a box of chocolate-covered cherries in a vanilla cream. Eleni loved those. Now that his drunk was wearing off, he could stand to have a couple himself.

"How much for the chocolate?" said Karras.

"We got more than one kind."

"The Miss America cherries."

"Forty-nine cents."

"Gimme a box of those. Also, a pack of Lucky Strikes. And a pack of Raleighs."

"The cigarettes are thirteen cents a pack. Two for a quarter."

"I said I wanted 'em both. I didn't ask you for the price." Pops was beginning to cut on Karras's nerves.

The old man shrugged and arranged everything together in a bag. Karras dropped a dollar bill on the counter and took the cigarettes from the bag, sliding them in the pockets of his topcoat. He looked out the storefront window while the old man rang up the sale. He saw the metallic flash of Recevo's car as it passed beneath the light in the street. Recevo was driving away, heading north on 14th. What the hell was he doing, anyway? Probably got antsy, sitting there. Probably just driving around the block, trying to stay awake.

"Take care, old timer," said Karras. He took his change and the bag of chocolates and exited the market.

Karras stood on the sidewalk, looked up the street. Recevo had stopped the Mercury a block or so north, kept it running there against the curb. The brake lights were engaged, and he could see exhaust coughing from the tailpipe. Karras hooked two fingers in his mouth, whistled for Recevo to swing the coupe around, bring it back.

The coupe didn't move. Karras stared at the coupe as the lights inside the market switched off behind his back. Reed stepped out of the alley, flanked by two men.

"What the hell," said Karras, under his breath.

Karras recognized the two other men as part of the group sitting around the living room of the house, earlier in the night. One was of medium height, medium build, wearing a badly tailored suit. The other was a little guy, short and slight, with sharp, severe features. He wore a topcoat cut short above the knees and a tall hat meant to give him size. On him the hat looked comical—a Tom Mix number, with nothing underneath. Karras glanced over their shoulders at the Mercury; Joe had moved it out to the street. He was giving the coupe gas, pulling it away.

Reed stepped up in front of Karras. The others fanned out.

"Reed," said Karras. "I thought I recognized your heap."

"It's mine all right. You always were the bright one."

"You guys are out of your neighborhood, aren't you?"

"We caught last call over at the Neptune Room. I just pulled over to drain my lily."

Karras moved his chin in the direction of the little guy in the tall hat. "What was he doin'? Shakin' it off for you?"

"Funny boy."

"Yeah, I'm funny." Karras sighed, looked in Reed's porcine eyes. "You're in my way. I gotta be getting on."

"Sure," said Reed, and he took a step to the side to let Karras pass.

Karras moved forward, dropped the bag of chocolates just as he saw Reed pivot and then the right coming straight in. He didn't have time to ball up against the sucker punch, didn't have time to raise his arms. Reed buried his fist in Karras's stomach, kept it there.

Karras went to one knee, fought for air. He coughed once, managed to bring some in.

"Joe," said Karras.

Reed laughed.

Karras heard footsteps behind him, felt two men lift him from beneath his armpits. They were alongside him then, dragging him forward toward the alley.

"Joey," said Karras. He watched the sidewalk rushing away from him.

Reed straightened his tie. "I gotta get somethin' out of the car."

The men took Karras into the alley, stood him up against the bricks. The light from the streetlamp blew down, illuminated half of him, left half of him in darkness. The two men stood at the head of the alley, blocking his way. Dorsey's orchestra was playing from the Packard, something with a more hopped-up tempo, the horns flying around and then kicking in. Karras relaxed, tried to catch a rhythm in his breath. He heard the car door slam shut.

Reed, the small man and the medium man were coming forward. The two others moved aside and disappeared. Reed held some kind of fat stick in his hand. No, it was a bat.

"Time to play," said Reed. He stood in outline against the light, his shadow falling in on the stones of the alley.

"I'm through," said Karras.

"You're through when we say you're through."

"This about Georgakos?"

"Georgakos? Yeah, I guess Georgakos tore it. But you been beggin' for this, Karras, for a long time."

"Why the bat, Reed? If you been wantin' a piece of me for so long, why don't we do it right?"

Reed's sharp teeth gleamed in the light. "On account of it's a special bat. I took a lathe to it, and I filled the dugout part with somethin' heavy. Then a nice cork on top to keep the heaviness inside. I want to try it out, see how special it can be."

"Come on, Reed," said Medium. "Let's get this done before someone comes along."

"I'm just givin' it a minute. I'm waitin' to see if his buddy comes back."

"You know he ain't coming back," said the half-pint.

"No," said Reed, with a chuckle. "I don't believe he is."

Karras was sick of listening to Reed, sick of looking at his face. He had been through worse, and he had been through it with tougher men. He smiled at Reed, put some poison in the smile.

"Fuck you, Reed. Fuck you and all of you."

"I guess I'm up," said Reed. He raised the bat.

Karras brought his elbows in tight at his stomach, tucked his chin, buried his face between his fists. For a moment, he caught a flash in his eyes as the bat passed across the light. He heard a great popping sound, felt his left leg go out from under him, felt a slice of pain shear into his spine and explode at the back of his head as he floated down. He landed on his back on the stones, felt nothing of the contact. He heard the bleat of his own voice echo in the alley.

"Jesus," said Medium. "Look what you done to his knee."

Karras rolled over on his side. The action sent another jolt up his spine. His stomach convulsed, bugged his eyes. An acid, steaming mix of booze and beer slopped from his mouth.

"Watch your shoes, fellas," said Reed. "Don't want to get any of that on you."

Karras watched his fingers claw at the stones of the alley. He saw the nail of his forefinger peel clean back, the blood pinkening the raw skin underneath. There was no pain there; it was as if he were watching the hand of someone else.

"Come on," said Medium. "He's had enough."

"Hey, Coach," said Reed. "I get three swings like everybody else, don't I?"

Karras looked up, watched Reed raise the bat over his head, gripping it like a club.

"Uh," said Karras.

He saw the little man turn his head away, the tall hat turning with it, the bat slashing through the image as Reed brought it down. He would remember that hat. And Dorsey's trombone. The sound of the horn was the last thing he heard for some time after that. Dorsey's horn, and a splintering sound. Jumping, happy music, and a sickening crack in the night.

FOUR

Farrell, Pennsylvania
1948

15

■■■■■ Michael Florek woke up around nine-thirty, looked across the room. The bed where his sister slept remained made up, untouched from the night before. It had been that way for several days. For the past year or so, it had not been unusual for Lola to stay away from home overnight, especially on weekends. Michael's mother knew what she was up to; so did Michael, and so did plenty of the folks around Farrell and in parts of Sharon. It was no secret to anyone anymore, and in time even the sting of embarrassment began to fade. But if Lola would be away for more than a day or so, she'd always call, leave word with one of the kids. No one had heard from Lola in the last five days.

Mike Florek sat up, stared at the unmade bed. There had been a blue and black afghan blanket on the bed for the past three years, but now the blanket was gone. He used to sleep with Lola in that bed when he was a kid. He would have liked his own, but there were four kids and both his mom and dad back then, two-and-a-half bedrooms for the six of them. At around twelve years of age Mike began to wake up in the middle of the night with a hard-on, pressed as he was against his sister's back. He knew then that a change in the sleeping arrangements was well overdue. His old man died of a cancer in the chest at around the same time, died young like plenty of the guys who worked at the mill, so the two younger kids moved into his mother's room and Mike got his own bed. Mike and Lola had shared the same room since.

Mike went out to the living room, saw his mother putting what was left of a chicken into a boiling pot. She could stretch a chicken out all week. The apartment was quiet, what with his kid sister gone for the day, at the high school getting things decorated for the game, and with Louis, his younger brother, into the Army now and gone three months. Lola might have made a little noise if she had been around. That Lola could laugh and she could talk, and she could make a little noise.

"Mornin', Ma."

"Michael." His mother winced, turning up an arthritic elbow as she pushed the chicken down into the pot. Her hair had fallen down in clumps about her plump face.

"I'm just gonna clean up, Ma."

"You slept plenty late. I'm going to need you to go down to the butcher this morning."

"I won't be but a little bit."

He went into the bathroom, stripped off his pajama top. In the mirror he tried to flex an arm, got barely a ripple. He looked at his bird-cage chest, the scary-sharp blades of his shoulders. Almost six feet, but he barely weighed a hundred and fifty pounds. Twenty years old, and still he hadn't put on any weight.

Mike washed his face, squeezed some Ipana out onto a brush and cleaned his teeth. He shook some West Point tonic into his palms, rubbed them together, and ran his fingers through his hair. He gave his hair a center part and combed the sides out and back. Then he returned to the bedroom, dressed in trousers and a sweater, and put his mackinaw jacket over that. It was November and already plenty cold.

"I'm leavin', Ma," he said as he walked past the kitchen.

"Here." She crossed the room and pressed a couple of soggy bills into his hand. "Pick up some of that special sausage they got down at the Colonial, okay? We'll have a good supper tomorrow, for Sunday."

Florek looked at his mother's face. The teeth in her mouth were near rotten and so spaced out that her tongue made sloppy sounds against them when she talked. And her eyes, once fierce in their blueness, were faded now and drooped at the corners. He could see that she had been crying, too.

"All right, Ma. I'll be back in a little while."

He left the apartment and went down the stairs to the street. They lived above a bakery off Broadway in downtown Farrell, had lived there as long as Florek's memories stretched back. That part of Farrell, where all the ethnics lived, straddled the line with the downtown section of Sharon. Italians, Poles, Slavs, Germans, Hungarians, Bulgarian-Macedonians, Greeks—if they had an accent, they lived downtown. Some of them had businesses, and most of them worked in the mills. They all had their own

102

associations, as well—the German Club, the Greek Club, like that. The Protestants and the Presbyterians—his father used to call them "the White People," with that thick Polish way of his—all lived up around Highland Avenue, on the high ground, where those who had money and power always seemed to settle in any town Florek had ever seen. The White People also worked in the mills, but in clerical and management positions. They didn't smell like Florek's father used to smell when he came home from his shift. They lived longer lives.

From the street, Florek could see the stacks of Sharon Steel down along the Shenango River, loosing steady blankets of charcoal-gray smoke into the air. At night, the molten sparks from the smokestacks lit up the sky. The mills had killed his father, he was sure of that. But he found a kind of beauty in the fiery orange line stretched out every night across the evening sky.

He walked over to Broadway, passing churches and taverns. Florek had seen a "Ripley's Believe It or Not" in the funny pages once which said that Farrell had more churches and pool halls, per capita, than any other town in the USA. They might have added basketball hoops to the list; hoops were nailed up on telephone poles all over town. Maybe that's why Shenango Valley teams were among the very best in the country. Some of the old-timers complained about all the hoops, but Mike Florek wouldn't have taken down one of them. He liked everything in Farrell just the way it was, the way it had always been. He knew he'd never leave his town.

Florek saw Anthony "Snake" DeLuca walking toward him on Broadway. DeLuca was a senior at Farrell High who ran with a bunch of hep guys. The rumor was that DeLuca and his boys were jazzing some of the student teachers who had come from Westminster College in Wilmington, PA, to instruct at the high school. Florek didn't doubt it; New Wilmington was a dry town, and DeLuca had probably introduced the girls to Farrell's bottle clubs. You put a little liquor into a nice Protestant girl and . . . well, Florek didn't actually know. He didn't know much of anything when it came to girls. He had heard, that's all.

"Hey, Mikey."

"Hey, Snake, how you doin'?"

"On my way to work." DeLuca ushered at the Capitol, the town's A-house. His brother Nunzio worked at the Colonial, which played B-movies and oddball pictures. Florek had seen all the movies by a guy named Preston Sturges at the Colonial. That Sturges character, he shot pictures that really made Florek double over, laugh down deep in his belly.

"Got a matinee today?"

"Sure." DeLuca smiled. "How's your sister Lola?"

Florek didn't like the smile, or the look in Snake's eyes. He kept his mouth shut about it, though. Snake DeLuca might have been a high school kid, but he had it on Florek by thirty pounds, and the extra weight was strictly muscle. On DeLuca's weakest day, he could take Florek down.

"I gotta get on."

"Take it easy, Mikey."

Florek walked on. He passed a workingman's hotel that housed single guys and immigrants without families, mill workers all of them. He passed Bessie Barnes's whorehouse at 518 Broadway, where as a kid he had once stolen a peek at the girls lounging around in silk dresses and feathered, fancy hats. Lola wouldn't have had anything to do with a setup like that. With Lola it was something else.

Florek stopped in the California Confectionery, where he worked as a soda jerk, to pick up his pay. His boss fixed him a banana split, which he ate while sitting at the counter. It wasn't much of a breakfast, but it was free, and it would do. Florek's friend Eddie Monetti told him that Johnny the Greek, who controlled the rackets in town, owned a piece of the confectionery. Mike Florek never asked his boss if this were true. His old man had always told him to keep his nose out of those kinds of affairs, and Mike didn't care to know.

The Colonial Market, owned by a couple of Greeks named George and William Tsimpedas, sat on Broadway at Adams, next to the Colonial Bank, which had gone down in the Depression. George Tsimpedas used the bank for storage now, flour and rock salt and the like. During the war, the market held the sole rationing license for meat, so the Colonial had become the place to go for chicken and beef and pork. People stuck with them, as Tsimpedas had the best butcher in town in Andy Langal, a knife artist like no one in Farrell had ever seen.

Langal was in the back of the market when Florek walked in. He was a large-boned Pole with typically big hands. Florek could see him back there, gloves on, standing next to the smoker. He came out after a while and stood behind the glass counter.

"Young Florek."

"Andy."

"What can I get ya?"

"Some of that special sausage you got. About a pound of it, I guess." Florek dropped the tone of his voice. "Is it fresh killed?"

Langal spread his hands. "What, has it ever *not* been fresh?"

"I guess not, no."

It was a dumb question, and Florek was sorry he asked it. The meat was always fresh in this place, and George Tsimpedas went to Youngstown three times a week to make sure the produce was fresh as well. Florek knew all of that. He was just trying to act like a guy who wouldn't get taken for a ride. It never came out right when he tried to act hard.

"Here ya go." Langal handed him the sausage wrapped in butcher's paper.

"Thanks, Andy."

"You owe a balance?"

"You better go ahead and check."

Langal went in the back again, returned with a figure. Florek settled his account from his own pay. His mother had floated what she owed Tsimpedas for the last three weeks.

"Take it easy, Andy."

"You too, young man."

On the walk back to the apartment, Florek tried to think about what had happened to Lola. He couldn't blame it all on the soldiers or the war, because Lola had always been the type to look beyond Farrell with wide-open eyes. But the war had started all this bad business with Lola, in a roundabout way. The war had played a part in it, that much he knew.

When the Army needed a disembarkation point for its soldiers, they built Camp Shenango between Sharon and Greenville, acres of barracks and new roads. Almost immediately, the towns and boroughs of the Shenango Valley changed. Sharon restaurants began to make good money selling whiskey to the soldiers, and the entertainment and bar dollars flew into the township of Brookfield and the strip at Masury, just over the Ohio line. The soldiers brought in girlfriends and wives before their ship-out dates, and many of those women stayed around. Florek had heard stories of drunken women, of gang bangs and pass-arounds. Everything was loose, wide open, different than what the hardworking mill workers and business owners of the towns were used to. But the war and the camp were a boon for the local economy, and the attitude in general was that nothing was too good for the soldiers. Hell, the Army had even flown in Judy Garland for a special show.

Lola had met a soldier in her senior year, a special soldier, she said. On the night after the soldier left for Europe, Florek found Lola crying in their bedroom. The soldier's buddy had phoned her that day, told her that his friend had recommended he call, and that she be "nice to him" too. Lola had met him, and when she asked him to slow down, he had gotten rough with her in a frightening way. It made Mike Florek angry, but realistically,

105

what could he do? He knew he wasn't going to take on any soldier. So he let it go, and then Lola made the same mistake, over and over again. She kept making mistakes, and the people of Farrell began to talk about her as someone who would continue to make mistakes, and by the end of the war she was sitting in bars in Masury on Saturday nights, waiting for the next mistake to walk through the door and have a seat on the stool to her right. If she was going to do it anyway, if this pattern was as unavoidable as it appeared to be, why not make a few bucks from it and just enjoy the ride?

That was the way Lola saw it, anyway. It was a cockeyed way of looking at things, but Florek knew that's the way she reasoned things in her mind. When you share the same room with someone all your life, you get to know them pretty good.

Mike Florek entered the apartment, put the sausage in his mother's hands. They stood there in the kitchen, unspeaking, looking into each other's eyes. Florek had unzipped his jacket when he walked in. Now he ran the zipper back up along its track.

"I guess I better go see about Lola."

His mother nodded. "Yes, Michael. Go see about your sister."

"I'll be home around dinnertime, Ma."

"Go on, boy. You go on and go."

Florek went into his bedroom, rummaged through his dresser, withdrew Lola's high school graduation picture. She had inscribed a short note to him on the back. There was a copy of the photograph, minus the note, in Lola's own dresser. He slipped the photograph into the side pocket of his mackinaw. He found the car keys where his mother always left them, in a handpainted dish that sat on a small table by the door. He left the apartment and went down to the street.

■

Florek's father had bought a '34 Plymouth for three hundred and twenty dollars just before the war. Mike Florek thought about the times the family would drive into Ohio, buy chickens there off a farm, tie the live chickens to the fenders of the Plymouth, then head back to Farrell. They were in bad shape then, what with his father laid off from the mills, working on the highway in a government program for beans and flour and the odd nickel and dime. He could remember being hungry then, really hungry, and cold up in the apartment in the bowels of winter, the only warmth rising up from the bakery below, a warmth that carried a soft, pleasant smell. Thinking back on it, it wasn't all that bad. They were together then, at least.

The Plymouth started with a cough. Florek pumped the gas a couple of times, let the engine idle. No heat in this one ever, and no radio. He could have done without the heater, but he really would have liked some music. Florek liked the lady singers and the big band sound. He had seen plenty of the bands and their singers—Misty June Christie with Stan Kenton's outfit, Doris Day with Les Brown—who came through Youngstown. He had caught Glenn Miller, too, at Yankee Lake over in Ohio, and boy, that had been a night. They had packed them in so tight for Miller, you couldn't even dance. Yankee Lake, it had its share of acts. But if you really wanted to see the big ones, you had to make the trip into Youngstown.

Youngstown itself was a world away from Farrell. The mob was deeper into Youngstown than New York and Chicago combined. It seemed that way, anyhow. You could find any brand of trouble in Youngstown, and you could find it right out in the open, from whores to gambling to narcotics. Florek had taken a bus there one Saturday night with a couple of his buddies, and they had looked in the front door of Youngstown's biggest and most notorious gambling house, the Jungle Inn. A couple of hard guys patrolled the upper deck, Tommy guns cradled in their arms. You'd have to be screwy to try and knock over a place like that. Those gorillas with the Tommy guns, they'd open up and kill every customer in the joint before you ever got a nickel. No, Youngstown was not the kind of place where Mike Florek wanted to hang out.

Florek pointed the Plymouth out of town and over the Ohio line. After another half hour or so of driving he reached the township of Brookfield and went on into Masury, a small commercial block which was little more than a post office box. He parked on the street in front of the Clover Club, looked down the block. The Gray Wolf Tavern was down there among a couple of other businesses. Florek had heard about the Grey Wolf's floor shows, but he had never seen one. The Clover Club would be closer to Lola's style.

Florek got out of the car, walked in the front door. In the middle of the day, the Clover Club looked like any other shot-and-a-beer tavern he knew. A couple of guys, millworkers from the looks of them, drank boilermakers at the bar, staring straight ahead. A solo drinker, a veteran whom Florek recognized but could not place, sat on the last stool nursing a mug of beer. Between the millworkers and the veteran were two large jars, one containing pickled pig's feet, the other filled with hardboiled eggs swimming in the juice of beets. The new Louis Prima came from the radio mounted above the rows of call.

Florek had a seat away from the others. The thick-necked bartender came down, gave Florek a good going-over. Florek knew he looked young

107

with his gangly wrists and undersized frame. But in Ohio, you only had to be eighteen to drink their 3.2. And in Masury, if you could reach up to the bar and drop your dime on it, you'd always get served.

"What's it gonna be?"

"A bottle of Green Pop," said Florek.

The bartender went to the cooler and withdrew a Rolling Rock, placed the bottle on the bar in front of Florek.

"Another one of these Dukes," said the millworker closest to Florek, the one with mean eyes. He wiggled his finger above his shot glass. "One more of these, too."

The bartender walked to the tap, drew a Duquesne, put a nice head on it. He carried the mug and a bottle of rail whiskey over to the millworker, poured the whiskey to the lip of the millworker's glass.

The millworker dropped the shot glass into the beer. It sank and settled at the bottom of the mug. The millworker looked over at Florek, raised the mug and drank. Florek raised his glass and did the same. He heard a soft chuckle come from the millworker's buddy, seated to his right. Were they laughing at him?

Florek drank his beer down, let it hit him. He ordered another and pulled out the picture of his sister as the tender put the bottle down on the bar.

Florek leaned in. "I'm looking for this girl. Lola Florek's her name. You seen her?"

"I don't think so."

"Here you go."

Florek smoothed out the photograph with his fingers, turned it around so the bartender could have a straight look. The tender's eyes flashed for a moment, then returned to their natural dull state. Florek had time enough to catch the recognition in the man's eyes.

"You do know her," said Florek. "Am I right?"

"I've seen her," said the bartender with a sloppy shrug. "It's been a while."

"I'm her brother."

One of the millworkers laughed.

The bartender looked away. "Like I say, it's been a while."

"I know she drinks in here on Saturday nights. She told me about this place—"

"She used to, maybe." The bartender drifted, drying the inside of a rocks glass with a rag as he moved.

Florek looked over at the millworkers, who were no longer laughing. Both of them had their eyes pointed down into their drinks. At the end of the bar, the veteran stared at the millworkers, kept staring as he killed his mug of beer.

Florek knew the guy was a veteran, but not from his getup today. He wore a carcoat ripped at the armpits, with a quilted flannel shirt tucked into dirty blue workpants. Still, when Florek looked at the guy, he pictured him in uniform, just back from the war.

The government had given its soldiers twenty bucks a week, every week, for the first fifty-two weeks after their discharge. A guy could live on that, and he could buy a lot of drinks with it as well. Some of them never even thought of looking for a job that first year. A few of them fell in love with the idea of sitting on a barstool, figuring ways to stretch the twenty out. The years began to fall away for guys like that. Florek's mother said that the government never should have given its soldiers such a gift. That was trouble money, she said, no kind of gift at all.

The veteran got up from his seat, walked across the boards in the direction of Florek. He slowed going by the millworkers, stared at their backs, then kept on. Reaching Florek, he clapped him lightly on the shoulder, slid himself onto the stool to Florek's right. He settled in with the slow and deliberate movement of a man inching toward an afternoon drunk.

"How you doin', friend?" The voice was scorched from tobacco.

"Doin' okay," said Florek.

"You don't remember me, do ya."

"I can't . . . no, I don't think so."

"I remember *you*."

"You do, huh?"

"Sure. I went to Farrell High, just like you. Graduated two, three years ahead of you. I grew up downtown, off Idaho."

Florek's hand tightened on the bottle. *It's Ted. Ted Something. A Bulgarian-Macedonian name. Lupoff, Luminoff, something like that. What the hell is it?*

"Ted Lupicoff," said the veteran. He put out his hand.

Florek took it. "Mike Florek. How's it goin'?"

"Good."

"Let me buy you one, Ted."

"Naw, that's all right."

"C'mon."

"Aw, hell. A beer, then, for luck. Yeah, I'll have a beer. Make it an Iron City."

The bartender served it. Lupicoff and Florek tapped bottles, drank off some of the beer. Lupicoff lighted a cigarette.

"You still don't remember me, huh?"

109

"It's coming back."

"Ted *Lupicoff*, Mike. I used to run around with your sister, back when. For Chrissakes, I been to your house once for Sunday supper."

It came to Florek then. He could see Lupicoff now, bright-eyed and smiling, without the two-day stubble and the stinking clothes. He could see him in uniform just back from the war.

Lupicoff smiled, the stain of nicotine splashed across his teeth. "Your mom still makin' those pierogies with the sauerkraut inside?"

"Sure. She makes 'em all the time."

"Those pierogies," said Lupicoff, "they'll make you cry."

"Yeah, my ma, she can cook."

"You said it, friend." Lupicoff wrapped his hand around Florek's thin bicep. "Listen, don't get the wrong idea about me and Lola. Like I say, we ran around together in the same crowd, is all. I'm talkin' about way back when."

Florek sipped his beer, placed the bottle softly on the bar. "You seen her lately?"

Lupicoff lowered his eyes. "Yeah. I seen her in here once or twice."

"When's the last time?"

"The last time?" Lupicoff's mouth twitched. He put his cigarette between his lips to stop the twitch. "Hell, I don't know, Mikey. She's been keepin' to herself lately, I guess. Last week or so, I hear she's been stayin' over at the hotel."

"In Brookfield?"

"Yeah."

Florek stood up, put a few dollars on the bar. He signalled the tender, pointed to Lupicoff's empty bottle. The bartender went to the cooler and pulled an Iron City from the ice.

"There's a bellhop over at the hotel," said Lupicoff. "Real hep guy by the name of Danny Auerbach."

"Auerbach."

"Right. See *him*."

"Thanks."

"You want I should come along?"

"Uh-uh."

"Take care of yourself, Mikey."

"You too."

Florek went out to the bright light of the street. He walked up toward Brookfield, thinking that the walk and the air would clear his head. Two beers and he was half-lit. He didn't much care for the feeling of being un-

110

steady on his feet, but the beer gave him confidence, put a can-do swagger in his step. He'd find Lola now, bring her back home for Sunday supper. He'd do that, and things would be all right.

Florek stepped into the hotel lobby. Upon entering, he could hear the sound of an old man talking to himself and cursing under his breath from a small adjoining room. Florek knew from stories that this room held a slot. Another old man sat behind the desk, reading a dime novel. He looked up at Florek, coughed consumptively into a yellow handkerchief, then returned to his paperback. Florek moved over to the desk.

"Yes," said the desk clerk.

"I'm looking for the bellhop who works here. Fellow by the name of Danny Auerbach."

"You got bizness with him?"

"Yessir."

"What kind of bizness."

"The personal kind." Florek shifted his feet. "I'll just wait till he comes out."

"Suit yourself. But he don't come out unless we got a new guest. And we ain't takin' on any new guests tonight. We're all full up."

"Can you ring him out, then?"

The desk clerk dabbed the handkerchief at the saliva glistening on the edge of his pink mouth. "Maybe I can locate him for you." He had never taken his eyes away from the book. Florek stood over him for a couple of minutes. Neither he nor the desk clerk said a word. Then Florek pulled a one-dollar bill from his trousers and placed it in front of the old man. The desk clerk took it, slipped it somewhere beneath the counter with a swift and unexpected dexterity.

"Straight back down the hall, then make a left. Auerbach'll be there, workin' on a cigarette."

Florek walked past the lobby's staircase and back into an unlighted hall, dark as it was deep. He felt along the wall, stumbled once, hooked a left at the light of the hall's end. Down the hall, a compact, pale man in a red bellman's uniform stood talking to a maid. He was smoking a cigarette, the cigarette dangling carelessly between his fingers. The guy was leaning into the maid like he was trying to make time. He looked at Florek, then back at the maid. He said something to the maid, and both of them laughed.

Florek squinted through the cigarette smoke that roiled in the hallway light. "You Auerbach?"

Auerbach nodded, smiled, saluted by lightly touching his hat in a wise

111

kind of way. He stabbed his cigarette into an ashtray by the maid's stand and walked down the hall toward Florek with an exaggerated spring in his step. He was a small one, with tiny blue eyes and the hands of a boy. He moved with the jerkiness of a windup toy.

"Yes, sir," said Auerbach, standing in front of Florek. "What can I get you?" Up close, Auerbach looked like a blond mouse.

Florek took the picture of Lola from his mackinaw, held it out for Auerbach. Auerbach studied it, looked up cheerfully.

"She's somethin'."

"You seen her?"

"She's a dish," said Auerbach.

"Her name is Lola. She's my sister."

Auerbach shrugged. "Consider yourself lucky, pally. Some guys got ugly sisters, they have to look at that mess all their lives."

"I heard she might be stayin' here."

"Maybe."

"A guy over at the Clover Club—"

"What guy?"

"Just a guy. He told me my sister might have a room here. Said you might be able to help me out."

"I might."

Florek didn't wait this time for the touch. It had already been a long day, and the smoke in the hallway had begun to sting his eyes. He reached into his pocket, withdrew the last of his money, a one and a five. He held the one dollar bill out to Auerbach.

"Uh-uh," said Auerbach.

"I'm just lookin' for directions. It shouldn't cost all that much."

"You got me confused with that old desk jockey, pally. That guy comes straight out of the last century. You can romance him with a one, maybe, but a one don't even begin to buy my drinks."

"What do you want?"

Auerbach pointed his sharp chin at the bill in Florek's hand. "The fin."

Florek handed it over. Auerbach folded it neatly, tucked it into the watch pocket of his trousers.

Auerbach stepped around Florek. "C'mon."

Florek and Auerbach went down the hall, through a door and into a back stairwell. Florek figured they would take the stairs up to the second floor, but instead Auerbach headed down toward the basement. Florek had been in a few hotels; he couldn't think of any, even the cheapest flophouses, with rooms in their basements. He followed Auerbach, watched the cocky roll of the little guy's shoulders as he hit the bottom of the stairs.

They went into another hallway, passed rooms housing cleaning supplies and a bathroom with a floor slick from grease. The hall ended at an open-doored boiler room, where Florek could hear the steady hum of the house furnace. It was warm down here, close to hot, the heat dry and raw. Florek pulled the zipper down on his jacket.

Auerbach turned the knob on a door adjacent to the boiler room. He pushed the door open, reached in and flicked on an overhead light. He waved Florek through, stepped aside.

"Here you are, pally."

Florek went inside. On the floor lay a mattress covered with tossed, wrinkled sheets and a blue and black afghan blanket. Next to the mattress a lamp with a scorched shade sat on an overturned lettuce crate. A glass basin topped a plywood dresser pushed against the wall. The walls, empty of decoration, had been painted a pale gray. The floor was naked gray concrete.

"Where is she?" said Florek. He stared at the afghan on the bed. His mother had knitted it for Lola one very cold winter, three years back.

Auerbach walked into the room, leaned against the wall. He raised one foot, rolled down his sock, pulled free a pack of cigarettes. He extracted one, covered the pack up with his sock, put the foot back down on the concrete. He rolled the cigarette elaborately in his fingers, examined it like it was something special.

"I asked you where she was."

Auerbach tore a match from his book, lighted the cigarette. He kept the cigarette dangling in his mouth as he glared impishly at Florek.

"I can't hear you so good," said Auerbach.

"What, you're gonna hit me up again?"

"You asked to see her room. Anything else is extra."

"You took my last nickel."

"Then I guess we're done." Auerbach rolled his shoulders. " 'Cause information like that don't come free."

"Information." Florek felt a tickle of sweat on his back. "Maybe I got a little information for the cops in this township. Maybe they might like to know that the bellhop in this place is a lousy pimp."

"Sure, they'd like that." Auerbach took the cigarette from his mouth and grinned. "And while you're singin' about it, don't forget to tell 'em about your sister. Yeah, and you might want to go back to your little town and brag about her, too. Tell 'em all how your sister ain't nothin' but a three-dollar whore."

113

Florek lowered his head, stared at the floor. "Where is she?" he muttered.

"See? That's a whole lot better. A guy like you shouldn't try and wear a man's suit. It just don't hang on you right." Auerbach flicked a speck of tobacco off his pants. "Aw, hell, you seem like a nice kid. I guess it's only right I give you a few details, seein' as how she's your sister—"

"Where?"

Auerbach dragged on his cigarette. "Gone south to the big city, pally. Washington, D.C."

The swirls in the floor's concrete vibrated softly in front of Florek's eyes. "Gone with who?"

"A man she met here last week. A man and a woman, it was. I don't have no names. He registered at the desk, but you can make book that the name was a phony."

"What'd the man look like?"

"Small and bald. Other than that, I don't recall."

Florek closed his eyes. "Why'd she go with him?"

"This man, see, he put her onto something nicer than what I was giving her. Your sister, she liked to have a good time. She really liked these pills I was gettin' for her. Nembutols. *You* know, goofballs. I get 'em cheap from a pharmacist friend over in Youngstown. But this guy, he showed her a really good time. Put a needle in her arm, made her feel real dreamy and good. Promised her more of the same, more needles, more good times, nice clothes and big city life, all kinds of fancy shit like that. It's kind of funny, you know. What's that word for it? *Ironic*. Yeah, it was ironic, like. I introduced this guy to her, and then he takes her away."

"You sound pretty broken up about it."

Auerbach shrugged. "Hey, he paid me and all that. Fifty bucks, it was. So I didn't lose out all the way."

Florek's voice shook. "You made out real good."

"Yeah, I made out all right. I'm gonna miss her though, is what I'm saying. I had a good thing with her. She never complained once about who I brought down those stairs. Long as I kept feeding her those goofballs, she never got particular on me. You gotta admit, it's not a bad setup down here. It's warm all the time, with the furnace next door and all, so warm she never even had to get dressed. I walked in on her once or twice myself, got a good eyeful. Like I say, your sister Lola, for a hophead I mean, she was some kind of dish."

Florek turned on his feet and took a step toward Auerbach. The bellhop grinned, dropped his cigarette to the concrete, ground it under his shoe. He didn't move back an inch.

Auerbach smiled, looked Florek over. "Aw, get a look at you. You got your fists balled up like you wanna fight. Is that what you want, stretch? You wanna go a few with Danny Auerbach?"

Florek let the heat in his blood pass. He unballed his fists. He felt a tear run down his cheek, hated himself for letting it go.

Auerbach's smile disappeared. "Get outta here. Go on and beat it before I kick you in the ass."

Florek walked from the room. He passed through a veil of heat coming from the boiler room, smelled the alcohol in his sweat, the stench of it turning his stomach. On the stairs, he stopped to retch, holding the banister for support. Then he was out on the street, walking down the strip toward the Plymouth, his head down, his hands buried deep in his jacket. There was little to remember of the ride home.

■

That evening, Florek went to the California Confectionery and spoke to his boss. On Sunday he had supper with his mother and younger sister, a special meal with dishes prepared especially for him. Later he and his mother sat at the kitchen table while the radio played standards in the room. His mother kept her hand over his as they spoke into the night.

On Monday morning, Michael Florek took the two hundred dollars he had saved since high school from the bottom of his dresser. He gave his mother half of it and stuck the remainder in the pocket of his wool trousers. He kissed his mother on the cheek, picked up his duffel bag, and went out to the street.

Florek walked along the highway until he reached the edge of town. A flatbed truck hauling vegetables stopped for his upturned thumb. Florek went to the passenger side, looked through the open window. The driver had a kind, welcoming face. He wore a red plaid cap with flaps that covered his ears.

"Can I get a ride with you?"

The driver made a motion with his head. "Throw that bag of yours in the back, son, and get in."

Florek looked behind him at the town. Down along the Shenango River, blankets of smoke flowed into the gray sky from the stacks of Sharon Steel.

Florek swung the duffel bag over the rail of the truck's bed. He climbed into the cab.

The driver put the shifter in gear, gave the truck gas as it lurched onto the highway. He reached for a cigarette from the sun visor, placed the cigarette between his cracked lips. He struck a straight match on the dashboard, paused to glance at Florek before he gave himself the light.

"Where you goin', anyway?"

"Washington."

"Warshington? Down above Waynesburg?"

"Not Washington County," said Florek. "Washington, *D.C.*"

FIVE

Washington, D.C.
1949

16

Lola Florek felt the plump hand of Lydia Fortuno pushing on her shoulder, shaking her awake. If she could just keep her eyes closed, pretend she was asleep . . . maybe Lydia would go away. When Lola felt like this, so good and right, all she wanted was to lie there, curl up like her mama's baby girl, fly on it for a while, be left alone.

"C'mon, honey," said Lydia. "I can see that smile on your face."

The smile. Lola always forgot about the smile. She couldn't help but smile, the way it felt. Just so good and right.

"C'mon," said Lydia.

Lola opened her eyes. "Now?"

"Mr. Morgan's got a date for you, honey. You don't want to keep him waiting."

Lola looked up at Lydia. The woman had a truly beautiful face: baby-doll eyes, shining, wavy black hair, a full mouth that snaked around suggestively when she smiled. Most folks would never recognize her beauty straight off, as they couldn't get past the first impression of Lydia's size. It was true that Lydia was an awfully big woman, what most folks would call fat. Lydia, she probably weighed upwards of two hundred pounds. Well, some men liked them big. Men had funny tastes, all right. Which is why Mr. Morgan kept all kinds around.

"C'mon, Lola, get on up."

Lydia got a hand underneath Lola's armpit, raised her so she sat upright on the bed. Lola watched the flicker of the flame from the candle on the nightstand. Shadows did the rhumba on the burgundy lace curtains of the bedroom window. It reminded Lola of a Warner Brothers' cartoon she had seen before the feature at the Capitol once, back in Farrell. Lola laughed.

"Now, you don't want to get old Lydia in trouble with Mr. Morgan, do you? You gotta help me out here, baby. Like I helped you out, just a little while ago."

It was true, all right. Lydia had given her the sweet shot just a half hour before. She had always given it to Lola when she asked. Lola loved what the sweet shot did for her, but could not bear to put the needle in her own skin. On those nights when Lydia had a date of her own, she had showed Lola how to snort the brown powder up her nose, or heat it up in foil and inhale the smoke. Those ways worked just fine, but not like the needle. With the needle, it was like an ocean of warmth was crashing through her, sending her down to the liquid softness of her bed where she could just curl up and close her eyes and let it move her back and forth. So good and right . . . and Lydia had always helped.

"All right, Lydia. Here we go."

Lola managed to get off the bed. She went to the makeup stand with the scrolled legs, had a seat on the miniature davenport, looked in the mirror. The dress she wore was sheer, a mocha color decorated with small, blood-red roses, with long sleeves that covered the marks on her arms. Her slip showed black beneath the dress. Lola fluffed the sides of her blonde hair, then brushed away a fork of bangs that tickled her forehead. She scratched her forehead at the tickle and saw that she had made it red.

"Put on a little lipstick, honey."

Lola found a tube whose color seemed to match the roses on her dress. It was hard to tell in the light. She smeared some on her lips, laughed a little because she saw that she was missing the line by a wide mark.

"Let me get that for you," said Lydia. She took a tissue and wiped away the excess, got the detail by running one finger along the top of Lola's lip. Then she bent in and kissed Lola on the side of her mouth. Lydia watched Lola's eyes in the mirror for a moment, looked away. "C'mon, baby, let's go downstairs."

And so they were down the stairs. They were in the bedroom one moment and in another were down the stairs. They were in a living room of sorts, where several women sat around listening to 78s coming from a Victrola set on a stand in the center of the room. There were plants in the room and a couple of cushiony sofas, with a small cart on wheels against the wall holding three varieties of liquor and one or two mixers and a bucket of ice. A set of tongs with clawed ends leaned upright in the ice.

A horn sounded from outside. Lola turned suddenly at the sound of it, her hand fluttering up to touch her face.

Mr. Morgan said, "That would be them."

"Them?" said Lydia, giving Mr. Morgan the eye as she draped Lola's coat around her shoulders.

"One man," said Morgan tiredly. "A conventioneer. A gentleman, Lola. You'll be fine."

"Sure, Mr. Morgan," and she began to scratch at her forehead. Lydia took Lola's hand away from her forehead and placed it at her side.

Mr. Morgan leaned in. He was a small man with a soft build, completely bald on top with patches of brown over each ear. To Lola he looked like a science teacher she had known years ago. The thought of Mr. Morgan standing at the head of a classroom made her smile.

"This one is all me," said Morgan, lowering his voice. "You owe it all to me for tonight's kick."

"Yes, Mr. Morgan."

"Go on, honey," said Lydia. "I'll wait up for you, hear?"

"Sure," said Lola. She walked out of the room, through the foyer and out the front door.

The wind stung at Lola's face. She drew the lapels of her coat tightly to her chest. From up on the steps she could see New York Avenue. Mr. Morgan's rowhouse sat on a side street, one block off New York. She had never bothered to learn the address, as the cabbies picked her up and dropped her off, and always knew where to go.

The cab driver gave his horn a short blast. Lola went down the concrete steps to the street, the concrete pillowy beneath her feet. There had been a boy once, back in Farrell, who picked her up at her house and blew the horn on his little coupe to let her know he had arrived. He'd honk his horn, try to get her to speed things up so they wouldn't miss the show. They were in a hurry then, to be together and get away from their parents and go out and have some fun. Like the man in the cab was in a hurry. In a big hurry to have a little fun.

Just like on a date.

17

◼︎ Mike Florek cupped his hands around his eyes, sealed his tunnel of vision as he peered inside the plate-glass window of Nick's at 14th and S. His breath fogged the glass. Behind the glass, several Negro men sat drinking bottles of beer, talking and laughing and having something to eat, while a couple of dark-haired, olive-skinned white men went about their business behind the counter, preparing dishes, capping bottles drawn from the cooler, serving the Negroes their food and drink.

It was mighty odd, that—white men, serving colored men food. But then, Florek had thought many things odd since his arrival in the city two months back. This thing going on in Nick's was just another to be added to the list.

Florek had a room next door on a month-to-month, three floors up. He had passed by Nick's every evening on the walk downtown to his night job behind the soda bar at the People's Drug. Tonight's walk would be another cold one, what with the freeze dropped down from Canada. Florek reckoned he could use a cup of hot coffee before the hike. He had the nickel in his pocket, after all, and it did look awfully warm inside. He passed beneath the oblong blue sign encircled with white bulbs and pushed on the glass front door of Nick's.

A chime sounded as he stepped inside. Inside the door, a huge Negro sat on a stool, perhaps the largest man Florek had ever seen, his arms folded across his broad high chest. From the first, Florek noticed the flatness of the man's head, the flatness exaggerated by his hair shaved close on the sides. The head looked like an anvil atop the bunched mountain of shoulders. But, aside from the size, this was not a man with meanness in his eyes.

This man's eyes were alive with amusement, curiously gentle. Florek guessed that a man that size could look at the world in any way he chose, with absolutely nothing to prove. The bouncer didn't even give Florek so much as a glance as he passed.

A couple of the Negroes turned their heads sharply as Florek walked across the wood floor. Just as quickly they went back to their conversations. Florek chose a stool at the end of the counter and had a seat.

A record spun on a nearby phonograph, a blues number sung by a lady. One of the Negroes down along the counter had a crate full of 78s on the floor by his side. The radio mounted on the wall was shut off, as was the television set which sat on a wood platform nearby. The lady on the record was singing about how she had changed the lock on her man's front door. The Negro man closest to Florek softly sang along.

"What you gonna have?" said the larger of the two white men to Florek, stepping up to the counter. He was a big man with thinning black hair and a small, raised pink scar on the right cheek of his wide, open face. He wiped his hands across a blood-stained apron.

"Just a cup of coffee," said Florek. "That'll do it for me."

"Costa!" said the big man, turning to the stocky one with the wild head of hair and the thick moustache. *"Ena cafe yia to aspros!"*

Costa went to the urn, drew a cup, put the cup together with a saucer, placed it on the counter in front of Florek. "Here ya go, boss," he said.

"I'm gettin' gray waitin' on those ribs, Nick," said a young Negro to the big white man.

"Check on those ribs," said Nick.

Costa stood at the swinging doors that led to the kitchen, yelled over the top of them. *"Pou eine ta ribs mou, vre?"*

A voice replied from behind the doors: "Hold on to your shirt, Costa. The ribs are workin'."

Florek looked down the counter past the bottles of hot sauce butted against the napkin dispensers and salt-and-pepper shakers to the plates of food in front of the men. He had never seen food like this. Well, he was in the South. This must be what they called a Southern Style place. But he had never seen food like this for himself.

"The goddamn ribs!" said Costa. *"Grigora!"*

Florek sipped at his coffee. The coffee was rich and good.

"Hey, Six," said the young Negro to the huge bouncer. "Who you got that money of yours on tonight?"

The bouncer just shrugged. Costa paced like a cat in front of the kitchen doors.

123

"How 'bout you, Nick?" said the young Negro. "Who you think's gon' win that fight tonight?"

"The Cuban," said Nick. "What the hell's his name again?"

"Kid Gavilan. You think he'll take Ike Williams? Williams beat him good in the Garden last year. And don't forget, the Kid's a bleeder."

"Ah," said Nick. "That Williams guy, he's too heavy. Look at 'im: He let himself get soft. I read in the *Star* how he weighed in at one-forty today. That's too heavy for that guy. And Gavilan's got them uppercuts. Whad'ya call them things?"

"You talkin' 'bout those 'bolos' of his," said the young Negro.

"Yeah," said Nick. "That."

"Don't matter no how anyway. The winner of this one's gotta go up against Sugar Ray. And you *know* what's gon' happen then."

"Hey, Costa," said the Negro with all the records, gently elbowing the man next to him. "Who you think's gonna do it tonight? The Cuban or the colored?"

"Cuban, hell," said Costa. "You call him what you want, they both look plenty colored to me, goddamn."

The men at the counter laughed.

Costa walked hurriedly over to Florek, nodded at his cup. "You ready for a refill?"

"No thanks, I'm okay."

"Refill's free."

"I'm just gonna have one tonight, thanks."

"Refill's free."

"I gotta get on my way."

"Hokay, boss. Suit yourself."

"Ribs up!" said the voice behind the door.

Costa spun on his heels, pushed in on the swinging doors, motored back to the kitchen. Florek heard Costa's voice then, speaking to the cook excitedly in that strange, jumbled language.

"How much I owe you?" said Florek to Nick.

"Nickel."

Florek put it on the counter. "Thanks."

"Coffee okay?"

"Yeah, fine. I'd stay for another, but I gotta get off to work."

"Yeah? Where you work?"

"People's, downtown."

"Doin' what?"

"Soda jerk."

124

"Uh," said Nick.

"I'll be back. I only live two doors down."

"In those rooms Mrs. Roberts keeps?"

"Yeah, those."

The large man in the apron put out his hand. "Nick Stefanos. That's my name on the sign out front."

Florek shook Stefanos's hand. "Mike Florek."

"Florek. What kinda name's that?"

"Polish."

"Me, I'm Greek." Stefanos smiled. "Hokay, boy. You come back soon, hokay?"

"Sure. I'll see you around."

Costa came bursting through the doors, running the ribs to the man who had ordered them. He put the plate down with a flourish, slid a bottle of hot sauce next to the plate. The man with the records held one out to Costa, who took it and placed it on the phonograph's platter. Florek walked across the wood floor. The young Negro, who was dressed stylishly in a suit and tie and velvet-banded hat, gave him a quick glance and a tight nod as he passed. Florek went by the bouncer named Six, heard the rolling piano intro to the song as the new record began to spin. A guy could really tap his foot to a record like that.

Florek pushed on the door, zipped his mackinaw up to the neck as he hit the sidewalk. He found himself smiling as he walked south. He was plenty glad he had stepped into Nick's.

■

Florek had hit town in late November. He phoned his mother first off to let her know he had arrived, then went straight to the YMCA where he found a cot and place to wash his face. His first night was virtually sleepless, as he felt the need to protect his hundred dollars from the vagrants, drunks, and drifters with whom he shared the space. He spent the first couple of days looking for a room of his own; he needed work right away, and he knew he'd have difficulty getting it without a local address.

An ad in the *Times-Herald* pointed him in the direction of 14th Street in the northwest quadrant of the city, where an elderly, straight-backed lady named Mrs. Roberts showed him a room on the third floor of a row house between R and S. The room was comfortably furnished, had steam heat, and a large picture window that faced east on 14th and caught a great block of morning sun. The promise of the sun blowing through the window each morning, along with the reasonable asking rate of five dollars a week, closed the deal for Florek. He assured Mrs. Roberts that he was both a sober and quiet young man. Her eyes betrayed her doubt—Mrs. Roberts suspected all young men, by design, of bad intent—but she took his ten dollars representing two weeks' rent.

Florek sought work immediately through the Restaurant Association, whose Northeast offices he walked to on his third day in town. He filled out some paperwork there and spent the rest of the week waiting to hear from them and exploring the city. It was an easy city to get to know. The trolley lines and Capital Transit buses were logically routed, and the streets—numbered north to south, alphabetized east to west—could not have been more plainly laid out for the first-time user. Of the streets themselves, he found a kind of open beauty in their width and clean lines. He did find it difficult deciding on which of these streets to avoid; unlike New York's Harlem or Chicago's South Side, there seemed to be no clear boundaries separating white D.C. from its Darktown. Often he would pass through residential neighborhoods housing Negroes, then whites, then Negroes again on alternating blocks without landmarks of any kind. But after a while he grew used to this, too, and at no time during the day, walking on those streets, did he feel unsafe. He did, however, feel the weight of loneliness pushing down on him as the days fell away; in that first week alone, he phoned his mother three times.

In early December, Mike Florek answered an ad in the *Evening Star* for counter help at a place called People's Drug. The Restaurant Association had not contacted him, and his money had begun to run low. He thought he might have a shot at such a position, what with his experience at the California Confectionery back home. The next morning he went to the employment office at 77 P Street in Northeast, filled out an application, and was interviewed on the spot. The interview did not go well to start, as Florek was not one to shine at first meeting, but then the man behind the desk, a Pole named Mr. Grieszefski, caught Florek's address of origin on the application, and broke into a smile. It seemed Grieszefski had an uncle on his mother's side by the name of Daniel Florek, who lived in western Pennsylvania near the Shenango Valley. Was he a relative of Mike's? Mike nodded with bright eyes and said that he was. In the big city it felt somehow natural to tell lies.

That evening, Florek started his new job as a soda jerk at People's on 15th and H. The shift went seven till midnight, the pay seventy-five cents an hour for twenty hours' worth of work per week. The pay was fair, and a meal came with it, and he figured he could sneak more food into his stomach on top of that. As for the job itself, he knew he could do the work in his sleep. A cherry Coke was a cherry Coke, wherever you were raised.

Florek thought, too, that he might make some friends at this new job. But his shift boss turned out to be a pale, middle-aged Baptist from the southeast part of the city named Mr. Simms, who seemed to frown on anything that smacked of fun, and the two of them clashed from the start. Florek did his job, though, took the constant negative comments and swipes quietly, and continued to report for work promptly at seven each evening. The pay kept him solvent, and even the company of Simms was preferable to the hand-wringing solitude he faced in his room late at night. Florek still phoned his mother three times each week, though he had nothing to report.

So far, he had made only one weak effort to find Lola. One night, after a month in D.C., Florek had gotten the nerve to pass by Thomas Circle on his walk home from work. Thomas was a safe bet to start, as even tourists and conventioneers knew the Circle as the city's major open-air market for prostitutes. Typically, Florek chose to approach the meekest-looking of the whores, a tiny girl still in her teens with a blond pageboy haircut who wrapped herself coyly in a fake sealskin coat. He assured her that he only wanted to talk; she replied that the price would be the same, talk or not. In the unheated hallway of a nearby flophouse, he showed her the photograph of Lola. The girl drew on her cigarette as she studied the picture with the passive interest of a woman glancing at her nails.

"She's a working girl?" she asked, in a jarring accent of high-elevation origin.

"I think so, yeah."

"Not around here, she ain't."

"You sure about that?"

"Honey, I know who works these few blocks. You best look for your girlfriend somewhere else."

"She's not my girlfriend," said Florek, instantly ashamed.

"Yeah?" The girl dragged on her cigarette, blew a ring at the photograph. The smoke exploded across Lola's face. "Who is she, then?"

"Nobody," said Florek.

That brief exchange cost him ten bucks, nearly half a week's pay. He walked back up 14th toward his room, a desperate hollowness inside him like he had never felt.

Florek made no further direct attempts to locate his sister. He continued to wander the city by day, hoping to run into her, and he continued to work the soda bar at night. Near Christmas, he visited the windows at Woodward and Lothrop on F Street more than once, taking pleasure in the faces of the children who had come with their parents to see the decorations and lights. He spent Christmas Day alone.

By January his relationship with Simms had deteriorated to the point where they rarely spoke. Florek concentrated on his work, trying to increase the speed of his counter service out of boredom more than anything else. His improved job performance, of course, only increased the resentment coming off of Mr. Simms. But by now Florek had something else on his mind: a redheaded girl named Kay who worked the cosmetic counter of the store. He had never spoken with her, though he had seen her with her friends at Truman's parade on Inauguration Day, and from across Constitution Avenue had gotten a smile. After that Florek tried to catch her eye now and then at work, and often did, and soon he thought that he might ask her out to see a picture or to have a bite to eat. But finally he lacked the courage even for that. Instead, in his room late at night, sitting on the edge of his bed, he often imagined her naked, her red hair clean and lustrous and fanned out on a pillow; those nights ended with his face contorted, his eyes closed tight as he beat off furiously into a dirty sock. Afterwards, he felt useless and sad.

Florek had not had many good days in D.C. There seemed to be few places in town for a stranger like him to go and sit and listen to other men talk—a place like any of the places on Broadway or Utah in Farrell, back home. So the cup of coffee at the Greek grill downstairs, earlier in the day, had been special for him. It had made him feel comfortable and good.

That night, by the picture window in his room, listening to the Gavilan-Williams fight on the cheap Emerson table radio he had recently bought, Florek began to think about that Greek place, and the people there, those behind the counter and the customers as well. He listened carefully to the ringside announcer, made mental notes as to the technical jargon, the jabs and the crosses and the footwork and such. He'd want to know what he was talking about when those guys at the counter started jawing about the fight. He could join in on the fight talk with those guys, join in and maybe be one of them, when he walked into Nick's the next day.

■

"What the hell's wrong with the greens?" said Costa.

The green-eyed Negro at the counter pointed to his dish. "I'm just tryin' to explain it to you, man. These here are collard greens, Costa, they got to

128

be cooked a special way. You don't want to be boilin' the flavor out of these, like you do with them bitter dandelion weeds you be pullin' out of some field for one of your Greek dinners. These greens here, they got to be stirred a little bit in a fryin' pan with some pork fat, 'long with a little red onion and garlic. And these greens here got taste, understand? You don't need to be coverin' up that taste with all this lemon. You people put lemon on everything you cook!"

Costa studied the greens on the man's plate. "So, lemme get it right. You fry these up with some onion, a little garlic. And no lemon."

"That's right."

The man next to the green-eyed one said, "And you might want to cut a little okra into it, too."

"Okra," said Costa. "I get it. Hokay, *vre mavroskila.*"

Costa went away as the two men as the counter grinned and touched hands.

"A little more coffee?" said Stefanos to Florek, seated away from the others on the same stool as the day before.

"All right, Nick. Just warm it up for me, will you?"

"Cafe, Costa. Yia to Kirio Florek."

Costa took a glass pot from a burner and filled Florek's cup. A show called "Dance Party" was coming from the radio, the dial of which was set at 1590, the city's Negro station with the call letters WOOK. Florek had been sitting there for over an hour, had listened to spirituals for the first thirty minutes.

"How about that fight, Nick?" said the green-eyed Negro. "You sure did call it."

"The Kid did it, that's right," said Stefanos. "Gavilan was bleedin' all over the ring, but he did it to Williams, all right."

"It was them rights of his," said one of the men.

"It was the uppercuts," said Florek, loud enough for all of them to hear. "That buzz-saw attack that Gavilan's got."

The green-eyed Negro looked down the counter at Florek, then at his friend. "You hear what the young man said? It was a buzz saw got Ike Williams." The two of them laughed.

"Those whad'ya-call-its," said Stefanos.

"Bolos," said Florek.

Florek glanced over his shoulder at Six, sitting by the door. The bouncer was looking back at him with amusement.

Business picked up a little after that. Men came down from the U Street corridor after quitting time and made their way either to Nick's or to the Sun Dial, Pete Frank's restaurant at R. Frank had recently turned his place into a Negro house as well.

Costa pushed on the swinging doors, sped back into the kitchen. Florek heard a door open, then Costa's voice as he yelled up a flight of stairs to a person named Toula. This had happened several times in the afternoon, and Florek had begun to recognize the pattern in Costa's voice. Costa used a different tone when yelling at this Toula person than he did when yelling at the cook.

Stefanos popped the cap on a bottle of National, served it to a newly arrived customer. The customer put some coin on the counter, and Stefanos rang the sale on a register facing out from the wall. Florek saw that no one, not even Costa, rang on that register but Nick.

Costa came out with a bowl of catfish gumbo, placed it in front of a man in a shirt and tie. He stood there watching in disapproval as the man shook hot sauce vigorously into the gumbo.

"Taste it first, at least," said Costa, "before you drown it in that stuff."

"It ain't hot enough for me," said the man. "I done had it here before, and I know."

"Okay, *arape*. You do what you want."

"*Sopa, re,*" said Stefanos, clearly annoyed.

Costa pushed off from the counter as Stefanos shot him a look. With the colored customers, Costa always punctuated his exchanges with a few choice words spoken in Greek, followed by a cheerful smile. Florek could see, and the colored men could see—hell, a blind man could see—that Costa was insulting them. Costa, in fact, was the only one in the place who believed he was putting one over on them, and the men let him go on thinking it. Playing with Costa was their sport. Getting the little guy excited was a large part of the entertainment at Nick's.

"Let me settle up, Nick," said Florek.

"Nickel."

Florek laid it down. "I'll see you later, hear?"

"You workin' tonight?"

"Uh-uh. My night off."

"Come on back. Tuesday night, we gonna watch the fights on the television. Ten o'clock."

"Okay, Nick," said Florek. "Ten o'clock."

■

Mike Florek woke from his nap in near darkness, the only light in the room bleeding in through the picture window from the streetlamp outside. Florek sat up, ran a hand through his hair. He rose and took a shower in the common bathroom located in the hall. Then he changed into a clean shirt, went down to the street, and headed toward Nick's.

The place was crowded, noisy, blanketed in smoke. Six had moved away from his post at the door and walked slowly through the crowd, eyeballing the men, his arms draped loosely at his side. The stools and booths were all taken, and several fruit crates had been brought out and overturned. These had been taken now as well. The men sat on the stools and on the crates and in the booths, drinking steadily from bottles, all of their eyes focused on the fight going on the television set mounted on the wall. The image was fuzzy, and the picture rolled occasionally on the screen, but no one seemed to mind. Everyone was laughing and carrying on, trying to speak louder than the guy next to him, all of them having a fine time. Nick's might have been a lunch counter during the day, but it was no different than any other beer garden at night.

A thin white man with slicked-back hair and a black moustache sat on the customer's side of the counter among the Negroes. He watched the fight without expression or comment, nursing a Ballantine Ale. Florek went by him, squeezed in at the open end of the counter, tried to catch Stefanos's eye. He and Costa were moving clumsily back there, rudderless, unable to catch a rhythm. They bumped each other and raised their voices when they did, though not in the good-natured way of the afternoon. There was a sloppiness in the way they moved; the place was just too busy for them to handle.

Florek stepped through the opening and behind the counter without thinking. Stefanos, fumbling for a beer in the cooler, looked up. His face was streaked with sweat, his hair damp and fallen about his face.

"What're you doin' back here?"

"I can help."

"Help how?"

Florek shrugged. "I'll jockey the drinks."

Stefanos glanced over at Costa, clearing dishes off the counter. Costa looked back at his friend and nodded once.

"Okay, boy," said Stefanos. "Get an apron."

"Where?"

"In the back."

Florek turned, pushed through the swinging doors that led to the

131

kitchen. A tall, lean man with a good head of gray hair stood over a set of large burners, stirring a pot of soup. He looked at Florek as he burst through the doors.

"What the hell," said the cook.

"I need an apron," said Florek.

The cook jerked his head behind him toward a stainless steel table used for prep. Beneath the table, Florek could see a stack of folded white aprons. He went for the stack, took an apron off the top, unraveled it, flipped it over so it made a clean rectangle. He tied the apron tightly around his waist.

"Thanks," said Florek to the cook. He moved back through the doors.

In the front of the house, more men had arrived. A guy raised a finger toward Florek and ordered a Carling Red Cap. Florek went to the cooler, found one, pulled it free. He looked around for something with which to open the bottle.

"On the cooler, *re*," said Stefanos from over at the register. "On the side!"

Flora saw the Coca-Cola opener screwed into the side of the cooler. He popped the cap, served the bottle to the man who had ordered it. He heard the register ring down, then a riot of voices as someone threw a knockdown punch on the television screen overhead. Through the shoulders of the men in front of him, Florek caught a glimpse of Six pushing a man out the front door. The man appeared to be taking flight. The chime sounded at the man's exit.

"A Ballantine Ale for me," said the white man with the slicked-back hair.

"Yessir," said Florek.

He bumped into Costa going for the cooler, hesitated trying to get out of Costa's way.

"All right boy," said Costa. "Get on your horse! Move it!"

Florek stepped aside. He found the Ballantine, served it to the white man.

"Thanks," he said, with a quick wink. "You keep doing what your doing, and don't worry about Costa. You just keep it up."

The crowd and its demand intensified, but Florek soon found his step. He and Stefanos and Costa found their own places behind the counter, Nick at the register and Costa back and forth from the kitchen and Florek from the cooler to the counter with the drinks. Florek forgot about the sweat on his back, never noticed the dryness of his mouth or the ache in his legs. He never noticed any of it until the fights ended and the noise settled and the crowd began to thin out. It was then that he looked at the Blatz Beer clock centered over the front door and noticed that he had been working close to two hours straight.

"Here ya go, *vre*," said Stefanos, handing Florek a cold bottle of National.

Florek took it by the neck, drank deeply. Costa walked by, clapped Florek on the shoulder as he passed.

"The new guy's pretty good," said the white man with the slicked-back hair.

"Yeah, he's okay." Stefanos pointed at the man. "Florek, meet my friend, Lou DiGeordano."

They shook hands. "Mr. DiGeordano."

"Pleased to meet you, son."

DiGeordano put some money on the counter, took his topcoat off a tree by the booths. He nodded at Nick Stefanos and went out the front door.

Stefanos cracked a Ballantine Ale, poured some into a glass. He raised the glass at Florek, drank from it, then wiped the foam off his upper lip.

"Well, how about it, Florek?"

"How about what?"

Stefanos put his foot up on the cooler. "How much they payin' you down at People's?"

"Seventy-five cents an hour, somethin' like that. Why?"

Costa walked over with an empty glass in his hand. Stefanos poured the rest of the Ballantine into Costa's glass.

"Business is pickin' up. I'm gonna need some help around here, four, five nights a week. I'm gonna match what they're payin' you down there. Only here, you're gonna get it under the table, cash." Stefanos rubbed his thumb and forefinger together. "You understand?"

"I guess so," said Florek.

"You work out here when we're busy like tonight, and sometimes you're gonna help the cook in the back. Unloading, stocking, preppin' food, things like that. There's a few things my cook can't do. Might put a little muscle on you, too, liftin' things like that. You could use a few pounds."

"Yessir."

Stefanos turned to his friend. "That okay by you, Costaki?"

"Me? I don't give a damn nothing!" He smiled crookedly at Florek, had a sip of beer. Then he went to the television set and pulled its plug from the wall socket. "Little bit of quiet, that's all I need."

"Come on," said Stefanos, pulling on Florek's arm. "I'm gonna introduce you to the cook."

Florek walked along through the swinging doors, a little dizzy from the beer and the heat. He wasn't exactly certain as to what had just happened, and he tried to remember if he had agreed back there to any of Nick's

133

terms. Not that it mattered—he knew that there really wasn't any doubt that he would take the job; it felt right, being in a place like this, with these kinds of men.

The cook was sitting on a tall stool, drinking a bottle of beer and smoking a cigarette. The cook's hair was all gray, but his face was smooth and unlined. Now that Florek had a longer look, he could see that this man was much younger than he had first appeared.

"Panayoti," said Stefanos to the cook. "I want you to meet our new counter man, Mike Florek."

The cook got off the stool, winced a little as he stood. He took a few steps toward Florek, limping deeply. Florek looked at the cook's left leg: even through the fabric of the trousers, he could see the bend, the awful twist at the knee. Florek stepped forward, met the man halfway, put out his hand. The cook reflexively touched at a black smudge on his face, then extended his own hand. The two of them shook.

"Mike," said Florek.

"Pete Karras," said the cook. "C'mon, chum, I'll show you around."

18

Peter Karras caught his breath sharply as his foot touched the floor. He tried to relax and let some air out, give it a few seconds to let the moment pass. Three years after the night in the alley, the mornings still gave him trouble. It was hell for Karras, getting out of bed.

After the operation, when he had been in rehabilitation for a while, the doctors told him that the knee was nearly useless, that the sack of smashed bone and cartilage that had been his left foot would never set just right. He'd have to wear a brace on his leg, they said, with the hope that maybe someday, if he was real good and lucky, he could graduate to a cane. There was also some talk of a special shoe for the foot, a Boris Karloff-looking number with a built-up sole and laces on the side. Of course, on account of the mangled knee, the bum leg would always be shorter than the other. But the Karloff shoe coupled with the cane would lessen the limp.

Karras asked the doctors if he had heard them right: that if he went along with the program, and didn't expect a whole lot, then a lucky guy like him, he might be able to make do with a gimp's shoe and *yero's* cane. Is that what the doctor meant to say? The young doctor had laughed skittishly and made several attempts to strike a match to a cigarette.

Dimitri was crying in the second bedroom of the apartment. Drowsily calling out, "Maaama, Maaama, Maaaaaa . . . ," probably standing up in his crib about now, his chubby olive hands wrapped around the wood rails. Eleni would be in the kitchen, cooking some breakfast, listening to her records, playing them just loud enough that she couldn't hear the kid. Karras figured he better get up and help the little guy out.

Those first few steps in the morning were always the worst. He always worked through it, though, like he had worked through the worst of it in the beginning, without the brace from the very start and later without the cane. As for the shoe, a cobbler in Chinatown had stretched out one of his brogues, fitted it with a couple of padded inner soles, and Karras had made do with that. He walked, and when it hurt so bad he thought he'd scream, he kept walking. Soon he learned how to keep the pain from showing on his face, so that after a while, except in the morning and on very cold days, the pain crawled away like a beaten dog to a black corner in the back of his mind. That was the mental part of it; it was the physical part he couldn't lick. Karras knew that he would always have that damned and goddamned limp.

"Maaaaa . . . ," said Dimitri.

Karras got off the bed, grunted as he walked across the hardwood floor. He pulled his underpants away from his sleeper's hard-on, scratched beneath his balls. The pain was rough this morning, rougher than most. He could take the pills he had in the bathroom, the ones he had gotten from a pharmacist on 14th and Colorado Avenue, a friend of a friend. Karras always thought it over, ended up never taking the pills. A doper was just another kind of cripple to him. Still, he kept the pills in the medicine cabinet, never considered throwing them away. It was good to know that they were there.

Out in the hall, he pushed on Dimitri's door, opened it to a wall of heat. He had told Eleni to leave the door open at night, what with the radiator in there, but she insisted on keeping it closed. And there he was, standing in the crib, his cheeks flushed like some living Raggedy Andy doll, his black hair as damp as if he had been sleeping beside a furnace.

"Da," said Dimitri, his eyes—the same shade of brown as Eleni's, the same exact shape—registering mild disappointment.

"Son."

Karras lifted him from the crib. Dimitri's sleeping outfit, the powder blue one with the sewed-on feet, was wet around the crotch.

"Eleni!" yelled Karras.

"What?" came the weak response from the kitchen.

"The *pethi* is wet!"

"Then change his diaper!"

Karras looked dolefully at the stack of cloth folded neatly near the cup of safety pins on the table by the crib. A picture of a bear wearing a baseball cap had been painted on the table. Karras felt ridiculous, standing there with the kid in his arms, the cartoon bear's eyes bugging idiotically in his direction.

"Diapers," he said to his son. "Someone ought to let your mom in on a little secret: I don't know how to operate these damn things."

Dimitri pointed to the door. "Mom."

Karras lowered the boy to the floor, steadied him on his feet, patted him on the rump.

"Yeah," said Karras. "You go on and see Mom. Mom'll fix you up."

Dimitri stumbled once, regained his footing as he went giggling out the door. Two years old—Eleni always corrected Karras, had to remind him that Dimitri was "eighteen months"—and the kid was already running around, putting a few words together. Karras watched him go, a stocky, dark boy, more Triandokidis than Karras. The old man had noticed it straight off, the day Eleni and Pete had brought the infant home from the hospital: "He's no Spartan, that one. *Miazi ti mitera tou, aftos.*" After that, Karras's father rarely paid attention to the boy, despite the fact that Dimitri was his namesake and his blood. Peter Karras should have been angry, but oddly, he was not. The boy did favor his mother, both in looks and gesture, and given a choice, young Dimitri would run to her over him every time. From the start, Karras felt disconnected from him, wondering sometimes if a bond would ever grow between them, if he would ever really feel like a father to the boy. And then he wondered if that was what he wanted after all.

Karras went to the bathroom, pulled his softening cock from his underpants and stood over the head. His urine split and went off in two directions, some of it splashing onto the black and white tiles of the bathroom floor. His first piss of the day was always like this, and it had been that way for his old man. Karras smiled, remembering the mornings he'd stand in the door frame of his parents' bathroom as a boy, watching the old man pissing two streams, hungover and pressing one palm flat against the wall. Back then, Karras believed that his father had more than one dick, that this was what happened when a boy became a man. He used to wonder when he would begin to grow his second one, too.

Karras washed his face, looked in the mirror. Twenty-seven years old, and all-the-way gray. His father, he had gone gray early as well. Gray or no, Karras could still get the looks, if the girls didn't happen to catch his walk. Then they'd look away. But on good days Karras could still pass for a blue-eyed Hodiak. John Hodiak with a limp, and a full head of gray hair.

Karras found his robe hanging on a hook behind the bathroom door. He put it on and went out to the kitchen.

The sound of Betty Hutton singing "Doctor, Lawyer, Indian Chief" hit him as he walked into the room. Dimitri stood in his playpen in the middle of the living area, holding onto the netting, squatting up and down in rough cadence to the song's beat. Personally, Karras couldn't stand those novelty numbers, and to top it off Hutton had the hardness of a man. But the kid liked the tune, and Karras knew that Eleni had put it on for him.

"Mornin'," said Karras to Eleni's back. Eleni turned her head and smiled, then went back to the bread she was soaking in a bowl filled with egg yolk beaten into milk.

She tossed her mane of brown hair. "I'm makin' a little French toast, honey."

"Okay by me."

"Pete?"

She wanted something. He could tell it by the singsong way she said his name.

"What, sweetheart?"

"You think we might be able to sneak out to a picture this weekend?"

"To see what?"

"There's this movie called *The Boy With Green Hair*, it's opening down at the Keith's."

"What's it about?"

"Robert Ryan's in it."

"I like Robert Ryan. Ryan's the McCoy. But I didn't ask you who was in it. I asked what the picture was about."

"There's this little boy, see, and he wakes up with a head of green hair. People treat him differently because of it, like he's some kind of freak—"

"Sounds like a million laughs. I don't think so, baby."

"You never wanna take me out."

Karras checked out his wife's backside. She hadn't lost much of the weight she had put on from having the kid, would probably never lose it now. And he had been warned about her ankles. He could remember when he just got back from the war, when he had brought her over to meet the folks. His father had taken him aside, made some negative comment about her family, the village they had come from, what they had not amounted to, like that. Then his father had gotten to the real point.

"And one more thing," Dimitri Karras had said. "She's got them fat ankles."

"So what, Pop?"

"You marry a girl with fat ankles, the rest of her's gonna get fat, too, goddamn right."

"Oh, for Chrissakes."

"I'm serious, boy. *Acous?* You marry a girl, there's a good chance she's gonna get fat anyway, they all gonna get fat, nothin' you can do about that. But why you wanna marry one you *know's* gonna get fat? Huh?"

Karras married her, and she had put on the weight, and she had kept it on, and that had been fine with him. He liked a woman with a little something on her. Anyway, he liked it on Eleni. She carried it well, her big-boned legs firm and strong, her breasts full and unsagging. Eleni, standing there in that red rayon robe he had picked up for her at Morton's for three and change—yeah, she looked pretty damn good. Karras began to imagine her beneath the robe, caught the dryness in his mouth, looked away. He knew he ought to save it for later in the day.

Karras picked the *Times-Herald* up off the kitchen table, glanced at the front page. The Reds in Hungary had kicked out Selden Chapin, the American foreign minister, after Chapin had gone and stuck his nose in the Cardinal Mindszenty affair. The Soviets had given the Catholic cardinal a life stretch for his anti-commie activities, but Karras thought, so what? Let the cardinal rot there, if it would keep a country of boys out of another war. If there was a God, and this God had any justice in Him, wouldn't saving young lives be His racket? Wouldn't that be what He would want?

"Take these empty bottles out, will ya, honey? The milkman's gonna be here soon."

"Sure thing," said Karras, not glancing up from the paper.

Below the fold, a story appeared about the new lead on the latest prosti killing, the third in as many years. This one had died like the others, a razor cut from throat to groin. The lead was a phony, a plant from a department eager to convince the public that they were on the case—Karras knew as much from a conversation with Jimmy Boyle. Karras wondered when the blueboys would figure this one out; overworked and plain stumped by the seemingly motiveless intensity of the killings, and not used to a repeat-murder case remaining unsolved for such a long period of time, the detectives appeared to be chasing their tails. At least it looked that way to Karras. And Boyle had told him that the department had *nada*.

"These bottles, honey."

Karras looked up at Eleni, standing there holding the empty bottles. Her robe had opened a little, giving to a view of the tops of her breasts. Goddamn her, she never wore a brassiere underneath that robe.

"Oh, what the hell," said Karras.

Karras went to the record player, took the Hutton off the platter. He found Stan Kenton's "Artistry Jumps" in the stack, put that on, let it spin. He limped across the room, doing a stutter step to the tune. Dimitri bounced up and down, holding the netting of the playpen walls. Karras moved toward Eleni.

"What's got into you, anyway?"

"Just feel like cuttin' the rug this morning," said Karras.

"We don't have any rugs, Pete," said Eleni, her nose crinkling from the repressed smile. "And you never could dance."

"Come here."

Karras took the bottles from Eleni's hands, placed them on the kitchen table. He danced her a couple of steps around the room, opened his robe, pushed himself against her and gave it some friction as he kissed her softly, running his tongue along her gums. Eleni's breath smelled of coffee.

"Pete."

"Aw, shut up."

"I haven't even brushed my teeth."

"Shut up, baby."

They moved to the living room, where Karras fell back into an over-stuffed lounge chair. He drew her down to him.

"Mom," said Dimitri from the playpen. He began to cry.

"The *pethi*." Eleni's breath had become short.

"He's all right."

Karras fumbled at Eleni's robe, opened it. He pinched the nipple of her right breast, kissed her roughly on the mouth. She pushed herself against him. He freed his cock, rubbed the head of it against her damp panties. Eleni bucked, made a grunting sound, pulled the fabric of her panties aside.

"*Esi eise etimi*," said Karras.

"*Ella*, Pete."

She made a small wave of her hips, forward and down again to let him in. And then he *was* in, deep into her pussy, which was wet and always hot.

"Um," she said.

"Quit complainin,'" said Karras.

She threw her head back; a string of saliva dripped from the side of her mouth onto Karras's chest. The Kenton band kicked it in the room, the sound drowning out the boy's crying. Karras watched Eleni's right leg convulse, watched it beat against the side of the chair.

Karras laughed. "Just look at you, baby. You're kickin' like a mule."

"*Scase*, Pete."

Karras did as he was told: He shut his mouth and closed his eyes.

■

"Hey, Pete," said Eleni. "Where you goin', all dressed up like that? You're not wearin' that suit to work, are you?"

Karras had taken his shower, dressed in his blue, chalk-striped, double-breasted suit. He stood in the kitchen buttoning the jacket.

"I guess I forgot to tell you. The new kid is handling lunch today. I'm gonna go in after that."

"The Polish kid?"

"Yeah, Mike Florek. It's only been a week, but he's catchin' on pretty good."

"You better look out. He might catch on good enough to bounce you out of your job."

"I'm not worried. There's plenty of customers now to keep all of us busy. Anyway, Nick'll always treat me right."

Eleni rested a fist against her hip. "So where you goin'?"

"I heard about a couple of businesses downtown that were up for sale."

"What kind of businesses?"

Karras fumbled with the change in his pocket. "There's this soda bar concession . . . and a little lunch counter I got my eye on, too."

Eleni's face brightened. "Oh, Pete!"

Karras moved his eyes away from Eleni's. "I said I was lookin', that's all. Just trying to get some kind of idea."

Dimitri sat cross-legged on the kitchen floor, banging a wooden spoon against a pot. Karras went to him, bent down, kissed him on the top of his head. The boy's hair was wet with sweat—Christ, the kid was gonna roast in this place.

"See ya, Jimmy."

"Da," said Dimitri.

"Pete?"

"Yes, sweetheart."

"Phillip's has a GE vacuum cleaner on sale this week, one of those new upright models. Thirty-nine ninety-five. You can pay on it, too, a buck a week."

"What's wrong with just sweeping out the place with a broom? We don't even have any carpets."

"I was thinkin' we could look into a couple of throw rugs, too."

You never learn, do you, sweetheart? You shoulda asked me for those things a half-hour ago, when all the blood had left my brain and gone down to my dick. I would've said yes to anything then.

"Let me think it over, Eleni. I mean, we just moved into this two-bedroom, and things are kind of tight."

141

"Okay. We'll talk it over later."

Karras kissed Eleni on the side of her mouth, got his topcoat from out of the closet, shook it on. He picked up a deck of cigarettes from the table by the door, slipped them and a book of matches into the topcoat's side pocket.

"See ya later, sweetheart."

"Oh, Pete, I almost forgot." Eleni moved in the direction of the icebox.

"Ah, no."

"Just run this around the corner to your mom." Now she had pulled a tray from the icebox and was moving toward him. "It's some of that *pastitsio* we had last night."

"What do I look like, some kind of delivery boy? You see some kind of paper hat on my head?"

"Pete, don't get sore about it." She put the tray into his hands. "And say 'hi' to your mom."

Karras took the tray and the empty bottles and left the apartment. He dropped the bottles in a hinge-topped container outside the door. On the stairs, he passed the milkman coming up. Karras pretended to trip, acted like he would dump the food on the man in white. The man flinched, then grimaced as Karras pulled back.

"You," said the milkman.

"Hurry up with that cow juice," said Karras. "I got a hungry kid waitin' on it upstairs."

Out on the street, gulls appeared overhead, dipped down toward the tray of food. Karras smiled, thinking of the milkman, how he got him every time. Then he thought of Eleni, and the smile went away.

Imagine me, ownin' my own business. That'll be the day.

◾

His mother was boiling a chicken when he got to the apartment. She was standing in the kitchen in her black housedress, her nylon anklets bunched about her black orthopedic shoes.

"Hello, boy *mou*," she said as Karras walked in. She frowned as he limped across the room.

"Hi, Ma." He kissed her on the cheek, handed her the tray. "From Eleni."

"*Pastitsio, eh? Entaxi.*" She took the tray and set it on the counter. "*Thelis cafe?*"

"Okay, Ma. I'll have a cup."

Georgia Karras served her son some coffee and placed a small plate of sweets on the table. Karras dipped a *koulouri* in his coffee, ate that one and

142

then another, then lighted a Lucky Strike and smoked it while his mother related some gossip about a woman she knew from church. When she had finished the story, she told him how the prostitutes' murders had made her frightened to walk the streets after dark. He listened to all of this passively, smashed out his cigarette when it had burned down to the brand name printed on the paper. He got up to leave.

"Gotta go, Ma. Got an appointment. Need any *lefta?*"

"Fiya, boy. I'm okay."

The old man had taken out a good insurance policy. Well, at least he had done one thing right.

"All right, then. I'll be on my way."

His mother patted his cheek. *"Pas sto kalo."*

Karras stopped at the door, watched his mother clear the table. He looked around the place: blankets covered the apartment's mirrors, and all of the window shades were drawn down tight. Karras went out to the hall, closed the door behind him. He gripped the banister, moved carefully as he took the stairs down to the street.

On H, Karras saw Su leaning against his new cab, smoking a cigarette, the butt dangling from his mouth, his hands deep in the flap pockets of his zip-up jacket. Su, a Chinese Alfalfa—that one fork of straight black hair still stood up on the back of his head, as it always had when they were kids.

Su smiled, his eyes disappearing with the action. "Hey, Pete!"

"Su."

Su ran a hand along the front quarter panel of his cab. "How you like my new sled?"

"Nice. Where'd you get it?"

"Up on Florida Avenue, at Cherner's. Gotta deal on it, gonna pay on time. It ain't so new how I'd like it, but you know what they say—"

" 'Next to a New Car, a Chernerized Car is Best.' "

"That's right! How 'bout a lift, Pete?"

"I'm headin' down to Southeast. I thought I'd take a bus and walk a little after that. It ain't so far."

"C'mon, Pete." Su opened the rear door of the Dodge, made a courtly handsweep pointing Karras inside. "I'll only hit you for one zone."

"All right."

Karras got into the backseat of the sedan. Su pitched his smoke, ran quickly and nimbly around the front of the car. He slipped into the driver's seat, put the Dodge in gear, pulled away from the curb.

"What'ya think about the Nats this year, Pete? They got anything?"

"I couldn't tell you. I haven't followed baseball much since the war."

Karras thought of Billy Nicodemus, pictured him running across H as a boy, his mitt hanging loosely on his hand. Billy had taken that mitt everywhere, even when the boys had pooled their change one summer and taken the open streetcar out to Glen Echo. Perry Angelos had brought Helen Leonides along as his guest, which didn't sit well with the other boys but which they had allowed—as everyone knew, even then, that Perry was sweet on Helen. They had caught the streetcar at the beginning of the line and watched the conductor walk the wheel from back to front, flipping the chair backs as he went along the aisle. Upon arriving at the park, they had swum in the pool until the early afternoon, then went to the funhouse, where they rode the big wheel in the center of the hall, which spun faster and faster until all the kids had been thrown to the side. Helen's skirt had blown up around her thighs while on the wheel, and Karras could not help noticing the blue print on her soft white underpants, feeling some degree of excitement tinged with shame. Later, as evening fell, Joe Recevo had suggested that they finish things off listening to the popular tunes of the McWilliams Orchestra in the Spanish Ballroom, but none of them save Joe knew how to dance. At the end of the day Angelos had gotten sick on the roller coaster, and Billy Nicodemus vomited from the motion of another ride coupled with too many sweets. On the trolley ride back home, Billy had smiled, remarking on what a fine day it had been, a crusty arc of vomit framing his wide grin. Yeah, Billy—he had always been some kind of happy kid.

Su brought Karras back to the world. "Think Feller will sign with Cleveland?"

"Like I say, Su, I wouldn't know."

Su tried again. "DiMaggio signed yesterday, d'ya hear about it? The Yanks are gonna pay him ninety grand."

"That so."

Karras shook a Lucky from the deck, struck a match to it, dropped the match out the cracked window. He looked at Su looking at him in the rearview.

Karras said, "You still running errands for the Hip Sings?"

"Hip Sings?" said Su. "What the hell is that?"

Su didn't say much after that. Karras figured the crack would shut Su up, and he was right. These Chinese, you brought up their secret societies, you might as well ask them to rat out their own mothers. Su drove quietly through the streets while Karras smoked his cigarette.

Su dropped Karras on the 4500 block of Alabama Avenue, let it idle by the curb. Karras went around to the driver's window, leaned in.

"Thirty cents," said Su.

"Here you go." Karras handed him four bits.

"Ninety grand for DiMaggio, Pete. Can you imagine it?" Su winked, put his fists together, broke his wrists in an abbreviated swing. "Joltin' Joe."

Karras smiled. "Take it easy, Su."

"You too."

Su gunned it down the street. Karras waited for the cab to make the turn at the intersection, then walked along the sidewalk to the middle of the block. He took the steps up to the front of a row house there and went through an open door into a common foyer. He rested for a moment in the foyer, then knocked on a door marked 1.

The door opened: A built, green-eyed blonde in a black slip stood in the frame. She wore black stockings with seams running down their backs; sling-backed, open-toed high heels finished things off.

Karras swallowed hard. The woman turned all the way around to let him have a good look, wiggled one foot in the air when she was done.

"You like?" she said.

"Cat-eyes, right?"

"That's what they call them. How'd you know?"

"I saw 'em down at Hahn's. I was walkin' down F last week, the guy was just putting them out in the window." Karras made an eye-sweep of the foyer. "You always come to the door dressed like this?"

"When it's you knocking, I do." The woman took Karras by the hand. "C'mon inside, Pete, it's awfully cold."

Karras looked her over, couldn't help but grin. "That much I can see."

"Quit clowning around. You know I've only got an hour for lunch."

"A whole hour, huh? How we gonna fill it up?"

The woman chuckled, reached out to touch his cheek. Karras stepped through the open door frame. He slipped his arms around her waist, pulled her to him gently. He kissed her open mouth.

"Vera," he said.

Karras breathed her in, a smell clean as spring.

19

Jimmy Boyle unwrapped his second hot dog of the morning, took a bite. With the mustard and the raw onions and a little of the vendor's green relish, God, the dog was good. He finished it quickly, drank off the rest of his Coke to push the mess down his throat. His burp brought the taste back up, making him think with some remorse that the two hot dogs had only made him angry; sometime soon he'd be ready for a serious crack at lunch.

"Hey, Mister, you gonna turn that bottle in?"

A kid had been sitting on the curb nearby, eyeing the bottle like he could have taken a bite out of the glass.

"What say?" Boyle turned so his good ear was pointed toward the boy.

"Your bottle. Would ya mind if I turned it in for the refund?"

Boyle went to the boy, dropped the empty in his lap. "Here you go, kid. Knock yourself out."

Boyle bought a paper at a newsstand, stood on the sidewalk facing a bank, had a look at the front page. The alleged lead on the killer in the latest whore murder almost made him laugh. The Department spokesman had told the *Times-Herald* that a walk-in confession was being looked into, but Boyle knew that was a flat-out lie. Confessions they had, in spades. What they needed was a killer. Every time one of these roundheels bought it, handfuls of phony confessors—terminal drunks and dopers looking for a permanent three-square, bedwetters crying for attention—turned themselves in. Some of them were capable of violence in certain situations; one or two of them qualified as drool cases or rubber-room candidates. None of them were gone enough to do what the killer had done. And only the

146

killer would know certain elements absent from the newspaper accounts—the press had been fed the facts minus several key details. So the few detectives still assigned to the murders took the confessions, noted the pertinent omissions, and slipped the reports in a thickening file.

Reading the story, Boyle felt a click in his chest. If he could just dig a little bit, turn up the right rock that had a genuine lead underneath, a solid lead on the murders . . . hell, he might as well forget about it—he'd been dreaming about cracking this case for the last three years. Why would he think *he* could uncover something when the homicide boys had come up with major-league goose eggs? They were the ones with the wheels and the departmental muscle. *They* had the access to the lab jockeys with all the scientific equipment, *they* wore the suits and ties. And here he was, a beat cop, wearing the same lousy blues given to him when he joined the force. To top it off, the Department had colored guys working Shaw now, walking the same beat, making the same amount of dough as him.

Boyle lowered the newspaper, looked at his reflection in the bank's window. Shit, did he really look like that? The window distorted things, that much he knew. But this wasn't some circus mirror like they had out at Glen Echo, the one that could make a skinny man look fat. This was him, more or less—a guy not even thirty years old, with a triple chin, a head like a cantaloupe, and a gut covering the buckle on his belt. Boyle looked away.

Most of the guys he came up with were now private sixth grade, the highest rank of nonofficer, and a few had already made the jump. These were the guys who had kept an eye on their physiques, made a few high-profile busts along the road. Boyle had not distinguished himself in looks or in deed, or in any way at all. When promotions came around, he had been passed up every time.

His father had told him long ago that a man is judged on how he looks. Not that his father—a frail, balding morgue attendant on and off the city payroll throughout his career—had ever looked like much himself. But Boyle had always listened patiently to every homespun bit of advice the old man had given out. And it was his father and uncle, now a detective, who had come through when Boyle had applied for the force—the two of them had managed to falsify his physical, get him into the Academy despite the bum ear. So Boyle had no reason to doubt that a man's looks could keep him from getting ahead. The knowledge, however, was of little use to him if he couldn't take off the weight. The truth of it was, Boyle just loved so goddamn much to eat.

Boyle would try this new thing Karras had suggested, though he had his doubts. A pill that could make you forget about food, give you energy all the time—a "pep pill." Now, what the hell was that? Karras had assured him that it wasn't any kind of dope, but Pete had always been on the blind side about things like that. Still, Pete had gone out of his way to drop his name to that uptown pharmacist he knew. He might as well go there, give the Doc a try.

Boyle took the U Street trolley over to 14th, caught a northbound bus. He rode it up through Columbia Heights and into Brightwood Park to the end of the line, got off at the depot at Colorado Avenue. The pharmacy stood on the corner there, where Colorado crossed 14th.

Boyle entered the pharmacy, passed a soda bar managed by a young, handsome guy, a Marine Corps veteran of the Philippine campaign. The vet was a friend of Peter Karras, but Boyle could not remember his name: Paleo-something, some shit like that. Whatever, the only thing Boyle would have bet on was that it ended in an *s*. These Greeks and their crazy names. Boyle nodded at the guy and the guy nodded back. Karras had told Boyle that this veteran was a good Joe.

The Doc was behind the counter in the back of the store, smoking a cigarette. He was tall and thin with sharp, elongated features, gray half-moons below his eyes, the caved-in cheeks of the often ill. His thin assistant, young and on the healthier side, stood on a platform working on an order. Boyle went up to the counter, waited for the Doc to look up. He was reading a paper he had spread there, smoke dribbling slowly through the flared nostrils of his long nose. He crushed the cigarette in an ashtray filled with dead ones, pushed the newspaper to the side. Boyle noticed the caffeine shake in the man's hand.

"Can I help you?"

"I'm Jim Boyle. Pete Karras sent me."

The Doc cracked a smile, everything on his face rearranging itself into a whole new wrinkled mask. "You the cop?"

"Yeah, but this isn't business. I'm here on my own time. You've got nothing to worry about."

"Who's worried? Pete told me what you wanted, I thought I might be able to help."

"I been puttin' on the pounds lately—"

"Not a problem. You just wait right there."

"Could you speak up a little?"

"I'll be right back."

Boyle watched him go up to the platform, talk to the young assistant. The assistant looked Boyle over from up on his perch. Then he disappeared for a couple of minutes, came back and put something in the Doc's shaky paw. The Doc returned to the counter, pressed a plastic canister into Boyle's hand. Boyle shook it, listened for the rattle before slipping the canister into his trouser pocket.

"Anything I ought to know?"

"Let's see. Well, they're going to make you a bit jumpy, in a pleasant kind of way. You'll find you have more energy, less desire to eat. If you have trouble sleeping, knock off taking them late at night. You should see the results you're looking for fairly quickly."

"That it?"

"That's all, I guess."

"I'm no doper," said Boyle.

"Neither am I." The Doc shrugged. "Neither is my assistant. But we use these all the time. They're simple pep pills. Everyone needs a lift at some point during the day. You can't always get to a cup of coffee."

Boyle reached for his wallet. "What do I owe you?"

"Nothing."

"You sure?"

"Please. Like I said, I'm just looking to help you out. Maybe you can do the same for me some time."

Boyle hesitated for a moment, then turned and left the store.

The Doc put fire to a cigarette. He coughed a little, felt a rawness in his throat. His assistant came up next to him, snatched a cigarette for himself from the house pack. The Doc struck a match, held it out.

"You and me are just smoking up a storm," said the Doc.

"It's these pills. They make you crave it."

"Brother, you said it."

The assistant drew in hungrily on the cigarette. "You fix him up?"

The Doc nodded. "He needs to lose a little weight."

"I'll say."

The two of them laughed.

"How much you give him?"

"About twenty tablets."

The Doc smiled. "He'll be back."

"I give him about a week," said the assistant.

"Yeah," said the Doc. "That's one thing about this Benzedrine—you start likin' it real good and quick."

∎

By the time Boyle had changed into his uniform and left the locker room for his foot patrol, he had started to feel pretty damn good. The Doc had been right about the energy, but he hadn't mentioned the incredible wave of confidence, the notion that he could kick right through a brick wall. It had come on him slowly, beginning with a tickling sensation at the back of his head married to a powerful thirst. He hadn't thought about food once in the last hour, either, and when he did force himself to consider it the notion sickened him, maybe for the first time in his life. If one tablet had done this for him, imagine how good he would have felt had he swallowed two.

On the walk west, Boyle had gone through Temperance Court near 12th and T, where any variety of dope or weapon could be bought, and he had seen a known tea smoker named Russell Edwards making a buy. Boyle had called Edwards's name, chased him on foot, lost the younger, thinner man two blocks south. Afterwards, he laughed at his own uncharacteristic tenacity while catching his breath. To go after a man in the Court unassisted was foolish, and mainly a waste of time. It was not something Boyle would normally do.

Boyle headed down U toward 14th, twirling his baton as he walked. He smiled at the sight of a young Negro on the sidewalk talking softly to a woman who leaned out of a second-story row house window. The young man was dressed to the nines, moving his hands elegantly, pleading his case in a very poetic way. Boyle looked at the woman, the fine chocolate skin of her thin arms, the curl of her lips, her teeth . . . he didn't blame the young man, understood the inspiration for his poetry and desire. Since Negroes couldn't come to see the shows in the white venues, but whites could go to the Negro houses, Boyle often went to the Howard Theatre to catch the revues. On those occasions, he spent more time studying the women in the audience than he did the acts. His preference was just another aspect of his character that would have to remain hidden from the departmental brass.

Boyle stopped at the head of an alley, noticed three men shooting dice against the bricks. The man running the game stood to the side, dollars fanned out in one tight fist. He was a jockey-sized man, balding, a Jew with a knotted nose and a glass eye. Boyle knew him as Matty Buchner.

"Buchner!" said Boyle, rapping his baton against the wall.

The three men collected what they could from the ground, bolted off down the alley, booked right at the T. Buchner stopped to collect the money they had left, then began to follow their path. His short wheels didn't take him far. Boyle caught up to him without effort and grabbed him by the collar of his shirt. He spun Buchner around, backed him up against the bricks.

"Matty, where you think you're goin'? I know where to find you anyway, you know that."

"I wasn't runnin' from you, officer, honest. I just wanted to catch up with those guys, they left a few scoots lyin' around on the ground."

"That's you, Matty, a Boy Scout all the way."

Buchner's good eye moved toward the T of the alley. The glass eye didn't follow. "I almost made it," he muttered.

"You weren't even close," said Boyle.

"You gonna take me in?"

"Depends. You got anything for me today?"

Buchner wiggled his closed mouth. He was a nervous little guy, a cold-finger man and gamer who had done a stretch for hitting the coatroom at the Shoreham during a high-society wedding reception in '46. Buchner had been going through unattended coats and purses for fifteen years before he had been caught. It was said around Shaw that Buchner had run his hands through more fur pieces in those fifteen years than Sinatra had in his whole career. All cops had informants, some more reliable than others. Boyle had Matty Buchner.

"What do you hear about the murder?" said Boyle.

"Which murder?"

"The latest hooker."

"Oh, her. I ain't heard nothin', officer. Honest."

Boyle ground his teeth together. That was another thing with those pills.

"That so," said Boyle. He went to the place where the men had been shooting craps, picked up the dice from the stones. He examined the dice, turning them in his hands. Boyle grinned. "These your sugar cubes?"

"Yeah," said Buchner, blinking the good eye, giving his mouth an involuntary wiggle. "Something wrong?"

"Nothing wrong," said Boyle. "Not unless you want to roll a seven with these things."

"Come again?"

"Two, four, and six. That's the only numbers I see on these dice. Any way you add 'em, it's kinda hard to roll a seven with these babies, isn't it, Matty."

Buchner slapped his own cheek. "Man-O-Manischewitz! Did I bring them novelty dice out with me today? My little nephew, he musta slipped them into my trousers when I wasn't lookin'—"

"Can it."

Buchner's shoulders slumped. "All right."

151

"Those men who just hotfooted it out of here, you think they might want to know about how their pal Matty was fixin' the game? Say, wasn't one of those guys that big spade that works behind the bar at the Yamasee on U? That was him, wasn't it?"

"I don't r-recollect."

"I'm gonna ask you again." Boyle got close into Buchner's face. "What do you hear around on the hooker murders?"

"Pasadeno. It's like I said, I don't know nothin', officer, honest. I mean, I know what you know. The hookers that got themselves dead, they were all big and fat. To each his own and all that, but you gotta figure this guy that turned out their lights has something against fat hookers."

"He hated them, huh? What're you, a head doctor?"

Buchner shrugged. "Hey, I saw *Spellbound*, like everybody else. Anyway, it ain't too hard to figure out. I mean, you saw what he did to 'em. It ain't exactly a love letter when you cut a girl open from her throat to her snatch."

"Maybe he was on a budget. Maybe he chose the fat ones on account of the fat ones come cheaper."

"Ixnay. Not these fat ones. We're not talkin' about five-dollar punchboards here. And none of them were known streetwalkers, I read that much myself in the *Evening Star*. It was all telephone trade, from what I understand. I mean, it ain't like the guy walked into a cathouse and ordered one up. He arranged a meeting through a third party, kept the date, then took the girls into an alley and opened them up. But you know all that."

"Yeah." Boyle backed off. "You can go. But I want some information quick. I'm gonna hold on to these dice, in case I run into that bartender from the Yamasee."

"I'll ask around."

"Do better than that. Find something, and find it quick."

"Thanks for—"

"Get out of here. I'm tired of lookin' at your face."

The little man went down the alley, cut left at the T. Boyle walked back out to U, headed west. He was feeling a little drawn, kind of blue, with less of the energy he had before. Maybe he'd go into Nick's place, say hello to Pete Karras, have a cup of coffee to pick himself back up.

Boyle thought of Buchner, twitching in the alley, shifting his feet like a kid who had to take a leak. The little Jew was tougher than he looked; it must have hurt awful bad when that guy in the joint had taken that spoon to Buchner's eye. The first trashcan Boyle came to, he tossed the pair of dice inside.

Pete Karras stood in the sunlight coming in through the window, straightened his Windsor knot, formed it right. He slipped on his suit jacket, went to where Vera stood reapplying her makeup in the dresser mirror. He kissed her neck, reached beneath her arm, slid his hand across her breastbone and into her slip. He felt the dampness of sweat, her heartbeat, the swell of her nipple.

"Pete. I'm going to be late for work."

"Me too. You just looked so good standing there, that's all. I just had to touch it."

She turned into him, kissed him, moved him back gently, her palms flat on his chest. "I've got to get into work."

Vera turned back to the mirror. Karras went to the bed, sat on the sheets, avoided the dark, slick area where they had been. He picked up a paperback novel off the nightstand, read aloud the words on the cover.

"Evelyn Waugh," he said. "Who's she?"

"It's a he."

"A guy named Evelyn, huh."

"You wouldn't like it."

"I haven't read a book since high school. And even then I didn't read it."

"He's speaking this weekend at Gaston Hall. Would you like to go?"

"Speaking? I don't think so."

"You ought to read once in a while."

"I'll get around to it one of these years." Karras watched her drag a tube of lipstick across her fine mouth. "What do you folks do over there at the Census Bureau, anyway?"

"We count."

"Hmm." He touched the mole on his face. "So it isn't the job that's keeping you in D.C."

"I come from Indiana, Pete. Anything's better than—"

"That's not what I mean. There's other cities to visit, if it's the big city you like. What I'm askin' is, what makes you stay *here*?"

Vera looked at him in the mirror, realized she was staring, forced a quick smile. "I like this town, that's all. That good enough for you?"

"It'll do."

Karras got up, shook himself into his topcoat. He walked across the room, stood next to her at the dresser. "What I'm getting at, I guess . . . what I've always wondered is, I mean, why did you call me up, six months after that night in Kavakos's? And after you had a look at me, what made you stick?"

Vera stopped what she was doing, gave him that throaty chuckle he was waiting for. Her green eyes were a little watery in the light. "I don't know, Pete. You noticed my shoes, I guess. And you were funny, and good looking, and honest to boot. And you didn't try to sell me on how smart you were, or how much money you were going to make, or what a hero you were in the war. You didn't have any illusions about what you were."

"How about when you saw what I had become?"

Vera grinned. "I took pity on you. Then you surprised me. You turned out to be a great lay."

"Aw, quit jokin' around."

"Listen, Pete—"

"I know, you gotta get into work." Karras kissed her lightly. "I'll see you later, sweetheart."

He went to the door, opened it, began to step through.

"Pete?"

"Yeah."

"You think you and me could go out one night? Just have a drink or something, someplace quiet? I'd like to go out one night, get away from this room."

"Sure, sweetheart. We'll do that soon."

"Want me to phone you a cab?"

"I don't think so. It's a nice day. I'm gonna walk a while until I get tired. Then I'll catch a streetcar."

"Bye, Pete."

"Goodbye."

Karras closed the door behind him. Vera got her skirt off the bed, shimmied into it, zipped it up along the side, hooked it at the top. She took her blouse off a hanger and went to the window. She began to button her blouse as she looked outside.

Karras had paused out on the sidewalk to light a cigarette, his hands cupped around the match. Smoke swirled out of his hands as the match caught.

"You ask me why I stick around," she said out loud, her breath fogging the window. "The answer's staring you right in the face. I don't know how dumb one man can get."

She saw a twitch of pain cross Karras's face, felt a dull throb in her own chest.

"You just don't get it," she whispered. "Do you?"

Vera Gardner watched Karras limp along the sidewalk until he was out of sight. She finished buttoning her blouse, tucked the blouse into her skirt.

20

Mike Florek slid the last of the dishes into the basin filled with steaming hot, soapy water. He gathered up the tail of his apron, used it to wipe the sweat from his face.

"I'm gonna let these ones soak for a while," said Florek.

"Hokay, boy," said Costa.

Florek rubbed his hands dry. Costa stood by the prep table, running the edge of a machete against a whetting stone. Next to the stone, a leather sheath lay on its side. The scrape of the blade against the stone had been ripping through the kitchen since after lunch.

"Where'd you get that, anyway?"

"From Karras. One of those Filipinos gave it to him in the war. It's a good knife. Now I'm gonna make it real good. Real good and sharp, goddamn right."

Florek heard a dull thud come from the second floor. That would be Toula, Costa's wife, calling him from their apartment upstairs, stomping her heavy black shoe on the wood floor.

Costa went to the door in the kitchen that opened to a straight flight of narrow stairs. He opened the door, yelled up into the black, got a two-minute reply that sounded like bloody murder.

"*Scaseeeee!*" screamed Costa, ending the conversation. He slammed the door shut, then walked across the kitchen, his hair going off in all directions, a crooked smile on his animate face.

It had taken Mike Florek a couple of days to get used to things at Nick's. Costa and Nick were friends, he could see as much in their eyes, but the stranger off the street wouldn't have known it. They were at each other's

155

throats all the time, parrying, constantly looking for an opening in which to place the knife. And Costa could not stand in that doorframe—he was incapable of it—without yelling at his wife, and getting the fury of her verbal wrath in return. It drove Florek crazy at first, all this wasted, meaningless emotion. But after a while he began to look forward to hearing the warm current of affection in their raised voices, their loud spontaneous laughter that came quick as fire and resonated off the high, pressed-tin ceiling of the grill. He liked the way their thick hands punctuated their speech, the way Costa and Nick rolled their *R*s, the strange, almost clumsy grace in the way they moved. And there was Karras, a cripple gone gray before his time, a Greek with no accent, a steady, unemotional man, not like Costa or Nick. Florek liked him fine, but Karras was a harder man to get to know.

Costa sheathed the machete, put it on a high shelf, grabbed a serrated knife and a two-pronged fork from a metal drawer beneath the table, went to a roast beef he had recently withdrawn from the oven and placed atop a cutting board. He licked his thumb, stuck the fork into the beef, began to slice the meat. Costa softly sang a tune in Greek as the slices of meat curled off and fell to the wooden board.

Nick Stefanos came through the swinging doors, a knife in one hand and a tomato in the other. He looked at Costa slicing the meat, moved his lips like he was going to speak, took a second to chuckle to himself and enjoy the moment before he opened his mouth.

"*Siga, vre,*" said Stefanos.

"I'm goin' slow, Niko," said Costa.

"You're bein' too rough with it."

"No, I'm not."

"What're you tryin' to do, kill it again? It's *already* dead!"

"Ahhh. What the hell's the difference, anyway? I make a nice roast beef, cook a nice steamship round like this, these niggers, all they want me to do is throw it on the grill with some onions, put a bunch of hot sauce all over it, goddamn!"

"Hey, Nick," said Florek. "You need some help out front?"

"Yeah, go ahead and watch the counter. I'm gonna slice up the tomatoes came in this morning. Karras ought to be in any minute."

Florek refolded his apron, turned the wet part inward, tied it tight around his waist. He went out to the front of the house, Costa and Nick's laughter trailing behind. The Negro with the records, who Florek now knew as a man named Oscar Williams, sat at the end of the counter with a friend, both of them drinking beers. A uniformed cop sat in one of the booths, sipping a cup of coffee.

"A coupla more beers down here, youngblood," said Oscar Williams.

Florek drew two Nationals from the cooler, served them, put a couple of hash-marks on Williams's check. Williams handed Florek a record from the boxful that rested next to his stool.

"Here ya go, man, put this one on the box."

Florek placed the record on the platter, let it spin. He snapped his fingers to the now-familiar piano style, the way it rolled fluidly against the rest of the arrangement.

Williams's friend looked at Florek going with the beat. "You like this one, huh?"

"I like it fine. What do they call this?"

"They call it race music," said the friend, nudging Williams. "This one here is Fatha Hines."

Williams said, "It's called 'boogie-woogie,' youngblood."

"What's that?"

Williams spread his large hands. "Boogie-woogie? Why, boogie-woogie ain't nothin' more than plain old blues, played eight-to-the-bar."

Florek didn't ask what that meant, didn't really care. He liked the sound, liked all the records, in fact, that Oscar Williams brought into Nick's. It wasn't just somebody reading music off a sheet, singing by rote. These people felt something when they played it and when they sang it, and they made you feel it, too.

Florek grabbed the coffee pot off the burner, went out to the booths, refilled the policeman's cup. The cop thanked him for his trouble, leaned against the wood. Florek walked back around the counter, replaced the coffee pot, found some dirty glasses and put them in the bus tray. Nick's revolver, a pearl-handled .38 Smith & Wesson, lay next to the bus tray on its side. The gun was never moved from its spot, and Florek was careful not to touch it.

Stefanos had come back out and was standing over the sandwich board, slicing the tomato that he held in his hand. Florek had never seen a man who could do it that quickly and without waste. Not that he did it cleanly every time—Stefanos always had cuts on his meaty hands where the knife had slipped. You could count on seeing Nick, every day, with odd pieces of tape hanging off his fingers, tape and bandages, and streaks of blood smudged across the lap of his apron.

"Hey, Nick," said Williams's friend. "What the number was yesterday?"

"I couldn't tell you," said Stefanos. "I don't play 'em no more."

"You don't need to," said the friend, and he and Williams laughed. "If I had your money, I'd throw mine away. Anyway, you fixin' on havin' one of those lucky dreams of yours, don't forget to let us know."

Stefanos did not respond. He picked up another tomato, began to slice it thin.

"You hear about Lady Day?" said Williams to his friend.

"Yeah, they caught her last night in Frisco with that opium in her room. Got her dead to rights!"

"You think she did it? Her manager said it was some kind of plant."

"What her manager said don't matter no way. They gonna get that girl whether she guilty or not. Shoot, boy, you ought to know that."

The record had stopped. Florek went to the radio, pushed its plug into the wall. "Dance Party" was on WOOK, and Williams head-motioned Florek to let it ride. Florek wanted to hear more about this opium thing, but he decided to leave the men alone. Oscar Williams always had a good selection of Billie Holiday's records on hand. Opium or no, that Holiday gal, she could really sing.

Karras came through the front door, hung his topcoat on the tree by the booths, had a seat across from the policeman. Florek took a cup of coffee to Karras, who introduced him to the pale, overweight cop. The cop's name was Jimmy Boyle. The two of them looked to be friends, so Florek left them to their conversation. Six came in soon after that, sat down on his chair by the front door.

Florek said to Stefanos, "You gonna need me tonight, boss?"

"What's tonight, Tuesday? Milton Berle's on tonight, huh? I'm tellin' you, that Texaco Star Theatre's killed my Tuesday business. This town's dead now, Tuesday nights. No, Florek, you sweep up out here, wait for Karras to dress, then you go ahead and take off."

The cop left, and Karras went back to the warehouse area to change clothes. Florek got the broom from the kitchen, swept the lunch dirt toward the front door. Costa had come out front, was arguing with Williams and his friend, something about the preparation of hog's jowls, and Florek tuned that out. He came up to Six, asked him to lift his feet up so he could sweep beneath the chair. When Florek was done, he looked up at Six, who was staring at him with those bear's eyes, big and round and deep brown.

"I been wonderin' about something," said Florek.

"Go ahead," said Six in that baritone of his.

"Why they call you 'Six,' anyhow?"

"'Cause I'm six feet tall, I guess."

158

"You don't mind my saying so, you look closer to seven feet."

"Maybe so, but you don't want to be callin' no man 'Seven.'"

"Why not?"

"Six *sound* good, comin' off your tongue. But, Seven? Seven, it just don't sing."

■

Florek showered in the common bathroom and dressed in clean wool trousers and a shirt. He put on his mackinaw jacket and slipped the photograph of Lola in the side pocket before leaving the room and heading down to Nick's.

Costa and Stefanos were behind the counter, Costa arguing with two new customers over the cooking method of the evening special. Lou Di-Geordano sat on a stool away from the Negro customers, drinking a Ballantine Ale. He was dressed in a single-breasted, brown-check suit which hung loosely draped on his thin frame.

"Young Florek," said DiGeordano.

Florek nodded, said to Nick, "Where's Pete, boss?"

"Out back, havin' a smoke."

Florek went directly to the kitchen, then through curtain doors to the warehouse area in the back of the building. Paper goods and industrial-sized cans of foodstuffs sat stacked on wood pallets pushed against the south wall. A room off the north wall housed a low toilet, with a wash basin outside the room. The middle of the area was kept empty, lit by one naked bulb suspended on a cord from the tin ceiling above. There was no switch for the light—it turned on and off by manual rotation, as Stefanos considered the installation of a switch an unnecessary expense.

Florek walked through the open door at the back of the warehouse. Karras was out in the alley that ran between R and S, sitting on a fruit crate, his wrists relaxed, his hands dangling between his knees. Two of Costa's cats figure-eighted Karras's ankles, ran off as Florek approached. A Negro boy washed Nick's Ford, a Custom V8 club convertible, a '49 that Nick had bought in the beginning of the model year at Wolfe Motors on 12th and K. The Negro boy looked chilled in the late afternoon air, dipping his brush in the bucket of cold, soapy water. Nick had the same kid wash the car, no matter what the season, every week. He gave the boy a quarter for his trouble, along with a hot meal.

"Pull up a chair," said Karras, pointing to an empty crate.

Florek turned the crate over, slid it next to Karras, had a seat. The boy scrubbed intently, the tip of his tongue breaking his lips as he worked at one tough spot. The sun had fallen behind the buildings to the west, the Ford glistening in the dying light that remained. Down at the end of the alley, a stylish woman stood at the rear entrance to the Sun Dial, her arms folded to her chest as she smoked a cigarette.

"Who's that?" said Florek.

"Pete Frank's wife, Alice. Everyone calls her Kiki."

"She takes care of herself."

"Yeah, she carries herself pretty good. Wears sharp clothes, always has on a nice pair of shoes."

"Pete Frank gonna make it down there?"

"Since Nick and Pete turned over to colored joints, there's business enough for everyone, I'd say. So, yeah, I think Frank's gonna do all right."

Florek rubbed his cheek. "Course, Nick doesn't really need the dough anyway, does he."

"Why do you say that?"

"These colored guys, they always joke with him about it, how he's got plenty of money, like that."

"Yeah, well. Nick hit the number in a big way, back in '46. Matter of fact, I was sittin' right at that counter the day he played it. That was the same night . . . well, anyway, I was there when he played that number."

"How big did he hit?"

"To the tune of forty Gs."

Florek whistled through his teeth. "Why the heck is he workin' so hard for, then?"

"On account of he loves this place, that's why. If you could see where he came from, you'd understand. Anyhow, he bought this building with the dough, and he's savin' the rest of it for his son, if he ever comes over from Greece. I hear the son ain't worth a damn, but Nick's his father, so . . . what are you gonna do. It's not the money with Nick, anyhow. It's the work. Hell, he'd probably give it away if you asked him. You know that customer, the white man, that Italian who's always dressed up?"

"Mr. DiGeordano. He's in there right now."

"Right. I knew him since I was a kid, and he was the poorest-looking bastard you'd ever want to see. He had this fruit cart no bigger than a shithouse, he used to push it down by the waterfront."

"He looks pretty good today."

"Sure he does. He was the runner that sold the dream number to Nick. When he delivered the forty big ones, Nick peeled off two thousand dollars from the roll and handed it to Lou. Costa says DiGeordano fell to his knees, kissed Nick's hand. Course, Costa, he don't know shit from Shine-

160

ola, but you get the idea. DiGeordano was major-league grateful to Nick. He'd do anything for the guy today."

"What's DiGeordano do now?"

"He opened a deli up on Georgia Avenue with the two, got into the loan business after that, diversified into a little bookmaking. He's got a couple of guys workin' muscle for him now, has a wife and a little boy, he's doin' okay. All because Nick was so generous. Like he's been generous with me."

"How so?"

Karras pulled a deck of Lucky Strikes from beneath his apron, shook one out, pulled the cigarette free with his lips. He held the pack out for Florek; Florek waved it off. Karras slipped a matchbook out from under the cellophane of the pack, put fire to the smoke. He thumbed a speck of tobacco off his lower lip.

"Just look at me, man. I mean, I'm not the kinda guy who's gonna be an asset to a man's business."

"What d'ya mean?"

"I'm a cripple!"

"You're a good worker, Pete—"

"I'm a cripple, Florek, just the same."

Florek looked Karras over. "You get that crazy knee in the war?"

Karras shook his head. "After."

"It hurt much?"

"Not so much anymore."

"You get around on it pretty good."

"I'm fakin' it, Florek. Since you came, I been pretendin' like it doesn't hurt so bad." Karras took a drag off the cigarette, grinned as he blew a stream of smoke out into the alley. "The reason I had to fake it is, I'm scared you're gonna take my job away from me."

"Pete, it's not like that. I swear—"

"Relax, kid, I'm only havin' a little fun with you. The truth of it is, we all been watchin' you. And every one of us thinks you're doin' a pretty fair job."

"Thanks." Florek blushed, scraped the sole of his shoe against the stones of the alley.

The Negro boy trotted over to Karras, stood in front of him. He rubbed his hands dry on his torn trousers.

"Finished," said the boy.

Karras made a brief mock-study of the spotless Ford. "Looks okay, chum. Go on in and get your money."

The kid ran through the open back door. Karras took a drag off the Lucky, hotboxed it with a tandem draw, pitched it away.

"Listen, Pete. I'm sorry I asked all those questions about your bum leg. I didn't mean nothin' by it."

"That's okay, kid. Most people don't ask a thing. They just make like nothing's wrong, or they look away. I'm tellin' you, with most people it's like I'm not even there. So don't worry about it, hear?" Karras touched the mole on his face. "Where you from, anyway?"

"Western Pennsylvania."

"God's country."

"I guess."

"You get tired of it? That's why you're down here?"

"Not exactly. My sister's here in D.C."

"You visitin' her for awhile?"

"I'm lookin' for her," said Florek.

Karras watched Florek pull a photograph from his jacket, smoothed the face on the picture out with his fingers as gently as if he were touching flesh. Karras took the photograph from Florek's hand. The girl had an unformed, plain, doughy face, with lively eyes set wide above a thick Polack nose. The blond hair came from a bottle; he could see a crop of black sprouting at the part.

"Pretty girl," said Karras.

"The picture's a couple years old."

"Well, she's pretty."

"You're being nice. But if you knew her, if you knew her personality that is, you'd think she was pretty all right. Lola, when she got going, she could really make you laugh."

Karras said, "She come down here with a guy?"

"Yeah."

"Some guy your parents don't approve of, or somethin'? Is that it?"

"It's worse than that." Florek swallowed. "A man she met introduced her to some kind of dope. A kind of dope you take with a needle. She fell in love with it, I guess, and then she followed this man down to D.C."

Karras brought up phlegm from his throat, spat. "Have any luck hooking up with her yet?"

"Uh-uh. I showed her picture around . . . I showed it to a girl over at Thomas Circle. I came up with nothing there."

Karras tried not to react. So the kid was down from some steeltown, looking for his hophead sister, now a whore. It didn't get much rougher than that.

"Your parents must be crawling up the walls," said Karras, because he could think of nothing smart to say.

162

"My father's dead," said Florek.

Karras nodded. "Mine too, kid. He died last year of a bad liver."

A brief silence fell between them. Karras looked the kid over.

"Sometimes I'm glad he's dead. I know it's bad to say, but if he were alive, and he knew about Lola—"

"That your sister's name?"

"Yeah."

"What've you done so far?"

"Well, like I say, there was the girl at the circle, which didn't amount to much. Other than that, I haven't done a thing. Truth is, I don't know where else to go. I don't know the city, after all. I guess I just keep hoping I'm gonna run into her somewhere. They say D.C.'s a small town—"

"Not since the war it isn't."

"Anyway, tonight I was going down to People's to see this girl I know from my old job, a friend of mine who works behind the makeup counter. I thought maybe I'd stop at Thomas again on the way down, show the picture around."

Karras looked at Florek: bone-skinny, shy, and just about as green as they come. A kid like that, walking around, asking questions to the wrong kinds of characters, that was a damn good way to get himself killed.

"This girl down at People's," said Karras. "She just a friend?"

Florek gave an aw-shucks grin. "Her name is Kay. Truth is, I was gonna ask her to take in a picture with me tonight. The Warner's got a new one, *John Loves Mary*. Ronald Reagan's in it, and this new gal—"

"Patricia Neal."

"Yeah, her. It's a romance picture, the girls like that. I was gonna see if Kay would want to go."

"You gonna take a girl out, wearin' that jacket?"

"What's wrong with it?"

"It looks like something you'd wear to go hunting in!"

Florek lightly punched Karras's shoulder. "Aw, come on, Pete, what would you know about hunting? You're a city animal, all the way."

Karras chuckled. "Tell you what. When you get a little money in your pocket, you and me, we're gonna go out and get you some decent clothes."

"Whatever. Look, I better get going." Florek reached for the photograph.

Karras drew back his hand. "You got another copy of this?"

"Yeah, sure. Why?"

"You know that cop I introduced you to? He's a friend of mine from back in the neighborhood. I want to show this to him, see if he has any ideas."

163

"I'm not looking to get Lola into any trouble."

She's already in trouble, thought Karras. He said, "Don't worry. I'm only gonna have him ask around. And I know a few people myself. Maybe I'll ask around a little, too."

"I don't want to put you out, Pete."

"Well, it's not like I'm all that busy now, is it? Anyway, you take off. Go enjoy yourself with your girl."

Florek and Karras shook hands. Florek got off the crate, began to walk away.

"Hey, kid."

"Yeah?"

"There's a little restaurant next to the Warner, place called the Crown. They got highballs there with bonded whiskey, only sixty cents. Take your girl there for a drink, have one after the show."

"I'm a little shy of the drinking age."

"There's a guy behind the bar, a veteran by the name of Jackie Harris. Tell Jackie I sent you by."

"Thanks a million, Pete."

"Sure thing, chum. You take care."

Florek went down to R, turned left toward 14th. Karras folded the photograph, slipped it into his apron. He fished out another cigarette, lighted it, watched the smoke of his exhale shimmer in the last of the sun's rays.

Costa came out the back door then, wearing his coat and hat, a fishbone in his hand. A half dozen cats appeared from various hiding places and blind corners, circled his feet. Costa tossed the fishbone out into the alley, smiled for a moment as he watched the cats pounce on it, bat each other away. He brought up some spit, looked at Karras.

"*Ella, re.* I need you to take over for me out front."

"Where you off to?" said Karras.

"Gonna go down to Hains Point, have a walk around."

"You're gonna go down to the Speedway in the dark?"

"What the hell I care? I just wanna get out of here a little while, that's all." Costa spat on the stones. "I'm sicka all these niggers."

Costa walked down the alley, the smallest cat of the bunch following his trail. Karras crushed the cigarette beneath his shoe, got up off the crate, grunted from the pain in his knee. He went back through the warehouse and the kitchen to the front of the house, where the Negro boy sat at the counter, eating a hot meal. Stefanos and DiGeordano were splitting a bottle of ale.

"Karras Jr."

"Mr. DiGeordano."

"Here you go, *re*." Stefanos took a business card off the counter, handed it to Karras. "Some *Americanos* left this for you."

Karras had a look at the card. "This bird's been after me, trying to sell me life insurance, some crazy veteran's deal he's got."

"Uh," said Stefanos. "You see Costa?"

"Yeah. What the hell's wrong with him?"

"He's a little guy, that's all, and I'm not just talkin' about he's short. Don't get me wrong, I love him like a brother. But he's always gonna be little, and he knows it. So Costa, he's always gotta blame someone else."

"Let me get goin'," said DiGeordano, getting off his stool.

Nick Stefanos killed his ale, put the glass in a bus tray beneath the counter. Karras slipped the insurance man's business card in the breast pocket of his shirt. He picked up the bus tray and limped back toward the kitchen.

21

Burke stood ramrod straight, his back to his desk, looking out the window to the street below.

"So what's it going to be, Joe? I'm going to let you make the call, since you've got a bit of a personal investment. That's a block of 14th Street we haven't touched yet, and I'd like to get a lock on it before someone else moves in. So here's the question: Do we talk to Pete Frank first or do we move straight in on Nick Stefanos?"

Joe Recevo gave a slight shrug of his shoulders. He withdrew a deck of Raleighs from his inside jacket pocket, blew his breath into the pack. A cigarette popped halfway out; he pulled it from the pack with his teeth, struck a match to the tobacco, dropped the match in the ashtray that sat on the large table in front of him. He let out some smoke, watched it inch across the room.

"What difference does it make?" said Gearhart, his hands folded in his ample lap. "We're going to hit them both eventually."

Burke turned, eased himself down into the seat behind the desk. "Yes, that's true. But the impression you make the first time, it dictates whether the rest of the players on the block fall in step or not. It's very important how the first one pans out."

"Neither one of those guys is gonna lay down," said Recevo. "You realize that, don't you? We're not talking about some frightened immigrants here."

Reed had been pacing the floor throughout the conversation. He stopped, leaned against the glass-fronted case that held the Thompson gun. "We've dealt with Greeks before. Greeks can be pushed like anyone else."

"Not these Greeks." Recevo tapped some ash off his cigarette. "Stefanos and Pete Frank, they're Spartans. You gotta understand—"

"Christ," said Reed. "Now you're gonna tell me that there's men that can't be pushed."

"Relax," said Burke.

Reed pushed off the cabinet, straightened the jacket of his sharkskin suit against his broad frame. He put his hands into his trouser pockets, began to pace. He passed beneath the overhead fixture, the Vitalis in his hair gleaming in the light.

"We've met resistance before," said Gearhart.

"Of course we have," said Burke. "It's the nature of the business."

"Well." Gearhart wheezed as he pushed his three hundred pounds up from his chair. He began to move himself into his overcoat. "You know, there *is* something we could do, just in case it doesn't go the way we planned."

"What's that?" said Burke.

"We could use that trick we used on those Jews, when we hit that liquor store of theirs, uptown. Send a second, more sympathetic team of men in after the first. Offer them a bit of a discount, make them feel as if they're getting a bargain. Play that game."

Reed snorted. "You could make a wig out of all the gray hair growin' on that gag."

"It's an option, anyway," said Burke.

"Well, it's not in my area of expertise. I thought I'd bring it up." Gearhart made a short tip of his head to the others in the room. "Goodnight, gentlemen."

Reed made a clownish gesture with his mouth, tried to catch Recevo's eye. Recevo did not look up.

Reed said, "Got a date, Gearhart?"

"Goodnight," said Gearhart.

He walked slowly to the door. Recevo listened to the creak of the floor beneath his weight, the horse-clomp of the two-toned gibsons on the fat man's feet. Gearhart closed the door behind him.

"Where's he off to so fast?" said Recevo.

"He's going out to find some release," said Burke, pouring a healthy shot of bourbon whiskey into the thick tumbler that sat on his desk. "Gearhart and his whores."

"He better find a big one that can take his weight," said Reed, with a smile. "But I guess he knows what he's doin'. He ought to, long as he's been around them. They say Gearhart's mother—"

"Shut up, Reed," said Burke. "We don't need to be getting into everyone's family history here. I would think that yours would have the makings of a good dime novel, too. I don't fault Gearhart for finding his pleasures out on the street. Every man needs a receptacle, I suppose."

Receptacle. Recevo listened to the smoothness of Burke's voice, the fancy words that he liked to use. He watched Burke take a long drink of the bourbon. The smoothness, the fancy words, that would all begin to wash away now with the drink. He'd better settle this quick before Burke turned mean. Burke always turned mean and sloppy when he crawled into the bag.

"Let's talk to Pete Frank," said Recevo. "Frank's the one we ought to go to first."

"I'm inclined to disagree with you," said Burke. "There's more men over at Stefanos's place, so I'll grant you that it's going to be a tougher job. But if we took on Stefanos as a client first, the rest of the block would tumble."

"Mr. Burke—"

"Karras works for that Stefanos character," said Reed, turning to Recevo. "That have anything to do with why you want us to keep our hands off?"

Recevo did not reply. He took a drag off his cigarette.

"Reed, go downstairs. Round up a couple of the men."

"Don't I have a say in this?"

"Do it."

Reed went quickly out the door, stared meaningfully at Recevo one last time. Recevo kept his eyes straight ahead. He took in a last lungful of tobacco and crushed the cherry in the ashtray.

Burke swallowed the rest of the bourbon, poured out four more fingers' worth. He swirled the whiskey around in the glass.

"You happy here, Joe?"

"Sure."

"You've done all right with me, haven't you?"

"I got no complaints."

"How do you like your new car? It's an Olds, isn't it?"

"A fastback '88. I like it all right."

"And that suit you're wearing. A Fruhauf, right? It must have set you back fifty bucks."

"Fifty and change. I like nice things."

"Sure you do. You got a real nice girlfriend, too. How's she doin', anyway?"

"Lois is fine."

"Yeah," said Burke, "you're doin' all right."

Recevo coughed into his fist, looked around the room.

Burke got out of his chair, took his glass with him. He stood in front of the window, looked at nothing in particular out on the street. Recevo suppressed a smile; Burke thought he looked pretty good, standing there framed against the glass. A big shot, giving it the big pause to lead into the big finish.

And here was the pitch: "Things are going to get even better for you, Joe. You know that, don't you?"

"Thanks, Mr. Burke."

"I mean it. You think I'm just blowing smoke up your skirt?"

Recevo shook his head.

"Well, I'm not. Take a look at the other men I've got in the organization. That alone should tell you that you're at the top of the list. You're going to go far with me."

"Those other men you're talkin' about. They been here longer than me."

"They don't have the qualities I'm looking for in my right-hand man. Gearhart is fine as far as counsel goes, but he's a strange one, and he doesn't have the guts. Reed has the guts but not the brains. And I'm getting tired of him bringing attention to us with his outside activities. That thing in Lafayette Park last year, where he beat those two fairies to within an inch of their lives—"

"I heard about it."

"A perfect example. Gearhart got him off, of course. But the point is, I can't control him much longer. I need someone levelheaded who can stand next to me, help me make the tough decisions. The man who can do that, it's going to be very good for him."

"I'm here whenever you need me, Mr. Burke."

"That's all I wanted to know." Burke turned to face Recevo. "So, that brings us to tonight."

"Go ahead."

"I want you and Reed and a couple of the men to go over to the Stefanos hash-house. I want you to explain to that Greek how things are going to be from here on out. Now, I know that your friend Karras works in that place. I want to make sure you don't have any problem with that. You don't, do you?"

"I work for you. If you say go, I go."

169

"Good boy," said Burke. "Let me know how things turn out."

Recevo took his topcoat off the chair where he had draped it, put it on. He smoothed out the brim of his hat, placed it on his head, cocked it right. He nodded to Burke and headed for the door. Burke kept his eyes on Recevo, tipped the glass of whiskey to his lips.

In the foyer, Face sat in a chair trying to make a ball on a string fall into a cup. Reed stood in front of a mirror, watching his reflection as he smoked a cigarette. Recevo came down the stairs.

"All right, Reed. Get two men together and let's go."

Reed smiled, walked into the living room where a half-dozen men sat around having highballs and trading wisecracks with a couple of women who smelled of house booze and off-brand perfume. He returned with a large Welshman in a blue twist suit and a medium-sized man in a double-breasted gray plaid. They arrived shoving revolvers into their waistbands, then retrieved their topcoats from the hall closet.

"We'll take my car," said Recevo.

"We going to Stefanos's place?" said Reed.

"Yeah."

"Now you're talkin'."

Recevo felt the eyes of Face upon him.

"Who's Stefanos?" said Medium.

"Some guy who can't be pushed around." Reed smiled, glanced at Recevo as he punched Medium in the shoulder. "Come on, fellas. Let's go have us a little fun."

■

Mike Florek crossed 14th Street, kept an eye out for traffic as he looked through the plate-glass window of Nick's. Nick and Costa were there, talking to a group of large white men wearing coats over suits who were standing spread out around the customers' side of the counter. Through the glass of the door Florek could see the big brown arms of Six, hanging loosely at his side. There didn't seem to be any Negro customers in the place, though that was not unusual, as it was Berle night anyway, and the ten o'clock fights had ended long ago. Florek decided not to stop by to shoot the breeze or anything like that; if Nick and the others were with their friends, having some laughs over a few bottles of beer, maybe they wouldn't want him around.

Florek went to the entrance of his building, opened the door, and headed up the stairs.

He didn't mind being alone tonight, not after the time he had had with

Kay. He had gone by People's in the early evening, made like he was surprised to see her working, and then, after the necessary small talk, suggested they take in a show. To his relief, she agreed without a fight of any kind. Despite the fact that she was dressed for work—a sweater and skirt, with a string of fake pearls around her long neck—Kay looked lovely to Florek, as lovely as if she had prepared for him all day. He watched her take a sampler atomizer and spray some perfume on her wrists and behind her ears before she ended her shift. On the way out the door, Florek gave a smart chin-nod to an unsmiling Mr. Simms.

"What do you call that stuff?" said Florek, as they walked south. "I can smell it, even out here in the breeze."

"It's 'Evening in Paris,' " she said. "You like it?"

Then Kay put her hand up to his nose, and the two of them stopped walking as he breathed her in.

"I like it fine," said Florek, and he lightly kissed the pulsing vein on the inside of her wrist. He didn't know why he had been so impulsive and forward—it was not something he had done on a first date back home with any girl before—but Florek felt older here, living on his own, more privileged in some natural kind of way. Thankfully, Kay laughed and patted his cheek; Florek knew he was in like Flynn.

The movie was okay, light and fairly plotless and easy to follow, which was okay by Florek. He and Kay sat in the balcony at the Warner, and by the end of the first act his arm was around her shoulder, and the arm was still there when the credits rolled and the house lights had come up. They both agreed that the new girl, Patricia Neal, had something to her, though Florek thought Jack Carson was the standout in his usual sidekick role. Carson always made Florek crack up.

Jackie Harris, the bartender Karras had recommended, was behind the stick at the Crown, and Florek and Kay had two rounds of cocktails there after the show. It went cheaply and without a hitch, though Florek noted with some dismay that Kay could hold her liquor better than he. It was she who had to figure out the tip, after Florek could not do the simple arithmetic in his head. They left three on a two-forty check, and went out into the night.

The two of them walked to a stop at 13th and F, waited for Kay's uptown bus. At a pause in the conversation, he found himself staring at her, admiring the light freckles showered on the bridge of her nose, the way her red hair fanned out in the wind. She took his face in both her hands and kissed his mouth, her tongue sliding against his. When she was done she butted her forehead lightly on his, then drew back and smiled.

"You were shaking, Mike."

"It's cold out, I guess."

Kay laughed, kissed him once more as the bus pulled to the curb. The doors opened and she went up the steps. Florek waved her off, thinking, *he* should have gotten on the bus himself. But he was very happy walking home, noting as he neared R Street that he had not thought once about the route he had taken in his journey from downtown to Shaw. He was beginning to know this city—its streets and bus lines, the best cups of coffee, the biggest slices of pie, where to walk to save time and where not to walk late at night—and he was beginning to like it, too. And then he thought: I haven't called my mother in the last week. I'll have to do that tonight, as soon as I get in.

Going up the stairs to his room, Florek felt a wash of guilt, imagining Lola, wherever she was, alone in this town without family or friends. Florek, he had friends, and it could be that now he had a girlfriend, and with Karras looking out for his sister, maybe, for the first time in months, he had a little bit of hope. He wanted to turn around, go back down the stairs, ask Karras exactly what he planned to do to help him find Lola. But Nick and the rest of them, they were down there talking to some of their buddies, and tonight was not the time to interrupt. Florek would just have to wait, ask Karras about it the next day.

22

From the kitchen, Karras watched the Olds fastback pull to the curb in front of Nick's. He watched the men get out, a man he didn't know and the medium-sized man from the night in the alley and, behind him, Reed. Recevo stepped out of the driver's side next. Something dropped in Karras's stomach at the sight of him, a feeling that was neither fear nor hate but something in between. It was funny, how he felt at that moment, happy almost—but also sorry, like finding something you lost as a kid, many years later, and realizing that finding it no longer meant a thing.

Karras followed Recevo's track to the door. *Joey, you finally got your fancy car.*

The door chime sounded as the four men entered the grill. Costa and Stefanos were behind the counter, and Six was on his chair by the door. The only customer, an old Negro who had stayed past the fights for one last beer, turned his head and had a look at the men, all in topcoats and suits. They were standing there spread apart, not making any kind of movement at all.

"Almost closing time, friend," said Stefanos, who had recognized the dark one with the expensive clothes as Karras's friend, the *Italos*. Dime-store gangsters, all of them. What the hell did they want with him?

Stefanos spoke to the Italian: "What can we do for you, eh?"

"We got time for a quick round of beer?" said Recevo.

"If it's quick," said Stefanos. "We gotta get this place closed up." He glanced over Recevo's shoulder, met the steady brown eyes of Six.

"Four beers, then," said Reed. "Make 'em Red Caps."

Costa had been rubbing his hands slowly on a damp rag, watching the

173

pig-eyed *Americanos* with the mean face. He looked at Nick, who nodded one time.

"*Beera, Costa. Ande, re.*"

Costa went to the cooler, extracted four Carlings. He jacked each bottle against the Coca-Cola opener screwed into the side of the cooler. He took his time.

Reed looked at the medium-sized man in the badly tailored suit, then jerked his head in the direction of the huge Negro who sat by the door. Medium dragged a stool to within four feet of the bouncer, had a seat. He opened his topcoat and let the tail of it fall over one thigh. The grip of a revolver showed then where it had been slipped beneath the waistband of his trousers. Medium brushed his fingers against the grip, stared at Six. Six looked straight ahead, showing nothing on his face.

Reed and Recevo stepped up to the counter, slid onto a couple of stools. The Welshman moved to the plate-glass window, put his back against it, opened his coat. He spread his feet wide.

It was quiet for a while as the old Negro drained his beer, dropped some coin on the counter, and left the store. Then the only sound was the sucking pop of the last cap, the hollow sound of it hitting the floor, and the tick of the Blatz Beer clock over the door.

Costa gathered up the beers and a couple of glasses. He put beers up for the Welshman and Medium, neither of whom stepped forward. He put a beer in front of Recevo and one in front of Reed, and glasses up for both. Costa slipped a hand into his right pocket.

"Costa," said Stefanos. "*Siga.*"

Reed lifted the Red Cap off the counter, threw his head back and drank. Costa studied Reed's muscled neck, the Adam's apple bobbing just below the shadow of beard. He fingered the switchblade in his pocket, which he had oiled earlier that day. It would be easy to bring the knife out fast, right now, and cut the throat of this American, a quick thrust in and then a clean, vicious red slash from left to right. Cut him down to the windpipe real good and quick.

"*Costaki,*" said Stefanos. "*Ochi tora.*"

Costa removed his hand from his pocket. He stepped back, picked the rag up off the sandwich board, began to wrap it tightly around his hand. Recevo lighted a cigarette, poured beer into his glass, drank down half of it at once.

Karras stepped forward so that his eyes cleared the swinging doors of the kitchen. He saw Nick's .38 lying on its side next to the bus tray beneath the counter. Nick's eyes went to the .38, then back in the direction of Recevo.

"You guys want somethin'," said Stefanos. "What is it?"

"Just came by to warn you about something," said Recevo.

"Warn me about what?"

"Some bad elements in the neighborhood we been hearin' about, that's all."

"Uh," grunted Costa.

Reed laughed.

Over the doors, Karras got his first good look at Joe: Recevo had kept his weight down, had gathered no gray in his swept-back hair. His eyes had begun to fall at the edges, but he looked pretty good. Karras almost grinned, looking at the velvet-banded fedora on Joe's head, the dent perfect, the hat cocked just right. Joe was still the sharpest of the bunch. He had always been the sharpest, in the old bunch and in this one, too. Joey and his hats.

"What kinda bad element you talkin' about?" said Stefanos.

Recevo shrugged. "We heard about some gangs been coming through this way, workin' their way across Shaw. My source tells me they're lookin' to take a piece of every hash-house and beer garden on this block."

"Thanks, friend." Stefanos forced a smile. "Thanks for the tip."

Recevo tipped his head back, emptied his glass. He wiped foam off his upper lip. He said, "We thought we might be able to help."

"We'll take our chances," said Stefanos, in a jovial kind of way. He pointed to Costa and waved his hand in the direction of Six. "This gang you talkin' about, they come in here lookin' for some trouble, they gonna get a big surprise. I got my own guys here, I don't need to worry too much."

"They do look pretty ferocious," said Reed, smiling at Costa. A nerve sent a twitch into Costa's lip.

"Ssh, ssh, ssh . . . " A hiss of laughter escaped from between Medium's thin lips.

Recevo took in some smoke, tapped the ash off in the tray. He looked around the room, his eyes stopping on the white-gray hair of Karras above the kitchen doors. Recevo closed his eyes, hoping that when he opened them that Karras would not be there. *Don't come out here, Pete. Don't come out here wearin' no goddamn apron. You just stay back there where you are.*

Costa slipped his hand back in his pocket. Stefanos stepped toward the bus tray.

"You finished with this?" said Stefanos, putting his hand around Recevo's glass.

Recevo nodded. "Thanks."

"Thanks," muttered Reed, mocking Recevo's tone. "We gonna sit around here all night sendin' love letters, or we gonna do some business?"

Recevo did not respond. Stefanos lifted the glass off the counter, dropped it into the bus tray. He pushed his stomach flat against the counter, let his left hand dangle so that it touched the smooth pearl handle of the revolver.

"My rude friend here," said Recevo, tilting his head toward Reed, "he doesn't always know how to talk to people the right way. But he makes a good point. I mean, no disrespect intended, but if we can walk in here like this and take over the situation like we did tonight, what do you suppose those other guys are gonna do when they're real good and serious about it. Huh?"

"Keep talkin'."

"Like I say, we're in a position to help you keep those guys off your backs."

"How much?" said Stefanos, getting the .38 fully in his hand and bringing it up so that the muzzle butted up against the counter board level to Recevo's gut.

Recevo said, "Hundred a week ought to cover my men."

Stefanos and Costa laughed. Reed began to laugh, too. They all had a good laugh about it, the laughter covering the click of the hammer locking back on the revolver.

Karras watched Stefanos smile with the others as he snicked the hammer back on the .38. Stefanos had the only gun, and Costa had the cheap Italian knife. The two of them might get Reed and Recevo on a very lucky day. Six was covered by Medium, who would shoot him dead where he sat and then move on the others. And then there was the Welshman, standing surefooted and armed against the plate glass. The Welshman would finish anything left standing.

Karras pushed through the swinging doors. He kept his eyes straight ahead, limped across the floor as the men in the room turned their heads.

"Well, look at that," said Reed.

Recevo tightened his grip on the bottle of beer in front of him. *Goddamn you, Pete. Why'd you have to go and come out here, lookin' like that?*

Karras felt their eyes upon him as he bent forward, stepping in front of Stefanos.

"Excuse me, Boss," he said. "Let me get these dishes out of your way."

Underneath the counter, Karras put his hand over the revolver's hammer, gently pulled the gun from Stefanos's grasp. Keeping his palm over the hammer, Karras squeezed the trigger, released the hammer, eased it back down to the chamber. He slipped the .38 beneath his apron. Karras picked up the bus tray, walked back toward the kitchen.

Stefanos stepped back, pale and shaken. He looked at Recevo and said, very quietly, "I don't pay protection money. You hear?"

Recevo said, "Sleep on it. I'll call you tomorrow. We'll see what you think about it then."

Reed and Recevo got off their stools. Medium got off his, buttoned his topcoat.

"You owe for the beers," said Costa.

"Pay the little man," said Reed to the Welshman.

The Welshman put a couple of ones on the counter, followed the group out the door. Six locked the door behind them as they left. Costa took the money off the counter, balled it up, threw it in the trash.

Out on the sidewalk, Reed looked back through the window of the store. "We shoulda heated things up a little more," he said.

"Come on, Reed," said Medium. "They got the message all right."

The four of them got into the Olds, Recevo in the driver's seat and Reed beside him. Recevo turned the key on the ignition, pulled the car onto 14th, swung it around in the middle of the street and headed south.

"How about your boy Karras?" said Reed, his face waxen in the dashboard light. "Big war hero, wearin' an apron. He don't look so damn tough anymore, does he?"

Recevo thought of how Karras had come out from the kitchen, cut the fuse that was getting ready to burn right into the powder. The crazy little Greek, the one called Costa, you could see it in his eyes, he was ready to open Reed's throat, right there in the grill. Yeah, Karras had stopped a lot of blood from flowing back there. But why?

"Didn't you hear me?" said Reed. He punched Recevo playfully in the shoulder. "Your pal used to think he was really something. Man, I sure did clip that Greek's wings."

Recevo looked over at Reed. "Don't ever touch me like that again, get it? Not even in fun."

"I was just sayin'—"

"I'm don't care what you were saying."

"Now wait a minute," said Reed.

"Wait, nothin'," said Recevo. "Just keep your mouth shut."

Nick Stefanos poured ale into the three glasses that sat on the prep table in the kitchen. He opened another bottle of Ballantine, poured again so the levels were even in each glass. Costa took a glass off the table, waited for the others to do the same.

Stefanos held a glass out to Karras. Karras reached out from his stool in the center of the kitchen, took the glass. Stefanos lifted the last glass for himself.

"*Siyiam*," said Stefanos, and the three of them drank.

"Ah," said Costa, wiping the back of his hand across his mouth. "That's good."

Karras fished a pack of Lucky Strikes from his breast pocket, passed it to Stefanos. Stefanos took a cigarette from the deck and passed it back. Karras lighted one for himself, lighted Nick's.

"I coulda killed the big one with the mean face," said Costa. "I coulda killed him quick."

Stefanos let out some smoke. "And then the one by the window would've blown you down. Or the guy holding the gun on Six. Either one, it wouldn't have mattered. Both of them had a clear shot. Right now, you'd be dead."

"Six," said Costa. "That *mavros*. Lot of good he was to us tonight."

"He did fine," said Karras. "He handled himself just right. Anyway, it wasn't his affair."

"Costa's right about one thing, Karras. We could've stopped all this tonight. Maybe someone might've got killed, but at least it would be over. If you hadn't of stepped in the middle of everything—"

"And saved your life."

"Maybe you saved your friend's life, too. I'm talkin' about the *Italos*, and don't you think I don't know. Maybe that's what you had in mind the whole time."

"You're wrong." Karras looked down at his cigarette. "Me and Joe are through."

"Then why'd you stop me? Why'd you take away my gun?"

"Cause you don't start a gunfight in a storefront on 14th Street unless you're ready to die or go to jail. You gotta think these things through. It's like any fight—you gotta pick your spots, and you gotta take a couple to give one. Just cause you take a couple of good shots, it doesn't mean you're done. *Katalavenis?*"

"Sure, Karras. I understand."

They all had some more to drink then, letting the alcohol relax the tension that had crept into their shoulders and backs. Karras dragged hard on his cigarette, tapped ash to the tiled floor.

Karras said, "Now you have to think about what you're gonna tell 'em tomorrow when they call."

"I already know what I'm gonna tell those bastards. This is *my* place. That's *my* name on the sign out front. I take care of my own problems, and I don't pay no protection money to nobody, goddamn right."

Costa ran a hand through his wild black hair. "I could've killed that bastard quick."

"They come back," said Stefanos, "you gonna get your chance."

23

██████ Peter Karras finished with the glasses and silver, mopped the kitchen, and swept the place out front to back. He washed his face and splashed water under his arms in the warehouse sink, then changed back into his suit and tie. He went out to the front of the house, where Stefanos sat on a stool behind the counter, doing the day's books, fingering a string of worry beads in his free hand.

"All done," said Karras.

"Hold on, Karras, I'm gonna be finished here in a minute. I'll give you a ride."

"It's not so cold out," said Karras. "I think I'll walk."

Karras saw Stefanos glance unconsciously at his bum leg. "You sure?"

"Yeah, I'm all right." Karras shook himself into his topcoat, patted his breast pocket to check on his cigarettes. "You think real good about what happened tonight, Nick."

"I already thought about it, Panayoti. Go on, I'll see you tomorrow."

Voices came from the second floor, a man and a woman screaming at each other unintelligibly, full on. Karras and Stefanos looked up at the pressed tin ceiling, then looked at each other and smiled.

"Costa and Toula," said Stefanos.

"A couple of lovebirds, those two."

"Hey, he ain't seen her all day. They got to get to know each other all over again."

"*Adio*, Nick."

"*Yasou, re.*"

Karras walked up to U, headed east. He took his time, stopped to put fire to a smoke, watched the stylishly dressed Negroes arm-in-arm with their women on the street. The night was colder than he had anticipated, but the sky was clear, bright, with moonshine pearling the streets. Karras listened to the blues singers' voices coming from the clubs, the strange jazz further along U, the occasional horn blast from taxis and cars, the hiss of tire on asphalt, the gentle, Southern rise and fall in the inflection of these people's voices, their laughter, all of it comforting him somehow, this warming, familiar symphony.

Karras loved to walk through his city, had always loved it. Of all the things that had been taken from him in the alley that night, the ability to walk across town without tiring, that had been the cruelest. The frustration hit him around 12th Street as the pain increased, and Karras stopped walking. He raised his hand to hail a passing cab.

The cabbie dropped him at 6th and H; Karras gave the hack two bits, stepped out into a neighborhood just gathering its second wind. Round about now, as the bars around town were posting last call, it seemed as if all the city's cabs moved east. Pimps, hookers, politicians, gamblers, off-shift cops—they all made their way into Chinatown late at night. Whatever it was that floated your boat—chow, opium, booze, pussy, dice, cards, or just plain conversation—you could get it, and get it late, in this part of town.

"Hey, Karras!"

"Su."

Su was leaning against his gleaming cab parked on H, speed-talking in Chinese to a friend. His eyes had disappeared behind a smile when he caught a look at Karras.

"You take care of your business in Southeast today?" said Su.

"Yeah, I did all right." Karras thought of Vera, his hand roughly kneading her beautiful breast, the slack look on her face as he fucked her up one side and down the other in her own bed. He thought of Eleni, the two of them on the chair, getting with it right there in front of the boy. And then he thought: I have not seen my wife and kid since early this morning, have not even stopped to drop a coin in a phone and give them a call. What kind of a man—

"On your way home?" said Su.

Home. What the hell.

"Maybe I'll catch a drink first," said Karras. "I need to talk to you about something, anyway. Wanna join me?"

181

"Sure thing." Su turned to his friend, threw rapid-fire Chink lingo at the board-skinny young man. Su said to Karras, "Let's go. My cousin'll watch my sled."

Above 6th was restaurant row, On Leong Tong territory. Below 6th were laundromats, owned by the Hip Sings. Both the On Leongs and the Hip Sings had gambling and prostitution operations, and both trafficked in drugs. The Hip Sings took care of the needle and nose trade—heroin, morphine, and coke; the On Leongs added opium to the mix.

Cathay, the restaurant at 624 H, took in white Washingtonians, tourists and conventioneers. Just next door sat a plain, unmarked eat-house, neutral to On Leongs and Hip Sings, that catered primarily to Chinese. Karras and Su went inside.

The joint was smoky, crowded, loud with the clatter of china and the high-pitched yipyap of a foreign tongue. Several white women, cheaply dressed and obvious, were scattered among the yellows. A man with the face of a frog seated them; Su gave the frogman their order. Karras went to a phone, dialed up Boyle, asked him if he'd like to meet for a drink, told him why. Boyle sounded plenty awake, said he'd be right down.

Back at the four-top, a stooped woman served a teapot and two cups. Karras got out of his topcoat, dropped his deck of Luckies and a book of matches on the table, had a seat. Su poured straight gin from the teapot into the cups. He winked at Karras, touched Karras's teacup with his; the two of them drank. Karras struck a match, held it to a cigarette.

"What'd you want to talk to me about, Pete?"

Karras shook out the match, dropped it in the ashtray. "I'm lookin' for a girl. A white whore. I was thinkin' that maybe she's workin' for a Chinese pimp."

"You want me to get you a whore?"

"Not for me, Su. I'm looking for one girl in particular. From out of town, new in D.C."

"Hey, Pete, I'm just a cabbie."

"The Hip Sings are deep into the roundheel action, Su. Everybody knows it."

"Hip Sings? What the heck is that?"

"Knock it off. I'm not lookin' to learn your secret handshake. I'm just lookin' for a girl."

Su looked around the room. His eyes stopped on a thin man in a three-piece suit seated in the corner of the house next to a bottle blonde. He looked back at Karras.

"Who's this girl?" said Su.

"A friend of mine had a sister went down the primrose path."

"*Primrose Path?* I saw that picture. Ginger Rogers was pretty good in it."

"I saw it, too. Only this isn't a picture. This pimp glommed onto her and got her fixed up with some high-grade dope. Something you take with a needle."

Su's face darkened. "You're talkin' about heroin, Karras. Morphine, maybe. Either way it's plenty bad."

"Whatever. To me it's like colored jazz—I just don't get it. All I know is, she's a hopfiend who spreads her legs for her next dream. And I don't know where to begin to look for her."

"I don't think I can help you."

"Like I say, she's the sister of a friend."

Su finished his gin, looked into the empty teacup. He set the cup down. "There's this guy. But this guy might not want to talk to you."

"Tell him I live here. Tell him you and I go back. You can tell him I opened the doors on the Enola Gay for all I care. I don't give a good goddamn what you tell him—"

"Okay, Karras. I get it." Su's eyes darted around the dining room. "Wait here."

Su got up from his chair, went to the corner table where the thin man sat with the blonde. Karras retrieved the photograph of Lola Florek from the pocket of his topcoat as he watched Su chin-dance with the man in the three-piece and the matching tie. The counterfeit blonde yawned as the two Chinese spoke. Karras dragged on his cigarette, tapped ash into the tray.

Su came back a few minutes later. "Go ahead. The man's name is Wong."

"Anything I ought to know?"

"He hates the Japanese. So do you."

"Right."

Su had a seat, poured more gin. Karras picked up the photograph, walked across the room. He stood over the table where the thin man and the blonde sat, waited for the man to speak. Wong was in his middle years, emaciated, with facial lines parenthesizing a small tight mouth housing a riot of crooked beige teeth. The woman appraised Karras, shook a headful of hair like straw off her shoulder, a siren's move she had seen in a Rita Hayworth picture and had been practicing all night. Karras found her sexy as a corpse.

"Kawwas?"

"Yeah."

"Please, sit down."

Karras dropped into a chair, shook Wong's clammy hand, checked out his threads. The suit cost more than a few bucks, but it looked to have been tailored by a butcher, the tie knotted with arthritic hands. The counterfeit blonde wore a rayon dress cut low, with a booze stain splashed between her breasts, a soiled reminder of another sloppy night and a future full of them.

"Join me in a drink?"

"No, thank you. I don't want to leave my buddy Su too long. He gets lonely like that."

Wong smiled, lighted a tailor-made, let the cigarette dangle from the side of his mouth. He kicked up his chin, squinted his eyes. "Su tells me you were in war. The Pacific."

"That's right."

"That where you get your leg?"

"Jap shell," said Karras. He caught the blonde's eyes flicking down to his knee.

"You kill many Japanese?"

"Tons."

Wong showed some rotten teeth. "Then I like you fine. The Japanese, they very bad people."

"Yes," said Karras. *Whatever it will take to get you to talk.*

Karras pushed the photograph of Lola Florek across the table. Wong did not look down.

"So now we talk."

"You and me alone," said Karras.

"I wanna stay," said the blonde, tossing the orangeish mane of straw off her shoulder.

"Beat it," said Wong, keeping his eyes on Karras as he jerked his head sharply toward the front door. "Brow."

Brow. It's "blow," you pimp.

Karras thought of Recevo, how if he had been here the two of them would have had a good laugh now at the expense of this flyweight. Seeing Recevo earlier in the night, Karras had been reminded that he had not laughed like that in a very long time.

The woman snorted, rolled her eyes. Neither Wong nor Karras paid attention. After a few more second-bill theatrics the woman left the table. Wong picked up the photograph, studied it. Some ash fell from his cigarette into his lap.

"She's not one of mine," he said.

"Maybe you've seen her around. Like over at the Eastern House."

"How you know about Eastern House, Kawwas?"

"I grew up in this neighborhood. We used to call it the 'Eastern Cathouse' when we were kids."

Wong nodded. "I know many woman at Eastern House. This is one I have not seen." He took the tailor-made from his mouth, crushed it in the ashtray. "Why you come to me?"

"You look like a businessman. I see you sittin' over here with a blonde hooker—"

"All my women blonde," bragged Wong.

"No Chinese?"

"One Chinese woman to every ten Chinese men. Chinese women too valuable to whore. We marry them, make whore of them like that. Whore who make baby, clean house."

"This one I'm looking for, she's taking drugs, too."

"Not unusual. Drugs make very loyal whore."

Karras tapped his finger on Lola's thick-featured face. "So you don't know her."

"No."

Karras took back the photograph. If not for Su, he might have slapped this creep around, just for fun. Instead he shook Wong's hand.

"Thanks for your time."

"Okay, Kawwas. I see you around."

Boyle was back at the four-top, out of uniform and having a little gin with Su. Karras limped across the dining room, letting the fisheyes from the patrons pass. He had a seat, lighted a cigarette.

"Jimmy."

"Pete."

Su knocked off the rest of his gin. "I seen you shake Wong's hand. How you like the way it feel?"

"Next time I'll pet a snake."

"You find anything out, though?"

"Nothing. Not even the secret handshake."

Su grinned. "Well, I tried. Anyway, I gotta get back to my cab, make a little dough."

"So long, Su."

"See ya, Karras. Boyle."

Su speed-walked from the restaurant. Karras poured gin from the teapot, watched Boyle's fingers beat out a rhythm on the table, Gene Krupa with flesh sticks.

"What's with all the energy tonight, Jimmy?"

185

"Couldn't sleep, that's all. I'm glad you called me, Pete. I stopped workin' nights, I'm crawling the walls, looking for something to do."

"You quit workin' the door for La Fontaine?"

"Yeah, that's done. La Fontaine's eighty-one years old, it ain't gonna be long before he kicks. And the feds are stepping up on those gambling raids out in the county. What's that DA's name, been in the papers every day?"

"You're talking about Fay."

"Yeah, him. His boys raided Snags Lewis's joint last week, got twenty grand from the Crossroads alone. And they got forty-five numbers-and-ponies men in a raid on Ninth Street last month, screwed up the handbook action for a whole week. Course, Charlie Ford'll get 'em all off. The point is, it just ain't kosher for cops to be pulling bounce jobs out at those clubs anymore. Eventually, the shit's gonna rain down on them, too. And it looks bad when promotion time comes around."

"I never liked that county action, myself," said Karras. "To tell you the truth, it never felt right to me, being outside the city. I was always lookin' over my shoulder."

"That's you, Pete. That's you all over."

"Here you go, chum." Karras slid the picture of Lola in front of Boyle.

"This that whore you told me about on the phone?"

"Yeah. You keep the picture, the kid's got another one for me. Lola Florek's her name—I wrote it on the back."

"I hear anything," said Boyle, "I'll let you know."

Boyle glanced nervously around the room. Karras tapped his cigarette ash off in the tray, studied his friend: pale, flabby, with shaded half-moons beneath hard, glassy eyes.

"Want a little soup or somethin', Jimmy? They got a hot and sour here, so good it'll make you sing about it in the street."

"I'm not hungry."

"Soup'll make you feel better. You look like you might be comin' down with something."

"I never felt better. You Greeks, always pushin' food."

"Okay, Jimmy. Suit yourself."

They had another teapot of gin, and Karras smoked a few more cigarettes, and somewhere in the middle of the night he decided he'd had enough. Boyle had done most of the talking, gone on about the prostitute murders and about their childhood and other silly things that began to make less and less sense as the time passed. It was like he was in love with the sound of his own voice. When Karras turned at the door to wave goodbye, Boyle was still sitting at the table, beating out a drum roll with his fingers, some elusive number he could neither name nor forget, like the strange tingle that came and went inside his head.

Out on the street, Karras headed for his building. A '40 Chevy coupe passed on H. The kid in the passenger side put his head out the window, yelled something at Karras. Karras kept walking, listened to their laughter fade.

He entered his building, began the long trip up the steps. He stopped once, bent over, rubbed at his knee, a habit that did little to erase the pain. He made it to the apartment, entered quietly, hung his topcoat in the closet. He checked on Dimitri, leaned into the crib, smelled the boy's hair. Karras left the door open as he exited the room. That way the boy would not be so hot.

Peter Karras undressed, slipped under the sheets of his bed. Eleni slept on her side, her breath deep and heavy. Karras lay beside her, let one arm fall around her shoulders. He pushed his groin below her buttocks. She shifted beneath him, his cock settling between her thick thighs.

"Pete."

"It's me, baby. Go to sleep."

24

■■■■ Mike Florek stood at the prep table, reached for a tomato that floated in a water-filled bus tray among a dozen others. Florek held a small instrument in his hand that looked like something from his mother's knitting basket, an orange-handled piece with a round, sharp-toothed cap on its end. He dug the cap into the edge of the tomato's stem, careful not to let it slip too deeply beneath the red skin. He cut around the stem in a clockwise direction, scooped the stem out, and dropped the tomato back in the water. Florek liked coring the tomatoes, getting them ready for Nick to slice. Usually, when Florek was done, Nick would come over, give the tomatoes a brief inspection, offer a mild criticism, and tell Florek he had done a good job. But not today. Today Nick just walked to the prep table, lifted up the bus tray with a grunt, and carried it back out to the front of the house without a word. It had been like that with Nick all morning, and with Costa as well.

Florek looked across the kitchen at Costa, who had not spoken more than a handful of words to him that day. Costa had opened his switchblade and was now making a two-inch cut at the top of the long leather sheath before him. He made another cut parallel to the first, then went down past the halfway point of the sheath and made two more identical slices with the knife.

"What're you doing?" said Florek.

"I'm makin' somethin'," said Costa. "You just keep workin', take care of that lettuce underneath the table there. We gotta get this place ready for lunch."

Florek picked up the cardboard crate of lettuce, dropped it onto the

188

prep table. Coring lettuce was not the same as coring tomatoes—coring lettuce was hard work. And after a few minutes of slamming his palm against the lettuce core, loosening it and then digging his fingers in and pulling the core out by hand, he was always ready to move onto something else. His first couple of days at Nick's, Florek's palms were bruised purple from the job.

"Ah," said Costa, who had removed his belt and had passed it through the slices he made in the sheath. "I'm gonna need one more belt. Then it's gonna work pretty goddamn good."

"What's that, Costa?"

"Nothing, Florek. I'm only talkin' to myself a little bit here. You just worry about that lettuce."

Costa folded the blade back into the handle of the knife, slipped it into his pocket. Yessir, there was nothing like a good knife when you wanted to get a job done. A gun, you had to clean it and buy ammunition and worry about the casings you left behind, and anyway, a gun, it could blow up for no reason right in your face. After all, look what had happened to Niko with that cheap Italian pistol of his, up in Batavia, New York. Yeah, you could have your pistols and your shotguns and everything else; close in, there was nothing like a knife.

Costa smiled crookedly, thinking that it was a knife that had brought him to America in the first place. That knife was beautiful, the best one he ever owned, a six-inch blade with an inlaid, onyx handle. Too bad he had to leave it in the man who married his sister. The bastard, he had reneged on the dowry he promised when he asked for Stella's hand.

The day of the wedding, after the *papathe* had made them man and wife, Costa had asked his new brother-in-law about the details and whereabouts of the promised dowry. The bastard had laughed then, told Costa to relax, to have a good time at the party—that the dowry, the *prika*, it was a myth he had dreamed up to secure Stella's hand. The *prika* never existed, it held no more value than smoke. The bastard laughed, like it was some big joke. Costa laughed then, too; he let them have their fun at the party, danced and ate their *fayito* and drank with them all, even wished his sister and her new husband well as they went off late that night to their wedding bed. And the next morning, as the lying, laughing bastard walked down the road to get his first *cafe*, Costa stepped out from behind a stand of olive trees beside the *cafeneion*, and plunged the knife with the onyx handle deep into the bastard's armpit, shoved it straight in and clean down to the hilt, twisted it there as the warm blood spilled over his hand. A cousin came from behind another tree as Costa stepped back, handed Costa a handker-

189

chief to wipe away the blood. Costa thanked him and walked away. He kept right on going that morning, to Cairo first and on to America, where he met a fellow Spartan named Nick Stefanos, a young immigrant running bootleg hootch in upstate New York. Costa had never looked back, had never spoken or contacted his sister again, knew he could not return—as the man whom he had killed, this man had cousins, too. He felt neither regret nor remorse, though occasionally he would dream about the incident, the dream ending with the look on the bastard's face: surprise at first, coupled with raw pain, and then fear, the fear of the black unknown that was swiftly rushing toward him as Costa gave him the knife, gave it to him real good and quick. Yes, close in, there was nothing like a knife.

"You workin' on that lettuce?" said Stefanos, stepping into the kitchen, a tomato in one hand and a knife in the other.

"Yes," said Florek, wondering why Nick was being so short and impatient with him.

"When you gonna work on it, huh? Next week?"

"My hand's sore," said Florek. "I bruised it coring that other crate of lettuce two days ago."

"Ah," said Costa with a dismissive wave of his hand. "You got more excuses than Carter's got liver pills, boy."

"I'll be done in a couple of minutes."

"Yeah, hokay. I'll be looking for it out front." He turned to Costa. "And what the hell you think you're doin'?"

"I'm makin' somethin'! Why you gettin' all upset about everything?"

"It's my *nevra*, I guess. I'm waitin' on that phone call, that's all."

"Uh," said Costa.

Stefanos walked back out to the front of the house. A couple of Negroes sat in a booth, talking quietly, drinking coffee and smoking cigarettes in the slow hour between breakfast and lunch. Stefanos went to the radio, pushed the plug into the wall socket. Music came from the speaker, some *mavros* going on and on about a woman who left him for another *mavros*. This colored music, Stefanos could take it or leave it. But it made the customers happy, so what the hell.

Stefanos looked at the phone on the wall. When was the *Italos* going to call?

He picked up a tomato, held it firmly in his left hand, began to slice it thin.

They thought they could squeeze him for protection money, they had another thing coming to them, goddamn right.

The knife slipped off the skin of the tomato, its serrated edge raking

190

across Stefanos's thumb. He pulled his hand back, shook it, looked at the thumb. The cut was not so deep, but it had already begun to bleed. He pressed his thumb tight against his apron to stop the blood. He took a deep breath, let it out slow.

There was no way he would let them push him around. In this country, he had learned straight away, an immigrant had to stand his ground.

From the moment he stepped off the boat at Ellis Island, Stefanos recognized the importance of that. After his young wife had died of tuberculosis in the village, Stefanos had left his infant son with a sister and had come to America where it was said there was money to be picked right up off the street. He worked a few weeks as a common laborer in New York City, then met a man in a speakeasy who offered him a job as muscle for a bootleg operation he ran upstate, in a place called Batavia. Stefanos looked at the man's fine suit, the way he wore his hat, and accepted the offer. Soon he was wearing a fine suit himself, riding in a car behind a truck full of hootch, armed with an Italian pistol, protecting the load on its weekly run. The driver of the car was a tough little *patrioti* named Costa, from a village in Sparta not unlike his own. The two of them became fast friends.

Stefanos and Costa made two runs each week without incident over the course of seven months. It was on the last of these routine runs that they were ambushed by rival bootleggers after being flagged off the road by a woman standing beside a broken-down jalopy. The woman was a plant, but Stefanos had been suspicious from the start —there was no steam coming from beneath the upraised hood of the car, and the woman looked cheap, way too hard to be as helpless as she wished to appear. By the time the two gunmen had come from out of the trees, Stefanos had already rolled out of the passenger side of their car. He came up firing, wounding both men with four shots. On the fifth pull of the trigger, the Italian piece blew up in his face, sending a hot shard of barrel into his cheek. Costa finished the two gunmen with his knife; Stefanos heard the gurgle of their final breaths as he watched the woman drive off.

Costa and Stefanos headed south right away, drove straight into the night for Washington, D.C., where Nick had the address of a third cousin who lived in the city's Chinatown district. The cousin put them up, stopped the infection in Stefanos's wound. Nick bought a pearl-handled Smith and Wesson at a pawnshop shortly thereafter, vowing never again to touch an Italian-made gun. Costa stuck to knives, and soon married the sister of Stefanos's cousin, a dour young woman named Toula.

From his first job in D.C., as a dollar-a-week-plus-tips busboy at the Hotel Washington, to his ownership of Nick's, it had all been plain hard

191

work. Stefanos believed in putting your head down, not getting distracted by looking too far in the distance, because getting ahead of yourself was what tripped a man up. He would always remind himself of the fable of the dog with the bone in his mouth who saw his reflection in a pool of water, dropped the one in his mouth to get the one he saw, lost the one he had forever. That was just an old story, he knew it; but hard work and focus, it had always produced for him. He loved this country, loved everything about it, the shiny cars and the tailored suits and the beautiful, laughing women, and he loved the feeling of walking down 14th Street and putting the key to the door, *his* door, every single day. And now, these sonsofbitches, they thought that they were gonna make him pay? He'd like to see them try.

The phone rang on the wall. Stefanos went to it, picked up the receiver, listened to what the man on the other end had to say. He felt a pressure rise in his chest, heard the emotion in his own voice, saw spit fly from his mouth as he spoke. He slammed the receiver into its cradle, stood there, saw the Negroes in the booth staring at him, saw them look away as they caught the blackness in his eyes. He turned and walked back through the swinging doors into the kitchen.

Costa and Florek had stopped working. Karras, freshly changed from his street clothes into his work pants and apron, had just come in from the warehouse. He shook a Lucky Strike out of his pack, put it to his lips.

"Well," said Stefanos. "That's that."

"What was all that racket out there?" said Karras.

"I was talkin' to your friend on the phone. The *Italos*."

"And?"

"I told him to go to hell."

Costa smiled crookedly. *"Tora thai thoome."*

"Yeah," said Stefanos. "Now we gonna see what's gonna happen next."

Karras struck a match. He lighted his cigarette, studied the big Greek through the dancing flame.

■

"Well?" said Burke.

Recevo ran his hand along the phone's receiver. "He told me to go to hell."

"Hah!" said Reed. He took his feet off the big table in front of him, stood from his chair. "Well, I guess that tears it. How do you want us to handle it, Mr. Burke? We go back over there right now, or you want us to wait until tonight?"

192

Burke slowly rubbed his temples. His hair had gone off in a couple of odd directions, and he needed a barber's shave. He looked like hell; Recevo would have bet his savings that Burke had gotten stinking drunk the night before, but even a track bum could have played that ticket to win. Burke had been drunk most nights since the holidays of '48.

"Relax, Reed," he said.

"What. We're gonna sit here and let that Greek tell us to shove it?"

"Of course not. But there's no reason to move forward with something that might result in gunfire. So far, we've been lucky in not attracting attention. No, I think that Gearhart had a very good idea when he talked about implementing that old shell game with the second group of men."

Gearhart moved his turtle eyes beneath their lids. Other than that, nothing moved. He sat in his oversized chair, his hands folded in his lap. "It's worked in the past."

"And so it shall work again," said Burke. "We bring in a second group of men to talk to this Nick character, they promise him protection from us at a cheaper price. He'll see it as a bargain."

He'll see red, thought Recevo. *And he won't pay a goddamn cent.*

"Well, Joe?" said Burke.

Recevo said, "It's worth a try."

"Who are we talking about here?" said Reed.

Burke had a sip of coffee, placed the cup back on the desk. "It so happens that Bender and his men are down from Philadelphia for a couple of days. They're doing some gambling out at La Fontaine's place. Bender owes me a favor from a couple of years back."

"Christ," said Reed, "not Bender. That guy's all queer."

"I know how that offends you, Reed. But the truth of it is, he's just . . . what's that word, Gearhart?"

"*Theatrical,*" said Gearhart.

"Yes, that."

"Well," muttered Reed, "he looks all queer to me."

Burke turned to Recevo. "How about you, Joe? Any objections?"

"Call Bender," said Recevo. He blew into his deck of Raleighs and pulled free a cigarette.

25

■■■■■ Vera Gardner reached behind her, wrapped her hands around the rails of the bed. Karras pushed himself into her, retreated, pushed in again, buried himself inside her to the base of his cock. The bed lifted off the floor, slammed down and bounced on its springs.

Karras tasted the salty sweat which had gathered at the fold of Vera's breast. He bit gently on her hard red nipple. Vera arched her back. Karras's hand traced the steps of Vera's ribcage.

"Pete," said Vera.

He slipped one finger in her mouth. Her lips closed around it, her tongue cool and dry. He went in, kept himself there, Vera pushing up with her hips, her buttocks off the bed. She held her breath and broke with a spasm; he came like a river, his thigh trembling against hers. He rested his head on her chest. She brushed her fingers through his damp hair. They lay in the wet pool that had settled on the bed.

Karras and Vera showered together, dressed together in the room. Karras went to a chair by the window while Vera applied her makeup. He moved the chair so that it sat fully in the light. He had a seat, lighted a smoke.

Vera ran a comb through her long blonde hair, looked at Karras in the mirror. "Take me out, Pete. You said you'd take me out."

"Sure, honey. We'll go out."

"There's a play finishing its run down at the National."

"You know I'm not crazy about plays."

"It's a Eugene O'Neill. *Mourning Becomes Electra.* Michael Redgrave's in it, and Rosalind Russell."

"Rosalind Russell? If they had Jane Russell in it, then maybe I'd go."

"Oh, come on, Pete, it would be fun. Why don't we see if they have tickets for tonight?"

Because I've got a date with my wife tonight. Because with you and me it doesn't go any further than this room. You don't get it, Vera. You never have.

"Not tonight, Vera. Tonight I've got plans."

Vera's shoulders slumped. Her eyes darted away. She reached for an eyebrow pencil, leaned into the mirror. Karras watched her hand shake as she ran the pencil across her brow.

"What's wrong with you, anyway?" said Karras.

"Nothing," she said.

But Karras knew. He had felt it pulse through her as they had lain together afterwards on the bed. It was that girlfriend of hers, a dark, brooding woman named Natalie, with whom Vera had shared an office at the Census Bureau since 1946. Natalie, who had worked support staff on the Manhattan Project throughout the war and had been on site at Trinity. The woman had filled Vera's head with a nightmare's worth of information on the bomb. She had made her obsession Vera's obsession, too. It was always crawling around in Vera's mind—who had it, what it did, when it would land on us—and when Karras held her sometimes, during one of their frequent afternoon naps, Vera's head would snap back and forth and she would often wake with a start. It was this Natalie character who had put the cancer into Vera's dreams.

"You're thinking about that bomb business again, aren't you."

"No," said Vera, wincing slightly at the unconvincing sound of her own voice. She looked at him again in the mirror. "What about you? What's your excuse?"

"What're you talking about?"

"You haven't been right all day."

Karras nodded his head in the direction of the bed. "Not right, huh. I didn't hear you complainin'."

"You know what I mean. When we make love, everything's fine. Other than that, you're off somewhere else."

Karras dragged on his cigarette. The smoke from it hung in the blocks of light coming through the bedroom window.

"I saw an old friend the other day. When I saw him walking into the grill, I felt nothing, like he had died or something and I had gotten all the way over it. But since then, I've been thinking about him more and more. It's like someone's tapping a finger on my shoulder, and when I turn around, there's no one there. But that finger on my shoulder, it won't go away."

"Your friend Joe," said Vera.

"Yeah."

"It's not going to go away, Pete. It's not going away until and you and Joe settle it. You know it, and that's what bothering you. You realize that, don't you?"

"Yes," said Karras. He squinted at the sunlight that had entered his eyes. "Somehow, me and Joe are gonna have to make things right."

∎

Lois Roman came up naked behind Joe Recevo, put her arms around his shoulders, ran her hands across his chest. Recevo was fumbling with his tie, trying to put together a quick Windsor. He pushed her hand out of the way.

"Move it, baby, I'm tryin' to get dressed."

"What's your hurry?" said Lois.

"We got some guys comin' in from Philly tonight."

"That's not for a few hours yet."

"I know it. I thought you and me would head over to Mark Gallagher's first, have a couple of beers."

Gallagher's was up on Georgia Avenue, near Recevo's apartment. It was just a bar, a place where he could watch the fights, jawbone with friends, sip fifteen-cent drafts. It was a man's joint mainly, a little bit on the dull side, and Lois didn't care for it one bit.

"Ooh, Gallagher's," said Lois playfully. "You better be careful, you might spend a dollar or two on me by accident."

"Maybe I'm savin' it up for somethin' nice."

"Like a ring, maybe?"

Recevo reached behind him, grabbed a handful of Lois's perfect ass. "What we got baby, you can't buy in a jewelry store." He slapped her one there. "Go get dressed."

He turned and watched her walk back to the bathroom. Lois's bottom half—God, that was some kind of temple. He smiled just looking at it, thinking that his face had been wet with it just a half-hour earlier. Lois had sat herself on the side of the bed, put her hands behind her and shook that black hair of hers off her shoulders, and Recevo had kneeled there in front of her like he was in church, and he had buried his face in it until she had called out his name. And all the while his hands had been working on that beautiful ass of hers. Recevo knew that there would never be anything better than that.

But marriage? Hell, Lois was a nice kid, and all that. You might be able

196

to stretch it and even say that he loved her. But weddings, steady jobs, a family, yatta, yatta, yatta, that kind of noise was not for him. He'd have to be careful how he danced around it, though, because a man would be a fool to let a flesh trophy like that get away. Lois and her goddamn beautiful ass. Recevo could live down there, never come up for air. What did Pete always call him when they were clowning around? "The Frogman," on account of he loved to dive for gash. Yeah, "Frogman," that was it. Pete Karras and his names.

Karras. It was funny about Pete. He hadn't seen him since that night in the alley back in '46, hadn't thought a whole lot about him after the first six months had passed. And now, having run into him at Nick's, it was like someone had pointed out to Recevo that he had been walking around for the last three years without a right arm. It was like some joker had tapped him on the shoulder and said, "Here, buddy, you musta dropped this back there," and then handed him his own limb. Like he had been some kind of cripple, all that time, and didn't even know it. A cripple, just like—

"C'mon, Joe," said Lois, walking into the room in a sharp-looking tight skirt and high heels. "I thought you were gonna fix that tie."

Recevo looked in the mirror. He hadn't done a thing to it in the last five minutes.

"You better get it for me. My mind's somewheres else."

Lois turned him around, fixed it for him, tightened the knot. She patted him on his chest, smiled.

"Thanks, baby," he said.

"We better get goin'," said Lois with a wink. "I mean, you never know—Gallagher's, they might run out of those fifteen-cent beers."

■

"Mike, you're shaking."

"It's cold, that's all."

Kay laughed. "It's not so cold in here, Mike. Look at the windows. How cold could it be?"

Florek had a look around the interior of the car. It was true that it had gotten plenty warm; the windows had even steamed up since the last time he had checked. It smelled sweaty and kind of briny in there, too. Florek wondered if Kay's father would notice the smell when he got into his car the next morning. He squirmed a little at the thought.

"Where you goin'," said Kay with a chuckle, "wigglin' away from me like that."

Kay put her hand behind his head and drew him to her. She kissed him

197

roughly, sliding her tongue across his. Florek thought he would burst from his trousers—God, this Kay was something! And then he felt her reach for his hand, take it, move it across the wool of her carcoat. The coarseness of the wool gave to the smooth heat of her skin, and now she was moving his hand inside her blouse, the top buttons of which had come undone somehow, and then beneath her loose brassiere, where his knuckles barely brushed the fine weave of lace. Then his fingers were tracing the bumps of her nipple as he listened to Kay's steady moan, and he opened his eyes to watch her even as they kissed. Kay's eyes were neither open nor closed, but kind of away and not looking at anything at all. Her scent was strong in the car now, and Florek felt something rising in his cock, and he wanted to stop it but he could not. He caught his breath at the point of his own dull explosion, a quiet ejaculation sending rhythmic, warm spurts into the underwear which he had cleaned in the sink that very afternoon.

"Why are you stopping, Mike?"

"I don't know." He pushed his hair away from his eyes. "I'm nervous, I guess, that we're going to get caught."

She kissed him again, but saw that the passion in it had passed. Kay dropped her head onto his shoulder. "You had a good time, didn't you?"

"I had a great time, Kay."

Kay smiled. "I did, too."

They sat there for a while, but not too long, because Florek really did worry that someone would come along. He thought that a parking lot in Rock Creek Park would be the first place a cop would look for couples necking after dark. So he and Kay drove around a little and listened to the radio, and then she dropped him off at 14th and U Streets before heading uptown to her parents' house in Shepherd Park. Florek kissed her through the open driver's window before she sped off. He pulled the tail of his shirt out so that it covered the damp gray spot on the front of his trousers, and he began to walk south.

Another good night! They had seen a show at the Uptown called *Hills of Home*, a Lassie picture that Florek would have yawned through if not for a very young actress named Janet Leigh, who did it for him and reminded him of Kay. He and Kay had made out in the balcony off and on through most of the feature, and afterwards, at her suggestion, they had skipped any kind of food or drink and driven into the park. Thinking of them in the car, Florek found that he was walking very fast, running almost, down the street. Tonight had been a night of firsts: He had felt his first bare tit, had shot off for the first time without his own hand on the trigger. His buddies back home, they would have laughed and said that a dry hump was no cherry-bust, but any kind of lovemaking with Kay was good enough for him.

Florek smiled, running down 14th, thinking of how happy he was that he had come to D.C. And then he slowed down to a walk and finally a dead stop as the image of his sister entered his mind. Lola . . . just where the hell was Lola now?

■

Lola Florek looked up at her reflection in the ornate mirror angled and suspended from the ceiling above. Her body was mostly covered by the man who was inside her, but she could see her face above his muscled back, her head inching backward with each violent thrust. The sheets were bunched tightly in one of the man's hands, while his other hand gripped the bed rails for support. The bed had moved slowly in a clockwise direction since she had been watching it. She'd made a game of it, to see how far the bed would move before the man was done. There was pain, and she could feel it, but the pain was happening to someone else: the girl in the mirror. The girl with the black streaks running down her face.

Lola heard laughter and colored music from down below. She took her eyes from the mirror, felt the ripping inside her. For a moment, she could not breathe in or out. Then the pain passed, and she let some air out of her lips.

"I'm too dry," she said.

"Sssh," said the man.

Lola said, "Daddy."

The man said, "You go on and call me anythin' you want."

■

"What's your hurry, officer?"

"We're done. And it's cold out here."

"If it's cold out here for you, how you think I feel, my backside up against these bricks? Anyway, why you so jumpy tonight?"

"I gotta go."

"Don't you wanna love me a little bit more, sugar?"

"Wouldn't do me any good to be seen with a whore. You know that."

"A colored whore, you mean."

"You know that makes no difference to me."

"Course not. Matter of fact, colored woman's the only kind of woman you like."

"What say?"

"Nothin', sugar. I was talkin' on the wrong side of you, I guess. You know, that bum ear of yours gon' get you in trouble some day."

"Listen, Delilah . . ."

"I like to hear you say my name."

"I was wondering. If a colored man had a little money in his pocket . . . if he wanted to pay for a white woman, I mean, where would he go?"

"You lookin' for white women now? 'Cause you know you got everything you need right here. You been pickin' me up at the same place every week, 5th and K, for the last—"

"I'm not looking for myself. I'm talking about one specific white woman that I'm trying to find."

"You want to talk to a pimp?"

"Not exactly. Someone that sets dates up, maybe *through* a pimp—white women for colored men. Is there a name that comes to mind?"

"Let me think about it a little bit, sugar. I might just know someone you could talk to, yeah."

"Thanks, Delilah."

"My pleasure, officer. Now you better get yourself out of this cold. You don't mind my sayin' so, you lookin' a little pale, even for you."

■

Sometimes, Peter Karras didn't know how Eleni talked him into these things. Who would have thought he'd be sitting at a table with his wife at the Casino Royal, watching a bunch of midgets doing some crazy juggling and acrobatic act on stage?

"Aw, come on, Pete, we'll have a ball," said Eleni that morning, just an hour before he had headed into Southeast to see Vera.

And that had been why, he supposed, he had agreed to go—his guilt over Vera, and what he was about to do. But first he had to put up a little bit of a fight. She expected that much of him at the very least.

"*Ochi, Eleni.* What do I wanna go watch a bunch of dwarves for, wearin' costumes, singin' songs—"

"Don't be such a bump on a log, Pete. I'll get your mom to babysit Dimitri. And they're not just dwarves. It's Hermine's Little People, honey. They're a national act!"

After a couple of cocktails, Karras had gotten into the spirit of things. And Eleni, in the new outfit he had bought her at Jelleff's, she was looking pretty sharp. He caught the way her nose crinkled up every time one of the midgets made a pratfall, and knew for sure that she was having a good old time.

200

Karras liked the Casino Royal as much as any nightclub in D.C. The dance floor was small, but the place had a certain kind of class, with Chinese waiters serving Chinese chow and dollar drinks mixed with liquor one step up the shelf. The house band, Jive Jack Schafer's outfit, they could jump, too, and no wonder—the bald-headed Schafer had come up playing first trumpet with Harry James. The midget act, they were all right, but Karras relaxed a little more when Schafer's band came out to play.

The dance floor filled up fast. Schafer went right into a swing standard, and the jitterbuggers hit the floor. Karras saw Tommy Rados out there, felt a rush of affection, as Karras had not yet heard that Rados had made it out of the Philippines in one piece. That Rados character could really dance. Through the dancers, at a deuce at the edge of the floor, Karras caught a glimpse of Face and his wife, having a couple of drinks. Face's wife, my God, she was almost as big and ugly as him. But he had his arm around her, and they were both grinning like teenagers, and their heads were bobbing and their oversized feet were making likewise-time beneath the table. Karras called his waiter over, pointed to Face's table, sent Face and his wife a round. A few minutes later, Face looked over at Karras, smiled and raised his drink.

The midgets came back out and did their song-and-dance for another forty-five minutes, and then it was Schafer again and more dancing, and by that time Karras was half in the bag. A Greek Eleni knew from Saint Sophia came over and timidly asked Karras if it would be all right if he and Eleni had a dance. Karras knew that Eleni was dying to take a spin around the floor, told the Greek that it was fine.

"You don't mind, Pete?"

"Knock yourself out, sweetheart. I'm gonna go over to the bar, I think, have a taste of something else."

"Thanks, Pete. I'm only gonna take one dance."

"Go on, baby, have some fun."

Karras picked his deck of Luckies up off the table, rose from his chair, limped across the dining-room floor. He found an empty barstool and had a seat.

"Yessir," said the bartender, who was working on a good sweat.

"A bottle of Senate and shot of rye. Make the rye that Pete Hagen's up there on the shelf."

The bartender served both neatly on two cocktail napkins. Karras threw the shot back at once. He chased the rye with beer and lighted a cigarette. A paw landed on his shoulder. Karras glanced to his right; the hand was slightly smaller than Rhode Island. Face had a seat on the stool to the right.

"You mind?" said Face.

"Hell, no."

"Thanks for the round, Pete."

"Sure thing, Face. That your wife?"

"Yeah."

"I never had the pleasure. She's a looker."

Face blushed. "I tell her that, you're gonna make her night."

"Then tell her," said Karras.

Face ordered a rum and Coke for himself, signalled the bartender to pour Karras another shot. They tapped glasses and drank. Karras blew a smoke ring over the bar.

"How's business?" he said, looking straight ahead.

"All right, I guess," said Face carefully. And then, by way of an apology said, "It ain't exactly like I'm on the decision end of things. You know that, Pete."

"Sure, Face. I know."

Face looked down at Karras's twisted knee. "You know, Pete . . ."

"What?"

"Aw hell, Karras, I'm too damn drunk."

"I'm three sheets myself."

"It's just that, you ought to know . . . about Recevo, I mean."

"What about him?"

"I never was no fan of his, you know that. But you ought to know that what happened that night with Reed and the others, in that alley . . . it wasn't how it was supposed to go."

"How's that?"

"Mr. Burke never told Reed to mess you up as bad as he did. He never told him to take no bat to your leg—"

"What about Joe, Face?"

Face took a long swallow from his drink. "I was in the office that night, when Joe called from the bar. Mr. Burke didn't give Recevo no choice—it was either deliver you to Reed to get slapped around, or they were going to take you out. All the way out, Karras, get it? They woulda killed Joe, and you, if it hadn't gone the way they said. Reed was only supposed to slap you around, that's all."

"So Joe was just tryin' to save his skin."

"And yours."

"You tellin' me that Joe saved my life? Is that it?"

Face nodded. "Yeah."

"Look at me, Face. You saw me draggin' my leg across this dining room a few minutes ago. How did I look? Did I look alive to you?"

Face stared into his drink. "Christ, Karras. I was only tryin' to set you straight, that's all."

Karras smiled to himself, shook his head. He took some tobacco into his lungs. "You're all right, Face, you know it? For the life of me, I don't know why a guy like you stays with Burke."

Face chuckled from somewhere deep in his gut. "Now it's your turn to look at me. I'm big and I'm ugly and I'm just plain dumb. Workin' muscle is the only thing I'm good for. What else *would* I do?"

"Well . . . " Karras cleared his throat, touched the mole next to his mouth. "I oughta get back to my wife."

"I better do the same. The drinks are on me, Pete."

"Thanks, chum."

Face dropped money on the bar. Karras drained his shot. He closed his eyes, dragged deeply on his cigarette. The blare of Jack Schafer's trumpet exploded in his head.

26

██████ Bender removed his topcoat, draped it across the back of a free chair. He had a seat in front of Burke's desk, crossed one leg over the other, smoothed out the fine fabric of his suit trousers down to the knee.

"Have a good night out at La Fontaine's?" said Burke.

Bender cocked his head. "I lost a hand or two. Thought I'd take a break, come over and see what you had on your mind. I'll head back over the line after this, see if I can't win some of it back. You know how I hate to leave money lying on the table."

"Drink?" said Burke.

"What're you having?"

"A little bourbon."

"Bourbon's fine. But yours looks a little dark to me. Cut mine with water, will you?"

"Reed," said Burke, making a head motion toward the liquor cart.

Reed went to the cart, fixed a bourbon and water for Bender, dropped a couple of ice cubes in the glass. He carried the bottle over to Burke's desk, because he knew that Mr. Burke would want the bottle close by, and then he placed the drink in Bender's hand. Reed didn't care to build drinks for anybody, and he especially didn't like putting one together for a swish. He jammed his hands in the pockets of his sharkskin suit, continued pacing the room.

Two other men in topcoats stood by the door: a red-haired pug with a beat-to-shit nose and a dark-skinned joker too big for his suit. Reed pegged the dark-skinned one as an Italian or some other variety of white nigger, but the reality was that the big man, who was called Moon, hailed from London. These two men were Bender's. Recevo sat at the big table, where he always sat, always alone.

"We walked right in the front door," said Bender. "I was expecting to see that giant of yours. What was his name?"

"Face."

"Where is he, out gathering bananas?"

"He took his wife to a show. Some midget act they got over at Casino Royal."

"Midgets, huh? Charming. You know, Burke, you ought to introduce your men to some real culture. Take me and those two by the door, for example. Sure, we're down here gambling. But we've also reserved tickets, two nights from now, to a play by the name of *Hamlet*. It's running at the Little Theatre. You know where that is, don't you?"

"I know where it is. On 9th above F."

"Then you've been there! Maybe you'd like to come along."

"I don't think so."

"Larry Olivier's in the title role."

Larry. Recevo looked over at Bender, bright-eyed and grinning in his seventy-five-dollar suit, a derby in one hand, a leather flower in his lapel. The guy was all over the place with his fluttery hands, and when he spoke it was up and down in tone, like he was singing a song or something. Fruit or no, this Bender was a real piece of work.

"I'll pass," said Burke.

"As you wish."

Burke poured his fourth bourbon into his glass. Some of the bourbon missed the inside of the glass and splashed onto the desk. Burke wiped it away with the sleeve of his shirt.

"Listen, Bender. I don't want to waste any more of your time tonight. Let me tell you why I asked you to drop by."

Bender nipped at his drink, jingled the cubes in the glass. "Go ahead."

Burke started in. Recevo pulled his deck of Raleighs, lighted a cigarette. He smoked through Burke's pitch. By the time Recevo felt the heat of the burning end near his fingers, Burke was done.

"It seems straightforward enough," said Bender. "Shall we discuss compensation?"

"Two hundred flat if he tumbles."

Bender frowned. "Is that fair? I take a flat fee and you collect protection money from the Greek in perpetuity."

"It's my town, Bender. Maybe when I'm up in Philly I'll do the same for you."

Bender brushed some imaginary lint off his trousers. "Maybe you shall."

"Then it's settled."

"All right. But you haven't mentioned the odds. I never make a move without hearing the odds."

"Joe," said Burke. "How many men at the Stefanos joint?"

Recevo thought it over. "Anywhere from three to five if you count the bouncer. My take is the bouncer will fade."

"But it's only the three of us on this trip," said Bender. "I can't say that those are odds I like."

"I don't like them either," said Burke, a drop of bourbon dripping down his chin. "So I was thinking that I'd give you one of mine. Someone the Greek's never met. Joe, whad'ya think of that?"

I think you're getting sloppy. You're getting good and goddamn sloppy now.

Recevo said, "I think it'll be fine."

"Reed," said Burke. "Go downstairs and bring up a man."

Reed stopped pacing. "A couple of those guys downstairs were with us when we went in the Greek's place the first time."

"Then bring one up who wasn't with you the first time! Goddamn it, Reed, do I have to explain everything?"

Reed walked quickly from the room. Burke rubbed his temples; he wished he hadn't given Gearhart the night off, so he could bounce some of these things off of him. Gearhart, he was a strange one, but he always knew what to do. Well, at least he had Joe around. Joe had a brain in his head, at least.

Bender looked around the room, an expression of bemusement on his face. Then Reed walked back in with a man half his size. The guy had a small-man's scowl; a cigarette dangled from the side of his mouth; he wore elevator shoes and a ten-gallon hat.

Bender smiled. "This your man?"

"His name's Sanderson."

"Hmm." Bender chuckled under his breath.

Recevo checked out Sanderson—comical, if he wasn't so pathetic. And then another Sanderson image entered his mind: Recevo pictured himself, three years back, looking in the rearview of the coupe, seeing Reed and Sanderson and the others stepping up to meet Karras on the sidewalk in front of the market.

Burke turned to Bender. "He look okay to you?"

"Fine," said Bender. "In fact, this thing is beginning to look like it might be fun."

Recevo studied Sanderson and his Tom Mix hat.

That hat. He was wearing that hat the night in the alley. I remember it now, clear as day. And Pete Karras will remember it, too.

"How about you, Joe?" said Burke. "You see anything wrong with the setup?"

Recevo leaned forward. "No, Mr. Burke. Not a thing."

■

Matty Buchner had a sip of scotch, let his eye move casually around the room. It was a slow night in this place, with a couple of out-of-town businessmen and a solo fat man seated at the bar. A B-girl had managed to get some sucker to buy her a watered-down highball, and she and this suit-and-tie hayseed were in a booth making small talk. In the booth behind them, two high-end hookers sat drinking Cokes, trying in vain to get the attention of the businessmen at the bar. The girls looked like the Doublemint twins, but Buchner knew they were hookers, as he had seen them work this room before. Their clean-scrubbed looks fetched twenty dollars each, but in the heat of the summer, when this town was stone dead, you could get either one of them for ten. Never less than ten, though, Matty knew, because he had tried.

No action tonight. The Hi-Hat lounge in the winter was usually good for a few bucks, but not tonight. The patrons at the bar had kept their coats with them, and the checkout woman at the cloakroom, a broad with a face that begged for a feed-bag, she couldn't be bought. Yeah, the Hi-Hat, it was usually prime territory for a cold-finger man like Matty Buchner. But not tonight.

Buchner liked the place, even if it was a freeze-out on nights like this. The lounge was in The Ambassador, one of the newest and nicest hotels in the city, with air-conditioning in every room, and it drew the visiting money. Yeah, this Cafritz guy who had built the joint, he had done it up right. Buchner supposed he could head over to the Madrillon at 15th and New York, see what was going on there, but they had that spic music real regular now, and that stop-and-start, cha-cha bullshit played hell with his ears. Even if nothing was happening, Buchner decided he would stay at the Hi-Hat, relax a little bit, see what came up, have another drink. He signalled the tender with a tilt of his chin.

The bartender was a ratty-looking fuck who didn't know Matty from Adam, which was why Matty was still on his stool. The previous bartender had caught Buchner with his hand in some other guy's cashmere coat one year ago, and had tossed him out. And then there was the house dick, a fat, bald-headed dude who'd also given Matty the fisheye from time to time.

But Buchner had heard that there was a new guy on barshift, and that was what had brought him back.

"What's it gonna be?"

"A scotch and soda."

"Any flavor?"

"The house. That's forty-five cents, right?"

"At happy hour it is. Thing is, pal, you're about four hours late."

"Come on friend, cut me a little slack."

The bartender tapped his finger on the face of his watch. "The drinks are regular price, *friend.*"

"Aw, go on and make it, then, if you're gonna be cute."

The bartender ran a finger along the ploughshare line of his weathered face, and went to fix the drink. Buchner narrowed one eye; the lid of his glass eye stayed put.

This bartender, he wasn't fooling anybody, he was nothing but a lousy pimp. Buchner had seen him talking with the fat bird at the bar, had heard the whole deal being cut. Ever since he had lost his eye, doing his stretch for that misunderstanding at the Shoreham, his hearing had improved. It was funny, how that worked. The fat bird at the bar, he had asked the bartender for "a big one," and then the bartender had gone to the wall phone, stuck a toothpick between his thin lips, and made the call. The two of them, they thought they were being real slick. But Matty, he had heard the whole thing.

The tender served the drink. Buchner drained the old one, pushed the empty glass across the bar.

Matty looked at the fat shmuck sitting there, his ass spilling over the sides of his stool. The guy reminded him of some movie actor who always played a heavy. He tried to think of who it was, but all he could come up with was Victor Mature. But this fuck, he didn't look a thing like Mature. Mature was a handsome sonofabitch, a star, and this guy—

The phone rang on the wall, and the bartender went to answer it. Then the bartender hung up the receiver and walked back over to the fat guy. The two of them whispered a little bit, which Matty couldn't make out on account of they had brought it down so low. Then the fat guy, he left a big bill on the bar, put on his topcoat, and headed out. Buchner watched the fat fuck go; he reminded him of some actor, all right. But who?

Buchner looked in the bar mirror at the wholesome hookers, and then he caught his own reflection in the glass. He could remember a time when the ladies found him pretty sharp, but now, with this cockeyed eye . . . anyway. He looked once more at the hookers. He smiled at them, tried to think if he had the dough on him to take the next step. Aw, what the hell. Even if he had the twenty for the both of them—and he knew he could get them down to twenty—how could he enjoy it, knowing that they'd be sick about it the whole time, that they couldn't stand to be with a single-peepered sad sack like him?

Matty Buchner sipped at his drink. The house brand, it wasn't all that bad.

27

"Lola . . . Lola, honey. C'mon, wake up."

Lydia Fortuno took her hand from Lola Florek's shoulder, pulled back the topsheet that covered her. Lola lay fetally on the bed, her mocha-colored dress bunched and wrinkled, her ankle-strapped heels still on her feet. A spot of blood had formed and dried now in the area of Lola's crotch. Lydia felt her jaws tighten—Morgan, that sonofabitch, he had sent her over to that colored reefer party at the blind pig off 7th earlier in the night, even after Lydia had warned him that the child might get hurt. The bastard she had been with, he had ripped into Lola real good. Afterwards, Lydia had seen her coming through the front door, trying not to double over from the pain, and she had taken her straight up the stairs and given her the sweet shot. It wouldn't fix what had happened, but it would take Lola away.

"Lola, please."

Lola's eyes fluttered. "What?"

"I need you to come with me, honey."

"Where?"

"Morgan's got me fixed up with a date. A fellow who asked for someone like me . . . you know, on the big side, honey, like me."

"I'm hurtin', Lydia. I'm hurtin' bad."

"I know."

"And it feels real good to lie here."

"I know it does. But I'm scared. All those girls that was killed, you know how they were . . . they were built like me. I'm askin' you please, you gotta come with me. I helped you out tonight when you needed it. Don't I always help you out?"

Lola looked up at her friend. "All right, Lydia. All right. Help me up outta this bed."

Lydia washed Lola's face, straightened out her dress. The two of them went down the stairs to the foyer of the house. Morgan was waiting there, slapping a pair of leather gloves against his palm. He frowned at the sight of Lola.

"Well, what's she doin' here?"

"She's comin' with me."

"The gentleman didn't ask for a pair."

"She ain't gonna be with me and the gentleman, Mr. Morgan. She's only going to be around."

"For Chrissakes, Lydia, look at her. She's all the way hopped."

Lola stood by the front door, her hands holding the lapels of her overcoat together, her eyes closed. She was smiling, bobbing her head a little, following some rhythm line that only she could hear. The Victrola in the living room was not running; the living room was dark.

"She'll be okay," said Lydia.

"She needs her rest."

"I'm not going without her." Lydia rested one fist on her waist, tilted her chin impudently at Morgan.

"You like it here, don't you? You like the heat in your room, and you like that soft bed. You forgettin' already where you came from? When I found you, you were spreading your legs for two bucks with those Filipinos down by Sailor's Row—"

"I'm not going without her."

Morgan scratched his dome, glanced at his watch. "All right, then. I don't have time to stand here listenin' to you run your hash-trap all night. So hurry up and get her in the car."

"You're driving? Why not a cab?"

"It's what the gentleman asked for. He told me where to drop you, and that's what I'm going to do. He's paying for his pleasure, and he's paying big."

"Who is this guy?"

"Hell if I know. A tender I do business with across town hooked it up."

"And he asked for me."

"He asked for your type." Morgan grinned. "Good thing I keep a big old thing like you in stock."

■

Lydia and Lola sat in the backseat of Morgan's big '48 Chrysler Windsor as Morgan drove east. Lola rested her head in Lydia's soft lap, stretched out her legs. Light came in the windows from the streetlamps above, passing over Lola's fishbelly-white calves, disappearing, then passing over them again. Lola counted the seconds between each spear of light, soon discovered a pattern in the intervals. She found this game pleasant. Lydia hummed a tune as she stroked Lola's hair.

The car slowed. Lola felt the downshift of the engine. Morgan stopped the Chrysler, did not cut the ignition. He turned his head to the backseat.

"Out," he said.

"There's nobody here," said Lydia.

"He'll be here."

"You're not gonna just leave us, are you?"

"He'll be here," said Morgan. "And I got some business to take care of. I'll swing back and pick you up in a couple of hours. Wait for me on that bench over there, by that bus stop."

"But—"

"C'mon, move it. You asked for company and you got it. Now get her up off the seat and the two of you get out. Like I say, I got business."

Lydia pulled Lola up by her arms. She got her out of the car and moved with her along the sidewalk as the Chrysler pulled away. They had a seat on a wooden bench beneath the sole streetlamp on the block. Lola had a sleepy look around: They were on a small commercial strip where a market, a lunch counter, a Dutch bakery, and a laundry sat in a neat row. An alley cut between the bakery and the laundry, where the light of the streetlamp spread and then faded. The windows of the businesses were dark; one pre-war car sat parked on the street.

Lydia hummed the same tune she had in the car, a quaver now in her voice.

"Where are we, Lydia?"

"Northeast somewhere, I guess. Morgan crossed North Capitol a few blocks back."

"Northeast?"

"Don't you worry about where we're at. Hold my hand."

Lola reached out, felt Lydia's large soft hand envelop hers. It was as if Lola had sunk her hand into a bowl of warm dough.

"Mmmm," said Lola.

"That's right, honey. You go to sleep."

Lola heard the screech of a cat. Like the sound a cat made when its tail got stepped on. Only more human. Sharp, rising in intensity, and then cut off. There and then gone. Lola opened her eyes.

She was lying on the bench. Her hand dangled off the bench, the cold air stinging her naked fingers. Her hand had felt so warm before, when Lydia had held it.

Lola sat up. She stared into her lap, brushed weakly at the dried circle of blood. She got off the bench, walked unsteadily across the street.

"Lydia?"

She tottered on one heel, watched her shadow do a liquid dance against the asphalt. She caught her balance, edged herself between the bumper of the old car and the grille of the newer model now parked behind it.

Lola heard a shoe scrape against stone from somewhere in the alley. That would be Lydia, having a pee. Big Lydia, she could squat anyplace when she had to. Lydia and Lola, in the few months that they had known each other, they had managed to have a few laughs over that.

"Lydia?"

Lola stood at the head of the alley. In the weak gray light of the street-lamp, she could see the outline of Lydia now, lying down on a bed of black. Lydia was holding her stomach as if she were sick. A small cloud of steam rose off her body.

"Lydia, you okay?"

Lola stepped into the alley.

She bent forward to shake Lydia. She slipped a little, looked down at her feet. She saw that Lydia's bed of black was blood. A tangled length of slick intestine snaked through Lydia's hands.

Lola felt her knees begin to shake. "Lydia?"

Lydia did not answer. Her eyes were open wide, filmed over. Lola could see between the tear of the crimson-splattered dress, where the heat of Lydia's organs emitted steam into the cold air.

Lola stood straight, as if electrified. She tried to but could not scream. She put her hand against the brick wall. She vomited on the bricks.

Lola Florek felt a blunt shock to the back of her head. She felt nothing after that.

Lola opened her eyes.

"Don't look up," said the man who stood in front of her.

213

She stared at his shoes. They looked to her like golfing shoes. She had seen shoes like this in Lydia's catalogues, back at the house. Shoes that were half one color and half another. Only, these shoes, their insteps were splashed with blood. Lola kept her gaze fixed straight ahead.

"I don't know what to do with you," said the man. His voice was desperate and soft.

"Please," said Lola.

"I'm sorry, you know."

A hot tear ran down Lola's face, and another soon gathered in the corner of her eye. The tear tickled her; she did not blink.

"Please," said Lola.

"You're too little," said the man.

The right shoe moved violently toward Lola's face. The shoe was the last thing she saw for a long while.

■

Lola lifted her head. A pain knifed through her sinuses to the back of her skull. She put her face down on the seat, felt the vibration of a motor moving through her. She watched the spears of light enter the windows of the car from the streetlamps above.

"I'm hurt bad," she muttered. Her voice sounded queer to her. She ran her tongue around the inside of her mouth. Her tongue slipped through the space where her front teeth had been. The gum was jagged there. She tasted the salt in her blood.

Morgan turned his head to look in the backseat. His eyes were wide and dirt tracks ran down his face.

"Help me."

Morgan's voice shook. "We're going home."

"I need a doctor," said Lola.

"I'm gonna fix you up at home."

Lola swallowed blood. The blood stung at the raw spot in back of her throat.

"I saw a man, Mr. Morgan."

"Shut up."

"But Mr. Morgan—"

"I don't want to know."

"Lydia," whispered Lola.

Morgan said, "Don't ever mention her name again."

214

28

"Hey, Panayoti, it's for you!"

Nick Stefanos shouted over the swinging doors into the kitchen. He waited for Karras to walk across the tiles to the kitchen phone. Karras picked up; Stefanos hung the receiver in its cradle.

"Yeah," said Karras.

"Pete, it's Jimmy Boyle."

"Jimmy. What's up?"

"I might have something for you on that Florek kid's sister."

"Keep talkin'."

"There's a spade runs a blind-pig joint over on Seventh Street around T. He's hooked up with Yellow Roberts somehow."

"Yellow Roberts. You talkin' about Jim Roberts, that dope boss?"

"The same. The spade goes by the name of DeAngelo Ray. Throws gin parties with reefer to go in the mix. My source tells me he orders in white girls for the out-of-town guests. Favors them young and on the blonde side, if you catch my drift."

"I get it. Where the spot?"

"Over there between the Off Beat and the Club Harlem." Boyle gave Karras the address.

"You sound a little jumpy, Jimmy."

"Hell, Pete, I didn't get a wink last night. I'm running on fumes."

"You been up to 14th and Colorado, is that it?"

"I seen that Doc you told me about, yeah."

"You be careful with that stuff."

"I already lost five pounds."

215

"You just be careful."

"I'm on a roll, buddy. With that murder last night, the department's gonna be focusing everything now on that case. If I'm going to catch a ride on that train—"

"I read about it in this morning's *Times-Herald*," said Karras. "It sounded pretty bad."

"You don't know the half of it. My uncle gave me the real dope. What the reporters don't know is, they found two types of blood at the crime scene, and two different samples of hair. The hooker who bought it had black hair, but a blonde had taken an injury there, too."

"But they didn't find the blonde."

"Uh-uh. That's the deal. Find the blonde and you find a witness. Which is what I'll be talkin' about this whole weekend to all those meatballs out on my beat. Which is what every detective in the department is gonna be talkin' about out there as well. Why, I'm tellin' you, Pete . . ."

Boyle kept talking, but his voice melted into one big jumble in Karras's ears. Karras was looking over the kitchen doors now, to a group of four men who had walked into the grill. The leader was a thin man with talkative hands who wore a very expensive suit and a derby. He had engaged Stefanos in conversation immediately. There was a pleasant smile on the thin man's delicate face.

A redheaded man with a boxed-in nose stood with his back against the plate-glass window, and a large dark man in a small suit stood by the door. There were no customers in the store; it was Saturday morning, and there was little in the way of business. On Saturday mornings Karras and Stefanos worked alone.

Karras looked at the fourth man: a half-pint wearing a tall white hat.

"This is my shot, Pete," said Boyle. "I deliver some kind of lead on this case, I'm gonna get right out of these blues. It's my ticket to a detective's shield—"

"Jimmy . . . Jimmy, I don't mean to cut you off. I got some customers, chum . . . I gotta go."

"All right, Pete."

"Thanks for the tip."

"Sure thing, pal. Talk to you later."

"Yeah . . . you, too."

Karras racked the talkpiece. He reached beneath his apron, pulled his deck of cigarettes. He put a Lucky in his mouth, lighted it. He touched the mole on the side of his mouth, took two steps back into the depths of the kitchen where they could not see him. From that spot he couldn't see much of them either. He could only see the peak of the tall white hat.

Karras drew deeply on his cigarette. He felt a vein throb in his neck as he squinted through the smoke.

■

Stefanos stood behind the counter rubbing his worry beads. He wrapped one finger around the leather string, swung the beads into his huge palm. The four men had been gone now for ten, fifteen minutes. Stefanos had been standing there, rubbing the *koumboloi*, thinking about things since then.

"*Ella, Panayoti,*" he shouted back toward the kitchen. "Come on out here, I wanna talk."

Karras limped out to the front of the house. He leaned his forearm on the counter.

"Yeah, Nick."

"Have a beer with me, *re.*"

"Okay."

Stefanos went to the cooler, pulled a bottle of Ballantine Ale, uncapped the bottle. He poured the ale into two glasses he had set out on the counter. Karras and Stefanos picked up the glasses, tapped them together.

"*Siyiam,*" said Karras.

"*Siyiam.*"

Karras drank down some of the ale. He wiped a sleeve across his mouth.

"You see those guys, a little while ago?"

"I saw them," said Karras. "Who were they?"

"I dunno. They said they heard about the *Italos* and his men, comin' in here to shake me down."

"And they thought they could help."

"Yeah. The thin guy in the pretty suit, he said he'd make the *Italos* and the others go away for half what the *Italos* was askin' me to pay."

"So he's gonna protect us from the others."

"Somethin' like that. That's what they said, anyway." Stefanos scratched his head. "Hell, I don't know. Gimme a cigarette, Karras, goddamn."

Karras shook the deck in front of Stefanos. Stefanos pulled a cigarette free, put it between his lips. Karras lighted it. Stefanos blew smoke at his feet.

"They're all in it together," said Karras, shaking out the match.

Stefanos looked up. "What?"

217

"I recognized one of the men in this morning's group. The little *skato* in the Tom Mix hat. He works for Burke. The *Italos*, he works for Burke, too."

"Goddamn."

"Yeah. It's an old gag, Nick."

"And I fell for it."

"You didn't fall for it yet."

Karras studied Stefanos. He looked shaken, disoriented.

Stefanos said, "What the hell I'm gonna do now?"

"You know what you're lookin' at. But you gotta make that decision yourself. Whether you give up a piece of your place to those guys or not, that's a call only you can make."

"My place." Stefanos's eyes flashed. "*My* place. I'm gonna give up a piece of my place, now, eh?"

Karras had a drink, eyed Stefanos over the rim of the glass.

Stefanos said, "You know where I come from, Karras?"

"You told me."

"My house was nothin' but a stone hut, built into the side of a hill. I slept on a dirt floor, *re*, next to a fire. My family, all of us, we lived up in the mountains above the village. *O pateras mou*, he was a shepherd, and that's where we had to stay. Away from everyone else. I lost two of my kid sisters one winter, Karras, you know about that?"

"Sure, Nick. You told me."

"Sure I did. I told you, I know." Stefanos pushed some hair off his face. "And now I got this. I got on the goddamn boat, and I came here, and I worked . . . for *this*. I got a brand-new car, and an apartment up in Mount Pleasant with steam heat in every room, and a closet full of suits. And I got this. This is *my* place. That's *my* name on the sign out front. *Katalavenis?*"

"I understand." Karras put the glass down on the counter. The sound of it cut the silence in the room.

"The thin one, the one who talked like a woman. He said he wants an answer by tonight. They're gonna come back later, after we close down."

Karras stared into Stefanos's eyes. "You know, Nick, once you start this thing, you gotta be ready to go all the way."

"I know. You let me worry about it, hokay?"

Karras shook his head. "I wish I could do that. But if you're in it, Nick, I'm in it, too."

"Forget about it."

"I'm tellin' you, I'm in."

"And I said forget it. This is my fight."

Karras glanced down at his twisted knee, then back at Stefanos. "It's mine, too."

Stefanos said, *"Entaxi."*

Stefanos picked up the broom that leaned against the cooler, tapped the end of the stick against the pressed-tin ceiling three times. He and Karras headed back to the kitchen. By the time they had gotten there, Costa had come through the door that led to the apartment upstairs. His hair was uncombed and his hands were covered with bits of meat and bone.

"What the hell you want, Niko? I'm right in the middle of cleanin' a little chicken."

"Relax. I got somethin' to tell you."

Stefanos filled Costa in. When he was done talking, Costa rubbed his hands off on his apron.

"So?" said Stefanos.

Costa smiled crookedly.

"Good," said Stefanos. "Tell your *yineka* to take in a picture show to-night, *acous?*"

"Toula hasn't been out to a movie in ten years," said Costa.

"Tell her to go out and visit a friend, then. I don't care what you tell her. Just get her the hell out of the building."

"Florek's on tonight," said Karras.

"Then go up to his apartment and give him the night off. Give it to him with pay. Tell him I said to take his *koritsi* out, the one with the red hair. Tell him I said to have a good time on me."

"And what're you gonna do?" said Karras.

"I'm gonna call Lou DiGeordano," said Stefanos.

"Now you're talkin, boss." Costa laughed sharply, clapped his hands together one time.

"Karras," said Stefanos. "What'd you use on those Japs over there in the Philippines?"

"I had an M-one."

"I'm not talkin' about your rifle, *re.* I'm talkin' about your *pistola.*"

"A forty-five."

Stefanos turned toward Costa. "How about you, *Costaki?* You need anything, before I call Lou?"

"I don't need no goddamn pistol," said Costa.

"What, you gonna face 'em with your bare hands?"

Costa shook his head. He spat on the kitchen floor.

219

29

Lou DiGeordano walked into Nick's around closing time carrying a paper grocery bag in his arms. He nodded to Six as he passed him and went straight back around the counter and into the kitchen where Stefanos and Karras were standing around drinking beer and smoking cigarettes.

"Lou," said Stefanos.

"Nick," said DiGeordano. "Karras Jr."

"Mr. DiGeordano," said Karras.

"How's your boy, Lou?" said Stefanos.

"Little Joey's good." DiGeordano stepped forward, tousled Karras's gray hair. "Good boy, like you."

Karras ran a hand through his hair, straightened it back out. He looked at DiGeordano, natty in his sharply tailored suit, a pearl-gray goose feather in the band of his hat. DiGeordano had dabbed a touch of wax in his moustache tonight; the smooth black hairs gleamed in the kitchen light. Karras smiled.

"Who's watching the front?" said DiGeordano. "The *titsune*?"

"All the customers are gone," said Stefanos. "He's all right."

"Where's Costa?"

"He's gettin' himself ready in the back."

DiGeordano looked back over the swinging doors one time, then walked across the kitchen and placed the grocery bag on the table. Karras and Stefanos formed a half-circle around him. DiGeordano reached into the bag.

"Here ya go, Karras Jr."

Karras ground his cigarette under his shoe. He took the .45 from Di-Geordano. He hefted the steel automatic in his hand. He pulled back on the receiver, straightened his gun arm, sighted down the barrel. He thumbed back the lanyard-style hammer, locked it, dry-fired the Colt into the wall.

"That okay by you?"

"Bullets," said Karras.

DiGeordano handed Karras a magazine. Karras checked the load, then palmed the magazine into the .45. He safetied the gun, measured the weight of it in his palm, holstered it behind the waistband of his trousers.

"Okay," said Karras.

DiGeordano pulled a small, blue-steeled automatic with walnut grips from the bag.

"What the hell's that?" said Stefanos.

"Double-action Beretta. Three-eighty."

"An Italian gun," said Stefanos. "I shoulda known."

"Don't worry," said DiGeordano, a light in his eyes. "Me, I keep my pistols clean. This one here, it's not gonna blow up in my face."

"Uh."

"How about you? You all set, Nick?"

Stefanos patted the front of his apron. "Yeah. I'm set real good."

Costa walked slowly into the kitchen from the warehouse. He wore a white button-down shirt pulled out over his trousers. He stood with his back against the wall, did not move his head.

"You ready?" said Stefanos.

"Sure, Niko, I'm ready. What's the plan?"

"I'm gonna get to that," said Stefanos. "But you look kinda stiff. You ain't worried or nothin', are you?"

"Me?" said Costa. "I don't give a damn nothing."

Six's head appeared over the doors to the kitchen. "Excuse me, boss. 'Bout time we locked up."

"You go ahead, Six. Take off."

Six looked the men over, grinned. "What you all fixin' to do, overthrow the gov'ment or somethin'?"

"Why?" said Stefanos. "You gonna stick around and watch?"

"Thought I might," said Six, "if this is about those lovers that was in here holdin' that gun on me the other day."

"It is," said Stefanos.

"Then I'll stay, if you don't mind. Only—"

"What?"

"It's gonna run you a little overtime."

Karras tipped his glass back to his lips and drank. The beer felt cool going down his throat.

■

Bender, the redhaired man, the big dark one, and Sanderson walked into Nick's shortly after eleven that night. The bell tinkled above the door as they moved in. Bender gave Six the eyeball as he entered, smiled a little to himself. The four of them fanned out. Standing next to Six in his tall white hat, Sanderson looked like a child.

Stefanos sat behind the counter, making entries in a ledger book covered in marbled green leather. He raised his head.

"Mr. Bender," said Stefanos.

"Mr. Nick," said Bender, rolling his *R* just slightly in faint mimicry. "Are we too late?"

"No. I got book work to do, anyhow."

Bender looked back at Six, chuckled under his breath.

"Your colored man. He looks like he ought to be standing under a tent somewhere. Did he escape from the circus?"

Stefanos did not answer.

"Because I was thinking," said Bender. "Between your giant shine and my little man Sanderson over here, the two of us have the makings of a freak show."

Bender laughed. The redhaired man with the bent nose laughed. Even Sanderson's shoulders jiggled once or twice. The big dark one in the tight suit showed no expression at all.

"Anyway," said Bender. He pulled a pint bottle from his breast pocket, unscrewed the top, had a drink. "Shall we do a little business?"

"In the back," said Stefanos.

Bender made a precise wave of his hand in the direction of the kitchen. "After you."

The four of them followed Stefanos back behind the counter and through the swinging doors. Six listened to the doors crying on their hinges. When the hinges stopped complaining he locked the front door and turned out the lights in the front of the house and extinguished the lighted sign out front. He sat back on the stool, folded his arms across his chest, and stared impassively into the darkness of the grill.

■

"Just a little bit more," said Stefanos.

"Hey, get offa me, mate," said one of the men. Stefanos guessed it was the big one.

"Christ," said the redhaired man. "I can't see nothin', same as you."

"I'll get it in a second," said Stefanos. "Jus' gotta find the light, that's all."

"Ain't you got a switch?" said Red Hair.

"I don't need a switch," said Stefanos. " . . . Here we go, I got it. Lemme just turn it a coupla times here."

Stefanos's eyes adjusted to the darkness. In outline he saw the figures of the four men converge toward the rear of the warehouse, where a sliver of light came through the doorframe from the lamp in the alley.

Stefanos rotated the bulb clockwise. The connection was made, and a harsh wave of yellow light flooded the room.

Bender was the first to see the men standing before him. Costa stepped off the pallet where he had been standing and onto the concrete floor. Karras and DiGeordano had walked from the bathroom as Stefanos turned the bulb. They stood to the right of him.

Karras kept his eyes locked on Sanderson's. Sanderson spread his short legs, let his jacket fall open. He blinked spastically, tried to hook a finger in his belt, jumbled the action.

Bender's thin upper lip twitched. He smiled.

"A surprise. I love surprises, don't you, Moon?"

He was talking to the big one in the small suit. Moon did not reply. He took a deep breath, puffed out his chest. Red Hair turned his head quickly, saw the padlock on the back door.

"It's locked, Mr. Bender."

"Then I guess we're trapped. Is that it, Mr. Nick? Are we trapped?"

Stefanos untied his apron, let it drop to the floor. He kicked the apron aside. He pulled the pearl-handled Smith & Wesson from the front of his pleated trousers, let his gun hand rest at his side. He snicked back the hammer on the thirty-eight.

Moon reached into his jacket. DiGeordano pulled the three-eighty, put one in the chamber in one fluid motion. He pointed the blue automatic at Moon.

"Hold it, Moon," said Bender. "We don't need to get ahead of ourselves here."

Karras drew the .45 from where he had wedged it in the waistband of his trousers. He flicked off the safety, pulled back on the receiver.

"Now," said Bender, "this isn't too sporting, is it? You've all pulled your

223

firearms before we've had a chance to talk. Except you, of course." He smiled at Costa. "My, you're a little fellow, too, aren't you?"

Costa made a step toward Bender.

"Costaki," said Stefanos, and Costa stayed put.

The naked bulb stopped swinging on its cord; the light settled evenly in the room.

Bender reached into his jacket. Stefanos raised the .38.

"Don't get excited," said Bender. "I'm only getting myself a drink." He pulled the pint of bourbon. He unscrewed the cap, tilted the bottle back. Air bubbles flowed up the neck.

"Mr. Bender," said Red Hair.

"Relax," said Bender. "You've got to learn how to relax." He wiped the back of his hand across his mouth. "Aaah. So, Mr. Nick. Maybe now you'd like for the two of us to sit down, have a little talk."

"I'm gonna talk," said Stefanos. "You're gonna listen."

"As you wish."

"Hokay," said Stefanos. "Here it is. You gonna put any guns you carryin' on the floor, right now. Then you gonna walk out of here, go back to your Mr. Burke. You're gonna tell him that Nick Stefanos, he don't pay no protection money to nobody. You're gonna tell him to leave me alone. If you come back, or if he comes back, or if anyone that looks like one of your boys or one of his boys—if any of 'em even walks out front of my store— that man, he's gonna die. You understand?"

Bender looked behind him, smiled at Moon. Moon smiled back. Bender turned back to Stefanos.

"Your American," said Bender, "it's not so good. Nevertheless, I do understand. The thing is, Mr. Nick, me and my boys here, we don't lay our guns down and walk away for anyone. Not for any white men I know. And especially not for a bunch of immigrant dogs like you."

No one said a word for a while after that.

And then Stefanos said, "Now you're gonna meet my men. This is Karras. This here is Lou DiGeordano. Over here is Costa."

Bender said, "I don't care to be introduced to your men. Why on earth are you telling me—"

"I thought you might wanna know."

"I might want to know what?"

"The names of the men who killed you tonight."

Bender threw his head back and laughed. The laughter was high-pitched and dramatic. Costa spat on the floor.

"Poosti," said Costa.

224

Bender's smile faded as he narrowed his eyes. "What did he call me?"

"Cocksucker," said Karras.

"Uh," said Stefanos.

Bender killed the bourbon in his pint. He tossed the bottle back over his shoulder; the neck of it caught air and made a whistling sound in the room. The bottle shattered against the brick wall.

"*Uh*," said Bender. "You hear that, Moon? All these Greeks and Italians, grunting, making noises like a bunch of animals. And these are the men that are going to kill us." He jabbed a finger roughly to his own chest. "Kill *me*."

"A buncha wogs," said Moon.

"Yes," said Bender. "Wogs. What did I tell you about these Greeks, Moon? They're one step off of niggers."

Costa moved forward. He reached behind his neck, gripped the handle of the machete, pulled it free from where it was sheathed beneath the back of his shirt. He raised it above his head; the blade flashed in the light.

Bender gasped. Costa brought the machete down violently, screamed as he did. The blade splayed the flesh at the base of Bender's neck, severed the carotid artery, cut diagonally into Bender's spine. Blood geysered, splashed across the naked bulb. Bender crumpled, his arms dancing wildly at his side.

Karras was the first to fire. His shot blew Sanderson's white hat and the top of his scalp clean off. Karras kept firing, pinned Sanderson to the warehouse wall with the bullets of his .45. He could feel the power of Stefanos's and DiGeordano's guns exploding around him then, could see the red-haired pug and the one called Moon blown off their feet, twisting horribly from the force of the lead. He could see the rounds sparking off the bricks, the ejecting shells, the men going down even as they reached for their undrawn weapons, their figures gray now, floating in the cloud of gunsmoke that had fallen in the room.

Then there was the click of a hammer falling on an empty chamber; the heavy exhalation of a man's last breath; and the thin sound of a copper casing rolling across the concrete floor.

"Karras," said Stefanos.

But Karras was already limping toward Sanderson. He stepped over the body of the pug, dead as Roosevelt, his red hair wet and matted with the burgundy of his own blood. Karras kicked Sanderson in the face. He kicked him again, loosing something thick and chunked from the pulpy area at the top of his head. Karras brought his foot back once again, was stopped by a meaty hand gripping his arm.

"Karras," said Stefanos, in a quiet way. "You can only kill him one time."

Karras stepped back.

Costa put his foot on Bender's face, pulled the machete free.

Lou DiGeordano went to Moon. The big man arched his back, struggled to take in air. DiGeordano touched the muzzle of the .380 to the center of Moon's chest, pulled the trigger. A spray of blood caught DiGeordano as he turned his head.

"Sonofa*bitch*," said DiGeordano.

"Here," said Stefanos, tossing his apron, which he had picked up off the floor. DiGeordano caught it, wiped his face.

The color had drained from Costa's complexion. "I'm gonna get that butcher's paper from the kitchen," he said.

He returned a few minutes later, Six walking behind him. Six stopped cold when he saw the bodies. He took in the blood and flesh showered on the brick wall.

"Anybody come by out front?" said Stefanos.

"Uh-uh," said Six.

DiGeordano went through Bender's pockets, found an envelope and some keys. Costa stripped the others of their effects while DiGeordano threw the keys to Six.

"Here ya go, Six. You see what they drove in with?"

Six nodded. "Late model Ford."

"Get it. Bring it around to the alley and park it by the back door."

"I'll do that."

"And then I'm gonna need your help," said Costa. "I'm gonna need a strong man like you to help me cut these bastards up."

"That ain't exactly in my contract," said Six.

"Go on," said Stefanos. "You did enough. Bring the car to the alley and get on home."

Six went back to the front of the house. DiGeordano opened the envelope, examined the contents.

"I got some tickets to a show here. Some kinda play or somethin'. Somethin' called *Hamlet*."

"I'll take those," said Karras, and he slipped the bloody envelope inside his shirt.

Stefanos took his own set of keys out and removed the padlock from the back door. He opened the door a bit to let out the smell of cordite and death. A couple of cats slipped in through the opening and went to the bodies. One of the cats jumped up on Bender's chest, touched its nose to

226

the crimson canyon between Bender's shoulder and neck. Costa pushed the cat away.

"Lousy *gatas*," said Costa.

"What're you gonna do with 'em?" said Stefanos.

"I'm gonna make the fish happy tonight, Niko, that's what I'm gonna do. Don't worry about nothin', hear? I'm gonna take care of these guys, and the *caro*, too. Don't you worry about nothin'."

"I'm not worried," said Stefanos. But he was already thinking of what God did to men who took other men's lives.

Karras released the empty magazine from the Colt. He slid the magazine into the pocket of his trousers.

"Mr. DiGeordano," he said.

"Yeah, boy."

"You got any more ammo for this forty-five?"

"It's in the bag."

"How about its holster?"

"The same bag."

"You don't mind if I hang onto this gun for a while, do you?"

"Sure, Karras Jr. You go ahead."

Karras hefted the Colt in his palm, wrapped his fingers tightly around the grip. It felt good there, fitted in his hand.

30

■■■■ The next morning was a Sunday, and Peter Karras went to church. He accompanied Eleni, little Dimitri, and his mother, who wore a black dress with stocking anklets and black orthopedic shoes. Karras had not been inside the church since the baptism of his son, over one year ago.

Stepping into the narthex, Karras saw several of the parents and some of the children he had grown up with, now with children of their own, and he nodded cordially to those who nodded at him but did not engage them in conversation. A few of the old *grias* stared unashamedly at his twisted knee and whispered among themselves. Karras paid them no mind. He lighted an orange candle for his father, crossed himself, then kissed the *icona* and had a seat with his family in a pew to the right of the altar toward the back of the church.

In the thirties, when Karras was still a child, the men took their seats on the right side of the church and the woman took theirs on the left. Karras had always sat on the left with his mother, as his father had rarely attended service. He was reminded of this watching Dimitri sitting comfortably between his mother and grandmother in the pew.

Father Laloussis performed the liturgy, the glass in his wire-rimmed spectacles occasionally flashing in the light. Laloussis had an unremarkable singing voice and was not particularly dynamic, but he had been attentive to Georgia Karras after her husband's death, and Karras had thought him to be a pretty fair priest as far as priests went. Karras listened to the liturgy, closed his eyes occasionally to enjoy the choir, and took in the pleasant smell of the incense smoke that hovered heavily in the church. He did not care to tax his mind over the meaning in the spoken verse or in those words being sung. But when Laloussis brought out the communion cup, Karras went dutifully forward to take what he had been told to be the body and blood of Christ, and he drank the wine and ate the bread, and crossed himself as he backed away, because he thought that a man who had killed another man the night before should at least hedge his bets. He sat back down in the pew and tasted the *antithoron* that he held in his hand. Laloussis went into his sermon, spoken in Greek; Karras looked around the room.

Perry Angelos was up front in his usual spot with Helen and their two little girls. Behind them sat Mr. and Mrs. Nicodemus, Mrs. Nicodemus dressed entirely in black, six years after Billy's death. Next to the Nicodemuses sat Nick Kendros, who had owned and operated the Woodward Grill, near the D.C. stock exchange, where men had stood on platforms writing the latest figures on a board. Karras knew Kendros's daughter, a girl named Ruby, and he thought that she was pretty nice. When Karras and his friends had gone into the grill as children, Kendros, a short, stocky man with a rug of black hair and huge, gentle eyes, had always greeted them the same way, in his rich, enunciated, theatrical voice: "Welcome to the Wall Street of Washington, boys!" The place was New York modern, and air-conditioned like many of the movie houses around town. Nick Kendros had often treated Karras and his friends to lunch; it was not unusual for Kendros to bring a man on his uppers in off the street and serve him a cup of coffee or a hot bowl of soup.

And it wasn't just Perry and the Nicodemuses and Nick Kendros whom Karras knew. Karras scanned the pews, realized that he knew the names or recognized nearly everyone in the church, knew them from his own days in Sunday school or from the public schools he had attended or from visiting their businesses, food service establishments mostly, scattered throughout D.C.

There were other times he'd see them all together like this, too. There was the annual picnic at Marshall Hall, which he had attended last summer. He had caught the *SS Wilson* at the 7th Street wharves with his family, and they had taken the boat down the Potomac and gotten off on the Maryland side of the river across from Mount Vernon. On the boat, the Greeks had carried their food in baskets, roasting pans filled with lambs and flat trays of *pastitso* and bowls of *salata choriatiki*. Once the boat docked, the Greeks would rush off to get the choicest picnic tables, and there would be potato-sack races, and rides on the roller coaster, and dancing to music performed by a band of musicians playing bouzoukias and cymbaloms and clarinets. The older men would sit at the tables and get served by their wives while they drank a little ouzo or *mastica* and played cards, while the younger men, those that had been Americanized, stayed with their women and children. Karras's father had been alive for that last picnic at Marshall Hall. He had been one of the card players, and Karras had sat there with him at the table, ignoring Eleni and his son.

Karras looked down the pew at Dimitri, whose hand was locked in Eleni's.

His eye wandered to the lovely young woman in front of him in the next pew. He bent forward slightly to see if he could catch her smell. There was a raised mole on the bridge of her exposed shoulder; Karras imagined his tongue on the mole, and how it would taste. He glanced over her shoulder to her long, thin hands folded in her lap, and he imagined the way those hands would feel, caressing him, stroking his cock. As the woman turned her head to the side, Karras studied the curl of her lips and her slightly open mouth. He imagined her lipstick smeared from his kiss, and wondered how her mouth would look, if it would be open slightly as it was now, as her breath became short and she began to come.

Watching this woman, and the two or three others he had singled out since the service began, Karras suddenly remembered the one thing he had liked about sitting in church. And he wondered if the other men around him looked at the women in the church and shared similar black thoughts.

Who *were* these men? He thought of these Greek-Americans, who came to church each Sunday with their families, who worked hard as their fathers had, who knew what it was to make the full commitment that it took to be a man, who understood how difficult it was to stay on the path, and how easy it could be to stumble, yet in the end kept right to it. And Karras wondered, where did *I* begin to stumble? Why didn't *I* stay right like them? How did I become *this?*

"Goddamn you, Pop," he muttered under his breath. Then he crossed himself and shut his eyes tightly, realizing that he had just cursed his dead father in the house of God.

■

After the service the congregation gathered out on the stone steps in front of the church, visiting, greeting one another and exchanging pleasantries, but not for long, as the day was clear but biting cold. Eleni and Dimitri and Georgia Karras stood on the corner where 8th crossed L, Dimitri circling the lamppost there, his fingers tracing its iron ridges. They were waiting for Peter Karras, who had been stopped by Perry and Helen Leonides at the top of the steps.

Perry and Karras shook hands.

"Your family looks great, Perry," said Karras.

"Yours too," said Perry.

Karras smiled at Helen, who held their toddler Diana, little Evthokia standing at her side. Helen, shapely as ever but with a pleasing touch of age in her face, a fan-shaped spray of lines coming off her eyes. Helen smiled back, a drop of pity now in the look she gave to Karras as she scanned his gray hair and the cocked posture he had learned to adopt when shifting his weight off the bad knee.

"Perry," said Helen. "It's cold for the *pethia.*"

"Take them to the car, sweetheart, I'll be there in a minute."

Helen leaned forward, kissed Karras on the cheek. "*Adio,* Pete."

"Take care of yourself, Helen."

Perry and Karras watched Helen and the children cross the street, head for a '48 Packard Super 8 sedan parked along the curb.

"Nice car."

Perry blushed. "Lotta chrome, Pete. You think it's too much?"

"Don't be bashful, chum. You work hard, you deserve to give yourself and your family nice things. You get that second store opened yet?"

"Last month. I'm puttin' in some hours now. Between that and the house we just put a contract on—"

"You bought a house?"

"Yeah, a little bungalow out in Silver Spring. If everything goes through all right, we're moving in a couple of weeks."

"Leavin' the city, huh?"

"For the kids. Everything's for the kids now, right?"

Karras looked at Perry: soft around the middle, no hair left on top, a pair of heavy, black-framed glasses resting on his thick nose. Not even thirty years old, but already looking like his dad. Well, Perry had always looked like a middle-aged man, even as a kid. It suited him, somehow.

"*Ella,* Pete!" yelled Eleni from the corner.

"You start walkin'," yelled Karras, "I'll catch up to you!" He turned back to Perry. "So, you got a new car, a successful business, a new house, a beautiful wife and a couple of beautiful kids. No wonder you look so unhappy."

Perry laughed. "Aw, come on, Pete, stop ribbin' me. You know I couldn't be happier."

"I know it, chum. I'm happy for you, too."

Perry shuffled his feet. "Only, I wish life wasn't moving so damn fast, Pete. I mean, I never even see you anymore."

"Yeah, it's been too long."

"Maybe you and me could hook up together one night. Go see the fights down at U-Line or something."

Helen honked the horn of the Packard. From the steps they could see her in the front seat, waving Perry forward.

"You better get going," said Karras.

Perry put a hand on Karras's arm. "I'm serious, Pete. I haven't sat down and talked with you since your father's funeral."

Karras looked around at the other men and women on the steps, lowered his voice. "You don't need to be hangin' around with me, Perry. You're doing fine without me, understand? You don't want to be gumming things up for yourself at this stage in the game."

"Aw, knock it off, Pete. Quit kiddin' me."

"I'm tellin' it to you straight."

Perry removed his glasses, folded them, slipped them in the side pocket of his topcoat. "It's funny, Pete, the way you look at yourself. That's one thing. And then the other thing is, the way people look at you."

"What're you talkin' about?"

"You think I'm some kind of altar boy, always doing the right thing, getting the right things back in return. Well, I have been pretty lucky, I guess. And that's the way that you see *me*. But the truth is, growing up, *you* were the guy I wanted to be. I wanted to get my pants dirty once in a while, just like you. I never could play stickball like you, make small talk like you, make time with the girls like you. Even during the war, I had desk duty, and you were over there doing your part, putting your life on the line like a man ought to do. As far back as when we were kids, I'd see you and your father walking down the street, and I'd think, those are a couple of real tough characters. I knew . . . I'm telling you, I knew, even then, that I'd never be that kind of man."

"My father," said Karras. "Yeah, I'm just like my father, all right. I drink too much, and I got no ambition, and I treat my wife like some kind of maid, like she's some kind of hired help. Most nights, I can't seem to make it home for dinner—"

"Pete—"

"—and I don't even know how to love my own son." Karras's voice broke. "Just like my father, Perry. Yeah, I'm some kind of man, all right. I'm so much of a man that one woman's not enough for me. I even got a woman on the side—"

"Goddamnit, Pete," said Perry, avoiding Karras's eyes. "I don't want to know."

Karras got close to Perry's face. "And you always wanted to be the kind of man I am. Why, that's good for about a million laughs, Perry. The truth of it is, you're more of a man than I'll ever be. You always have been. Don't you get it?"

Helen honked the horn once again. Perry looked at the car, waved his hand. When he turned back, Karras could see a redness in Perry's eyes.

"I better take off. I haven't even read the Sunday paper yet. Gotta get to those funny pages. Skeezix is out at the family farm with Nina and Chipper right now. Chipper thinks you can make milk by mixing bran and water, see—"

"Save it, Perry. I haven't read 'Gasoline Alley' in over ten years."

"I still keep up with it, I guess."

Karras smiled. "Go on. Go on and get up with your family."

"*Adio*, Pete."

"*Yasou*, Perry."

Perry Angelos took the steps down to the sidewalk, crossed the street. When he reached the car, he stopped, put his hand to the handle, looked back. Eleni, Dimitri, and Georgia Karras were walking slowly northwest, in the direction of their apartment. Peter Karras was limping down the sidewalk in the opposite direction, heading south. Perry got into the driver's seat, turned the ignition, and pulled away from the curb. He gave the Packard gas, headed uptown.

"What's wrong?" said Helen.

"Nothing," said Perry. "The wind must have got to my eyes."

"You better put on your glasses, honey."

"All right."

Perry got the glasses from his pocket, slipped them on his face. Helen scooted over on the seat, leaned her head on his shoulder.

"Pete didn't look so good, did he?"

He looked like it's all closing in on him. Like he's walked into an alley that's all bricked up.

Perry said, "He looked all right."

Helen kissed Perry softly behind the ear. He smiled.

"What'd you do that for?"

"I'm happy, that's all."

Perry said, "I'm happy, too."

Evthokia slapped Diana on the arm in the backseat. There was an argument, and Diana began to cry.

233

"All right, you two," said Helen. "Cut it out!"

"Let 'em play," said Perry, listening to the emotion in his daughters' voices, liking the sound. He put his arm around Helen. He pulled her close.

■

Vera Gardner opened the door. She stood in the frame in her half-slip and black brassiere. She held a tumbler full of scotch and ice in one hand. She put the tumbler to her mouth and drank.

"Little early for that, isn't it?"

"I suppose. You want one?"

"More than one."

Vera laughed, wiggled her foot: a calfskin, platform heel with a slave-bracelet strap. "You like?"

"Seymour Troy. I saw 'em down at Hahn's."

"Twelve ninety-five. But I had to, Pete."

"Let me in, baby, before you catch your death."

"Don't you like me like this?"

"I like you every which way," said Karras. "I'll like you even more when we get inside."

He entered the room, kicked the door shut behind him. He threw his fedora on the bed. Beneath the bed, he could see the handles of Vera's suitcases protruding from behind the sheets.

"Scotch all right?"

"Fine."

She fixed him a drink from a tray she had set up, and carried it across the room. He took it, drank hungrily. Vera got close to him, took the tumbler from his hand, placed it on the dresser. Karras studied her jittery eyes; she was halfway lit, and there were dirt trails on her face.

"You been cryin'."

"I guess."

"About what?"

"Things."

She crushed her mouth against his, kissed him desperately.

"Hold me, Pete."

Karras said, "I will."

■

Karras opened his eyes. He yawned, read the time off the rectangular face of his Hamilton: almost two o'clock. He got up on one elbow, rolled onto

234

his side, leaned into Vera. His finger traced a circle around the cherry-red nipple of her right breast. God, she had those perfect tits—the most beautiful he'd ever touched.

Vera swiped dimly at a tickle on her nose. Karras watched her eyes jerking around behind closed lids. She moaned a little, moved her lips, tossed her head from side to side. A line of sweat had formed on her upper lip. The sheets beneath her were wet, and they were wet and slick from their lovemaking as well, just a half-hour before. Vera's slightly rank perspiration and the tang of booze hung in the air.

Her head suddenly came up off the pillow. She looked at Karras with wide and questioning eyes, as if she were seeing him for the first time that day.

"Relax, sweetheart. It's just you and me. You were dreaming, that's all."

Vera sighed, dropped her head down on the pillow. Karras draped his arm over her, fitted himself between her thighs. He listened to the tick of his Hamilton and felt the drum of Vera's heart pulsing through his fingers. He went to sleep.

∎

Karras woke alone on the bed. The light had changed in the room. He glanced at his wristwatch, saw that another half hour had passed.

He sat up and let his feet touch the floor. He scratched under his balls and brushed a dry patch of white from the inside of his thigh. Vera stood naked in front of the window frame with her back to him, staring at the gray window, completely steamed over from the cold outside and the bowl of water which Vera kept on the radiator below the sill. Vera smoked a cigarette with one hand and in the other held a tumbler of scotch over ice. An ashtray sat on the radiator next to the glass bowl. Vera tapped off a bit of ash which drifted down and missed the tray.

"Hey, kiddo," said Karras, but she did not turn around.

Karras got up, went to his suit jacket laid neatly across the miniature chesterfield by the makeup stand. He drew an envelope and his deck of Luckies from the inside pocket. He lighted a cigarette and limped across the room. Karras put his hand on Vera's shoulder.

"Been up long?"

"A little while, I guess."

"Here ya go, Vera. Thought you might like these."

He put the envelope in her hand. She studied the envelope and then its contents, smiled oddly, blinked her eyes.

"It's *Hamlet*," said Karras helpfully. "One of those Shakespeare plays."

"Oh, really?" she said mockingly.

"Laurence Olivier's in it."

"But there's blood on this envelope, Pete. There's a little blood on these tickets, too."

Karras chuckled unconvincingly. "I know. I was showin' them off to Nick Stefanos at the grill. You know how he's always cuttin' his fingers, slicing up those tomatoes of his—"

"That's nice. That was real nice of you, Pete. Were you thinking of coming along?" Her tone was queer.

"You know me and plays . . . I thought maybe you and your friends might use 'em."

"You're right, my friends might like to go at that. But the truth is, I won't be able to use them myself." She dropped the tickets carelessly on the radiator. One of them slipped through a gap in the tubes and fell to the floor.

"Why, you got other plans?"

"Plans? Yes, I've got plans."

Karras ran a hand along the curve of her hip. He put his cigarette to his mouth, dragged deeply. His exhale streamed toward the window, exploded as it hit the glass. He felt her tremble beneath his touch.

"What's wrong with you, baby?"

Vera took a drink. Her teeth made a clicking sound against the tumbler. She set the glass down.

"I was just thinking, Pete. You know how I do. About the bomb."

"That again."

"Yes."

"Well, what about it?"

"They say the reds have it now. Do you think they do?"

"Hell, Vera, I don't know."

"If they had it . . . if they had it and decided to use it, I mean . . . they'd drop it right here on D.C., wouldn't they. D.C. would be the first place they'd send it, isn't that right?"

"Christ," said Karras.

Vera drew some smoke from her cigarette. The smoke dribbled from her lips. "You were over there, Pete, when they dropped that bomb."

"So?"

"You know what it did."

"It ended the war."

"I'm talking about what it *did*. To human beings, Pete. To children. They say it turned them into little lumps of coal. Boiled their organs from the inside out—"

"Vera," said Karras, speaking softly. "The bomb ended the war. That's what it did. That's what it did for me and all the other GIs who were lucky enough to make it home. And it couldn't have come quicker. You know, after Leyte, they sent us back to Guam. Lambs for the slaughter, baby, keeping us fed and rested for the invasion of Japan. Towards the end we were out there on those troop ships, just waiting to go in. By then, most of us had been in combat, so in some ways it was worse than our first landing, because by then we knew what to expect. By then we had seen all that death. And we knew the Japanese would fight to the end—theirs and ours—on their own turf. Most of us figured we were never coming back alive. What I'm telling you is, I know everything I need to know about that bomb. That bomb, it took a lot of lives to save even more. And that's all I need to know."

Vera made a fist. She pressed it to the window, swirled it around in the condensation. The action opened a peephole through the fog to the outside. She stared through the hole.

"You ever see for yourself what those bombs do, Pete?"

"No."

"Natalie has."

"Natalie," said Karras, with unmasked disgust.

"That's right. She was on the Manhattan Project. She saw the films."

"You're talking about Trinity."

"Not Trinity. Trinity was just sand and scrub and desert. I'm talking about another test they filmed, where they let one go near some ghost town or something."

"Vera—"

"Natalie told me how it was. How this old town, it was standing there, still as a picture. And then there was a flash, and the town was just gone. Like a big wind had come along and flattened it all out, blown it all away. Like a big blowdown, Pete. There one minute and then just gone. I'm telling you, Pete, sometimes I stand here at night and look out this window, and I imagine that I see that flash, and then everything coming toward me, the cars, the buildings, the bodies, everything, coming at me at a thousand miles an hour in one big rush. And then nothing, Pete, not even black. Less than black."

"Vera." Karras turned her around. He took the cigarette from her hand and crushed it in the ashtray. He held her clammy, rigid body against his.

"I'm sorry to go on about it, Pete. It's just that I'm afraid."

"I know it, baby. So am I."

But he wasn't afraid. He knew that he should be, but he was not. In the end, Karras feared the image of himself as a useless old cripple more than he feared death. And for a moment, looking over Vera's shoulder through the clearing in the steamed window, he began to visualize this thing that Vera spoke of, this maelstrom of sound and flesh and architecture, hurtling toward him in one screaming, final rush. And for that one crazy moment, Karras had the peculiar wish to see this blowdown for himself. He knew with certainty that it might be pure and absolute horror. But he had the feeling that it could be something beautiful, too.

31

Recevo blew into his open pack of Raleighs. A cigarette shot out of the deck. He pulled it free with his mouth, struck a straight match off the sole of his shoe.

"Nothing yet," said Burke.

Recevo lighted the smoke. "That phone hasn't jumped since the last time you asked, Mr. Burke."

"That swish," said Reed. "I knew we shouldn't of sent him over to the Greek's."

Recevo sideglanced Reed, pacing the floor. "It's only been since last night."

"You'd think he would've called," said Burke, "to let us know, at least." Burke turned to Gearhart, stuffed into his chair, his fingers laced across the balloon of his lap. "What do you think, Gearhart? Is there cause for alarm?"

Gearhart shrugged, moved his turtle eyes curiously beneath their lids.

"Maybe he skipped," said Reed.

"Without his compensation?" said Burke. "I don't think so. And Bender is a peacock who likes to show his colors. If things had gone off right, he would have been right over here, bragging about the details, embellishing the story."

Burke poured bourbon from a decanter into a glass. Recevo watched him take it in one swig.

"There's something wrong," said Burke.

"Maybe not," said Recevo. "Maybe they turned Stefanos, and Bender just slept in. He had tickets to that show tonight, remember? Maybe he's getting himself ready for that."

Burke poured two more fingers of bourbon.

Reed dragged on his cigarette, snapped off some ash. "I don't know why we're dancin' around about it. What we ought to do, we ought to go over to that grill right now and settle it right. Just us, like we shoulda—"

"They'd take you apart," said Recevo.

Reed's eyes flared. "Oh, so they'd take me apart, huh? Is that it?"

"That's right."

"Who? That sawed-off little Greek, the one with all the hair? Or maybe your buddy Karras. You tellin' me that gimp pal of yours would take me apart?"

Recevo didn't respond. Burke sipped his drink.

Burke said, "Reed's got a point, Joe, in his own primitive way. We went outside of our own backyard to solve a problem that we should have handled ourselves. Perhaps we should pick up Karras, have a talk with him, see if he can't act as an intermediary in all this mess."

"We're getting ahead of ourselves, Mr. Burke. We don't even know if there is a problem, not yet."

"I'm supposed to just sit around and wait?"

"Give it another day," said Recevo. "I got this feeling, see? By tomorrow, it's all gonna work itself out."

Peter Karras stood on the corner of 7th and T, shook his wrist out of his topcoat, looked at his watch. He squinted in the darkness to read its face: 5:45. This time of year, night fell early in the city. Karras adjusted his fedora, buried his hands in his pockets, walked south.

A thick Negro in a camel-hair overcoat and brown suit did not step off as Karras approached. Karras walked around the man. He passed the Off Beat Club, a favorite of slumming jazz musicians, and the Seventh and T Club, a kicked-up version of "St. Louis Blues" coming from its open door. A Negro couple moved quickly toward him, and Karras stepped out of their way. There were not so many folks out, as it was early yet, and Sunday night. Sunday in D.C. meant beer and light wine, but that did not apply to the city's blind pigs and bottle clubs. Karras had one particular address in mind.

He found it in the middle of 7th, near the Club Harlem, a row house with a simple walk-up to a concrete stoop. He took the steps, knocked on the forest-green door, waited for the speak slot to open. It did, and a set of perfectly round eyes appeared in the space.

Then a deep voice: "Yeah?"

"How about a drink?"

"You got a membership card, boss?

"Do I need one?"

"Yeah."

"How's this?" Karras passed a couple of bucks through the slot.

"It's startin' to look like one."

Karras slipped another dollar through. The door opened. A big Negro with a pockmarked face stood before him.

The Negro grinned. "Tell you the truth, boss, I don't think this here's your kinda place. But things been kinda slow tonight, and I ain't had nary a bit of fun. So why don't you step on inside."

Karras walked by the bouncer, heard the door close behind him. He noticed that the windows had been bricked up. Tobacco smoke hung midchest in the room, cut with the smell of perfume and something else that was heavy and sweet. A phonograph played a Louis Jordan record— "Is You Is or Is You Ain't My Baby"—rather loudly; Karras recognized the tune as a favorite at Nick's grill. A Negro man slow-dragged a woman to the Jordan near a table of stud players by the far wall. The woman wore a sequined cap and a low-cut gown. Her grin was sloppy and her right eye dropped lower than the left. She was young and happy and half in the bag.

The place was no more than a fancy living room with a long bar against the north wall. Three Negroes in suit and tie sat at the bar. The bar was tended by a bow-tied Negro wearing red suspenders over a thinly striped shirt with French cuffs. All of them gave Karras the fisheye as he limped across the floor. He removed his topcoat, placed his Luckies on the mahogany, and had a seat.

"What you gonna have?" said the tender.

Karras could see no bottles on the shelf. "What's the choice?"

"Gin."

"I'll have gin, then," said Karras.

The tender reached below the bar, retrieved an unlabeled bottle, and poured liquor to the lip. He waited for Karras. Karras took a healthy swallow, stifled a cough: raw ethyl cut with juniper. The tender smiled. Karras lighted a smoke.

He looked down the bar. At the very end, a tall, thin man sat staring at Karras, smoking a cigarette, curiosity shading his face. The man looked like a brown mantis. Near him sat a light-skinned man in a fancy hat. He also stared at Karras. The hatred in his eyes was uncomplicated, simple as a fist. Karras looked at the man to his right. He knew the man from Nick's, a friend of the green-eyed record player whom Florek always chatted up.

241

The colored guys in Nick's, they called the guy Dinky, or Winky, some shit like that. *Pinky*. Yeah, Pinky, that was it.

"Hey," said Karras. "Pinky, right?"

Karras leaned to the right, extended his hand. The one he knew as Pinky ignored the gesture, got off his barstool. He walked slowly to the table of stud players, had a seat.

The tender leaned his elbow on the bar. "What you think, you was gonna walk in here, make a few friends?"

"But I know that man," said Karras.

"Not in here, you don't. Maybe in your own world, you do. But that man's nothin' but a stranger to you in here."

The Louis Jordan number ended. The phonograph's tone arm reached the end of the record and made a hissing sound in the bar. No one made a move to lift the tone arm off the wax.

"I'm here to see DeAngelo Ray," said Karras.

"Boolshit," said the man in the funny hat. He slid off his stool and walked toward Karras.

The tender said, "Finish your drink. Finish it and get on out of here. I ain't got nothin' for you and I ain't got nothin against you, understand? But you don't belong here. You stick around here another city minute, you're gonna get stuck for sure. And nobody in this joint's gon' do a damn thing about it 'cept sit around and watch you bleed."

Karras glanced toward the door, twenty feet away: the bouncer had leaned his back against it, folded his arms. Karras turned to the tender.

"The name is Pete Karras. Tell Mr. Ray I'm here to see him."

"I'll be gotdamn," said the light-skinned man in the fancy hat. "This motherfucker, he just don't listen."

Karras could feel the man's hot breath on his face. In his side vision, he saw Fancy Hat reach into his jacket. A voice from the end of the bar stopped him.

"Ike," said the tall thin man. "Back away." Then he spoke to the tender. "You just keep things real good and cool for a minute or so till I get back."

The tall thin man stood and walked through a door that led to the back of the house. Fancy Hat went back to his stool. Karras stared straight ahead, finished his drink, smoked down his cigarette. The tall thin Negro returned, tapped Karras on the shoulder.

"All right, Karras. Go on straight back and have your talk with Mr. Ray. You got five minutes to do it."

"Thanks," said Karras. But the man had walked away.

Karras draped his topcoat over his arm, slipped his cigarettes into his trouser pocket. He left a dollar on the bar and limped toward the door. He went around the dancing couple, who were still at it though the music had stopped. The stud players and the one Karras knew as Pinky did not look up as he passed.

Karras entered a room through an open door. He closed the door behind him. A dapper young Negro sat behind a desk, sipping from a goblet of brandy and smoking a thin cigar. On the desk sat a water chaser over ice. The Negro wore a double-breasted slate suit with a chalk stripe running through the slate, and a red carnation in the lapel. A crescent scar curved around his left eye and made a clean white slice through his brow.

"You're Karras," said the man.

"Pete Karras." He leaned across the desk, shook the man's manicured hand. He had a seat in a wine leather chair in front of the desk.

"My name is DeAngelo Ray."

"You're the man I wanted to see."

"So I heard."

A windowed door was situated behind the desk giving to a view of a screened porch and then an alley. Karras could see the shadow of a tall figure moving out on the porch. Then there was the sound of some crazy kind of music, a saxophone dancing all over the place, brushed cymbals and bass. Colored jazz, thought Karras, and damn if I can figure it out.

Ray jerked his head in the direction of the porch. "That would be Junior. We ran an outlet out there so he could listen to his records. He does love his New York jazz. But the folks out front, the cardplayers and the studs and the ladies and all the rest, they go for that straight jump. So Junior, he sits out there in the cold, and he listens to his music."

"Who's Junior?"

"The gentleman that saved your life."

"He saved it, huh?"

"Ike would've opened you up from ear to ear."

"Colored man kills a white man in this town, he's gonna do life if he doesn't fry first."

"Ike wasn't too worried."

"Neither was I."

"You're tough, Karras."

"I didn't claim that. I just knew that it wasn't my day."

DeAngelo Ray allowed a smile, looked Karras over. "That limp of yours looks pretty real. You in the war?"

"The Pacific."

"Army?"

243

"Marine Corps."

"Kill many men?"

"I killed a few."

Ray sighed. "I was over in Europe myself. Colored outfit. Had us digging latrines for the enlisted men. I envy you, Karras. I would've liked to have killed a few myself, 'specially when I got a good look at some of the prisoners. Why, those German boys, they were some of the palest motherfuckers I've ever seen."

"It's a long life. Maybe you'll get your chance."

Ray threw his head back and laughed. Karras saw gold fillings in the man's teeth.

"Yes," said Ray, "I really wanted to do my part for my country over there. They just didn't seem to want to trust me with one of those M-ones. Why do you suppose that is?"

"On account of you might have tripped or something, jerked your trigger finger, shot one of your lieutenants by accident in the back of the head."

"I might have, at that. I never thought of it, to tell you the truth." Ray snapped his fingers. "You could have a point."

"So you got a raw deal," said Karras.

"Yes. They gave us colored boys quite a raw deal."

"I wouldn't take it too hard. Things look like they're gonna start to turn around for you people soon."

Ray sipped brandy, eyed Karras over the glass. "And what makes you think that I would want 'things' to turn around?"

"I don't know. I thought—"

"You thought. Well, from where you sit, you're right. There's a lot of folks out there, thinkin' the same way. They're talking about equality, equal rights, all of that. And if they want that, then fine. Me, I'm a successful businessman. In *my* world, Karras. I got my own music, my own women, my own way of dressin'—my own *style*. Any place where I really want to be, I can go. I go where I want and I see who I want to see. When I was a kid in this town, over in Southwest, I rarely saw a white man or woman in my neighborhood. When I did, it was like I was looking at somethin' that flew in from another planet. You people looked different, talked different. You even smelled different. And I grew up just fine. So why would I want to change that now? Why would I want to sit next to you in a soda bar now? What's that really gonna do for *me*?"

"I have no idea."

"That's right, Karras. You haven't got a clue." Ray puffed lightly on his

244

cigar. He rolled a cylinder of ash off in the tray. "So what can I do for you this evening?"

Karras took the photograph of Lola Florek from his topcoat, tossed it on the desk. It slid neatly in front of Ray. Ray picked it up.

"Go on and say your piece," said Ray. "You're near out of time."

"The girl's name is Lola Florek. My source tells me you organize parties for out-of-town businessmen. That you're a middleman for Yellow Roberts. That you recruit the entertainment—white whores for colored men. Reefer and gin parties, like that. I thought you might have seen the girl."

"Your source."

"A cop I know."

"This cop on my payroll?"

"I wouldn't know. And if I knew, I wouldn't care. And I wouldn't sell him out."

Ray sipped brandy, chased it with water. "Tell me about the punchboard."

"Small-town girl imported to D.C. Hooked on hop from what I can make out. The hop's what keeps her tied to her pimp. Her brother's a friend of mine. He's looking for her, and I'm helping him out."

"Why?"

"I haven't figured that out yet."

"What's your cut of this?"

"No cut."

"Tough nut like you? It ain't like a man like you to be ridin' a white horse."

Karras shrugged. "What can I tell you, Ray? I been ridin' that black one all my life. Thought I'd try something else, see how it felt. You know, throw the changeup ball. Just to keep things interesting."

Ray laughed. "You're somethin', man."

"Yeah, I'm somethin', all right."

"And," said Ray, "you're a lucky man. 'Cause I'm about to help you out tonight. See, Karras, you show me this picture, and I'm lookin' at it, and I realize, all of a sudden—I *know* this girl."

Karras felt his heart jump.

"See, this girl, she was at one of my parties the other night. Got treated kind of rough by this boy from South Side Chicago. When I saw what he'd done, I had to tell that boy that he ain't welcome back. 'Cause I don't stand to see a woman treated that way. Don't matter to me whether it's a lady or a punchboard, neither, understand what I mean?"

Karras nodded.

245

"Now, I thought when her pimp came to pick her up, he was gonna be mad, do somethin' about it. Even expected some trouble out of him. But this pimp, all he did was, he yelled somethin' fierce at this poor girl for complainin' about how she got all ripped up inside. And I just didn't care for that. 'Cause you got to take care of your women, see. This pimp, that's a man I'd never do business with again."

"What's the man's name?"

"White man. Goes by the name of Morgan."

"Morgan—he retails women?"

"That's his business."

"You got a phone number where I can reach him?"

"I'll do better than that. I got an address for you, too."

Ray checked a notebook in his desk drawer. He wrote down the information on a sheet of paper, pushed it across the desk to Karras. Karras read it, folded it, slipped it and the photograph in his jacket pocket. He stood up, shook himself into his topcoat.

"I won't take up any more of your time."

"Yeah, you better go. And don't be comin' back around my place either, hear? You just happened to catch me on one of my generous nights."

They shook hands.

"Leave by the back door. You don't want to be runnin' back into Ike."

"See you later."

"I don't think so."

"Thanks, Ray."

"Go on and go. And Karras—"

"Yeah."

"Don't forget to thank Junior, too, on your way out."

Karras opened the back door, stepped down onto the porch. He pulled the door shut. The tall thin Negro, the one called Junior, sat in a weathered wood rocker, the brim of his brown hat pulled down, throwing shade upon his eyes. A lit reefer cigarette rested between Junior's fingers. His hand tapped along the arm of the rocker to the saxophone coming from the phonograph set by his side. Karras couldn't pull a tune from the melody to save his life, but that saxophone, he had to admit, it did sound right.

Next to the phonograph sat a kind of open briefcase holding records. A cord ran from the phonograph to a makeshift outlet set in the wall. Karras had a seat on a schoolroom chair near the rocker. He looked out into the dark alley, colored faintly from the pale yellow lights spilling out from the back windows of the adjoining houses.

"Thanks," said Karras.

"Say what?"

"Your boss asked me to thank you. I did it once already, back in the bar, but you were already travelin'. It doesn't hurt to say it again."

"Thanks for what?"

"For saving my ass back there, I guess."

"I owed you one, man. Now we're square."

"You owed me one."

"I did."

Junior pushed up on the brim of his hat. He dragged on the reefer cigarette, kept the smoke in his lungs. He held the reefer out to Karras. Karras liked the smell of it, rough and overpowering but at the same time pleasing and sweet. But Karras had no desire to give it a try. He shook his head.

"Some other time."

Junior exhaled, blew ash off the reefer cigarette. "Suit yourself."

Karras followed the cord to its outlet, flush but unframed against the wood. "Nice work on running that line. You do it yourself?"

"I wouldn't touch it myself. You know what they say about us colored boys, don't you? There's only two things we afraid of: alligators and electricity."

Karras smiled, chin-nodded the phonograph. "What are we listening to?"

"Cat by the name of Charlie Parker. On the Dial label."

"I mean, what do you call this kind of music?"

Junior grinned. "Call it Jazz."

"Jazz. Swing music, you mean?"

"Naw, man, I ain't talkin' about no swing. I'm talkin' about jazz. Hard bop, Karras. *Head music.* Kind of music, you can't really read it straight off. Real crazy, man, like any damn thing can happen, but beautiful that way, 'cause you don't know where it's goin'. Like life itself."

Karras scratched his chin. "I saw Harry James once."

Junior, suddenly animated, leaned forward in his chair. "Harry James? Shoot, Karras, James and the Dorsey Brothers and Stan Kenton and any other of those gray faces you care to name, you know they don't know nothin'. And everything they *do* know, they copped from Mr. Louis Armstrong and Mr. Fletcher Henderson. You can *believe* that. Now, you wanna stick to the big band sound, you go on and stick to it, that's up to you. But if you're gonna listen to that swingin' orchestra thing, you might as well go on and listen to Duke Ellington, or the Count."

"I'm just ignorant, I guess."

"Naw, you ain't ignorant. But you only know what you done heard. And you ain't heard nothin', not until you heard a man who can blow like Bird."

"Your boss said you're into that New York sound."

"Well, seems like I'm up there every chance I get. I was up there Christmas Eve past, the night Miles Davis stepped down from Bird's quintet, and Kenny Dorham stepped in his place. Saw Ted Dameron's outfit at the Royal Roost, up there on Broadway and Forty-eighth. Been to Bop City, and the Clique. I even do a little dancin' sometimes at the Savoy, on Lenox at One-fortieth. They got a dance floor there, must be a city block long. And everywhere I go—" Junior patted the briefcase at his feet—"my records and this here portable-model phonograph go with me. But don't let me give you the impression that I don't dig what we got goin' on here in D.C. 'Cause we got our own sound here, too. Yes we do. Got musicians comin' out of this town, good ones, people like Earle Swope. Swope, with that trombone of his, climbed on down into the city from up in Hagerstown, he's got that Southern style of playin', real relaxed. You won't find a trombone sound quite like his anywhere else, I'll tell you that. Uh-uh, man, Earl Swope can play."

"You know, you're makin' me feel like I been tucked away all these years in my own world."

"Don't worry, man. You got your own thing, that's all. I jus' been tucked away in my own thing, too." Junior leaned forward. "Sure you don't want none of this tea?"

"I don't use it. And I got a night ahead of me still." Karras stood. "One thing's botherin' me, though—you said you owed me one. How could that be? I don't even know you, Junior."

"You just don't recall that you do. But you do. I met you one time, 'bout fifteen years back or so. We weren't nothin' but kids."

"What's your full name?"

"Round my way—in Bloodfield, that is—they called me Junior Oliver."

"I don't—"

"Me and my boys, one summer day, we rumbled you and yours over on a field around Fifth. You had me dead to rights, right up on me. You coulda beat hell out of me. But you backed off. You let me go. I owed you one, Karras. Now we done squared things up."

Karras shook his head. "I still don't remember. How'd you recognize me, anyway?"

Junior Oliver smiled. "By those blue eyes of yours, and that fucked-up mark on your face. You had it then, and you still got it. I never saw too many white boys when I was a kid. You and that mark, it stuck with me."

Karras touched the mole with his finger. "I'll be goddamned."

"Head music, Karras. The shit is plain crazy, sometimes."

Karras put his hands in his pockets. "I guess I'll see you around."

"I doubt it," said Junior. "Most time, you and me be walkin' through two different worlds. This thing here tonight? This was just an accident."

Karras turned and pushed through the screen door. He took the steps down to the cobblestones, cut right. He quickened his pace. The colored jazz trailed him and faded as he limped down the dark alley.

Out on the street, Karras hooked his forefinger and pinky in his mouth, whistled for a cab. A yellow Dodge pulled over and Karras climbed inside.

"Where to, pal?"

"Shaw," said Karras.

"Express, or you wanna see the monuments?"

"Fourteenth and R." Karras dropped a one over the front seat. "Make it fly."

32

Jimmy Boyle picked up the ringing phone.

"Hello?"

"Officer Boyle?"

"Go ahead."

"Matty Buchner."

"Buchner. What's up?"

"Somethin' maybe. I don't know. Somethin's been botherin' me since Friday night. It might be nothin', but—"

"Talk, Goddamnit."

"Why, you don't have to be so impatient."

"I got the caffeine shakes, is all it is. I'm tellin' you, I'm just plain jumpy."

"Well, let me tell it from the beginning. I was in this bar the other night—"

"What bar?"

"Jeez, officer, I don't remember."

"So you were running some cold-finger action in a bar. Listen, Matty, I'm gonna get it from you anyway—"

"All right, I was in the Hi-Hat. Now can I just tell it?"

"Go ahead."

"So I'm in the bar, minding my own business, enjoying a cocktail or two, and I overhear this conversation between this customer and the house tender. The customer, he's ordering up a punchboard through the tender, who's nothing more than a pimp who builds drinks on the side."

"Keep talking."

"I wouldn't 'a thought anything of it, see, but this customer, when he's giving the bartender his order, he asks him to make sure the broad's a big one. A big one, just like him. What with that murder on Friday night, I don't know, I thought the two things might connect."

"Why?"

"On account of the dead punchboard was a big one. And it's on the street already that this one went like all the others."

"When'd you say this was?"

"Friday evening."

"You gotta speak up, Buchner. You know I got a dead ear."

"All right."

"Describe the customer."

"Big and round and ugly. Wears clothes real neat and clean, like—whad'ya call that?—a dandy. Not the criminal type, if you ask me—the guy doesn't look like your average yegg."

"What else?"

"Here's the part that's drivin' me nuts. The guy reminded me of some character actor. At first I thought it was Victor Mature, but I knew straight off that the guy was too ugly to remind me of Mature. And then it hit me yesterday: This actor I was thinkin' of, he was in a picture *with* Mature, see?"

"What picture?"

"I can recall the story, but for the life of me, I can't remember the title of the pic. There's this guy, see—Vic Mature—and he's in love with this dame who gets scratched."

"Who's the actress?"

"Carole Landis is the one gets murdered. My God, Landis has this set of tits on her like—"

"Go on, Matty."

"So Mature, he falls in love with Landis's sister, played by Betty Grable. It's the only picture I ever saw Grable in where she didn't sing. Anyhow, there's this cop, he's after Mature for the murder, even though Mature, you know from the start he didn't chill Landis. But this cop is screwsville over pinning the crime on Mature. He can't let go of it. In the end, you see the cop, he's gone over the deep end with his obsession. He's built a shrine in his apartment to Landis, like a church or somethin', with candles and shit, the whole nine yards."

"Who plays the cop?"

"I don't know! I seen him in a lot of pictures, but I don't remember his name. Funny thing is, he killed himself a couple of years ago, on account of he couldn't live with being so ugly and fat. Ugly and fat, officer, like this character I saw in the bar the other night."

"You didn't happen to lift this guy's wallet, did you, Matty?"

"Ixnay. I wouldn't of thought of such a thing in a million years."

"Matty—"

"And anyway, he never checked his coat."

"I'm gonna get back to you on this."

"Always happy to keep you up on things."

"You think of the name of that actor, you let me know."

"Believe me, it's killin' me that I can't."

"You just keep thinkin'."

Boyle racked the phone. He looked across his apartment to the hall mirror. He'd had the appetite of a bird for the last week, and he'd lost a good ten pounds. His cheeks looked drawn, and black circles ringed his hollow eyes.

Boyle went to the bathroom, got his pep pills from the shelf. He palmed one into his mouth, threw his head back, dry-swallowed the pill. He'd felt himself notch down in the middle of his talk with Buchner. The pill, that would shoot him back up; if he was going to catch a break now, he'd need all the energy he could get.

■

Karras spun the wheel of the big Custom V8, cut left off 14th onto New York Avenue. The Ford fishtailed, straightened coming out of the turn. Florek glanced wide-eyed across the seat.

"I ain't much of a driver," said Karras. "To tell you the truth, I haven't done it all that much."

"That's all right," said Florek.

"Anyway, you ought to be happy right now, instead of worryin' about my driving."

"I am happy. Happy and a little nervous at the same time."

"I know it, kid. I'm a little nervous, too."

"It was nice of Nick to loan you his car."

"Nick's all aces. But he doesn't have to know anything about your sister. As far as he was concerned, I was just running you across town to see your girl. Get it?"

"Sure."

Karras had trouble getting the shifter into third gear. An awful sound came from beneath the car. Florek sideglanced Karras.

"You know what they say," said Karras. "If you can't find 'em, grind 'em."

"Pete?"

"Yeah."

"How are we going to get Lola out of there?"

"We're gonna take her."

Five minutes later, Karras slowed the Ford, stopped beneath a street-lamp, read the address on the piece of paper given to him by DeAngelo Ray Karras parked the car in front of the house.

"Let's go, kid."

Florek got out of the car, walked quickly up the stone steps to the front door. He waited for Karras, who had to use the handrail for support as he made his way. Karras stood next to him then. He tapped Florek on the arm.

"Go on, Mike. Ring the bell."

Florek pushed on the buzzer. The door opened quicker than he had expected, and a soft, small man stood before them in the frame. He kept himself behind the door as he leaned his bald head forward.

"Yes?"

"We're here to see Lola Florek," said Karras.

The man looked Karras over, ignoring Florek. "There's no Lola at this address."

Karras put his good foot to the door. The small man stumbled back-wards, caught himself on a foyer table. Karras and Florek stepped into the house. Karras shut the door behind him.

A healthy-looking woman sat drinking a highball in the living room, while two women in satin dresses danced together to a Bing Crosby num-ber coming from a Victrola set in the center of the room. They continued to dance slowly, their bodies pressed together, as they watched impas-sively the entrance of the two strangers.

"You Morgan?" said Karras.

Morgan held his nose where the door had bumped it. "What of it?"

"Just want to know I'm talking to the right man."

"I'm going to call the cops," said Morgan. "That's what I'm going to do. And I'm going to do it right now."

"Call 'em," said Karras.

Morgan did not move.

"Where's Lola?" said Florek.

"You fellas have an appointment?"

"Where is she?" Florek balled his fist.

253

"Why, you lookin' to bust your cherry or somethin', sonny?"

"We're takin' her out of here," said Karras. He slipped his hand inside his topcoat, scratched his chest. He kept his hand there, looked down menacingly at Morgan.

"Go on and get her, then," said Morgan. "She's useless to me, anyway. The way she looks now, I couldn't give that snatch away for free."

Florek moved forward, pivoted his back foot, threw a straight right. He connected at the bridge of Morgan's nose. Morgan was on the carpet before Florek even realized that he had thrown a punch.

Karras looked at Florek. Florek rubbed the skinned knuckles of his right fist, smiled thinly through a tight jaw. The dancers stopped moving; one of them stifled a grin.

Blood dripped out of Morgan's nose and inched down over his lip. He got himself up on one elbow. "Upstairs, second door to the right. Take her and go."

Florek glanced briefly at Karras, then took the stairs two steps at a time. Morgan began to get to his feet.

"Sit there," said Karras. "Get up and I'll knock you down myself."

"You bastards," muttered Morgan.

Karras said, "And keep your mouth shut."

Five minutes passed. Karras stood over Morgan while the dancers in the living room took a seat on the sofa and the healthy woman built herself another drink. Karras said nothing more to Morgan. Then he heard the creak of footsteps and looked up.

Florek had his sister by the arm and was leading her down the stairs. Lola wore a dirty beige dress decorated with blood-red roses. An overcoat had been draped around her shoulders. As they took the last step, Karras saw her face, colored almost entirely by a large gray bruise. The bruise obscured the great swelling in the area of her nose. Smaller purple bruises sat gorged beneath both eyes. Her two front teeth had been knocked out, a white line of pus oozing there along the gums.

Tears ran down Lola's face; tears clouded Mike Florek's eyes. Karras looked away.

"Get her in the car," said Karras.

Florek led Lola out into the night.

Karras said to Morgan, "Who did that to her?"

"I don't know." Morgan caught the look in Karras's eye. "I'm tellin' you the truth, buddy—I don't know."

Karras turned.

"Wait a second," growled Morgan. "I wanna know who did this to *me*."

Karras shifted his shoulders beneath his topcoat. "Pete Karras. Remember it."

Morgan said, "I will."

Karras felt the throb of a vein on his neck. He headed out the door.

33

Karras drove Mike and Lola Florek back to Florek's building on 14th. He let them off out front, then took the Ford up to S and swung it into the alley, parked it behind the grill. He moved along the alley, negotiating his way around the cats who sniffed and circled his feet, went in the back door to Nick's, and walked through the warehouse, which smelled heavily of detergent and pine disinfectant and perfume. Costa had scrubbed down every inch of the floor and walls Saturday night, leaving no trace of Bender or his men when he had finished close to Sunday dawn. Not a hair or a shard of clothing remained, and not a spot of blood.

Karras found Stefanos drinking a bottle of ale on a stool in the kitchen, a string of worry beads wrapped tightly in one hand. He handed him the keys to the Ford.

"*Efcharisto*, Niko."

"*Tipota*. You put any dents in it?"

"I didn't beat it up too bad. Costa around?"

"He's at the Hellenic Club, playin' cards."

"Toula?"

"She's up there. Why?"

"Just want a word with her, that's all."

"Uh."

Stefanos seemed listless or in thought, so Karras did not engage him further. He opened the kitchen door and took the stairs up to Costa's apartment. Toula was not busy and more than eager to listen to Karras and do as he asked. She especially liked the idea of keeping the matter hidden from Costa and Nick; the promise of conspiracy seemed to delight her.

Karras delivered Toula to Florek's room. She went in with a small satchel filled with home remedies and herbs. Karras stayed out in the hall and smoked a cigarette. When he was done with it he crushed the butt beneath his shoe. A thin, middle-aged tenant emerged from another room wearing only a towel around his bony waist; the Big War vet nodded at Karras as he tiptoed toward the common shower. Karras listened to the pipes wail and then a tapping sound as the tenant turned on the hot spigot. Mike Florek came from the room, closed the door softly behind him. He stood next to Karras, leaned his back against the wall.

"Thanks, Pete. Thanks for everything."

"Forget it. Here, have a smoke."

"I don't use 'em."

"Have one anyway."

Karras shook the deck in front of Florek. Florek took one and Karras took one for himself. He lighted his own, lighted Florek's.

"Toula got to work on her right away," said Florek. "She practically pushed me out of the room."

"She'll fix her up."

"She put an empty water glass lip-down on Lola's back, and lit a candle near the glass. I could see Lola's skin getting sucked up into that glass. I had to look away—"

"*Vendouzas*," said Karras.

"What the heck is that?"

"The cure. Some kind of Greek voodoo. Don't ask me to explain it, 'cause I can't."

"Does it work?"

"Hell if I know. My mother use to give 'em to me when I got sick. It can't hurt. And it doesn't matter whether it works or not, because Toula's gonna go ahead and use it on her either way. She'll do some other stuff, too, on the more legitimate side. Look, from what I saw, the damage is cosmetic. And anyway, you got bigger things to worry about than that bruise on her face and couple of missing teeth."

"Like?"

"Like getting her off that junk. Like turning her back into the girl she was. Making her forget about what she's become."

Florek took a short drag off his cigarette. "How am I supposed to do that?"

"Get her somewhere so she can't move around too much. Put her in a room and tie her down if you have to. It's gonna be hell for her, but it's the only way I ever heard of that works."

"Where do I do that?"

"Home. With you and your mother, back in that steeltown of yours, wherever you come from. She doesn't belong in this city, Mike. Neither do you."

Florek looked at Karras. "Tonight?"

"No, not tonight. Tonight she needs her rest." Karras put his cigarette to his lips, inhaled deeply. He glanced at the skinned knuckles of Florek's right hand. "You gave it to Morgan pretty good."

"I guess I did. I never hit nobody before, Pete."

"A lot of firsts for you down here, huh? You even look different than when I first met you. With all that work, you put a few pounds on, too."

"You think?"

"Sure. How'd it feel, hittin' that guy?"

"It felt all right, I guess. There's no magic to it, if that's what you mean."

"Remember it, chum. It doesn't take any brains to slug a guy or to hang out with hoods or to get yourself off track. No brains and no magic."

"Maybe not. But I'd like to run into the guy who did that damage to my sister."

"You better put it behind you. You can't change it, so you might as well go on and do what's right for her now."

Florek dropped his cigarette to the wood floor, stamped it out. "She talked about it, you know. While you were getting Toula. She talked about what happened."

"Yeah?"

"Fever gab, Pete. She was rambling on about a whole lot of things. Even claimed she was with the hooker that got sliced the other night. Claimed the hooker was a friend of hers. That the killer opened up her friend, then kicked Lola in the face before he walked."

"She claim she saw this killer?"

"She saw nothing. Only a pair of shoes like rich guys wear on the golf course. You know, two-tones. Brown-and-whites, only without the spikes. I don't believe a word of it. I gotta think that every working girl in this town is seeing killers, on account of they're so scared. You don't think there's anything to it, do you?"

"No. Hop talk, I'd say."

"Yeah. But I'd still like a minute in the same room with the guy—"

"Forget about it, Florek."

"Right. That's what I gotta do. Just forget."

Karras butted his cigarette against the door frame. "Let me get outta here."

"Where you headed?"

"Home. For a change, I'm gonna beat the stroke of midnight. See if I can't catch up with my wife before she hits the sack."

Florek tugged on the sleeve of Karras's topcoat. "Pete, I—"

"You told me already." Karras smiled. "Go on inside and see how she's doin'."

"I'll talk to you tomorrow, okay?"

"Yeah. Tomorrow we're gonna work everything out."

Karras headed for the stairs. Florek watched his shadow on the wall as he descended. Then there was the creak of the building's front door and the solid sound of it being shut.

Florek rubbed his swollen knuckles, thinking of the man who had just limped away. A man taller than his own shadow—that's who Pete Karras was. And the guy didn't even know it. Florek smiled to himself, seeing for the first time how maybe Lola could be all right. He pushed off from the wall, opened the door to his room, stood there for a moment in the frame. He went inside.

34

■■■■■ The next morning, a Monday, before Dimitri woke in his crib, Peter Karras made love to Eleni to the sound of car horns on H and Eleni's own gasps and sobs. They had joined violently at first, caught a rhythm soon thereafter, and taken it slow to the end. Karras came first, quietly and for what seemed to be a long while; Eleni broke with a spasm, her one leg kicking at the air, as it always did. Afterwards they laughed about that, Karras giving her the treatment about the leg and not letting up about it, causing her to blush. She forgot about her anger over not having seen or heard from him, except for that one hour of church, for the last few days.

Eleni cooked Karras a couple of eggs over easy with fried slices of scrapple from Maryland's eastern shore. Karras took his eggs unbroken and preferred his scrapple browned deeply on both sides. Eleni served both in perfect form, and Karras enjoyed his breakfast while listening to Eleni's new Jo Stafford record and the sound of the boy trying to sing along to it from the playpen set in the middle of the room. Karras thought: You know, this isn't bad, hanging around here like this. If I tried it out once in a while I could maybe get used to it. Yeah, this could be all right.

Karras pushed his plate away and read the sports page of the morning *Times-Herald*, and had a cigarette with his second cup of coffee, and then he took the boy from the playpen and tried to start a game with him involving a blue rubber ball. But the boy went straight to his mother after the first turn, and Karras had a seat in the living room armchair, thinking: *Now what do I do? I've gone at it with my wife and I've eaten my breakfast and I've tried to play with my son. I've done all that, and now I've got the whole rest of the day to do . . . what?* And then: *I'm just not cut out for this racket.*

260

Some guys can sit around with their families and get used to it and even like it, but I'm not built for it. Who the hell am I kidding? It's just not right for me.

So Karras showered and dressed in a blue suit and slipped his cigarettes in the jacket of the suit and shook himself into his topcoat and walked for the door.

"Where you goin', Pete?" said Eleni.

"Out."

Two minutes later he was limping east on H, his back to the morning sun.

■

The bell chimed as Karras pushed through the door and entered Nick's. A couple of Negroes whom Karras did not recognize were seated on stools, with Costa back behind the counter, alternately halving lettuce heads on the sandwich board and keeping an eye on the customers. A show called "Rhythm Special" on WOOK came from the house radio, and the two customers moved their heads in unison to the bass line of the beat.

"Hey, Costa."

"Karras."

"Busy?"

"Yeah. Your boy Florek called in sick."

"Where's Nick?"

"*Sto kouzina.*"

Karras went through the hinged doors, entered the kitchen. Stefanos sat on a stool next to the prep table, a newspaper spread out on the table, an empty bottle of ale and a glass half-full of it beside the paper.

"*Yasou,* Panayoti."

"*Yasou,* Niko."

"C'mon and have a little *beera* with me."

"It ain't even noon."

"*Ella, re!* I been waitin' for you to come in. Go get a bottle and let's talk."

Karras went out to the front of the house, retrieved a bottle of Ballantine Ale from the cooler, uncapped the bottle, took it back to the kitchen along with a clean glass. He removed his topcoat, put his cigarettes and matches on the table, found a stool. He dragged the stool next to the table. He and Stefanos touched glasses.

"*Siyiam.*"

"*Siyiam, re.*"

Karras and Stefanos drank. Karras wiped foam off his upper lip.

261

"Anything good in the paper?"

"There's this one thing." Stefanos leaned forward to get a good look at the newspaper, touched one thick finger to an item above the fold. "The law fried some colored guy in Alabama last night. A blind guy. *Mavros* by the name of Buster Snead. First blind man ever put to death by the state."

"He do it?"

Stefanos nodded. "He confessed. Hacked a woman to pieces in her bed. Says she owed him twenty bucks for over a year. He got tired of askin' for it, I guess."

"Twenty bucks. Not much for either one of them to die for."

"Uh. But here's the funny part. Not laugh funny, but, you know, strange. They asked the guy for his last words before they threw the switch. He says—" Stefanos squinted as he read directly off the page—" 'I'm going to see Jesus and I'm glad.' "

"He say anything else?"

"Yeah. He said, 'Goodnight'."

"That about covers it."

"I guess."

Stefanos folded the paper, crossed one leg over the other.

Karras said, "You been hittin' it kind of early lately, haven't you?"

"I been thinkin', that's all. The *pioto,* it helps me think."

"About what?"

Stefanos spread his big hands. "The other night, mostly. Those men we killed. How maybe we moved too fast. How we coulda done somethin' else."

"It's a little late for that."

"I know it. And I'm not sayin' that they didn't deserve to die, because they did. If not for this, then probably for somethin' else. But I'm tired of it. I don't have the stomach for any more killin', *katalavenis?*"

"I understand. But I told you then that when you start something like this you gotta be ready to go all the way."

"I remember."

"And you know, somebody's gonna come looking now for Bender—his own men or Burke's men, it doesn't matter which—and when they find out what happened back in that warehouse, believe me, they're going to want to take it out in blood."

"Sure, they'll come. What I'm sayin' is, I don't know if I have the *orexi* anymore to fight back."

"You turnin' over a new leaf, huh."

"Go ahead and grin about it. But that's exactly what I'm gonna do. I'm gettin' into my middle age now, Karras. I got a little lucky with that number a few years back, and I want to be around to share it with my family. I wanna get that good-for-nothin' son of mine over from Greece, get him workin' here, too. I got a letter from him last week, said he met a nice *koritsaki* in *Sparti*. I'm thinkin', maybe he marries her, comes over with his new wife, I'm gonna get real lucky now, have a grandson of my own some day, too."

"You'd like that, wouldn't you."

"Goddamn right I'm gonna like it! Wouldn't you?"

"I don't know. I can't see that far ahead, to tell you the truth."

Stefanos caught himself staring at Karras. He looked away, grabbed his glass off the table, had a swig of ale.

"Ah," said Stefanos, "that's good. Anyway, so like I say, I been thinkin'. I wanna slow things down around here, no more hoods hangin' around. And no more guns and no more knives. I gonna slow down myself—on my drinkin', and my gamblin', and everything else. And you, *vre*, you need to slow it down, too."

"I don't know about that."

"You and your friend, the *Italos*. Maybe you ought to talk things over. Get a few things straightened out."

Karras looked down at his shoes, shook his head. "Me and Joey don't know how to do that."

"Bullshit. What you gotta do is, you gotta get off the bus."

"What?"

Stefanos leaned forward. "I got this idea about life, see. That life, it's like a bus ride through town. Lemme give you an example: You take the U Street line over to Seventh, right? You transfer over to a southbound bus, transfer again to the F Street line, head west on that one across town."

"So?"

"So. When you're on the U Street line, you gonna see the same people all the time, all doin' the same kinds of things. The Seventh Street southbound is gonna be different. On the F Street bus, same thing, but maybe you see some of those old people from U—"

"What the hell are you talkin' about?"

"Just this. You and the *Italos*, you been on the same bus all your lives. That bus you been on, the brakes are wearin' down on it, *katalavenis?* I know, 'cause me, I been on the same kinda bus myself. But now I'm thinkin', maybe I'm gonna pull down on the cord, jump off at the next stop before it's too late. Catch a new bus, I mean. You and that Italian friend of yours, you gotta get off that old bus, too."

Karras lighted a cigarette. He shook out the match and tossed it on the tiled floor. The phone rang loudly from the front of the house.

"Like I said, Nick. I don't know how to do that. I'd like to, but I just don't know how."

"Aaaah," said Stefanos, waving a hand at Karras. "You just don't know yourself, that's all. You look in the mirror, you're not seein' the same man I see sittin' here right in front of me."

"Listen, Nick . . . "

Costa pushed halfway through the swinging doors. "Karras! It's that Irish cop on the phone, lookin' for you."

"Boyle?"

"Boyle, Doyle, what the hell do I know? I'm busy out here, goddamn! Come on out here, *malaka*, and pick up the phone."

Karras went out to the front of the house. He mussed Costa's hair as he took the phone.

"*Ella, vre bufo!*" said Costa. He cursed Karras creatively as he walked away.

"Jimmy?"

"Yeah, Pete, it's me."

"Jimmy, I was gonna call you this morning myself, thank you for that tip on DeAngelo Ray."

"Anything there?"

Karras dragged on his smoke. Lola had claimed that she had witnessed the murder; hop dream or no, he didn't want her involved with the law just yet.

"Nothing yet," said Karras. "But I'm still checking things out."

"Glad I could help."

"So what's on your mind?"

"I got a movie question, Pete. You always knew the pictures inside out, what with you workin' that usher job at the Hippodrome before the war."

"What's this about?"

"Nothin', most likely. This street snitch of mine says he saw this fat sonofobitch ordering up a whore the other night from the night tender at the Hi-Hat. Says he ordered a big one, the same night that big hooker got herself sliced. Could be nothin' at all—"

"Slow down, Jimmy. What night was that?"

"Friday."

Karras felt his pulse quicken. "You talk to the bartender yet?"

"I was waitin' to get somethin' else straight first. That movie question I wanted to ask you about. Then I was gonna drop by the Hi-Hat tonight, when the tender comes on."

"All right. Go ahead."

"My snitch said the fat boy looked like a character actor he knew. Guy who always plays a heavy—at least he used to, before he croaked himself on account of he couldn't live with the way he looked. Anyway, this actor was in a picture where he played a screwball cop, chasing after Victor Mature, who's falsely accused of murdering some dame."

"Who plays the dame?"

"What's her name, she's got this beautiful set of personalities—"

"Carole Landis."

"Landis, right. Okay. Now, Betty Grable was in this picture, too, only not in a singin' role. And that half-pint, Elisha Cook, always looks like you woke him out of a bad dream. Anyhow, this cop, he's got a, whatd'ya-call-it, an obsession with Landis—"

"*I Wake Up Screaming.*"

"What?"

"*I Wake Up Screaming.* That's the name of the picture."

"And who played the cop?"

"Laird Cregar," said Karras, tossing it right off. And then the name came off his lips again, because he saw the man who looked like Cregar in his own head. A dandy, and a fat one—the worst kind. Sitting in his chair, with his hands folded across his fat lap. And at the end of his feet, a pair of two-toned gibsons. Two-tones, brown-and-whites . . . Laird Cregar . . . *Gearhart.*

"I'll be goddamned," said Karras.

"Come again?"

"Nothing."

"Yeah. I couldn't think of that actor's name to save my life. Who knows, maybe now I'll get to the bottom of—"

"Jimmy, I don't mean to cut you off. But I really gotta go. Thanks again for the tip with Ray."

"Thank *you,* pal. Take care."

"Yeah, you too."

Karras racked the receiver. He walked back to the kitchen, took a last drag from his smoke, crushed it on the floor. He picked up his topcoat and got himself into it.

Stefanos cocked an eyebrow. "You hokay? You're lookin' a little *steni-chorimenos.*"

"I'm fine. I gotta get to an appointment."

"Go on, then. But you think about what I told you, *acous*?"

"Yeah, I hear. Catch you later."

Karras limped toward the swinging doors. He turned around.

"Hey, Nick."

"Yeah."

"Just in case I don't manage to get off that bus you were yakkin' about—"

"*Ella, re!*"

"I'm serious. Listen to me—there's an envelope in my locker, back in the warehouse."

"Well?"

"You'll know what to do."

Stefanos looked in Karras's eyes. "You're on the schedule tomorrow. I'm gonna see you, right?"

"Sure, Nick."

"*Yasou*, Panayoti."

"*Yasou*, Niko. *Adio.*"

Karras walked from the kitchen. Stefanos watched him go.

35

▄▄▄▄▄ Peter Karras hailed a cab and told the driver to point it down-town. He had no destination in mind but he wanted to get away from Nick's and he needed a place to think. He got out around 13th and H and gave the cabbie two bits and walked into a lunch counter called Dag-wood's situated at the corner there, fronted by an inviting, brightly col-ored sign. Karras was not awfully hungry, but he was looking to come in from the cold while he sorted things out.

The gimmick in Dagwood's was the sandwiches, Dagwood Sandwiches they called them, straight out of the funny pages' strip. Karras had a seat at the counter and ordered a Cookie's Delight without looking at the par-ticulars.

"Anything to drink?" asked a man in a white paper hat.

"Co-cola," said Karras.

A few minutes later the hash jockey brought out a chicken and bacon on white toast trimmed with lettuce, sliced tomatoes, and mayonnaise. The jockey dropped a platter of sweet gherkin chips, slaw, and pickled tomatoes on the side. Karras drank down half the cola at once, asked for a cup of coffee, got it. He sipped the coffee, which he recognized straight off as a product of National, the vendor over on 9th. Nick Stefanos used the same blend in his urns.

Karras downed the sandwich and got a refill on the coffee and lighted a cigarette. He smoked that one and then another. He stabbed the butt in the ashtray and signaled the guy behind the counter.

The hash jockey delivered the check. "Let's see . . . that's fifty cents for the sandwich and a nickel on the coffee. Plus your tax."

Karras slapped a one onto the counter. "Keep it."

"Thank you, sir."

"You got a phone book back there, chum?"

"Yessir."

"Bring it here."

Karras found Recevo's number and address in the book. He was not surprised that Joey hadn't moved—he still had that one-bedroom affair off Georgia, up there near Fort Stevens. Karras carried the book over to the in-house booth, closed himself inside it as he settled onto the bench. He dialed Recevo's number.

"Hello?"

"Joe?"

"Speaking."

"Pete Karras."

And then there was a silence. Karras half-expected it. He reached into his jacket for a cigarette, decided against it, pulled his hand out.

"Pete, you there?"

"Yeah, I'm here. And I'm gonna make it quick. This isn't a social call."

Recevo said, "Go ahead."

"You know about those whore murders been goin' on the last few years?"

"Sure, I know."

"Well, this is gonna sound crazy to you. But the guy who's been openin' up those punchboards, he's in bed with Burke. In fact, he's been sittin' on his fat ass right next to you in that office of yours all this time."

"What?"

"I'm tellin' it to you straight, Joe. The killer is Gearhart."

"What the hell . . . "

"Yeah."

Dead air. And then: "How do you know?"

"I couldn't prove it with a gun to my head. But I got more than a real strong hunch. Don't ask me how it came to me, 'cause I won't tell you. You're just gonna have to trust me. Gearhart is the one."

"You got a witness to any of this?"

"No."

"Well, let's just say it's true. What the hell am I supposed to do about it?"

"You gotta get this Gearhart monster off the street. And I mean all the way off—don't go sending him out of town or anything cute like that. Because a bolthead like that is just gonna go on and do the same thing somewhere else. And Joey, Goddamnit, you know that's wrong. You and

268

me, we did some bad things, but this isn't even in the same ballpark. It's just all the way wrong."

"You tellin' me I gotta take this to Mr. Burke?"

"That's a start."

"But I gotta know *somethin'*, Pete. I gotta know how Gearhart got found out—at least where it started. I can't go to Burke with this without a source. Otherwise, he's not gonna believe a word I said. I swear to you, I'm not gonna tell him nothin' about you—"

"I don't give a good goddamn what you tell him."

"Give me something, then."

"The ball started rolling at the Hi-Hat. The night man who works behind the stick there, he's retailing women."

"That'll help."

"Then we're done."

"Listen, Pete—"

"Forget it. And Joey . . ."

"Yeah?"

"One more thing. I wouldn't mind if you guys decided to take care of Gearhart your own way. But if you decide to do it the straight way—turn him into the law, I mean—promise me you'll let Jimmy Boyle take him in."

"Boyle still walkin' that beat?"

"Uh-huh. And he's lookin' to earn his detective's shield. You and me, Joey, we got the opportunity to do somethin' right here. You understand?"

"I get it, Pete. I can reach Boyle at his old address?"

"Right. That covers it, then."

"Wait a minute."

"What?"

"I'm curious about somethin'. Burke sent a guy by name of Bender to look for Nick Stefanos and the rest of you."

"So?"

"I was just wonderin'—"

"He found us."

Recevo said, "Nice talkin' to you, Pete."

"Yeah," said Karras. "You too."

Karras cradled the receiver. He stared at the phone, brushed his fingers across the mole on the side of his mouth.

∎

Joe Recevo dialed Burke.

"Mr. Burke, it's Joe."

"Yes?"

"You alone?"

"Yes."

"Gearhart around?"

"He's down in the living room with Reed and a couple of the others."

"Good. There's something I gotta tell you."

Recevo gave it to Burke straight down the middle. When he was done, Burke sighed audibly into the phone. Recevo could hear the jangle of cubes bouncing off the side of a glass.

"Who tipped you to this?"

"A guy I know was in the bar of the Ambassador Hotel the other night."

"The Hi-Hat?"

"Yeah. He saw Gearhart put his order in for a hooker from the barman. The tender there doubles as a middleman pimp. The order fit the description of the woman who got herself chilled. Fit it to a T."

"Lot of fat whores around. That doesn't prove a thing."

"No. But suppose there's something there. The law's gonna be deep into our business, and quick."

"Yes, I see your point. Who was your informant?"

"Like I say, just a guy. A jamoke who's seen me around with Gearhart, knows we're in the same outfit. He was doin' me a favor, but he doesn't want any part of it from here on out. He won't talk to anyone, and he knows what would happen if he did."

"Hmm."

"Mr. Burke."

"Okay, Joe. I'm going to bring Gearhart upstairs, have a little talk with him. Can you come by?"

"Yessir."

"And Joe? Good work."

"I'll be right there."

Recevo cut the line. He put on his topcoat, creased the brim of his fedora, placed it just so on his head. Lois Roman came into the room.

"Where you off to, Joe?"

"Business. Come over here and let me give you one."

Lois walked to him, smoothing her skirt out against her thighs. He crushed his lips against hers, pulled back, looked thoughtfully into her eyes. Then he kissed her the same way, one more time.

Lois smiled. "What was the second one for?"

"It just felt so good, I had to hit it again."

"Don't be too late."

"Love you, baby."

Recevo patted Lois's behind, broke away. She watched him march quickly across the room, a cocky spring in his step.

"I love you, Joey," she said.

But he was already gone.

■

Karras took a cab into Southeast, left the driver idling at the curb along the 4500 block of Alabama Avenue. It was a workingman's afternoon, and a Monday at that, with little activity on the street.

Karras limped up the concrete steps to the row house door, took the entrance to the common foyer. He knocked on the door marked 1. The force of his knock pushed the unlocked door inward by a foot. Karras stepped inside.

The landlord owned the furnishings, and they were there, but other than that the place had been stripped. The closet had been left open and empty, its wooden rod holding a row of bent wire hangers. A half-inch of gray water remained in a lipstick-stained glass sitting alone atop the cheap dresser.

Karras went to the window. He bent forward, picked up the theater ticket fallen between the radiator's tubes. He rubbed his finger along the dried blood smudged across the word *Hamlet*. Karras dropped the ticket, watched it float back to the floor.

He walked from the room and straight out to the street. He settled in the backseat of the cab, fitted a cigarette between his lips.

"Where to, mac?" said the cabbie.

Karras said, "Chinatown."

■

Recevo passed Face in the grand foyer, saw the Welshman and Medium and a few of the others sitting around in the living room as he hit the stairs. He went up to the landing, cut right. Reed was leaning against the wall, smoking a Fatima outside the closed door of Burke's office.

"He's in there," said Reed.

"Who?"

"Gearhart. He's in there and he's bawling like a girl. He spilled it to Mr. Burke straight off. It all came out when Burke asked him. Like he's been waitin' for someone to ask him about it: 'Hey, Gearhart, by the way, I was just wonderin', was it you who chilled them broads?' I'm tellin' you, he couldn't wait to sing about it."

"What did he say?"

"Somethin' about his mommy. His fat whore mommy, who used to do it for a buck on Sailor's Row. She never loved him, and like that. Only loved the niggers, and the white niggers, and anybody else who could come up with eight bits. Blah, blah, blah." Reed dragged on his cigarette, blew a smoke ring across the landing. "You ever horsefuck a fat girl, Joe?"

"Shut up, Reed."

"It ain't so bad."

"I said, shut up."

Reed grinned, brushed ash off the lapel of his sharkskin suit. "You're somethin', you know it? You lucked out and came through with this Gearhart thing before the law could step in. A real hero, aren't you. Let's put another star on the report card from Mr. Burke."

"I'm going inside."

"But now we got a problem don't we? What are we going to do about our fat friend?"

"I'm going in."

"Who tipped you, anyway?"

"That's my business."

"Oh?"

"It's mine if I say it's mine."

Recevo knocked on the door. Burke yelled for him to enter. Recevo turned the knob, went in, was followed by Reed. Reed leaned himself against the gun case; Recevo had a seat at the big table.

Gearhart sat in his usual spot, his hands tented over the balloon of his lap. There were tear streaks running down both puffy cheeks. His shoulders were scrunched up, burying what was left of his neck, and he stared straight ahead. All he needed was the dunce cap to complete the picture: a three-hundred-pound boy, humiliated in class.

"I'm so sorry," whispered Gearhart.

Burke reached over his desk for the bottle of bourbon, poured three inches straight. He tasted the whiskey, considered the glass. He turned it in the light.

"You talked to Reed outside?"

"Yes," said Recevo.

"Then you know."

"Yes."

"We'll figure this out now. We've just got to figure this out."

272

"That's right, Mr. Burke."

"But we've got another problem we have to deal with first."

"What's that?"

"A witness to that last one on Friday night. Another working girl who was at the scene. For some reason, Gearhart over here decided to spare her life."

"Who is she?" Recevo glanced at Gearhart, still staring ahead. He considered asking the fat man, but Burke seemed to be ignoring his presence. Recevo figured he'd go that route, too.

"Gearhart doesn't know."

"Go to her pimp, then."

"He doesn't know the pimp. Gearhart was in the habit of ordering his women through middlemen. The cabbies at the hotel hackstands, the bartenders, like that."

"So you go ask the night man at the Hi-Hat. It was him that arranged things."

Burke said, "That's right, isn't it Gearhart?"

Gearhart nodded one time.

"Yes," said Burke. "He'll know the pimp. Through the pimp we'll get the girl. And we'll have to convince the bartender and pimp to keep their mouths shut. Reed."

"Yeah?"

"Would you like to take this on?"

Reed smiled, pushed away from the gun case. "It's my meat, Mr. Burke."

"I know it is, Reed."

"There's something else," said Recevo.

"What?" said Burke.

"The murder weapon. Gearhart used a straight razor on those women, right?"

"Gearhart?"

"Yes," said Gearhart. "I'm sorry . . . "

"Never mind that. Where's that razor now?"

"In my apartment," said Gearhart. "In my bathroom. Right there in the medicine cabinet—"

"What's it look like?"

Gearhart looked down at his lap. "An ordinary razor. It folds into a brown, tortoiseshell handle."

"Okay, Reed. Talk to the tender and find out the name of the pimp. Then get over to Gearhart's dump and get rid of that razor."

Reed said to Gearhart, "Gimme your key."

"My key," mumbled Gearhart. "I keep my key beneath the mat. I always lose my key . . ."

"Okay, Reed," said Burke. "Do it."

Reed smiled at Recevo, clipped him roughly on the shoulder on his way out. Recevo listened to the heavy footsteps fade. He removed his hat, brushed back his hair, replaced the fedora neatly on his head.

"Don't worry, Mr. Burke. We'll figure this out."

"Yes," said Burke, taking a healthy swallow of bourbon. "I only need to think."

Recevo looked at Burke, slumped down in his chair. *You need to think, all right. And that goddamn whiskey is really gonna help.*

Recevo stood up. "Well, I'm gonna grab a little chow. I'll swing back around later on."

"Go on, Joe. Go have a little dinner. But come right back. I need you around here. You're the only one I've got with any sense in his head."

"Sure, Mr. Burke. I'll be right back."

Recevo walked quickly from the room. Gearhart and Burke sat in silence for the next five minutes. Then Gearhart moved his turtle's eyes curiously beneath their lids.

"Mr. Burke?"

"Yeah."

"Do you mind if I go downstairs? I'd like to sit around with the boys a little bit, if you don't mind."

Burke looked into his empty glass. "Go ahead. Don't drift."

"I won't."

Burke said, "Then go ahead."

■

Joe Recevo pulled the Olds to the curb, parked in front of the Patio Lounge, a beer garden at 13th and F. He bought a mug of draught from the barman and took it into the phone booth back by the head, left the booth door open so he could smoke. He found Jimmy Boyle's number in the book, dialed it up.

"Jimmy."

"Yeah?"

"Joe Recevo."

Boyle didn't answer. Recevo listened to him breathe.

Boyle said, "What do you want?"

"I got somethin' for you, Jimmy."

"I don't want nothin' to do with you, pal."

"Sure you don't. You hate me straight down to my guts. But I'm gettin' ready to hand you the biggest break of your life."

"Yeah? What for?"

"On account of Pete Karras asked me to, that's why."

"You talked to Pete?"

"Yeah. I talked with him this afternoon. But we don't have time to go into all that. Now listen, you write down this address . . ."

Recevo gave it to him.

"I got it," said Boyle.

"Good. Now you get your ass over to that apartment. Go to the bathroom and then in the medicine cabinet. You'll find a straight razor there. The razor folds into a tortoise-shell handle. Wear gloves when you get it, then take it out of there and get it to your lab boys."

"Why would I do that?"

" 'Cause that's the razor that killed them whores."

Recevo lighted a Raleigh, waited for Boyle to sort it out.

"How do you know?"

"Karras tipped me, and don't ask me how. Get goin', Jimmy. You gotta move fast, on account of someone's gonna be there in an hour or two lookin' for the same thing."

"Who?"

"One of mine."

"Who's the killer, Joe? One of your guys, too?"

"Never mind that. Get the razor first. I'll deliver you the killer later on."

"How am I supposed to get in?"

"There's a key under the mat."

"Joe—"

"Get goin'."

"I just wanted to thank you."

"All right, you thanked me. Now go."

Recevo racked the receiver before Boyle could have a chance to say anything else. He leaned back against the wood of the booth. He closed his eyes.

■

Jimmy Boyle got his service revolver from his dresser, checked the load, watched his hand shake as he sighted down the barrel. He spun the cylinder of the .38, wrist-jerked the cylinder back in, wedged the gun barrel-down behind the waistband of his trousers. He stuck it on the left side of his gut with the grip facing in so he could cross-draw with his right hand.

Then he practiced the drill in the hall mirror, as he had done so many times before.

Boyle put a carcoat on over his street clothes. He reached into his side pocket, found the vial of Benzedrine there, dry-popped the last pill on his way out of his apartment. He took the stairs two at a time, blowing by an old woman who pressed her back against the wall to let him pass. A moment later he was out on the street and running, full speed, toward his old coupe.

36

At 13th and Euclid, Boyle slowed his Buick coupe to a crawl in the middle of the street, double-checked the scrap of notepaper beside him on the seat. He pulled over, parked behind a late-model sedan, cut the engine. He looked around the block of three-story row houses, some crowned with grand turrets, some plain and nondescript. Two starlings lifted off the roof of the corner house, their black wings spread as they glided down to the asphalt to pick at the open skull of a dead squirrel. No one was out on the street; the slate-gray veil of night had fallen. The cold cut right through Boyle's carcoat, hit his face with the shock of a hornet's sting.

Boyle got out of the car, felt the finger-dance at the back of his head. He had come to know it well in the last week. The pep pill gave him that; and it gave him a powerful and unquenchable thirst. Taking the steps at a bounding trot, he tried to raise spit, found that he could not.

Jimmy Boyle had a sudden image of a lifeless naked boy lying on a concrete slab. The image had not entered his mind since he himself was a child, and here it was again. It had begun to haunt him the day his father had brought home the shoes from the morgue. His father had removed the shoes off the corpse of the boy just the night before, and early the next morning had laid them neatly side-by-side at the foot of Jimmy's bed. Jimmy Boyle awoke that morning to the sounds of his parents in the adjoining room, their voices raised in argument. "Let's be practical, honey," his father had said. "You know we ain't got a pot to piss in or a window to throw it out of, and Jimmy needs shoes. That boy got hit by that flatbed, he can't use them shoes today any more than he could use a shirt collar on his broken neck. We gotta be practical!" Jimmy Boyle had closed his eyes then, tried not to picture the boy, lying on that slab with his bruised and twisted neck. And Boyle wore those shoes, all that summer and into the next. But for a long time, he could not stop that boy from entering his dreams. Eventually, the image of the dead boy went the way of all his childhood nightmares, buried and forgotten, but sleeping, not dead. Now, as he walked through a common foyer towards Gearhart's apartment door, the image was back.

"Stop it!" said Boyle aloud, his voice echoing in the hall.

He shook his head vigorously. The dead boy was gone. He knocked on the door. He knocked again. He bent down, lifted the straw mat that sat before the door: no key.

Boyle stood, turned the knob. He pushed lightly on the door, let it open halfway. He looked around the foyer, stepped into the living room, closed the door behind him.

A woman lives here, thought Boyle, or a fancy kind of man. The place was neat and orderly, clean smelling, with magazines stacked on side tables and books shelved fussily in order of ascending height. A Lawson sofa, covered in wine matelasse, sat in the center of the room. A Duncan Phyfe loveseat, mahogany-framed with a beige striped fabric, sat facing the sofa. Between the two was a long mahogany table, its top brilliantly waxed and finely beveled, with intricately scrolled feet. Next to the sofa sat an RCA Victor Crestwood model radio-phonograph console, also constructed in rich mahogany wood.

Boyle walked quickly across a rose, tone-on-tone broadloom rug. The thickness of it muted his steps. He moved into a hall past two open bedroom doors. The hall ended at another open door leading into a bathroom. He moved toward the bathroom; queerly, it seemed to move toward him.

And then he was in the bathroom. The layout was simple: a sink and a toilet and a bathtub. The tub was large and sat free. Its feet were fashioned as lion's paws, heavily clawed and leafed gold. A white curtain was drawn around the tub, hung from a semicircular rod. The mirrored wood medicine cabinet sat flush in the plaster of the wall, centered above the sink.

Boyle looked in the mirror at the black circles ringed around his eyes. His flesh sagged gray on his face. My God, he thought: Is that me?

He reached for the cabinet, winced at the shake in his hand as his fingers grabbed the handle. He pulled back on the door, opened it, looked inside. He saw a pack of Feenamint, some Eno salts, a styptic pencil, a tube of Kolynos toothpaste, a brush, a bottle of Mistol nose drops, a bar of Old Spice soap, a jar of Pond's Cold Cream . . . no razor. And for the first time he thought: It stinks a little in here. Rusty, kind of, like some guy just took a big shit.

Boyle closed the cabinet door. The outline of a man flashed in the mirror. He turned to the right.

The man was in the doorway—a huge man in a flannel suit with a sickening grin spread wide across his fat face. The brown handle of a straight razor was tightly grasped in his upraised fist.

My ear. That goddamned bum ear of mine. I didn't even hear him coming down the hall.

"I'm a cop," said Boyle.

The man said, "Then you must be looking for this."

The man brought the razor down violently. Boyle felt as if he had been pushed with a hammer. He stumbled back, turned to grab the bath curtain, saw a diagonal line of blood splash against the white curtain as he turned.

"Momma," said Boyle.

The curtain ripped free from its rings. Boyle tumbled into the empty tub. His head hit the porcelain. He heard the sound, like the sound of a muffled bell, but he couldn't feel a thing. He couldn't feel it because of the other pain. There was the other pain now and it was pulsing and horrible and somewhere else. The air had gotten to the cut.

The fat man walked toward Boyle.

"I'm a cop," said Boyle, his voice rubbery and weak.

The fat man laughed.

Boyle fumbled his right hand to his left side. The hand was numb, clumsy. He found the grip of the .38. His hand slipped off the slickness there.

"I'm sorry, you know." The fat man raised the razor.

Boyle reached, found the grip. He pulled the gun, slipped his finger inside the trigger guard, fired the gun as the man's hand slashed down, fired again, screamed something as he fired a third time, watched the revolution of the cylinder through the smoke that had exploded into the room.

The fat man hit the floor, bucking in convulsion, the heel of one brown-and-white shoe kicking wildly at the tiles. Boyle aimed, put a round through the sole of the shoe. The fat man stopped kicking.

Boyle laughed senselessly, pulled the trigger, watched the dead man jump from the force of the lead. He pulled the trigger again. The hammer snapped on an empty chamber.

Jimmy Boyle dropped his service revolver as his head lolled to the side. He heard a splashing sound. A steady high note rang in one ear. It was all warm below his waist. His hand fell away, touched the wetness at the bottom of the tub. It was warm there, too. Boyle's eyes began to cross.

The room tilted. The room went black.

37

████████ Burke placed the phone back in its cradle. He rubbed his hand roughly across his face.

"That was Reed."

Recevo's fingers ran around the brim of the fedora which he held in his lap.

"And?"

"He called in an hour ago to report on his progress, right after I discovered that Gearhart had booked. I told him to get over to Gearhart's place right away."

"He found Gearhart?"

"Not exactly. There were a bunch of cops and an ambulance out front of Gearhart's when he got there. Reed parked, hung around, listened to some of the crowd and a couple of the blueboys jawboning about the details."

"Reed get any dope?"

"Yeah. Gearhart's dead."

"Damn." Recevo frowned in counterfeit remorse.

"A cop out of uniform took him down after Gearhart sliced the cop from top to bottom. The cop really let him have it. Reed says he saw them bring out the body. Even with the sheet, you could see it was a mess." Burke sipped at his drink. "I shouldn't have let Gearhart out of my sight. He panicked, I guess, went to get his things before he skipped. The thing I can't figure out is, what was that cop doin' at his place?"

"Hell if I know." Recevo paused. "The cop buy it, too?"

"I don't know if he made it or not. They had already taken him away by the time Reed got there." Burke looked at Recevo. "What's it to you, Joe?"

Recevo spread his hands. "Cops go bananas when you kill one of their own. They'll be all over us—"

"True. But I don't know if he made it or not."

Recevo watched Reed pour from the fifth which had been full that afternoon. The bottle was nearly empty now.

"You know, Mr. Burke, no disrespect to Gearhart or anything like that, but we might want to look at this as some kind of blessing."

"What do you mean?"

"This thing with Gearhart is over now. They can't tie anything to us now."

"Well, yeah. But there was that bartender, and the pimp, and that girl that Gearhart let go. Witnesses, all of them. I don't know what he told them. We'll never know until we talk to them. Don't you agree?"

Recevo did not respond. He was studying the slumped posture of Burke behind his desk. He was wondering how he ever could have followed a guy like that.

"Anyway," said Burke, "we'll know in a couple of minutes. Reed told me he talked to the bartender and the pimp. He sounded real excited about something when we talked. Said he couldn't wait to get in here and spill it."

Recevo withdrew a cigarette. He lighted it, tossed the match in the ashtray in front of him. He took a drag, watched smoke settle in the room. A little while later he butted the cigarette. A door slammed from the first floor at the front of the house. Heavy footsteps ascended the stairs.

"There's Reed," said Burke.

Recevo said, "I know."

■

Peter Karras got out of the cab, went straight into Garfield Hospital, asked the first cop he saw as to the whereabouts of Boyle. There were plenty of cops to ask. They were in the lobby and in the halls, some in uniform, some not. Uniforms or no, to Karras they all looked like cops.

Karras was told that Boyle was in recovery; he found the room, guarded out front and crawling with more cops. Karras saw Boyle's father, frail as always, and his uncle, a detective named Dan Boyle. Karras shook the father's hand, limped across the room to the uncle, a big man in a raincoat who was leaning against the wall, drinking coffee from a mug and dragging hard on a cigarette.

"Detective?"

Dan Boyle looked up. "Yeah."

"Pete Karras."

They shook hands, Dan Boyle giving Karras the hard lawman's eye.

"Thanks for callin' me."

"He was askin' for you before they put him under."

"He gonna make it?"

"Yeah."

Karras smiled, bit on his lip. He looked down, saw that he had been wringing his hands.

"How is he?"

"The bastard cut him bad. They got him stitched up and stable . . . whad'ya call that, *stabilized*. The main thing was he lost a lot of blood. Me and my brother—his father, I mean—we gave what they let us give. Plenty of other cops, they gave, too. Well, he ain't gonna look so good at the beach. But he's gonna make it all right. He's gonna make it fine."

"Can I look at him?"

"Come on."

They went to a window that gave to a view of the recovery room. Karras looked in, saw Jimmy laid out with tubes going in his arm and another running beneath the sheet. He saw a couple of white-coat characters standing nearby, talking something over, and a nurse with her palm on Jimmy's forehead.

"Those doctors," said Karras. "They know what the hell they're doin'?"

"I suppose." Dan Boyle nodded. "I can get you in there for a minute if you'd like."

"That's all right. Just do me a favor—when he wakes up, tell him that Pete Karras sent his love."

Boyle chuckled wryly. "What, are you two queer for each other or somethin'?"

Karras said, "Just tell him I love him, that's all."

Boyle studied Karras. "Jimmy told me about you. Said you've been friends since you were kids."

"Yeah."

"Funny, him havin' friends outside the force. Me, I don't have too many friends who aren't cops. Even family. My own kid just got out of the academy. Hell, *his* kid will probably be a cop someday. It's just in our bloodline, I guess."

"I guess it is."

"I sure would like to know what happened in that apartment today, though."

"You mean you don't know?"

Boyle shook his head. "We don't even know why Jimmy was there. The lab boys are going over things now, and we're interviewing everybody in the neighborhood—"

"Your nephew's a hero," said Karras.

"What?"

"I'm telling you, Jimmy's a goddamn hero. That guy that he killed, the fat man?"

"Yeah?"

"He was the whore murderer you guys have been trying to nail for the last three years."

"You don't say."

"I'm serious. The lard-bucket, he sliced Jimmy with a razor, right?"

"So?"

"You tell your lab boys to check out that razor. I bet they're gonna find some traces of that hooker that bought it last Friday night."

"What the hell are you talkin' about?"

"Jimmy told me all about it. How he found this piece of evidence, and how he was gonna follow it through."

"What evidence?"

"Damn if I know. You're the detective, you figure it out. But you better get on it and phone the station real quick."

Dan Boyle stared into Karras's eyes. He walked away, turned once, gave Karras the eye again, kept walking to another group of men. He said something to them in a very blunt and officious manner, and two of them broke off and stepped down the hall at a fast clip.

Dan Boyle rubbed his chin. He looked over toward the recovery room window. His nephew's friend, the cripple with the gray hair and marked face, was gone.

■

Reed stopped pacing for a moment to allow his audience the opportunity to absorb the drama in his account. He grinned widely, his pigs' eyes closing completely on the action. Recevo reached across the table, tapped ash off his cigarette. Burke broke the seal on a virgin bottle of bourbon, slopped a few inches into his glass.

"All right, Reed, get on with it. So you went to the Hi-Hat and spoke to the tender—"

"Right. And I got the name of the pimp."

"You didn't hurt the tender, did you?"

"Naw, he was John Wayne's sister. He gave the pimp right up. I went over there to the cathouse, had a talk with the guy, little fellow by the name of Morgan. Him I hadda rough up, but not much. I could see right away that someone else had already landed a good one on his beak. I gave him a short right in the same place, made his eyes tear up—"

"Get on with it, I said."

"All right. So I give this guy the business and find out about the girl. I get her name and her description and a few other things, too. Only, the girl, she ain't around no more."

"So where is she?"

"Well," said Reed with a tight giggle, "you're really gonna like this next part. Turns out an old friend of ours pulled her out of that cathouse."

Burke said, "Who's that?"

Reed smiled in the direction of Recevo. "Pete Karras."

Burke put his glass down on the desk. Recevo stared straight ahead.

"Yeah," said Reed, "it was Karras, and he hasn't learned a goddamn thing. Seems he couldn't help from bein' his usual tough-nut self. Before he walked out of the cathouse, he even gave Morgan his name. Don't that take all? Told Morgan to make sure and remember it. Well, he remembered it, all right."

"But why? What connects Karras to the girl?" Burke rubbed his temple. "Joe, you have any idea?"

Recevo said nothing.

Burke looked at him oddly. "Gearhart. Gearhart connects them. Isn't that right, Joe?"

"Yes," said Recevo, not bothering to lie, knowing then that it was all coming toward him too fast.

"It was Karras who tipped you to Gearhart, isn't that right?"

"Yes, Mr. Burke, that's right."

Reed clapped his hands together, laughed loudly.

"Why didn't you tell me, Joe?"

"Karras did us a favor fingering Gearhart. That's the way I read it, anyway. But I didn't know how you were gonna take it, so I kept it to myself."

"You feed me information," said Burke in a grim and even way, "and I decide how to take it."

"Yes, Mr. Burke."

"You hear me, Joe?" Burke stood, stumbled a bit, leaned forward. He brought his fist down on the desk. "I decide!"

"Yessir."

Burke fell back in his chair, narrowed his eyes to focus. He lowered his voice. "All right, let me think. Just give me a minute here so I can think."

Go on. Go on and think, you sloppy bastard. Have another shot of wisdom and think.
Recevo dragged on his cigarette.

So they all stayed where they were while Burke let the whiskey form a plan in his head.

Burke cleared his throat. Then he said, "This is what I want, Joe: I want you to bring Karras in."

"Like I said, Mr. Burke, he did us a favor."

"Then I'm gonna do him one, too."

"How's that?"

Burke smiled thinly. "I called Philly this morning, Joe. Bender and his boys never arrived. It's a lead-pipe cinch that Stefanos and the rest of them buried Bender. So now we've got to save face and bury the Greeks."

"Now you're talkin'," said Reed.

Recevo had to think quickly. "Mr. Burke—the reason Pete Karras tipped me . . . well, I didn't want to bring it up before, on account of you had so much on your mind. But the reason he tipped me is, he's tryin' to be a hero here. What I mean to say is, he wants to come back in. He wants another chance here with us."

"After what we did to him?"

"Bullshit," said Reed.

"Forget about what we did to him. He's seen his future. It's in the back room of a hash-house, with an apron tied around his waist. He's got a kid now—"

"All right, I believe you." Burke eyed Recevo. "I don't know why, but I do. Which is all the more reason to bring him in. But first he's gonna have to prove himself to me."

"By doing what?"

"He's gonna have to deliver the whore. I want to talk to her, see what Gearhart told her about us. I don't want her chirping about our business to the cops. I wanna make sure she's not going to trip us up."

"What the hell," said Reed. "So he brings her in—so what? Like we got use for a cripple around here. What are we gonna do next, bring Harold Russell on board?"

"Shut up, Reed," said Burke. And then to Recevo: "Whad'ya think, Joe?"

"I'll talk to him, Mr. Burke."

"Talk to him. Yes. And if he has any ideas about doing something noble with the Greeks or the whore, give it to him like this: He stays with the Greeks, he dies. He tries to protect the girl, he dies. Get it?"

"Yes, Mr. Burke."

286

"And Joe. You ever think of crossing me . . . you ever hold back on me in any way again . . . well, Joe, you're going to die, too. Believe it."

"Y-y-yes, Mr. Burke."

Recevo put a twitch in his lip. He put it there, just like he had put the stammer in his reply. He had made it happen, like an actor would in a picture. Because it hadn't come naturally. It hadn't come naturally because it wasn't there. The fear was not there anymore.

"Tonight, Joe. Bring Karras and the girl in tonight."

"Okay, Mr. Burke. We'll settle this tonight."

■

"Okay," said Karras. "I'll see you then."

Karras hung the phone in its cradle. He stood in the middle of the living area of the apartment, touched the mole on his face. Eleni walked from Dimitri's bedroom and through the hall.

"I got him down," she said.

"Good. Listen, sweetheart, I gotta go out for a little while."

She studied his face. "Who was that on the phone just now, Pete?"

"Joe Recevo."

"You're goin' out with Joe? Why?"

"He wants to see me."

"So he calls and you jump."

"I'm goin' out."

Karras walked to the bathroom, washed his face, ran some tonic through his gray hair. In the bedroom, he opened the top drawer of his dresser, withdrew a fifty-dollar bill that he had slipped in a rolled pair of socks back in 1946. He tucked the bill into his wallet. He went to the closet, found the rest of what he needed on the top shelf, attached what he had found onto his body and put his suit jacket on over that. He dropped a fresh deck of Luckies into the jacket. He shook himself into his topcoat, stood in front of Eleni's full-length mirror, smoothed the topcoat out.

John Hodiak. He winked at his reflection in the glass.

Karras walked out of the bedroom and down the hall and opened the door to where his son slept in his crib. He leaned into the crib, kissed the boy on his sweaty scalp. He breathed in deeply; Dimitri's black hair had the scent of Johnson's shampoo. He ran a finger down Dimitri's cheek.

"My good boy," whispered Karras.

He limped from the room, leaving the door ajar so the child would not be hot.

Eleni waited for Karras at the entrance to the hall. She put her arms around him, kissed him on the mouth. She looked in his eyes.

"What is it, Pete?"

"It's nothin'."

"Yiati eise stenichorimenos?"

"I'm tellin' you, it's nothin'. I'm not worried about a thing."

"Don't be late, okay? I made a pot of *dolmathes.*"

Karras kissed her. His thumb brushed a fallen eyelash off her cheek.

"I love you, baby."

"Come home early, Pete."

"Sure. And keep Dimitri's door open, will ya? Christ, the kid's gonna roast in there."

Karras smiled and Eleni smiled back. He went to the door, opened it, walked out into the common hall. Eleni listened to his irregular footsteps as he made his way across the hall to the stairs. She waited for a minute or so, walked over to the window that gave to a view of H. She looked through the window.

Eleni could see him down there, standing beneath a streetlamp, his head cocked to one side, his hands cupped around a match as he put fire to a cigarette. A funnel of smoke swirled around his head as the match took. She watched him as he tossed the match to the pavement. She watched him walk east.

38

Joe Recevo leaned against the rear quarter panel of his Olds, watched Karras move from the darkness and into the light of the street-lamp at the corner of 8th and K. He thought he saw a smile on Karras's face as he approached, but as Karras drew nearer he realized that he had been mistaken. It was a wince that had made Karras's mouth twist up like that. Recevo wondered how bad the leg still hurt.

"Joe."

"Pete."

They did not shake hands. Recevo dragged hard on his cigarette, flicked it to the ground. The butt sparked as it glanced off the concrete.

Karras chin-nodded the Olds. "Nice sled."

"Yeah, it's all right."

"What's the model?"

"It's an eighty-eight. The lines sold me. The fastback really gives it somethin', don't you think?"

"Hell, Joe, you know I don't know cars."

"You don't have to know about 'em to know they take you places quick. I mean, you could of caught a cab over here, couldn't you?"

"Been waitin' long?"

"You said a half-hour. It's been over an hour."

"It wasn't so cold out. I thought I'd walk. I can't get around so fast any-more, but I can still walk."

"You always loved it."

"Yeah. Anyway, you didn't have to stand around out here. You could've gone inside and had a seat at the bar."

Recevo's eyes moved to the Kavakos sign that hung on the building. "I thought it'd be better if I waited for you. It's not like anybody's gonna run over and give me a kiss in that place."

Karras said, "Come on."

They walked together down the sidewalk, cut in at the head of the line, went through the side door. No one objected. Jerry Tsondilis let them in, greeted Karras, did not greet Recevo.

Inside, they took a couple of stools at the bar. The nightclub action was thin, but the house band played as if the club were full. They were hitting the intro to Glen Miller's signature, "Moonlight Serenade," and couples were making their way slowly to the floor.

"I always liked this one," said Recevo. "Listenin' to Miller sometimes, it's so pretty it makes you wanna cry."

"It's pretty all right. But Miller took everything he knew from a guy by the name of Fletcher Henderson."

"Fletcher Henderson? Who the hell is that?"

"Hell, I don't know."

"Then what are you talkin' about?"

"Never mind."

A Kavakos brother stepped up, cocked his chin as he wiped his big hands dry on a yellowed bar rag. His eyes moved from Recevo to Karras.

"What's it gonna be, Pete?"

"A bottle of Senate and a shot of Pete Hagen's."

Recevo said, "The same way."

Recevo put his cigarettes on the bar. He removed his topcoat, removed his fedora, brushed his hand back through his hair, rested the fedora on the topcoat which he had draped over the stool to his right. Karras did not remove his coat.

The drinks were served. Karras and Recevo tapped their glasses, drank their shots at once. They followed the rye with swigs of beer.

Karras reached into his jacket, withdrew a cigarette. Recevo blew into his deck of Raleighs, pulled free a smoke. He lighted his, lighted Karras's off the same match. Karras let a stream go and watched it drop over the bar.

"How's Lois doin'?" said Karras.

"Good."

"That's nice. I always liked Lois."

"Yeah, she's a good girl. How about Eleni?"

"Fine."

"And the boy?"

290

"He's fine."

Recevo grinned, gave Karras a soft elbow. "I heard you finally made time with that Lizabeth Scott lookalike you were after."

Karras did not answer.

"You two still shacked up?"

"No."

"There'll be others."

"It ain't like I'm proud of it."

"But you can't help it, can you. Gash-hound like you." Recevo smiled. "Hey, Pete. You remember that girl—"

"Can it, Joey. I didn't come here for all that."

Recevo said, "All right."

Karras exhaled slowly. "On the phone you made me a proposal."

"Yeah."

"So Burke wants me back in the fold."

Recevo nodded. "I talked him into givin' you a chance to come back in."

"And all I gotta do is give up the girl."

"That's right."

"What're they gonna do to her?"

"Listen to her tell what she knows about Gearhart. What she knows about the business."

"And what if they don't like what she tells them?"

"We didn't get that far with it, Pete."

Karras dragged on his cigarette.

"There's somethin' else," said Recevo.

"Tell it."

"That thing with Bender. Burke knows Stefanos buried him and his boys. He's obligated to make things right there, too."

"So, what, he wants me to deliver Nick Stefanos to his door as well?"

"Don't be cute. He just wants you to step aside, is all."

Karras drank off some of his beer. He put the bottle down on the bar. "It's easy for that to come out of your mouth, isn't it, Joey."

"What do you mean?"

"Step aside and let Burke take down a friend."

Recevo looked down at the acned wood of the bar. "Cut it out."

"Because it ain't so easy for me. Nick Stefanos was the one who propped me up when I thought I'd lost everything—"

"Pete . . . "

"You don't get it."

"It's you that doesn't get it. What happens to Nick is going to happen to him whether you stand by him or not. I'm tellin' you, Reed and the rest of them, they're gonna burn that place to the ground."

"I'd like to see 'em try."

"Sure you would. You and your boilin' Greek blood. You just don't give a good goddamn, right? I mean, what is it with you, Pete? You wanna die, or somethin'? Is that it?"

"No. But you've got to stand for something sometime. At least you gotta try." Karras snapped ash off his cigarette. "Like I say, Joey, you just don't get it."

Recevo signaled Kavakos for another round. Kavakos brought the bottle, placed the beers in front of them, free-poured rye into their glasses. Recevo knocked his back. Karras sipped at his own.

Recevo said, "How's Jimmy?"

"He's gonna come out of it all right. They gave him some fresh blood, flushed that junk he's been takin' out of his system. Hell, the truth of it is, he looked better in that hospital than he has in weeks."

Karras saw Recevo's mouth turn up in a kind of smile. The smile passed as quickly as it had come.

"I screwed up, Pete. I was concentrating on getting Jimmy in and out of there before Reed showed up. I didn't even think that Gearhart would double back to his place. He slipped out of Burke's office, is all it was."

"I should've been there with him," said Karras.

"Maybe I shoulda been there, too."

"You did okay, Joey. You did plenty. When he gets out of that hospital, Jimmy's gonna get his shield out of all this. You went way out on a limb, tippin' him off like you did. Thanks."

"Just trying to help. You know, it ain't always like you think it is with me." Recevo found Karras's eyes. "Listen, Pete . . ."

"Stop it."

"I know you hate my guts—"

"I don't."

"But I want you to know what happened that night."

"I already know. I ran into Face one night at Casino Royal, and he told me how it was. I know and I don't care. Because you should've stood next to me that night, Joey. You shouldn't have driven off and left me in that alley. There's nothin' I wouldn't have done for you, man, and you tore it right in half. I can't get past that now, because in the end that's all that matters. You might want to change it with your explanations. But you can't change it, Joey. So forget it."

"What I did to you I did *because* we were friends."

"You did it because you were plain scared."

"There was that. But there was the other thing, too. I was tryin' to help you out, Pete. Back then, you couldn't even see enough to get out of your own way. I was tryin' to save your life."

"That what you're tryin' to do for me now?"

Recevo looked away. "Yes."

"So now I come back in and go to work for Burke. Shakin' down immigrants and their sons for loan and protection money. Like these three years never went by. Like I'm not the cripple that I am. I just go on and forget about it, right?"

"I didn't ask you to forget about it. But what other options have you got? What else you gonna do, Pete?"

Karras nodded slowly. "I guess you got a point."

"Sure I do. You gonna flip hamburgers the rest of your life? Wear a goddamn apron? Is that what you wanna do? Come on, man, that ain't you. You and me, we weren't cut out for that."

"That's right, Joe. You and me have always been on the same bus."

"That's what I'm sayin'! Listen, you can leave that nine-to-five bullshit to your buddy Pericles and all those other altar boys we knew back when. I'm tellin' you, Pete, the way you're goin' now, you got no future."

Karras dragged deeply on his cigarette. "You know somethin', Joey? I do believe you're right."

"Sure I'm right."

Karras stared into the bar mirror, smiled sadly at his reflection.

And Karras said, "I'm gonna need your car."

"My car? For what?"

"So I can deliver the girl."

Recevo grinned. "You know you can't drive for shit."

"I'm gonna need it all the same. I can't very well walk her across town, can I?"

"So she's across town, is she?"

"Never mind where she is. I'll bring her to you and Burke. But I'm gonna need the car."

Recevo reached into his pocket, put his keys in Karras's hand. Karras downed his rye, finished his beer in one swig. He stabbed his cigarette out in the ashtray. Recevo did the same. He put on his topcoat, put on his fedora, left a heap of ones on the bar.

"All right," said Karras. "Let's go."

They went to the side door. Jerry Tsondilis gave Recevo a cool eye-sweep, patted Karras on his shoulder.

293

"*Yasou*, Pete."

"So long, *Kiriako*."

Then they were out on the sidewalk, moving along together smoothly, Karras keeping pace despite the limp, not out of synch, but in rhythm, like two halves of the same man.

They passed a cab idling at the curb. The cabbie leaned out the window. "You fellas lookin' for a lift?"

"Keep it runnin'," said Recevo.

They stopped at the Olds. Recevo leaned his back against the car.

"You sure you know how to drive it?"

"I'll figure it out. This thing got any juice?"

Recevo nodded. "Overhead V-eight."

" 'Cause I wouldn't wanna make you wait."

"When should we be expecting you?"

"An hour, hour and a half."

"Greek time or American time?"

"I'll be there."

Karras reached out, took Recevo's fedora off his head. He flicked a finger into the crown, dented it right. Recevo took the hat, placed it back just so on his head.

"You and your crazy hats, Joey."

"What about it?"

"Nothin'."

Karras opened the door, dropped into the driver's seat. He turned the ignition, put his foot to the gas, revved the engine. He revved it again until it screamed, sideglanced Recevo.

"Hey, what're you doin'?"

"Just warmin' it up."

"Warm, hell. You're gonna make it catch fire."

Karras fitted a Lucky to his mouth, lighted it. He tossed the spent match at Recevo's feet.

"Take care of my car, Greek."

"Don't worry, Joey. I won't screw up."

Karras pulled away from the curb. Recevo whistled for the cab.

39

Karras shifted the Olds into third. It went in smoothly, without a grind, the three-on-the-tree transmission easing into gear like a hot knife through butter. Karras ran a hand along the gray broadcloth upholstery, checked out the dash layout, the clock laid into the nacelle at its center. Recevo had gone for all the options, hadn't missed a trick.

"You did good, Joey," said Karras aloud.

And then he thought: You know, this car is swell and all that, but who needs it? You're cooped up in one of these things, and you miss it all—the smells, the sounds, all of it. In the city, you're cutting yourself off from everything like that, and with cabs and busses and streetcars going everywhere you'd want to go, you really don't need a fancy sled like this to get around. You just don't need it.

Karras rolled down the window a notch so the air would take the smoke from his cigarette.

He drove into Chinatown.

Karras parked at 6th and H, crossed the street to a pay phone situated on the corner there. He dialed Costa's number, was relieved to hear Toula's voice on the other end of the line.

Karras told Toula to get over to Florek's room without tipping Costa, and to tell Florek and his sister to get ready to travel. He told her that he'd be there in fifteen minutes.

"*Hokay*, Panayoti. *Tha kano tora.*"

"*Efcharisto*, Toula. *Kali nichta.*"

Karras cut the line. He glanced down the block at the unmarked chow palace next to Cathay. Su was out on the street, leaning against his cab, his

295

face close to another Chinaman's, the both of them animated and rapid-firing words into the night. Karras lighted a cigarette, watched Su go at it. Su still seemed trim and energetic, and he probably would be for a long while. Su was a good Joe. A damn good little athlete, too.

Karras looked up at the building in which he had grown up. He looked at the window to his old apartment, the light inside yellow through the heavy curtains. He dragged on his cigarette.

Karras sunk a nickel in the slot, listened to the ring on the other end of the line. He looked up through the window, watched the stooped, heavy shadow of his mother as she crossed the room slowly to get to the ringing phone. He could see the bun, even in silhouette, done up on the back of her head. He thought of her hair when she had worn it long, when she had let it out at night, when she had run through it so many times with her silver-backed brush. He could picture himself as a boy, sitting on the edge of her bed, watching her pull the brush down through her long and beautiful hair.

"Hallo."

"Ma, it's Pete."

"*Panayoti, pou eise?*"

"*Sto magazi.*"

"*Thoolevis?*"

"Yeah, I'm workin'."

"*Thelis na fas?*"

"I already ate, Ma."

"*Ella na fas. Tha fiaxo ligo fayito, tha copso-sou ena microoli salata . . .*"

"Ma, I already ate."

Karras looked through the window at the still black figure of his mother.

"Ma."

"*Ti eine, pethi mou? Eise arosti?*"

"No, Ma, I'm not sick. Got a tickle in my throat, is all. Listen, Ma, I gotta go—"

"*Panayoti . . .*"

"Ma. I just wanted . . . I only called to say hello."

"Hokay, boy. *Pas sto kalo.*"

Karras hung the phone. He dragged on his smoke, dragged on it again until it was hot, flicked it out into the street. He limped to the Olds, got inside of it, fired the ignition. He drove west.

■

296

Karras went down U, rolled the window all the way open so that he could hear the life on the street. He passed the theatres and the bars, saw the young Negroes dressed carefully and with style, walking arm-in-arm and talking and laughing together against the live and recorded music coming from the open doors of the clubs. He saw a bartender he knew, standing outside the door to the Yamasee; he waved to the big man, and the man waved back.

Karras turned left on 14th, drove past S, swung a U in the middle of the street, parked the Olds on the east side facing north. From there, he could see across the street through the plate glass to the lighted counter of Nick's. Out front, the blue sign encircled with the white bulbs had been extinguished. Karras checked the Hamilton on his wrist, saw that the evening had somehow fallen away.

Nick Stefanos and Costa were behind the counter, gesturing wildly with their hands, speaking to each other excitedly, two glasses half-filled before them and between the glasses a bottle of Ballantine Ale. They could have been arguing or they could have been making a friendship pact sealed in blood. From the expressions on their faces, it was awfully hard to tell.

Karras smiled.

So you'll burn it down. Like hell you will.

He got out of the Olds and crossed the street.

Karras entered Florek's building, took the stairs up to the landing, stopping once to rest and to rub ineffectually at the knee. Then he was on the landing and at Florek's door and he was knocking on the door.

Mike Florek opened the door. He was wearing his mackinaw jacket and his duffel bag was at his feet.

"Come on."

"I gotta get Lola."

"Get her," said Karras, reaching down and picking up the bag. "I'll start the car."

"You got a car?"

"More than just a car. A nice Olds fastback with an overhead eight."

Karras went back down the stairs and out to the Olds. He stashed the duffel behind the front seat, turned the key on the ignition. By then Florek had begun to cross the street. He had his arm around his sister, and he was moving her slowly toward the car. An army blanket lay draped around her narrow shoulders.

"Lay her down in the back," said Karras.

Florek did it with care and got himself into the passenger seat. He chin-nodded in the direction of Nick's as Karras pushed the trans into first.

"I should say something," said Florek. "He's been mighty good to me, Pete."

"No time for that. I'll explain everything to him myself. And then maybe you ought to write a letter or somethin' tellin' him how it really was. You know I'm not too, whad'ya call it, articulate."

"Why tonight, Pete? Why like this?"

"On account of I got this nice car. I mean, you gotta go, right? Why not go with a little style?"

"Where we headed?"

"You and your sister are goin' home."

Karras pulled off the curb. He swung another U, went south on 14th. He took 14th to New York Avenue, made a wide left turn.

"How is she?" said Karras.

"It's been rough."

"Well, the worst is over, right?"

Florek did not respond. He opened his window, let the air hit his face, breathed in the city smell that he had come to know. The light from a streetlamp passed across his face.

"Pete?"

"Yeah."

"I had this girl down here."

"That little redhead."

"Kay was her name. I know I ought to be thinking about Lola and all that—"

"It's all right."

"But I sure do wish I could see her one more time or something."

Karras downshifted smoothly. "You'll be seein' that girl the rest of your life, kid. And you'll see her the way she was. Even when you're old, and she's old, you'll see her the way she was. Consider yourself privileged for that."

"I guess."

"Anyway, there's gonna be plenty of girls. Plenty of girls for an operator like you."

Florek blushed slightly, settled in his seat.

Karras parked the car across from the Greyhound Terminal on the 1100 block of New York Avenue. Men and women, some in uniform, moved quickly in and out of the terminal doors. A soldier sat nearby on a low concrete wall, smoking a cigarette in the shadows.

"Why are we stopping?" said Florek.

"Get out."

298

Karras went around the hood, met Florek on the passenger side of the car. Karras reached for his wallet, pulled the fifty-dollar bill from the fold, handed it to Florek.

"A fifty," said Florek. "What the heck is this?"

"A guy owed it to me. The same guy who owns this car."

"What—"

"Take it. Get your sister in there and buy a couple of tickets to Pittsburgh or someplace close to wherever the hell you're from. If you can't get a quick bus there, then get on one that's goin' anywhere north. Just get on one quick, hear?"

"Sure, Pete. But why?"

"It's like I told you once before. You don't belong here, chum."

"But fifty bucks. I can't use all this on a couple of bus tickets. I'll mail you back the change."

Karras smiled, patted Florek on the sleeve of his mackinaw. "I thought you might use the rest to buy yourself a new jacket. Something with a little more style. Might come in handy, with all those girls you're gonna get to know."

Florek looked down at his feet. The wind caught his straight hair, blew it back. "Why you doin' all this for us, Pete?"

"Hell, Mike, I don't know. I never planned anything my whole life. Now, get on out of here. Go."

Karras and Florek shook hands. Karras turned and began to walk away.

"Hey, Pete, you on foot?"

"I told the guy he could pick his car up here."

"I could drive you somewhere, bring the car back myself."

"It's a nice night," said Karras, glancing up at the sky. "I think I'll walk."

Florek went around the car, retrieved the duffel bag, got Lola up from the backseat. He pulled her out gently, got her on her feet. They walked together to the terminal doors, the overhead lights coloring Lola's pale, drawn face.

"Mike," said Lola.

"All right," said Florek. "We're almost there."

Mike Florek turned his head, looked back through the traffic on New York Avenue. Karras limped slowly past the soldier sitting in shadow on the concrete wall. A crowd of couples came down the sidewalk, seemed to envelop Karras, then went on, laughing and talking loudly among themselves. And then it was just the soldier there, looking down at his boots, smoking his cigarette. The soldier and the night and nothing else. And Peter Karras was gone.

40

Peter Karras stopped to put fire to a cigarette. He cupped his hands around the match until it took. He drew in smoke and sulfur, kept it in his lungs, savored the pleasure of it, let it out slowly and watched it fade in the icy, biting wind. He walked on.

He cut southeast onto Mass Avenue. Massachusetts, he felt, was a good Washington street. It was wide and it was orderly and the houses were kept with care. Karras had always liked the width of D.C.'s streets, the quad-grid layout, the circles and the lines. The buildings were not so high, restricted so by law, and on clear nights and standing on certain spots you could see much of the city just by looking straight out. Tonight was such a night: The moon shone bright and cast a pale and immaculate light through the cloudless, starred sky. Karras thought the city looked especially fine tonight.

He pitched his cigarette and went down Massachusetts and angled off onto New Jersey Avenue, passing into a mostly Negro neighborhood of darkened row houses whose residents had long ago gone to sleep. He was a block away from North Capitol now, around 1st, between E and F. The lighted Capitol dome loomed up ahead. Karras looked at the dome, unmoved by its majesty. He looked around the street. He saw some familiar cars parked along the curb, two or three coupes and a luxury sedan. Then he was on the corner in front of the turreted row house crowned with the crenellated battlement. And then he was going along the walk there, and up the steps, and he was standing at the front door. It occurred to him then that he had walked a dozen city blocks; oddly, he had not given his leg a passing thought.

Karras knocked on the door. The slot on the door opened, and a blood-rimmed set of eyes appeared in the space. Then the door itself swung open.

"Face."

"Karras."

"How's the family?"

Face issued a gassy grin. "They're good, Karras. Thanks for askin'."

"I'm expected."

"C'mon in."

Karras stepped into the grand foyer. He looked through the open French doors to the right, where several suited men were sitting on the sofa and in chairs sipping highballs and shooting the breeze. The Welshman and Medium were among the men. A blue steel pistol lay on the kidney-shaped marble table in front of the sofa. Karras caught Medium's eye; Medium looked away.

"I oughta frisk you, Karras," said Face.

"Yeah. And right after that why don't you just sock me on the jaw and hang me on a meat hook."

"Christ, Karras, you don't have to get so cute about it. I was just sayin' what I oughta do. I didn't say I was gonna do it."

"Face, you don't have to do anything but stand around and be big."

"Yeah, I guess you're right. Well, go on up."

Karras went up the stairs, running his hand along the veneered oak banister. Then he was on the landing, cutting right, and standing in front of Burke's closed door. He raised his hand to knock on the door but did not. Instead he stood there for a good two minutes without moving, listening to the muted voices behind the door. He went back down the stairs.

Face sat in the foyer chair, his thick fingers intertwined, his forearms coming out of his suit jacket like hairy beams of pine. He stared through the French doors into the living room, smiling at something wise someone had said from in there, his eyes heavy and dull. He looked to his left at the sound of Karras's feet hitting the bottom of the stairs.

"What," said Face, "you all done already?"

"Uh-uh. Burke sent me back down here to have you run an errand for him."

"Normally he sends Reed."

"He sent me."

"Yeah? What's Mr. Burke want me to do?"

"He wants you to run out and buy a box of cigars."

"Mr. Burke don't smoke no ceegars."

"He's gonna smoke one tonight. We all are. You know, Face, like a cele-bration. On account of I'm coming back in."

Face's jaw opened, stayed slack while he tried to think. "Any particular brand?"

"People's has those Dutch Masters Belvederes on special this week. A box of fifty for five and change."

"I gotta go all the way to People's?"

"That's what Mr. Burke said. Anyway, what else you doin'?"

"All right, I'm on my way."

"And Face—there ain't nothin' serious goin' on here tonight. So don't break your neck gettin' back."

Face dragged his weight out of his chair, went to the front door. His hand enveloped the knob.

"Hey, Face."

"Yeah?"

"Just in case I'm gone when you get back—give my best to your lovely wife."

"Okay, Karras, I will." Face grinned sheepishly. "Take it easy, hear?"

"You too, chum."

Karras watched him leave. He gave Face a minute or so to get to his car, and then he went back up the stairs. Then he was in front of Burke's office door. He rapped his knuckles against the wood.

A pillowed voice came through the door. "Yeah."

"Pete Karras."

"Come on in."

Karras turned the knob, stepped into the room.

Burke sat slumped behind his desk, one hand on a tumbler of whiskey, his eyes waxed and unfocused. Recevo was at the big table, a lighted Raleigh between his fingers, his fedora situated casually atop his head. Reed stopped pacing, shifted his shoulders beneath the sharkskin fabric of his suit, leaned against the gun case as Karras came in.

"Pete!" said Burke with a shaky smile.

"Mr. Burke."

"You're looking well."

Karras ran a hand along the lapel of his topcoat. "I'm doin' all right."

"Last time I saw you," said Reed, "you was in an apron." Reed laughed at his own joke.

Burke kept his eyes on Karras. "He's not in any apron now, are you, Pete?"

"No, I'm not."

"Well, no hard feelings, and all that." Burke raised his tumbler. "To better days ahead."

Karras watched Burke drink his bourbon dry. A drop or two spilled out of the glass and fell to the desk. Burke reached for the fifth, poured another couple of ounces into the tumbler. He turned his wrist, squinted so he could read his watch.

"You're right on time," said Burke.

"That's me," said Karras. "Johnny-on-the-Spot."

"Funny," said Recevo. "I didn't hear no car pull up to the house, Pete."

"The truth is," said Karras, "I walked over."

"I don't care if you fell out of the Hindenburg and crashed through the roof. I'm askin' about my car."

"Never mind the car," said Burke, making a limp and awkward wave of his hand. "Where's the girl, down in the foyer?"

Karras looked over at Recevo. He gave Recevo a small smile.

Reed took his hands from his pockets. "Mr. Burke asked you a question, Karras."

Karras stood still and expressionless in the center of the room.

"Frisk him," said Burke.

Reed smiled, made a step toward Karras. Karras put his palm out in a halting gesture.

"I'm not gonna let him touch me," said Karras, speaking to Burke. "He gets near me, I walk right now."

Burke sighed heavily, pointed his chin toward Recevo. "You brought him back in, Joe. He's your responsibility. You frisk him."

Recevo got up from his seat, went to Karras, patted him down. His eyes made contact with Karras's as he ran his hands over the front of the topcoat.

"Where's my car?" muttered Recevo.

"Sorry, Joe," said Karras.

Recevo abruptly stopped what he was doing. He stepped back and stood straight. "He's okay, Mr. Burke."

Recevo went back to his seat, picked his cigarette up from the ashtray, dragged on it, exhaled slowly. He shook his head, staring off somewhere past Burke through the office window. His jacket opened as he reached over to flick off some ash. As it opened, Karras caught the curve of the checkered grip on Recevo's .38.

"Now," said Burke, "about the girl."

"The girl," said Karras. "Well, the girl is gone. She's heading south, gone back home with her brother. Down to some shitkicker's town in Tennes-

303

see, or wherever the hell they're from." Karras glanced at his Hamilton for effect. "I'd say they're on the interstate right about now. I imagine that overhead V-eight is purrin' pretty good."

"Goddamn you, Pete," said Recevo. He stabbed his cigarette savagely into the ashtray.

"You're a dead man," said Burke.

Karras smiled grimly. "Whatever made you think that I would've turned that girl over to a broken-down lush like you?"

"Joe made me think it," said Burke, his voice growing very quiet. He stood slowly from his chair. "Isn't that right, Joe?"

Recevo jumped up, brushed by Reed, went to Karras, stood before him. His eyes were hollow and enraged as he raised his right fist.

Karras stared into Recevo's eyes. Recevo slowly lowered his fist.

"You scared, Joe?"

"No."

"Our day," said Karras.

Recevo placed his hand on Karras's shoulder. Karras brushed the hand off. They looked at each other for a moment, and then they laughed.

"Hey," said Reed. "What the hell is this?"

Karras put his hand inside his topcoat. He reached beneath his suit jacket, drew Lou DiGeordano's .45 from its holster. He pulled back on the slide, put a round in the chamber.

Reed wheezed, took in breath.

"So long, Reed."

Karras straightened his gun arm, squeezed off two rounds. Gunshots thundered from the jerking .45. A piece of meat that had been Reed's face jumped off to the left. The rest of Reed was blown back straight; his body dropped heavily to the floor, bounced one time, did not move further.

"Joe," said Burke dreamily. His hands went up, palms facing out in surrender. "Joe."

"Yes, Mr. Burke."

Recevo drew his .38, pulled the trigger. The whiskey bottle exploded on the desk, shards of it slicing into Burke's grimacing face, the bullet entering his groin, the hole there ejaculating blood. Burke cried out, raised his hands to shield his face. Recevo shot him in the stomach two times. Burke began to pitch forward, his tongue thick and darting comically from his mouth. Recevo blew him back with two quick shots to the chest. Burke spun and fell.

Recevo pointed the revolver down, squeezed the trigger; the hammer fell on an empty chamber. He dropped the .38 to the floor.

"You," said Karras, tossing the Colt to Recevo.

Recevo released the magazine, checked it, slapped it back into the butt.

Karras picked up a chair, heaved the chair across the room. The glass of the gun case imploded, the sound of it loud as a bomb. Karras walked to the case, reached inside, pulled free the racked Thompson gun.

"This loaded?" said Karras.

"All the way," said Recevo.

Karras hefted the Thompson, pulled back the bolt. "How many?"

"Thirty-shot mag."

"Now," said Karras, "we're gonna see."

The men were organizing down in the foyer; their voices were shrill and bursting with nerve and anticipation and fear, and Karras and Recevo could hear them well. Then there were footsteps on the stairs, heavier as they ascended and without hesitation, because now they were charging up the stairs and the charge itself had conquered the fear.

"Here we go," said Karras.

Recevo spat to the side as the first man rushed through the door.

Karras saw the muzzle flash from the blue steel pistol even as Recevo blew the man off his feet. Karras was driven back from the lead that slammed flat into his shoulder, shattering his clavicle on impact.

"Ah!" said Karras.

Recevo kicked the big table over on its side, crouched behind it, came up firing as the next man entered the room. This one screamed as he fired, moving diagonally across the room, firing wildly, his legs twisting up from the shots spitting from the Thompson gun, the bullets stitching him thigh to chest as Karras blew him down.

"I'm hit!" said Recevo.

Then Medium was in the room, running straight in through the gunsmoke that was heavy now and nearly impenetrable, firing straight at Karras, Karras firing back, the hardwood floor splintering at his feet as he lowered the gun, thinking how it felt to be shot, thinking how it was like being punched, body blows landing over and over again. Medium lay dead in front of him, a large purple rip steaming in the middle of his throat.

Karras gripped the leg of the overturned table. He bit down on his lip, feeling the warmth of his own blood flowing down his leg.

"Joey," said Karras.

"I'm here, Greek," said Recevo. And he was there, just to the right of Karras, holding the bloody .45 tight to his gut where a slug had opened him up.

305

A look passed between Recevo and Karras. They could hear the rest of them crowded outside the door.

Karras cradled the Thompson gun, pressed the butt tight against his ribs.

"Well," he whispered. "Come on if you're gonna come."

They charged into the room.

Karras saw white fire as he heard the reports, heard Joey's gun explode, saw one man fall, heard Joey scream, watched Joey's fedora tumble by as if it had been blown by a strong wind. Karras squeezed the trigger, saw men diving through the gunsmoke, the doorframe disintegrating in spark and dust. He fell back to the floor from a blunt shock that felt like a hammer blow to his chest.

Karras winced, got himself up onto the balls of his feet. He leaned his face against the table, rested it there, caught his breath. He listened to the others move about the room.

Swim, you Greek bastard.

And he was over the table, landing on his feet as softly as if he had landed in water. And they were there, the Welshman and the others, moving toward him, emptying their guns at once, the sound deafening now and riding over their caterwauling screams and the bottomless scream coming from his own mouth.

Karras went forward, humming as his finger locked down on the trigger, the Tommy gun dancing crazily in his arms, the gunmen falling before him through the smoke and ejecting shells and the white gulls gliding against the perfect blue sky.

Red flowers bloomed on the chests of the men who had come to take Peter Karras to the place where he was always meant to be.

SIX

Washington, D.C.
1959

41

▬ Nick Stefanos downshifted, gave the car gas. The Chevy kicked smoothly into gear, cruised south on Beach Drive through Rock Creek Park. Through the emerging leaves, the sun brightened the wild white dogwoods and planted daffodils, adding color to the muted brown and flat green of the woods. Stefanos patted the knee of the toddler at his side, hummed along to the song coming from the dash radio. Next to the boy sat Costa, reading the morning *Post,* one arm out the open passenger window, the wind blowing back his unruly, uncombed hair.

Stefanos chuckled. "The *pethi,* he likes the music."

"Aaaah," said Costa, not looking up from the paper.

The boy moved his head arrhythmically to the stuttering guitar, smiling as the smooth vocal came back into the mix.

"Whatsa matter, *re,* you don't like Elvis Presley?"

"I take him or leave him," said Costa.

"The girls like him all right. They're goin' nuts over that *choriati.*"

"What do they know, huh? He sings like a nigger, that guy."

Stefanos changed the subject as he changed lanes. *"Sou aresi to caro mou?"*

"Yeah, it's all right. You know me, boss, I don't know one model from the other."

Stefanos had recently purchased the Belair, a used '57, from Star Pontiac at 4th and Florida in Northeast. It was a sporty V-8 with a beautiful turquoise-and-white finish, whitewall tires, and continental kit complete with Power Glide. Stefanos went for the turquoise color, and he really liked the classic lines.

"It's all paid for," said Stefanos, "that's what I like. Seventeen hundred and seventy-seven dollars, cash money, and I don't have to worry about makin' payments. No interest, nothin' like that."

"Good, Niko. That's good."

"Sure, you don't care. You're too busy with your newspaper."

"Just readin' about Ike. He really gave it to the Reds in this speech he made. He said that the Reds 'promote world revolution, destroy freedom, and commun . . . communize the world.' He's tellin' 'em, goddamn."

Stefanos turned his head to the left, brought up some phlegm, spat out the window. "Anything in the sports page?"

"*Mia stigmi.*" Costa found the section. "Here we go. Bob Addie's talkin' about some Cuban ballplayer here. Says the kid is the fastest thing to come out of Cuba since the Batista sympathizers. That's supposed to be funny, right?"

"Yeah, that's pretty good."

"And here's an article on the Nats. They lost six straight in preseason ball."

"They gonna do anything this year?"

"They'll end up in the cellar, like last year. It's a race for second place in the American League, anyhow. The Yankees have it sewed up. I'm tellin' you, it's the Yankees and everybody else."

"Okay, Costa. All right."

Costa screwed up his face. "Niko, turn that goddamn music down, will ya?"

"The kid likes it."

"The *pethi.* Everything for the *pethi.* I saw you this mornin', watchin' that show with him on channel nine, what the hell's that *bufo*'s name, wears the uniform like he's in the Navy?"

"Captain Kangaroo. And right after that we watched Ranger Hal."

"That's what I'm talkin' about! The next thing, you're gonna be cancel-ing our card game so you and the boy can watch cartoons!"

"Well, I might."

"Everything for the *pethi.*"

"That's right."

Costa shook his head, shuffled the pages, turned to a large display ad. The sun came through the open window, highlighting the gray hair crowding the black of his moustache.

"Here we go!" said Costa excitedly. "Jumbo's got chicken fryers for twenty-seven cents a pound. I'm gonna pick up a few later on for the *magazi.*"

"What, you're gonna take a bus all the way out to Benning Road because the chickens are a penny cheaper than our regular food vendor?"

"A penny's a penny, Niko, goddamn right!"

Stefanos glanced down at the boy sitting at his side. The boy wore his first pair of blue jeans, bulged in the middle from the diaper underneath, and a set of red suspenders over a green striped shirt. Stefanos smiled.

"You gotta learn to relax," he said. "Enjoy things a little bit, *re.*"

They came out of Rock Creek and rode along the Potomac and around the Tidal Basin and drove on into the park at Hains Point. Stefanos parked beside a black '56 Coupe de Ville and cut the engine. Costa blinked hard, stared at the Negro man waxing the Caddy carefully in the shade.

"A *mavros*, hangin' out at Hains Point like he owns a piece of it. Time was you could sleep in this park on summer nights, not worry about nothin'. I remember—"

"Sure, you remember. And I remember when the movies were a nickel. So what? Come on, Costa, let's get out and walk a little, enjoy the day."

Costa tossed the newspaper over his shoulder, into the Belair's backseat.

"Careful, *re*, you're gonna crush the flowers!"

"All right!"

Stefanos pulled the boy out of the car.

"*Opa!*" said Stefanos. The boy smiled.

They walked beneath a blooming cherry tree to the concrete walk that ran around the edge of the park. Stefanos set the boy down carefully, steadied him on his feet. The boy went to the rail and Stefanos followed close behind.

"Watch him," said Costa. "You don't keep an eye on him, he's gonna go right in the drink."

"I am watchin' him, what do ya think? He just started walkin' a few months ago! Anyway, I'm not worried. If he went in, you'd go in after him."

"I wouldn't go in that water even if I fell in it."

"You'd go in all right. 'Cause you know how much I love this boy."

"I know, Niko." Costa looked at his friend. "You think your son and daughter-in-law's ever gonna come over to this country and help raise their boy?"

"They said they'd be right behind him when they sent him to me. But, you know what, Costa? I don't even care anymore if they do."

They stood at the rail there, keeping track of the child and looking across the Washington Channel, brilliantly reflecting the afternoon sun.

Across the channel, the fish markets were open for business and thriving along Maine Avenue.

"I remember when Lou DiGeordano had a stand over there."

"Me, too. How's Lou doin'?"

"He's all right."

Costa spat over the rail. "You read the *Star* last night? The New York Boxing Commission's gonna make Sugar Ray Robinson defend his title against Carmen Basilio."

"Ray's a good fighter. Maybe the best who ever stepped into a ring. But he's what, thirty-seven?"

"Thirty-eight." Costa reached down, pulled on the boy's suspenders, brought him back from the rail. "Speakin' of old fighters, I saw Steve Mamakos, walkin' down M Street."

"I heard Mamakos was all punch drunk."

"Punch drunk, hell. That was just some crazy rumor went around. He looked all right to me."

Stefanos said, "Pete Karras loved that guy."

"Yeah, Karras. That who those flowers are for in the back of the car?"

"Yeah, I'm gonna run out to Glenwood after this. I'm gonna do my *stavro*, leave the flowers on his grave."

"Between you and that fat detective friend of his, he's got flowers every month."

"Yeah."

"How's Eleni?"

"Okay. I see her at church, her and the boy. Dimitri's twelve, thirteen now, somethin' like that. Karras took care of them with that insurance policy he took out. Bought it from this guy, always used to come around the grill, bug him all the time about this veteran's deal he had. Yeah, Karras, he did something right there. He did one thing right, at least."

Costa followed the glide of a gull against the perfect blue sky. "Those were some times, Niko."

"Yes."

"You ever hear from that Polish kid, worked for us back then?"

"Not for a while. I got a couple letters in the beginning. He opened a tavern up there in Pennsylvania, found a girl, got married, like that."

"Toula told me somethin' about a sister."

"He never mentioned no sister in the letters. I don't know what happened to her."

Costa looked over at Stefanos. His friend had gotten heavy, and his features had begun to sag, and what remained of his hair was thin and gray. But the laugh lines and character were deeply etched into his face.

"Hey, Niko."

"Yeah."

"You ever know what it was that happened in that house? Karras and his buddy, they didn't leave one thing alive. I mean, what *happened?*"

Stefanos looked out across the water. "Karras and the *Italos* . . . sure, I know what happened. Those two, they didn't know enough to get off the bus."

"What?"

"Nothin'. It's just a story." Stefanos stood straight. "C'mon, let's take a little walk around the speedway, *re*. That okay with you?"

"Me?" said Costa. "I don't give a damn nothing."

Nick Stefanos picked up the boy, who was also named Nick Stefanos, and the three of them walked over the lush green grass, passing a Negro couple who sat together, their arms intertwined, in the shade of a flowering tree.

Praise for *The Sweet Forever*

"One of the best crime novelists alive, George Pelecanos is an American original. *The Sweet Forever*—a sweeping, blistering thriller set on Washington's mean streets against the cocaine rush and underground music explosion of 1986—is a beautiful, brilliant book. Volcanic, violent, exhilarating, it is also poignant and savagely tender, bearing a sad and knowing love for the hustlers and schemers, the innocent children and simple working men and women trying to get by in a brutal, tattered world. Gritty and flawlessly paced, this is the finest novel I've read this year" **Dennis Lehane**

"Pelecanos at his very best—telling a story that is urgent and moving, full of wisdom and the gritty truth of the street. You can't put this book down or out of mind. It is one of the best novels I have read in years" **Michael Connelly**

Praise for *King Suckerman*

"This book smokes" *Kirkus Reviews*

"Packed with Pelecanos's usual meticulous details of pop life . . . comparisons to *Pulp Fiction* are inevitable. But Pelecanos is more than merely slick; there's heart behind the Tarantino-esque ephemera" *Publisher's Weekly*

". . . wonderfully evokes both the real and mythic 1970s in all their sleazy glory. King Suckerman is down. King Suckerman is nasty. King Suckerman is outta sight" **Peter Blauner**